PRAISE FOR **Things I Didn't Do**

"*Things I Didn't Do* masterfully portrays the precarious lives of a hard-scrabble Utah family grappling with haunting pasts and uncertain futures. Unflinchingly unromantic—yet wonderfully tender and hopeful at its core—this novel transports readers to the harsh landscapes and circumstances of the real American West, where everything depends on who and where you come from. Anderson is a brave, compassionate storyteller, and this is an extraordinary book."

—SHELLEY READ, *Go As a River*

"This novel moves like memory. The shape of what's missing stays with you, like something forgotten until you see it again—familiar, and changed. Anderson writes without sentiment, without apology [...] in favor of something harder, and truer. What a wonder!"

—MORGAN TALTY, *Night of the Living Rez*

"*Things I Didn't Do* is a capital-L life story, told in shimmering prose. In Ryder Mikkelson's life—despite or because of his constraints—we recognize our own: how others' expectations shape us, how family and friends are both shelter and storm, and how getting from here to there is often about degree, not distance. With deft storytelling and deep heart, Anderson guides us through."

—CRAIG LANCASTER, *Northward Dreams*

"Daring, lithe, and mesmerizing… Conjuring a bear, shapeshifters, river chasms, and abandoned mines, Anderson again shows new, irreducible ways of seeing the American West—and kept me reading late into the night. I am in awe of the limitless power of Anderson's prose to match the beauty and terror of all it describes with a precision that will leave readers, as it has left me, changed."

—KATHLEEN BLACKBURN, *Loose of Earth*

THINGS I DIDN'T DO

Things I Didn't Do

A Novel

KARIN ANDERSON

TORREY HOUSE PRESS

Salt Lake City • Torrey

First Torrey House Press Edition, August 2025
Copyright © 2025 by Karin Anderson

Published by Torrey House Press
Salt Lake City, Utah
www.torreyhouse.org

International Standard Book Number: 979-8-89092-026-3
E-book ISBN: 979-8-89092-027-0
Library of Congress Control Number: 2024949526

Cover design by Kathleen Metcalf
Interior design by Gray Buck-Cockayne
Distributed to the trade by Consortium Book Sales and Distribution

Torrey House Press offices in Salt Lake City sit on the homelands of Ute, Goshute, Shoshone, and Paiute nations. Offices in Torrey are on the homelands of Southern Paiute, Ute, and Navajo nations.

Pied Beauty

Glory be to God for dappled things—
For skies of couple-color as a brinded cow;
For rose-moles all in stipple upon trout that swim;
Fresh-firecoal chestnut-falls; finches' wings;
Landscape plotted and pieced—fold, fallow, and plough;
And all trades, their gear and tackle and trim.

All things counter, original, spare, strange;
Whatever is fickle, freckled (who knows how?)
With swift, slow; sweet, sour; adazzle, dim;
He fathers-forth whose beauty is past change:
Praise him.

—Gerard Manley Hopkins, 1877

PART ONE

THE FALL

Etna, Utah

ONE

His night friend flashed a tiny green light as it clung to the ceiling.

Flash. Flash. Flash. Flash.

Deeper inside, a slower red light. Ryder could only see that one if he lay against the wall and looked up sideways.

He understood, but could not believe, that the small presence was only a contraption.

"What is it?" Ryder asked his mother one urgent, sweaty, restless night. Sometimes she came to sit with him after bad dreams. She slept "light," she said, while Ryder's dad, once in bed, slept "like a rock" after a long day of bricking.

"It's a smoke detector," she answered from the old Band-Aid-colored chair beside his bed. "It makes a loud noise when there's a fire. Wakes us up. It's way more sensitive than a human nose. Even a dog's. Just a whiff and off it goes."

He tried to imagine it. Fire in the kitchen. Flames in the fields. Orange light in the high canyons. Invisible smoke, to smell, before the billowing black, to see. The comforting little spaceship on the ceiling squalling like an angry cat.

He tried to make sense of it. A puzzle required the strain of pronouncing.

"H-h-how did they teach it how to smell?"

His mother laughed. "You really are a cute one. Where in the world did you come from, boy?"

.   .   .

He talked funny. Almost they didn't let him start kindergarten. Said he needed to be *intelligible* before enrolling in school.

Ryder thought they meant *intelligent*. This frightened him.

"What in the dickens are you going on about?" his mother asked the principal, poking in the large man's direction. "He's been in Sunday School since he was three. Plays with the same friends and cousins he'll be in class with. They can tell the teacher what he means if she don't listen well enough."

His mother was right.

"He wants a yellow one," his Primary friend Wendy translated when bright frosted birthday cookies came around.

"He means nine. That's the right answer," his cousin Kenty affirmed between bounces when Ryder couldn't assemble the exact word, taking the long way to it with *that one before ten*. Ryder drew the tailed loop in the air—backwards, even, so it looked right from the teacher's eyes.

"Well sure enough," Mrs. McFarland affirmed. "You're a smart little whip, aren't you, Ryder? You can't pull the wool over my eyes."

Speech therapy didn't hurt his mouth, or teeth, or throat. It hurt something deeper, like the hidden flash in the smoke detector. After a hard session, the grim therapist pushing for one more round of *flat tire sounds. Okay then, let's do J-j—jeep noise. Come on, Ryder, just a little more. Let's get this done. We all want to go home.*

Ryder earned one tiny pastel brick from the Pez after every ten tries. A plastic Batman's head tilted alarmingly back from its post. Ryder felt sorry for him. He ate the candy solemn as sacrament, hoping it would somehow organize his unruly lips and stubborn tongue.

Nights after speech therapy, twice a week after the resource lady came to his school, he would roll and toss in his bed, sweat dripping through his tangled hair. He'd cry out half-awake but dreaming: a lamb sagging on his teacher's head. Tiny Batman tripping over his own fused feet. His mother, teaching a smoke detector how to smell.

But, sometimes, in the mornings after, new sounds came like they'd hatched. Perfect and new.

TWO

Good thing talking came easier as he learned how to read. First, blotches of color-sound in his head honed into petroglyph shapes, telling him what to say. Then, spelling words connected his good eyes to his tricky tongue. Finally, whole sentences, written on a glass window in his mind, spoke themselves when he opened his mouth to read them. As he got faster at reading, the space between seeing and speaking got smaller. But had to remember to not float around to the other side of the mind window, or he'd read the words backwards.

Sometimes Ryder's dad went to work before the light. On those mornings Ryder heard his parents' low voices in the kitchen, and the start of his father's truck outside. He went back to sleep until his mom came to awaken him. Other times he got up by himself and came downstairs, where his mother was making numbers on paper. She was always happy to see him. She'd put the pencil down and stand up to start Ryder's day.

"Ryder, what do you want for breakfast this morning?"

Yellow box truck on the highway. Letters on the side. His name on the panel. Ryder.

Blink. Blink.

Yellow eggs, which he did not want. He wanted toast and jam. Orange juice. If he made enough mind-pictures, sorted them out, letters followed.

Blink.

E-G-N-A-R-O (no) O-R-A-N-G-E

"Orange juice?"

"Sure thing, buddy."

"And br—no, I mean t-t—"

"Toast?"

"Don't say it for me."

"Okay."

"Toast. Raspberry … *(J-A-M)* jam."

"Good talking, Ryder! I think maybe we got this."

He knew enough by now to keep going, once the words flowed.

"M—om."

"What is it now?"

"How do airplanes fly?"

"I don't know. You'll have to ask your dad that one."

"Wha—where does the train go?"

"Over the mountains, Denver. Across the desert, San Francisco."

"What makes it. Go?"

"Back when my daddy rode trains, it was coal. He shoveled it into a fire hole in the engine. The fire made steam. Steam pushed the pistons. Don't know, now. Diesel?"

Ryder risked a moment to put his thinking together. Didn't want to lose the words as they came. Jammed out one more question.

"Where is your daddy?"

"Long gone, Ryder."

"On the train?"

His mother raised her eyebrows, squinted how she did when she didn't know the answer. "After a fashion. Trains come back to where they started. People don't. Not always."

THREE

For the six-year-olds advancing from Mrs. McFarland's kindergarten class, first grade with Mrs. Willins felt like keeping an eye on a flash flood.

"It's like they were chumming us," Kent said, much later. "Then, the hook."

Mrs. McFarland had gushed over every kindergarten accomplishment. *Ryder! My goodness! You can draw ponies better than most adults! Sami, you must have learned subtraction from somebody smart, and you are, too! Kent Mikkelson! Come up here right now, mister—don't gallop in the classroom, okay? I want you to show us the difference between sedimentary and metamorphic rocks.*

Mrs. McFarland seemed to think she was in the company of five-year-old geniuses.

But Mrs. Willins, poky elbows and poodle-haired, was on to them. She knew Emery County six-year-olds grew up plenty quick to be delinquents, underaged parents, drug addicts, welfare cheats. The ones with real potential were hurtling toward the penitentiary.

Mrs. Willins knew their older brothers and sisters. She'd taught some of their parents and aunts and uncles. She knew where Sami came from, and where her kind was headed: *squalid reservation indolence.* In Mrs. Willins' class, Ryder's brain churned up ugly pictures that made no sense. Weird sounds. Sami dropped her head, face blank and arms folded. Ryder's cousin Kenty bucked and whinnied like the wild pony he was. He bounced against the walls. He shoved everything out of his desk looking for his pencils. He stood on his chair to see out the window when he heard truck sounds. He made honking noises at them until Mrs. Willins yanked him down.

For now, Kenty was quiet, pushing his pencil around his desk like a car in a canyon. He made tiny car sounds while Mrs. Willins stalked through the classroom, looking for other kids to scare.

Ryder knew from Primary that children came from the Pre-Earth Life, where they had been everlasting grown-ups who came to earth to prove their valiance. They could return to God if they were obedient. But Kenty's mustang heart put doubt in Ryder's about that. Ryder tried to see Kenty as a grown-up angel in white robes, smiling calmly and holding his hands in angel ways. Billowing heaven-clouds and blue sky. It was impossible.

"Ryder Mikkelson!" Mrs. Willins interrupted, here, not in Sunday School but in every-day school. "You're daydreaming again! Stand up and tell your classmates what we're supposed to be learning in our classroom."

Ryder's pulse jumped into his eardrums, which made his brain make bad fireworks. His teacher's worrisome rubber smell under flower perfume made him dizzy. Her dress was the same color as mustard.

"Stand up! If you can't tell us what we ought to be learning, why don't you explain what's going on in that rattling head of yours?"

Ryder stood, small as he could make himself, shoulders hunched and rounded, knees bent. Face to the floor.

Mrs. Willins, an angry insect, blocked the ugly light above him. "Speak up!"

He made a sound in his throat.

"Aren't you in speech therapy?" she said. "Doesn't seem to be doing any good."

Kenty spoke up. "Hey Mrs. Willins, he don't—"

"You! Kent! Shut your mouth. We're all eager to hear from Ryder. Use your words, Mr. Mikkelson."

Ryder knew his cousin would not let this go unavenged, which only made the words choke up tighter in his throat. He tried again, only to manage a small frog sound. Sami, one row to the left and two seats up, scraped her chair backwards, hard. Ryder rolled his eyes up without lifting his head. Her fingers hung limp below her long shiny black hair, then dropped straight, signaling. She made a fist. She released one finger, slow, then another, and one more. She made her fingers make an *M*.

"Mmm—m—" Ryder said.

"What's that? I can't understand you when you don't speak clearly," Mrs. Willins said. "Spit it out."

The word spelled itself on the brain window.

"Mmmm—math."

Mrs. Willins said, "Now hold your head up and say that again."

Ryder lifted his chin. He could see the numbers on the board. His head cleared and his tongue relaxed. A little bit.

"Math, Mrs. Winn—I mean Willins. Minuses."

"What do you mean, *minuses?* That's not a word."

Kenty banged his hand on his desk. Then he climbed on up and stomped. The desk slipped and rocked but Ryder's cousin stood steady. "It is too, you stupid lady! Minuses means subtracting! You're just being mean to him, right, everybody?"

No one dared answer. Wendy turned her head from the far side of the room, sympathetic but she made no sound. She had enough to fear when she went home, and Ryder knew it. He heard shouting every time he walked past.

Mrs. Willins said, "Kent Mikkelson! Get off your desk at once." Kenty took a flying leap, slipping on the landing because of his cowboy boots. Mrs. Willins looked like she might pick him up and throw him against a wall, but another voice distracted her.

Jerusha Beeson, in Ryder's opinion the worst person in the class, said, "Mrs. Willins, I saw that Indian girl tell Ryder the answer," and Mrs. Willins spun around.

"Samantha Begay! Did you help Ryder cheat?"

Sami sat so still she was mostly invisible. She would have been, if she were in the right place, out where Indian kids used to live their days. Ryder saw Gilbert Nez, two rows beyond, fade into the walls and floor as well.

"*Did you?*" Mrs. Willins shouted. "This is what we get for providing a free ride for certain people. Native cleverness waxes devious."

"Leave her alone, you poopy-poo witch!" Kent hollered. He kicked a notebook off somebody else's desk and pandemonium broke wide. Suddenly, Ryder, Kenty, and Sami were sitting together in the secretary's office, waiting to see Principal Ivie.

The principal, a big man in a thick tan suit, said, "Look, you three. I know we don't have an ideal situation here. But not many qualified teachers apply for positions in an area like this. We must adapt to circumstance. Do you understand what I mean?"

"No," Kenty said, the only kid in the room with a working hinge for a jaw. He squirmed like a puppy on the beat-up talking-to couch. "Why are you talking like that?"

"I'm attempting to be tactful. You need to respect your teacher, even though—even if—"

"She's mean! And she's a—prejudice. My mama gots cousins out to White Mesa could come teach that crazy lady to—"

"Kent Mikkelson, that's enough from you! I'm attempting to forbear but you simply cannot—"

"I ain't scared of bears, you stupid jerk. Not even four of 'em. My mama told me any time I hear that kind of talk about Indians, I better speak up, don't matter who or what—"

"Would you like me to call your mother, Kent? Want me to invite your dad over here to shut your disrespectful mouth?"

"Go ahead!" Kent hollered, kicking the heels of his pointy boots against the cushion. "Make 'em drive out from Sunshine. They'll be really mad by the time they get here."

Ryder and Sami sat on each end of the couch, gripping the armrests. Kent's bouncing and wiggling took up all the space between them.

The principal said, "Ryder? What about your folks? You want me to call them in to remind you how to behave in first grade? This is the real thing now. Not just fun coloring in baby kindergarten. You can't be losing yourself in daydreams."

Ryder's tongue felt heavy as a river stone.

"But he wasn't doing nothing wrong!" Kent said. "He knew the answers! He don't say things the same way as other people. Why don't you cuss out Mrs. Willins for not listening good?"

Kent bounced up again. Principal Ivie stood up on the other side of the desk, leaning toward the kids. Kent threw himself back into the yucky couch, almost into Sami's lap. Kent scooted toward Ryder, then wiggled back to the exact middle.

No windows looked out to trees or cliffs or even sky in the principal's office. Ryder tried to take in a couple of big gulps of air, but there was nothing good to breathe. The principal's face was pink and sweaty. His dry stand-up hair made Ryder think of his grandma's bathroom carpet, which made his fingers curl into his palms.

The principal said, "Listen, you're all here for misbehaving, one way or another. Ryder was daydreaming. Kent, you are one hundred percent disrespectful, and we can't have it. You have got to sit still and be quiet in class. And you—" the principal turned, suddenly even bigger than before. "Samantha Begay. You made a sacred commitment to be grateful and to fit in when you came here to go to school, to live with a generous family. Are you straying from your promise?"

The principal sucked in some principal-office air. "Cheating, even if your intentions are kind, is not acceptable. Ryder must learn to stand on his own two feet. At our school we educate our students to become self-sufficient citizens, not welfare laggards."

Sami hadn't moved since sitting down in the office, even when

Kenty almost jumped on her. She didn't move now. Her lips were closed. Eyes to her lap. Her hands held one another.

Principal Ivie turned to plead with the one kid capable of answering. "Kent. I've got to do something, don't I? I have to support my faculty, or we'll be short a first-grade teacher fast. How about we get your brother down here as intermediary."

Kent raised a suspicious eyebrow. He kicked at the metal wall of the principal's desk. "Are you calling Ferron a mean thing?"

"Stop kicking my desk. What? No. *Intermediary* means someone who can speak effectively to both sides."

Kent stood up, because he couldn't sit down anymore.

"Sit down, young man! We're not finished here!"

Kent bounced himself down again.

"Okay. Fine." His boots clicked against each other.

The principal sat down to push a button on his phone, which made the awful shriek that always came before the booming voice over the intercom.

"Mr. Milavich," Principal Ivie boomed.

"Yes?" answered the speakers.

"Could you excuse Ferron Mikkelson to come down to my office?"

A long pause.

"Why?"

The principal's voice ticked with irritation. "Are you really asking me to explain over the intercom?"

More silence. Then: "Is he in trouble? He's just sitting quietly. He's reading. He's finished his work for the hour."

"Ferron is not in trouble! Send him down here, for hel—for heaven's sake! Why does every little request in this place have to be so difficult?"

Silence.

Principal Ivie scraped his chair on the office carpet. "I'll just go get him then," he muttered, but Ryder, seeing his approaching cousin through the secretary's window, finally found his words.

"There he is. Coming."

His cousin Ferron had been, from the beginning of Ryder's memory, more grown up than all the grown-ups. Ryder imagined Ferron might be a shapeshifter, come from the canyons, skimming along slopes and summits, dipping low enough to take on a body every few hundred years. Ferron was thin as paper, dark-tanned like his mother's family, made (as she reminded everybody) of French trappers, sinful priests, and supernaturally sneaky cattle-trafficking Utes. Maybe that's why Ferron's voice sounded like quite a few different people speaking together. When he talked, teachers, aunts and uncles, bishops, principals and drunks turned to listen. Everybody but Ferron and Ferron's dad knew Ferron was magical. Other boys wanted to be near him. Stray dogs and unbroke horses too. Girls changed their voices when they talked to Ferron.

Ferron drew everything outside in and put it where it belonged. The principal's office seemed to get bigger when Ferron came.

"What's the matter?" he asked, speaking to Kenty.

"Mrs. Willins was being mean! She told Ryder to use his words, and then when he did she yelled at him. She said Sami was—I don't know what the words meant. But I know what she said."

"Sami, are you all right?" Ferron asked.

Sami looked up. She nodded.

Ferron said, "Kent, what did *you* say?"

Kent scrunched his eyebrows. Kicked his legs like he was swimming.

"I said poopy-poo witch."

"To Mrs. Willins?"

"I ain't sorry."

"Why was she going after Sami?"

Now Sami piped up. "Because Ryder got lost a minute. I was just helping him come back."

Ryder said, "Mrs. Willins—she—she said it was cheating."

Ferron's cat-colored eyes moved from face to face, window to doorway, little brother to cousin to Sami to large principal. To Principal Ivie, he said, "Ryder needs help staying in words, but he's really smart. Doesn't Mrs. Willins know that? Sami was just helping him get back on track. Isn't helping people at school okay?"

The principal looked relieved, like he, too, needed help with the right answer.

Principal Ivie said, "Okay, you three. I'll walk you back to class. I'll talk to Mrs. Willins and clear up the misunderstanding. But Kent, you can't call your teacher a poopy—anything. You may not cast aspersions in class."

"I still ain't sorry. She casts stuff."

Ferron said, "Kenty. You can think things, but don't say the rude ones in school. It just turns into a mess. And if you can keep thinking about all the things you can do outside when you get home, it will help you sit still in class. I know it isn't easy."

"Well she deserved it."

"She doesn't understand kids. She doesn't have to matter to us. Don't make it harder for her. It will just make it worse for you and everyone else. Especially Sami."

Kent dropped his bottom lip. "Fine. But I'll make Ryder draw a poopy-poo witch at art time."

"Make the poop look like clouds, okay Ryder? Don't color them. Then you'll be the only ones who know."

Sami laughed, quiet but real.

Ryder made the picture in his mind, hoping it would make Sami laugh again when he drew it. A witch on a broom, flying through poo-shaped clouds, making more of them as she went. *Poop ... poop ... poop ...*

The principal stood up. "Let's get you all back to class," he said, and leaned toward Kenty and Ryder and Sami, eyebrows and lips scrunching to look serious: "Ryder! Clouds! You hear? And only at art time! I better not see any one of you back here in my office."

Ryder said, "Okay, Principal Ivie."

"What did I say?"

"C-clouds."

It took a long time after that for Sami to talk to them, even when they weren't at school. But now all three sat on the same seat on the bus. In the mornings, Ryder and Kent clambered on together, along with Ferron, who sat in the back with the big kids. After three stops from home, Ryder slid closer to the window to watch for Sami, who waited with the two moon-faced white girls and pudgy boy who were her school-year sisters and brother. Ryder knew their names from church. Charity was in third grade and Harmony and Ephraim were both in Ferron's class, fifth grade, but that was because Ephraim had been held back. He didn't seem any stupider or smarter than his sisters, but none made any sense to anyone but each other. This was a family that picked up roadkill if it looked fresh enough. "Not our kind," Ryder's dad said once, driving by as the Johnstons loaded a smashed doe into the back of their truck. "Although I guess you could admire the thrift of it."

The Johnston kids kept to themselves at school, grubby and pale. If they had something to say they said it together, a group screech after a family huddle.

Sami didn't seem affected by them one way or the other. When she was outside, her eyes were on the horizon, drifting toward sky, looking for something. In church and school, eyes to the ground. Or her desk. Or lap. Or shoes. Ryder watched for things that made her look up. Like horses grazing at the fence lines. Birds. Especially jays.

The things that made her laugh, like secret poop clouds. Cute dogs. Yellow leaves.

He drew pictures for her.

And even though he didn't show them to anyone, *of* her.

FOUR

His father was a small guy, even among his up-to-midsized siblings and cousins. Wiry. He was big to Ryder until Ryder hit a growth streak in eighth grade. He shot past Alma's five-six like a Fourth of July rocket.

Didn't sit well with Alma. "Think you're something, that right?"

"Didn't do it on purpose."

"You're too clumsy for basketball. So what's all that for anyhow?"

Ryder's dad had a way of coming out swinging. He came from a fists-and-boots family. But he also had a way of recalling himself, remorseful. Ryder understood him better once he got grown. But ninth grade is not grown. And Ryder *was* clumsy: the ground seemed further away. His arms reached too far, swung too wide. He had to adjust to new distances, sometimes one week to the next.

"Dad. I don't even like basketball."

"Good thing. You walk like a broke-leg heron. Couldn't even stay up on a pack mule, height's just gonna make it worse."

"Dad! Stop! You set me up on a three-foot load! I was seven!"

Alma stanced up to retort, then clamped his mouth shut, sorry. Ryder watched his father's brain grind into reverse. Bad clutch. In. Out. In again.

"I know it. Sometimes I feel so bad when I see you hitching along, I got to make it worse. But my daddy used to set me up there, younger than you was. All over the Books and Roans, the Swell. I never hit ground. Not once. Why would I think you wouldn't cling?"

"Cling to what?"

It was more than the femur, and tibia, and fibula. The rubble of metatarsals. Hospital. Surgeries. Money drained. Moving to Opex, a backwards landscape with no river. Mountains on the wrong side. Returning. Not hard to connect the parts looking back. Like a pack of firecrackers lit all at once: pop pop pop pop pop. Ryder came to see age seven as the last year of true childhood, the tipping event. How old was his mom that year? October 1986: forty-six in April. Old as some grandmothers. In Ryder's mind she'd always looked the same, which probably means she looked old then and young later. Not freakishly tall but she could seem so against Alma, who was two inches shorter (and three years older). She was heavy boned. Thick, short waist. Long legs.

Supernaturally strong when she needed to be, which was pretty often.

Deer hunt, 1986, Evaleen said, "I got a bad feeling about this. It's snowing. Looks to keep snowing. Why's he got to start hunting this year? He's not old enough to be baptized."

Alma: "What's hunting got to do with baptizing? You keep telling me he's our boy. Any son of mine's a hunter. I been riding deer season since I was five."

Evaleen rolled her lips between her teeth. "Put him on a real saddle then. He can hold on to the horn. On the steeps anyhow. No shame in that."

"He can ride on the pack. Needs to learn balance. And only dudes grab the horn."

"Put him on behind you. In front, even. He's a little boy."

"Evaleen. You want grandbabies or not?"

Ryder didn't know what that meant, but something got through to his mother. She turned and strode into the house. Then she came back out.

"Ryder."

"What, Mama?"

"Do you *want* to go hunting up in the cliffs, in the cold?"

Why did mothers wonder about such things?

"A course I do."

"Do you think you can stay on, way up there on the pack?"

Ryder had been thinking of the Bedouins he'd seen in a school library book. They rode high on the camels' humps. They must be able to see everything! His new teacher Mr. Aramospe had told him—told the whole second grade class, "If people can learn to do amazing things, so can you. You're people, smart as anyone."

"Mom! I'll be fine."

Alma shot him a man-to-man grin. That was it.

"Mom. I need to learn how to hunt."

"You're seven. You don't *need* to learn how to hunt. This is the twentieth century. And you don't know if you'll be fine or not fine."

Alma cut in. "How we gonna know anything if we don't get out there? Ain't that what you say? Ain't that why we got us a son in the first place?"

"Besides, Mama. Kent and Ferron are coming."

"They're on saddles. Uncle Doug's got Kenty an extra small one. Stirrups slide way up. Ferron's four years older than you. Don't understand why your daddy's trying to kill you so early on."

"Because we only got two animals, Evaleen. Ryder weighs about as much as a saddle blanket anyhow. Want *me* to get up on that pack? Let him ride Cadillac? I'll end up walking anyhow, once we got a buck to bring down. You're the one likes the freezer full."

Evaleen frowned. "You're the one likes booming away. Don't put this on me."

Alma laughed. "I seen you drop your share, Miss Big-Buck-Record. Why you're acting all delicate now—"

"Just don't like freezing anymore. And, like you said, only two mounts. So I get on one, leave Ryder here to fend?"

"I'll walk if you want. Hell, you're more like to bag one than any of us. And I bet Maura's coming, even though we said this is a man trip."

"I told you. I don't want to kill anymore."

"But you'll eat if I shoot? Come on, girl. Help me load the trailer. Everything's strapped in and ready to go."

"Mama shot a deer?" Ryder asked in the cab.

Heat blew from the vents at his face. Johnny Cash sang from the scratchy speakers.

"Not just once. She'd peg one every single year. Everyone older than you knows your mother's the best shot in Emery County. And Tintic and Carbon. Her record buck is mounted in the Elks Lodge up to Gemini. Head, anyhow. I'll show you when we're out there sometime."

Ryder watched gray-curtain cliffsides whiten under thin but steady snow. The truck rounded the Sunshine bend and shot south toward Nile Valley, where Grandpa and Grandma Mikkelson lived. He couldn't see out the front window, but the side was lower. The Swell opened and closed with hints of peach and orange, sandcastle ridges and, he knew, a maze of hidden canyons. He wished he could unlatch the seat belt and sit up on his shins.

Ryder watched for the Green River, took pleasure in passing over. Alma kept adjusting the rearview mirror to check the trailer.

Beyond, no towns left to watch for, Ryder asked, "That why you married her?"

His dad must have been still thinking about it, too. "Well, one of the reasons. The girl was up for things. Still is, find her in the mood. Life comes hard though, and it changes us."

"How come she won't shoot anymore?"

"Ask her when you're older."

"How come we're going to the far away part of the Book Cliffs?"

"Doug drew a Ute permit. Going in on their land."

Wet gray clouds hung low, hiding the Henry summits.

"All the way to Colorado?"

"Nope. Westwater. You know where. We'll meet them by the old corral. Where that French guy carved his name on the cliff wall, clear back."

"Aunt Maura says he's her great-great grandpa or something."

"Aunt Maura says a lot of things."

Big hill on Ryder's side. No tourists up top at the rest stop. Because, cold.

High Tukuhnikivatz, in and out of mist, poked up from the red desert. Like his dad, Ryder liked knowing the names of things. It would take a long life to catch up.

"About your mother. It's hard to explain," said Alma. "You're too young for this talk."

"What do you mean? I'm old enough to go hunting. So I'm old enough to talk about hunting."

Alma turned his head toward Ryder, then shouldered back to the job of steering. "Is that sass I'm hearing?"

"No, Dad. I'm just saying."

"I don't want to hear it. Ever. My dad knocked me over the head, first whiff of sass."

Alma had never knocked Ryder over the head. Never hit him at all. But Ryder's dad had his own dad on his mind. A lot. Alma always said he didn't want to be the same kind. Still, Ryder knew the law. No whiffing of sass.

Alma eased up. "Open up them Atomic Fireballs. Let me get something hot in my mouth."

"Can I have one too?"

"Sure, buddy. We're leaving civilization behind for a whole week. We can eat candy in the morning. Think you can take the heat?"

Ryder rummaged through the grub box at his feet, folding himself over the seat belt to reach. He found the package of red candy balls, pulled off the bright paper label and then opened the see-through bag with his teeth, exactly the way his mother had told him never to do. He extracted one hard red ball wrapped in its own neat package.

"Want me to open it for you, Dad?"

"Nope. Just give it to me. Watch."

Alma put the ball into his mouth, wrapper and all, but held one crimped edge between his fingers. Then he bit down, pulled, and the wrapper came free. "Whoo-ee!" Alma said after half a minute, his cheeks reddening. "There's a wake-up call! You ready to try?"

Ryder picked another red candy from the bag, put it still wrapped in his mouth the way his dad had showed him. He bit his front teeth together, pulled the wrapper. First it wasn't bad. Then cinnamon set his tongue on fire. Hot candy smell shot up his throat into his nose. Ryder jolted against the seat.

"I'm not crying, Dad. It's just the hot making my eyes water," he coughed. He didn't spit it out, but he held it between his teeth to give his stinging tongue a rest.

Alma laughed. "Well, we got something in common, don't we? Burning hot sugar. Don't bite down. Can't come home to your mama with your teeth broke."

It occurred to Ryder that his dad was throwing him off the scent of a more important conversation. Ryder could hardly breathe, let alone talk. But he got back to it as the candy turned into a regular white jawbreaker, as they approached the Westwater turn.

"I'm not sassing, Dad. But why won't Mama hunt? I really want to know."

Alma hummed to himself.

"Dad."

Little pyramid hills skimmed by.

"Look, Ryder. Your mother's been through a lot. She had it rough as a girl and rough in other ways as a woman. But she picked up skills. Like rifle aim. She grew up in big desert. She knows them west mountain ranges well as any man.

"I don't think she'd change anything if she had the choice, but it was a hard upbringing. Her mother was broken. Her father was a philanderer."

"What's a palander?"

"Spends too much. Wrong kind of dreamer. Worked hard on the railroad when he was young, then I guess wanted a way out. Thought he could find one last silver lode. And he was a drinker. Her mama had kid after kid after kid. When I married Evaleen, she could out-tough me in just about every category, and I was raised plenty hard."

Cliff walls rippled alongside the pickup, closer now. Ryder didn't know why they were called Book Cliffs. They looked like curtains.

"But women got their own sorrows, Ryder. Boys are raised to pick a direction and keep going. Women though, circumstance turns them every which way."

"What ways?"

"Pay good attention as you get older. You'll see. Be kind."

Alma worked the steering wheel leftward as the road followed the base of folding walls.

"Not that she's gone soft or scared. Just—"

Flat, cracked stone, distant pitches on Ryder's side. He knew the big Colorado river rolled in its hidden chasm—lazy enough for inner tubes, wild enough to tear a raft to ribbons, oars to tooth-picks. Thinking of the river made him remember things: hot sting-ing tongue, snowy peaks like pirate sails. Hove pink stone and the image of his mother, a girl in the Topaz hills, plinking at rabbits with a .22, bringing them home to pelt and eat. Shouldering a rifle for winter provisions.

Ryder spoke, careful. "But, Dad. Still."

"We got a turn coming. Let me keep an eye out."

Alma's sharp eyes watched left. Stick shift eased into the dropping speed. A knowing turn onto graded gravel. Trailer—big brown horse and sturdy black mule—followed smooth.

Finally, against the washboard rattle, Alma said, "Buddy. Your mother tried and tried to have babies. How she was raised, she thought she could figure out how to do about anything. This should of been easy. Every woman in her family, blink at her and she's pregnant."

"What?"

"I just mean them Woodward women have babies like mad. Like nature. But something was wrong. Don't say this word around her, but do you know what miscarriage means?"

"No."

"It's when the baby dies before it has time to get born. Dies inside the mother."

"Like Aunt Nora's baby."

"That's right, but it only happened to Nora once. She had plenty of kids already. Plenty since. Evaleen – before you were born – lots."

"Lots of kids?"

"No. Of course not. Where would they be? Lots of miscarriages. You've seen calves, lambs. You get the idea. Evaleen seen some awful stuff, all in the way of what she wanted and loved most. After long enough, she just didn't want to see…"

Alma drifted off.

Ryder spoke carefully. "See what?"

Alma sucked in a heavy breath. "Well, blood, of course. To her every one of them unborn babies was her child. She was done with the hard facts of bodies. Any. Somebody else brings meat home, fine, but she wasn't going out to get it. Not from the wild, not from the grocery store. She started planting tomatoes, and all them carrots, and peppers and squash."

Alma's calloused fingers squeezed the steering wheel. "It should be Evaleen telling you this, her own way."

Something in Ryder's mind opened like a heavy trap door. Whatever was down there, he couldn't make it out and he didn't want to. He tried to close it again.

Alma said, "I got to respect it. Like I said, when it comes to certain things, women and men live on different sides of the mountain."

Heavy clouds, curdling from clear sky, spun up behind the sharp skyline edge ahead. Mist fingered into nooks and canyons, but the atmosphere above the pickup was blue and bright. Slanting sun warmed Ryder's neck through the rear window.

Sometimes, at the edges of unmanageable information, Ryder's mind unplugged for a minute. This time it was more than a minute, because by the time he asked, "Can I have another hot candy ball?" they were all the way up the bumpy gravel road to the old cowboy corral, the cliffs gapping into canyon.

"Sure. Give me one, too." Alma said.

The cinnamon jolt helped him ask one more question.

"What about me, then?"

His father was ready this time. "We figured out another way to get your mama a baby."

"How?"

"Don't matter now, does it? It worked. Here you are."

FIVE

Ryder saw Uncle Doug's deluxe Chevy pickup parked at the corral. A sleek new trailer, horses still in it, was hitched behind. Ferron was perched on a high chute crossbar, watching for Ryder and Alma. He waved and hopped down. Ryder glimpsed a familiar mop of stringy hair bobbing along wet boulders on his father's side.

"Don't hit Kenty," he said, garbled because of a hard candy fireball.

"That boy has got no common sense." Alma rolled his window down.

"Kent! You see me, don't you? Don't come hopping off there without looking!"

"I see you," Kenty hollered. "I seen you coming a mile away. What took you so long?"

Alma rolled his eyes. Kept the window down. "That kid. I swear. Can't believe my brother survived long enough to have a child just like him. Ferron's only one's got sense. Comes from Maura. She was smart before drinking caught up to her."

"Dad, Kent's smart. He just doesn't do good closed up. Did Aunt Maura come?"

"Can't see yet. I hope not. I came here to hunt, not listen to them two fight."

Alma eased the truck and trailer alongside Doug's. Doug was further on, making big jerking gestures at Maura, who was gesturing back, flapping her arms.

"Yup, she's here."

"Aw, hell. Didn't we say this was a men's only hunt?"

Uncle Doug was a lot younger than Ryder's dad, but some ways he looked older. Alma was bent, skinny and bug-eyed from heavy work, and his face had some lines. Doug had a smooth face and big shoulders but his beer gut hung a good way over his belt buckle. He walked heavy, leading out with his head like he was making his way through the dark. He hadn't lived harder than Alma, but, Evaleen said, he'd lived stupider. A surprise baby, he grew up "feral." Everyone was too busy or too tired to raise him.

Uncle Doug came to church because Grandma Mikkelson made him, but that didn't keep him from smoking on his own time. He was smoking now. Beer cans littered the ground around the trucks. Ryder could see the cooler was packed with ice and silver cans. He hoped Maura had put in sodas for the kids, but you couldn't count on her that way.

Maura wasn't raised Mormon at all, didn't think much of them, even though Ferron and Kent showed up scrubbed on Sundays with their father. Maura was Catholic but didn't particularly appreciate her own faith either. *Just stay out of the confessional. Goddamn nosy priests.*

"She just wants free baby tending," Evaleen sometimes muttered, but Ryder was happy for his cousins' company in Primary and Sunday School. Ryder kept himself and Kenty quiet in Sacrament Meeting by drawing pictures in a little drugstore notepad—dogs and ponies, curly-horned sheep, monster trucks. Kenty in capes and heroic poses, Ferron in clown suits or part animal. Ferron didn't mind. Ferron read stuff: comics, school encyclopedias, tiny pulp novels he could hide in his hands at church. Hymns if that's all there was, just to keep the words coming. Ferron knew things, but, unlike anyone else Ryder knew, if he didn't he'd say so.

"Most of what you hear in this town is horseshit," he'd said to

Ryder. "Don't let it go too deep in your head. You'll have to pull it all out again when you grow up."

"Yeah, but how do I know what parts?" Ryder asked, anxious. That old fear that he wasn't *intelligible*.

The clown pictures were only meant to keep Kenty quiet, giggling as he passed them to his brother. Ryder wished he had a brother too, but only if he was like Ferron. Most of Ryder's friends had brothers who ganged up to throw them in the river, kidney-kicked, or knocked the wind out of them and left them stranded and afraid on cliffy slopes. Locked them in sheds or abandoned outhouses. Ferron was distracted, like he lived in two different worlds at once, but he was gentle like a medicine man. Or a wandering priest.

Ryder figured Kenty would be wild forever. Here he was now, swooping from rock to rock like an airplane in high wind. He took a flying leap, landing hard in the dirt. He galloped over to Ryder's open window.

"Come on Ryder!" he called. "Lemme show you something."

Ryder looked at his dad.

"Can I go with him?"

"Sure. But don't go where you can't see the trucks."

Ryder reached for the handle.

"Wait," Alma said. "It's deer season. What do you wear every minute?"

"Orange vest. Orange hat."

"That's right. Let's zip you in."

"Kenty's not wearing one."

"That's why your mother packed extra."

Kenty banged on the door. "Open up! Ryder! Come out!"

"Kent!" Alma called out Ryder's side. "Ryder's not coming out until you promise to put on a orange vest! You hear me?"

"Yeah, I know! Mom said Aunt Evaleen would send me one! I'll put it on!"

"We can't have you get shot! I need a promise!"

"I promise, Uncle Alma! Let Ryder come out!"

"You got a hat?"

"On the post, see? I'll put it on."

"Okay go then," Alma told Ryder, who nearly fell out onto gravel and wet dead grass from Kenty helping the door swing.

"Come see something," Kenty said. "Scary."

"What is it though?"

"Come look before Ferron watches us. Or your dad."

Kenty beelined for the ragged corral. Ryder followed. They ducked under the rails, cut across, ducked again. Kenty led Ryder along a twisty trail, then thrust his way into boulders and brush. Kenty's orange vest glowed against the sunburnt wall holding up the plateau.

Ryder proceeded with caution. Kenty could be up to anything.

Ryder stopped behind his transfixed cousin. An awful smell shot through his throat and lungs.

"What is it?"

"Come see, stupid."

Ryder crept forward. The brush opened to flat clean sandy floor, cavelike under a hovering wall. Indian writings quivered in the desert light, but Ryder was distracted by the disturbance on the ground, a frightening thing he recognized quicker than he could spell it in his mind.

B-E—

"Dead bear," Kenty murmured, reverent.

The high mound of the bear's butt lay toward them, still covered in fur but thinning. Black tufts lay about her like petals. Rotten flesh and whitening bone showed through naked patches at the ribs. Ryder could see a front paw sticking outward, heavy pad and long curving claws, but the head was hidden behind the shaggy body.

Cousins stood together. Ryder breathed lightly, partly because the smell came strong whenever the cold wind rose. The bear was smaller but also bigger than he'd imagined a real bear would be. He knew black bears lived in the high country, but he'd never seen one. Not up close and dead, nor alive in the distance, the way he was learning to sight deer and elk.

"I wanna see it closer. Come with me," Kenty murmured.

"I don't want to. I think I saw it move."

"No you didn't. Look at it. It's starting to fall apart. And it stinks. That means it's totally dead."

"You go first then."

"No. I done a lot already. I showed you it."

Ryder took a step forward, then took it back. "Let's walk around it more. Get where we can see the front."

"'Kay, yeah." Kenty nudged Ryder sideways. "Like a compass. The kind that makes circles. The bear's where the pokey thing is."

Ryder stepped, toes toward the bear, right foot, slide foot, right foot, slide, engrossed in tracing a perfect circle around the worrisome center. For a minute this allowed him to forget the scariness, but when he bumped into stone he looked up from the sand, into the black hole of an up-staring eye socket. A white jawbone in a horribly long animal smile. The leathery nose was falling off but still clinging.

"Hooooly shit," Kenty whispered. "What you think killed it?"

Ryder could only make sideways talk: "*Why, Grandmother ... what big ... big teeth you have!*"

Kenty giggled. "That was a wolf, Ryder. She brought lunch to a *wolf.*"

"*Mama Bear's ch-ch-chair was toooo soft.*"

"Go sit on it then." Kenty snorted, and then, "Do you think that's what it is? A mama?"

Ryder's loosened tongue said, "Don't see no balls. I think it's a girl bear."

"Did she have babies, you think?"

"Don't know."

The bear gazed blackly up. Ryder felt his stomach churn like a flushing toilet. No, clogged. Up it all came, a geyser, red hot and candy pink. Kenty leaped backward, but too late to miss the show. Kenty also heaved, humped, and spewed like a dog.

They stood, matched in fluorescent orange, coughing. Wiping their mouths with their flannel sleeves. Wide eyes. The bear gazed up from her empty eyehole.

"Sorry," Ryder whispered to her. "I'm really sorry."

SIX

The grown-ups were calling.

Ryder's brain couldn't stop making pictures of long sharp teeth, a black empty eye, fur fallen like flowers. Indian messages—a bear paw, even—glowing on the wall above.

"Should we tell Ferron?" Kenty asked.

"No. I don't want to talk about it."

For once Kenty agreed. And Alma was hollering.

"Boys! What did I tell you? Make sure you can see the trucks at all times! Come out to the road!"

Two orange vests popped out of the brush. Jeans and hand-me-down cowboy boots.

"We're right here, Uncle Alma!"

"That's what I'm talking about." Alma pointed them forward. "Doug thinks he's gonna pull his trailer up to the flats. Ryder, we're taking our animals out. Down here."

"Come on, we're all riding up!" Doug said. "Alma's a pussy!"

"Doug, shut up!" Maura barked. She kicked gravel in Doug's direction. "I'm not getting in that truck with you. Been suckered too many times."

She sat down on the cooler, stood up, opened the lid, retrieved a beer from the unnecessary ice, shut it, and sat again. "Might as well open a bev and enjoy the show. Ferron, Kenty, get ready to hike. You're heading up that horse trail, see? Ryder, you too. You'll get a good view of Uncle Doug rolling his rig over the edge."

Maura flicked a red-manicured finger toward the doubletrack, angling steep to high terrain. It hardly looked like a road. A slash hardly wide enough for a Jeep.

"I don't intend to leave my rig on the main road where every white trash hunter in the county has a chance to vandalize it." Doug had a whiny voice like a honky-tonk cowboy. "What I got all that power for if I can't climb a little hill? I want that cooler up there before we set out serious. We got beer. And steaks."

"You're white trash," Maura said. "That's why you're a white trash magnet."

"That's why you oughtn't buy a brand-new pickup every damn year," Alma said. "Let a truck get scratched up, nobody's tempted to rough up a rig set here to attract mischief. And then maybe you ain't broke all the time, too."

Ferron said, "Dad. Let's just get the horses out and ride up. This is the parking place."

"Shut your mouth, you little fuck. I need you to ride shotgun and spot the edge."

SEVEN

"It was Ferron who figured out how to carry you back to the trucks," Kent reminds Ryder, more than three decades later—same trail, different horses, more oil and gas rigs. "Do you remember any of that?"

"I remember it like dreams. Don't know what parts were purely in my mind, which were really happening. I thought that dead bear was with us the whole time. Alive. Flames from her mouth as she coaxed us along."

"Oh, man. I dreamed about that bear too. For years. Sometimes I still do."

Ryder stirs coals. Sparks rise into cobalt night.

Kent arranges fallen fir in the fire pit. "We were way up in here. Further than now. Hadn't crossed any other hunters, but in some spots we could hear horses and voices."

"I remember seeing the bear. The real one. You had that little rattail hanging down your back. And your dad had to take that hill. Your mom made us hike up the horse trail to wait, super pissed that Doug made Ferron spot. Then he's cussing Ferron for 'letting' the trailer tires slip off the edge." Ryder laughs, not happily.

"Not funny," Kent says. "Too many times with my old man. What the hell. Lost in talk radio fantasies. He thinks the pandemic is a liberal plot to scare us into compliance."

"Compliance with what?"

"You know well as I do. Turn us gay. Let the Blacks and Mexicans take over. Turn our women against us. Let's get back to the story."

Ryder recalls it in flashing scenes: him and Kenty on the crest. Alma shouting from below. Ferron's vulnerable head, bobbing out the window. Maura clambering scree, cursing like a miner, beer in hand. Horses in the trailer, white-eyed, whinnying. Uncle Doug's half-Morgan kicking the sides in fear and fury.

The right rear wheels of the four-horse trailer dropped as rocks and dirt gave way, threatening to drop the whole outfit two hundred feet.

"Your dad popped the clutch couple times before he got hold," Ryder remembers. "Then he gunned it to the top. Bashed the door so bad he had to kick it open."

"He was so mad I thought he'd shoot the horses. They were spooked, made a little stampede coming out. Your dad comes up the trail on Cadillac, all smug, leading the pack mule. What was that mule's name?"

"Kit Carson. When I told Sami that part, she about threw me out of the house. 'Don't you ever say that name again, not for any reason.' She was not joking."

"What did you expect, shithead?"

"I didn't know about Carson and Navajos. Or I didn't pay attention until I married her. She said, 'What did you think would happen, climbing up on a mule named . . .' She wouldn't let his name come out of her mouth. Had her own word for him."

"I've only seen her fired up a couple of times. She holds it close. Then, whoo—ee."

"Big mistake to light that fuse."

"Don't do it, then. What man ever got so lucky as you?"

Kent lies back to take in the stars. "You smoking these days?"

"Sometimes. Up here. What you got?"

"Good Colorado flower. Bought it in Fort Collins. Legit."

"Roll and light, cousin."

EIGHT

Kit Carson (the mule, not the murderer) was a docile creature of rough wilderness. Likely descended from Ute and Diné stock. His name wasn't his fault. Evaleen would not have objected to her seven-year-old riding him anywhere, desert or mountain. It was the pack frame, loaded high, she didn't like.

First morning, once Doug and Maura quit sniping at each other, once Ferron got the bridle right on his cowpoke brownie and the cinch tight enough to pass his mom's approval, once Kenty was hoisted astride the long-suffering paint, once Ryder was settled on the canvas pack like a Bedouin on a camel, and once Uncle Doug had run back to grab a couple more cold cans to tuck into the saddlebags, the turn toward the wooded plateau was like riding into a sky island, the dry desert below an inaccessible sea.

Shedding aspens filtered blue skylight onto carpets of yellow leaves. The trail meandered around jagged juts and gentle knolls. Every curve revealed undulating slopes, lonely towers, meadows cut with streams, flood-ripped arroyos. Sudden canyons.

Chilled winds cut the sun's perfect warmth, then dropped, and rose again.

Very old Ute and Paiute messages, and some from even further back in time, made by people harder to know, signaled from stone outcrops. Goat-like herds, horned humans, map-like trails. Snakes. Ghosts with wings. Sometimes spotted horses and sometimes just spots. Maura—Ute enough to have spent summers with cousins at White Mesa—bowed her head in respect as she rode by. Ryder wished he was a Ute boy, the old-time kind, before his own people came. His mother had told him their lives were plenty hard. But they lived here, travelers familiar with each rise and valley. Thinking of it made Ryder ache with yearning. No school. No church. Ponies and beautiful places. Family.

This part of the Book Cliffs belonged to the Ute people even now. "Like them Utes think they own nature," Doug complained.

"Like it's yours?" Maura snapped. "Don't start, Doug. Just shoot your buck, bring it home, hang the head on the wall."

"I'm just saying."

"Well, quit your saying."

If Ferron got set for a good shot, he could take it under Maura's tag. It was hard to know what Ferron wanted, but Doug was after a monster buck. A record to beat Evaleen's. He said no shots until they were two days in, far enough to follow unculled herds. Ferron and Kent would double up to free a horse for hauling the carcass. All of this was fine by Ryder, a sultan on his high perch. His father had packed carefully—hard stuff on the bottom against the wooden frame. Soft things—tent canvas, bedrolls, coats—on top. Ryder could lie on his stomach, absorbing the rhythm of Kit Carson's gait, turning his head right or left to see the glittering quakies, smell the scented evergreens.

Kent and Ferron were nimbler in their saddles, free to flit along animal paths and flicker though the groves. Sometimes Doug pointed one or the other up a high ridge to report on the larger view.

"How you doing up there, Ryder?" Alma asked every hour or so.

"Fine."

"You say that to your mama when we get home, all right?"

"Yep."

"Got anything to hold on to up there?" Maura said.

"Not really."

"Not a rope or nothing?"

"Yeah, but it's tight."

Alma said, "How about everybody lay off the damn subject. I'll loop one tomorrow when I re-pack. Trail will get rougher."

They made camp late afternoon. Cold came on fast as the sky darkened. Everyone, even Kent and Ryder, helped unload the horses, who shook themselves and trotted toward browning but delectable grass. Doug and Alma pitched tents, secured the rifles and shells, and fortified a fire ring while the boys brought in fallen branches. Maura stacked the boughs for a clean, quick light—a single match. After a few minutes the fire was blazing hot and nearly smokeless.

"Not as useless as you think, huh Alma?" Maura said.

Alma said, "I know you ain't. I'm a jerk. I just wish Evaleen was here too."

"Yeah, you are," Doug said.

"Real witty, Peewee Herman," Maura said, but the mood settled as the fire grew.

Light snow. Flakes hissed into vapor above the flames. Ferron, plagued by the tight hug of fabrics, sat close to the fire, coatless. Ryder and Kenty sat together on a log, sharing a woolen army blanket until suddenly they were too hot and threw it off.

"Come on, Alma," Maura said, as if they'd already been talking about this. "Have a beer. I'm sick of the way them Mormons got you hog-tied."

Alma shot a glance toward Ryder. Put his head down. "It's not the Mormons. Not exactly. I drank plenty when I was younger, even if I was Mormon. But you know what Evaleen's been through. I can't go against her fear that . . ."

"What kind of God would take that away on account of a goddamn beer?" Maura tilted her head in Ryder's direction. "God don't operate like that. Why would he jam a hand into a good solution?"

Ferron watched. His firelit eyes darted from Maura to Alma, then quick to Ryder.

Kenty said, "Take what away?"

Doug said, "Look, we got plenty of respect for Evaleen. She's been through a lot. But all this has turned her fanatical. She'll eat you up and Ryder too with the fear she's put in you."

Kenty: "Made her what? What does that word mean?"

"Shut up, Kenty," Doug said.

Ryder felt like he ought to know the answer. He pushed another marshmallow onto his whittled stick. He focused on holding it just the right distance from the embers.

Ferron said, "Here, Kenty. More chocolate. Make another s'more."

Kenty did.

Alma said, "She's the one did all the suffering. Right to the last moment of hope. Every time. Of course it changed her. But she's a good wife. A damn good mother."

"We know that, Alma," Maura snapped. "No question." Then, more gently: "But it changed you too. You suffered and worried as well. How long you got to pay for things you didn't do? Evaleen can believe what she wants about cause and effect. I respect her more than all the present company combined. But God's got better things to worry about than Evaleen's—" Maura's voice dropped, low as the embers, "—ovaries. All she went through has nothing to do with some piss-poor Mormon God getting worked up over who drinks a beer. Or who got bumped up and who collected. Catholic God tallies up and calls it good."

"That's right," Doug chimed in, and Maura said, "Doug, you ain't got a stick in this fire, except you want to beat Evaleen's hunt record. Fuck that for now. We're talking about higher things."

"What, beer?"

Ferron said, "Hey, Ryder. Kenty. Let's go look for owls."

Kenty: "No."

Ryder: "I don't know . . ."

Alma: "Ryder, you know I love you, don't you? I'm your dad.

One beer on a deer hunt don't affect that."

Ryder was confused, but he said, "Uh-huh."

Maura: "You boys know I love Evaleen, right? I got nothing but respect. But some things you don't have to go blabbing once we're out of the hills. Hunting's got its own rules."

"Are we still talking about beer?" Kenty asked.

"Yes."

"Let's call it a sacrament," Maura said, cracking open a can. She passed it to Alma.

Ryder knew drinking beer was a sin. Both of his parents had told him so, as well as his teachers at church. It frightened him to see his father partake. But also, he felt relieved. And then he turned his eyes to the hills above him, and the stars above them, and the whole subject emptied from his mind.

NINE

Ryder woke, warm in his bedroll, a cousin on either side. He blew steam into the freezing air, then pulled the blankets over his chin and nose. Ferron was murmuring in his sleep. Pleading. Kenty was still as stone.

Orion had swung around, kicking up his heels in black sky, chasing the invisible swan.

The big star bear shone bright for her little one.

Ryder remembers the next day in garish pastel: ecstatic visions, crescendos of pain. Except for one arresting detail in the hospital, sensations replay in continuum: pieces of sky gesturing. Scent of juniper. Rustling aspen. Light beams blocked by shouldering clouds.

A trickster surprised in her heedless tracks.

Kit Carson stepping back. Heave, shudder. Side buck.

High throw, falling, stone-studded stop, dull black.

His father's voice fearful. Doug's mosquito whine Ferron's resonance Maura's ruthless capable urgent probing hands. Commands. Kenty rising small from the saddle, rat tail trickling, twisting to see from the pinto's back.

"That's about right," Kent says. "Damn coyote came out of nowhere. We were winding around a knoll. Dome. Slope rocky as hell, and it was drizzling. Coyote might have had pups in some hollow, but suddenly she was on the trail, right there in front of you and Ki—I mean, the mule. Snarling, yipping, like she had it in for you. Proba-bly you and the mule and the pack all stacked up looked monstrous to her.

"Mule freaked. I heard your dad shout. Coyote was writhing like she'd been stepped on. Ferron was off his horse, running toward the coyote. The 'yote calmed, because you know how Ferron is, and she stood up and loped away. But you were already flying up, and then falling. If you would have fallen to the right, maybe a five-foot drop. Left, though – ten? Fifteen? Mule scrambled uphill, dirt and rocks came raining down. I thought you were a goner."

According to grown-up geology professor Kent: Maura said to leave the crumpled boy untouched until they could lift him, one motion, for transport. She told the men to saddle up fast, leave extra weight behind for retrieval. Maura sat with Ryder, holding his head between her warm hands, speaking more gently than Kent had ever heard his mother speak.

Ferron remembered a merit-badge way to make a stretcher: zipped or buttoned coats with their sleeves pushed in, aspen poles running through on each side. They chose the pinto, least likely to panic and smoothest gait, and Ferron lashed the front ends of the poles firm to the stirrups. Kenty held the reins while Alma, Doug, Maura, and Ferron lifted Ryder prone and laid him on the flattened coats. Doug and Alma lifted the back end while Maura padded Ryder's head, tucked him in tight with rolled shirts, trousers, socks—anything soft she could find. Ferron lashed his cousin fast and blanketed him with military wool.

"He cannot drop," Maura said. "We'll take turns carrying the back end. Keep him flat. No bounce."

Alma was so pale he was nearly blue. Doug was, maybe, resentful about the aborted hunt, but he didn't dare show it. He lifted Kenty abruptly, swinging him up to the pinto's saddle.

"You got no stirrups on the way out," he said. "Push your knees up tight against the saddle wings, see? It'll pin your butt down on the seat."

They walked—except Kenty and Ryder—leading the horses or taking turns at the stretcher until the sun set and the night rose. They traveled through snowflakes and stars, mist and moonlight, one twenty-minute barrage of sleet, then deep starry night to the slope above Doug's Silverado.

"Take the fall line down to your rig," Maura said to Alma. "Clear the truck bed. Turn it around. We'll be down with him by the time you're ready."

Doug took the stretcher poles. Ferron and Maura scrambled down to the Silverado for horse blankets and extra pillows.

By the time Kenty, pinto, and Doug angled Ryder down the doubletrack, Alma was ready. Headlights toward the distant highway. Cadillac and Kit Carson latched in the trailer. Maura and Ferron padded the truck bed, secure and extra soft.

They set Ryder in.

"I'll call the doctor, soon's I get home," Alma said.

"What the hell, Alma?" Maura said. "Are you in shock? This boy is broken to pieces. Get him to Grand Junction. Straight to St. Mary's. Drive fast as you can but keep it smooth."

Alma shook himself into clarity.

Maura said, "Ferron, get in the back with Ryder. Got you a sleeping bag, right here. Knock on that window if anything looks wrong. We'll follow, but we'll stop at Kathy's in Fruita to call Evaleen."

Alma wailed, "Evaleen's gonna kill me."

"Quit crying like a dog. Get that boy to the hospital. Ferron, up you go."

Ferron was already in, wrapped like a slug, spine to the cab.

"I'm ready."

Maura said, "Don't let him drive like a fool."

Alma said, "I'm okay now. Call Evaleen, soon as you can get to a phone." He shut the door and eased the truck into gear.

"That night was probably closest we ever came to being a functional family," Kent says. "In that one way it's a good memory for me. Thanks for that, Cousin."

Sure thing, Kenty.

Ryder suspects Alma still believes it was the beer that triggered their own family spiral.

TEN

Ryder awakened to vibration. Still dreaming as he gained thought. The rumble of the tires deepened and slowed. The beasts in the trailer sensed the change; the hitch yanked on the ball as they shifted weight. Stars among the clouds gave way to unnatural highway lights, flickering against gray flannel sky.

Ryder felt each gear slip down, and down again. The truck stopped. The rifle window opened.

"Ferron, stand up. Can you see it? I'll keep still."

Ryder thought to stand up too, to help Ferron look for whatever they were looking for. But the bear was asleep on his leg, heavy.

Ferron rose like a sapling, hair under his hunting cap blowing in the cold wind. He slapped his mittened hand on the roof.

"Down there, see the lights? Right, then maybe left to go in. Close!"

"Is he breathing?"

"Yes."

The bear sat up to see where Ferron pointed, her enormous butt smashing Ryder's leg. Her flat head and little round ears blocked his view.

"What are we looking for?" she asked in bear words. Ryder was surprised that Ferron, of all people, could make no sense of her question.

"Settle down, Ryder," he said, dropping back down to sit. "We're almost there."

The bear said, "It's too late for me."

Ryder said, "Get off my leg," and suddenly the lights above them were organized and strange.

"Stay still. They're coming to lift you out," Ferron said.

Kit Carson said from the trailer, "Look, buddy, you got a fight coming. Take time to study the terrain," and big Cadillac kicked the trailer wall so hard it sounded like a gunshot.

"Easy, pal," Ryder heard his father say, either to him or to Cadillac, and human faces leaned over the panels.

"Hello boy," said a man with thick black hair and a mustache. "Okay, amigo. We're taking you in. We do the work. Not you. Lie still."

Down went the tailgate, waving unnamable colors across the floating atmosphere, exciting a galaxy of buzzing neon flies talking in human voices but in bug language and the bear said, "I can't go with you," and she rolled over him, heavy, to emphasize what she meant, and rolled again but then a small, nimble woman—barely a grown-up—came into view, speaking quiet and earnest. Now it was Ferron conversing with the bear, persuading her to rise and follow the glowing flies *just for now / please / you'll know us / I'll find you at the summit / won't forget.* The bear rose into the night, large and light, turning on her axis, eyes aflame, and the small woman in scrubs told Ryder's father to stay back.

"I rode with my mom and dad," Kent says. "Stopped real quick at Mom's cousin's house in Fruita. My mom called yours, told her to get on the road. We pulled into St. Mary's just as your dad was hollering outside the ER. Couple of EMTs ran out. Jumped up into the bed with you. They picked Ferron up under the arms, set him on the ground like a butterfly. Extra guy pulled up in an ambulance truck. He lifted me up on the roof of it so I couldn't run around howling like a dipshit. Ferron climbed up and sat next to me."

"I can just picture the two of you when that thing got a call,"

Ryder says. "Two little cowboys flying in the wind."

"Nobody was going anywhere. Whole staff out there, working to bring you in. You kept blubbering about that bear until somebody asked your dad if you'd been attacked by one. Alma had no idea what that was about. Give him credit: he calmed down and explained the whole thing, straight up lucid. But he kept berating himself for stacking you up on that pack."

"Well, he knew Mom was on her way. Must have been purely terrified."

Kent takes time to fill his lungs with fragrant smoke. "Yeah, but it was you, Ryder. He couldn't stand that he'd let you get hurt. I know it went to hell for a while between you two, but if you ever wondered how much your dad loved you, you wouldn't have if you'd seen that."

The wind keeps circling back on itself. Pines lean one direction, then another. Aspens rattle their new-leafed branches. The atmosphere is gray one minute, yellow-blue the next.

The horses twitch under the saddles, stretch their lips for thickening grass.

"My dad did right by me," Ryder answers. "Even when I was a pain in the ass. Our dads weren't raised to have kids. Scares the shit outta me, thinking how unready they were to be husbands. Fathers. Because—damn. I was too."

"Your dad was just a nice ignorant country guy. That's forgivable. He learned as he went. Mine never learned shit."

"Yours wasn't made to be a whole person. He must have had something hiding in him though, or how would he have made Ferron?"

"Mom made Ferron."

"She needed a little help."

"Whatever that was, it's not going any further. Like I said a long time ago, you're lucky there's none of it in you."

"Yeah. Well. I might have worse. And I don't even know what to watch out for."

Kent pulls off his perfect Stetson. Runs his fingers through his hippie university hair. Lies back in the damp grass and puts the crown over his face. "Well, you're about to find out now, ain'tcha, cousin."

"I don't know if I am. I don't have to."

"Too late. Your girls won't let you off the hook now."

"Starting to think I got more freedom not knowing what made me."

"Nobody's free, Ryder. You and I have no more liberty than those animals we rode up here on. Hobbled, bridled, saddled, trained."

"Did you pick that up in some philosophy class?"

"Nope. Learned it from Ferron, growing up in Doug and Maura school."

"You sure aren't what you should have grown up to be. Wish I could raise Mrs. Willins from her weedy grave and tell her that."

"What would it change? Stories always come after nobody can do a damn thing about it."

"So we have to let a whole lot of people off the hook, then."

"Sure. Everybody but Doug. And maybe the dumb fuck who boinked you into existence. Foisted you off as my cousin."

"We'll see, jackass."

The pretty nurse talked to Ryder in the truck bed while the big men trussed him tight as a roped goat. "Okay, honey. We'll carry you in, get you feeling so much better, but stay calm while these big guys do their job. Try not to move. We know your leg is hurt, but we don't know what else."

Moving his leg was impossible, but when he tried to do what the lady told him, he panicked and thrashed his arms until the big men made sure he couldn't.

Pony collar around his neck. Something soft but confining at each side of his head.

He feared the pain of being lifted, rolled, turned. Terrifying as she was, he wanted the mother bear to come back. He wanted Ferron beside him again.

He heard his father's voice. "Just let me touch his hand. I won't interfere."

"In a minute. Let us Spider him down safe and we'll lift him out. Don't worry."

"His mother is coming, you know. Coming from Wellington. Near it."

"Utah?"

"Yes."

"You're his father, isn't that right?"

"Yes."

"Was a gunshot involved? Do you think he's been losing blood? Bleeding internally?"

"What? Gun? No! Guns had nothing to do with it. He fell off a mule—"

"Head? Do you think he has a head injury?"

"He fell. Far. It's my fault. I put him on the pack, too high. He fell on the down slope. I'm so sorry. So stupid!"

"We'll check everything. His airway is obviously patent because he's talking. He seems to be hallucinating, but he understands what we're saying, so it might be shock. We'll settle him and you can tell us what you remember. Don't worry. He's a tough little guy. Why don't you go on in ahead of us? You'll see us coming from those big windows."

Maybe Kent needs to reconstruct the story even more than Ryder does.

"Mostly for Ferron and me, it was just a long night of waiting. A nurse came out every little while to tell us what was going on. IVs. X-rays. I'm sure they were giving you oxygen. Couldn't kill the pain until they'd run all the diagnostics. Once, the nurse came out and made a chicken balloon out of a latex glove. She blew it up, tied it, drew eyes and some feathers. Maybe any other time I would have popped it, but I was scared and it made me feel better. Ferron told me some of our mom's old Ute stories to keep me distracted.

"Other patients came in, mostly small stuff, so they had to wait you out. But then an ambulance screamed in. Guy got shot up on Grand Mesa. His brother thought he was a four-point. Everyone rushed to stop the blood, but he didn't last long and they turned back to you. The nurse said we could come in and say hi to you, help you buck up before they took you in for surgery."

"First surgery. God."

"Yeah, bud. Bummer."

"I remember when you came in," Ryder says. "Ferron chewing his lip. You were staring like a baby owl. Main thing on my mind, the nurses had cut off my clothes. I was scared you'd grab the sheet and yank it off."

"I would have, if I'd known."

"Then of course—"

Kent laughs. "Alma spilled the beans."

Ryder: "Freaked out trying to answer the questions. Didn't know when I might get a growth spurt. How tall I might get. Didn't know what kinds of genetic conditions run in the family—"

"'I DON'T KNOW! HE'S ADOPTED!' I would have been less surprised if that bear walked in to bite your hands off."

"That's the last thing I remember before I woke up in traction." Ryder hoists his long—but not as long as the other—pinned, screwed, re-broken and re-set, re-casted (but fixed, good enough) leg in the air.

Kent says, "Does it still hurt?"

"Who cares? I can walk. I can swing up on a horse—"

"—long as you mount from the wrong side, like a fool."

"I can still run faster than my kid, at least from the pasture to the house."

"That won't last long. How tall are those folks up on the Front?"

"Men, pretty tall."

"And they look like you?"

"I guess so. I can see it now."

Ryder stands up to stretch. Put an eye on a rising hawk.

Kent says, "After all that hospital madness, best part of the story . . ."

"I know. I know—"

"Aunt Evaleen comes tearing into the parking lot—"

 "—on a dirt bike."

"Almost two hundred miles. In the dark. In October."

"Out of her damn mind."

ELEVEN

He awakened in a hospital room, his mother beside him. Her hand on his shoulder. A nurse on the other side of the bed held the other.

His leg was hung in a little hammock and wrapped in white bandage, mummy-ish. He could see his bare toes in the distance.

He tried to sit up. Their hands held him down. Pain made him shout and sink back.

"Ryder, you have to be still."

"Where are we?"

"Provo."

"How did we get here?"

"You came in a helicopter. Cool, huh? Your dad and I drove up in the car."

That made him cry. "But I don't remember it."

"You were unconscious. But it's a good story anyhow. A true one."

"Where's Dad?"

"He had to be at work. He'll come back."

Images of high plateau. Pale yellow sun.

The sensation of riding high on Kit Carson's canvas pack.

The bear.

Darkness.

TWELVE

Christmas was not exactly coming soon, but his mother brought a cardboard advent calendar and taped it to the wall beside his bed. Santa held his arms up like a band leader as elves, bunnies, and fawns scurried about making toys. Mrs. Claus stood at the door with a silver tray stacked with cookies. Rudolph stuck his head through a window, lighting a corner with his bright red nose.

"Look," Evaleen said. "When you come home, we'll still have Christmas coming up. We can start a new calendar if we want, because December will be right around the bend. But this here, see? It will show us the progress. There's twenty-five little doors and there's a chocolate candy behind each one. You can open a door and eat one every night after dinner, and then you'll know you're another day closer to coming home."

Ryder put a finger on the little door that said "1." He found 2, 3, 4, 5 . . .

"Twenty-five days?"

Evaleen put a finger on his hand. "Well, let's count them to twenty-five. And then if we have to plan for more, we'll find a new way to do it."

"Mom, what? *More?*"

"Maybe! Ryder, we don't know yet. You need to keep that IV in you a good while. It's holding back pain you wouldn't hardly believe. It's keeping infection out. And that leg has got to stay hung for three more weeks at least. If we don't do it now, and right, you might never be able to walk on it again. They'd maybe have to amputate."

Ryder thought he knew what that word meant, but he wanted to make sure, even if it made him sound *unintelligible*.

"What's amputate?"

"Cut it off. Ryder, I couldn't bear it."

Ryder said in a small voice: "I could get a pirate leg."

"Not if you don't have to, buddy. I know this is a lot to understand at your age, but no matter how long this lying-in feels to you, you're going to live a lot longer. The doctors say they can get you up again. Ryder, you'll be so glad you stayed tough and seen it through. I *know* you will. Time won't mean a thing, once it's behind you, except it will have all went too fast."

Ryder stared up at his suspended toes, purple but looking more familiar. His unbroken ribs chafed against the binding that held the cracked ones firm.

"How do you know?"

"I got polio when I was even younger than you."

Ryder tried to sit up but remembered, quick, that he could not. His mother's shoulders seemed frail against the white wall. Her face looked very tired.

He needed to put some ideas together. Talking meant all the things in his head had to line up and take turns. His body was sinking into something fuzzy and dark, which made him urgent.

"What's polio?"

"A bad sickness. We have shots to stop it now. But when I was your age, it swept across the world. Mostly hurt kids. Burned up nerves that helped them walk. Or breathe. I was lucky—just got hot and sick and then I don't remember some of it, but when I woke up my best sister had already died. My mother was pregnant, so my aunt sat with us the whole course of the fever. She moved away once I could stand up again and she never came back, she was so torn up. So Mama lost her best sister too."

Ryder tried to imagine it, but there were too many parts, especially making his full-grown mother a little girl in a fevered bed. He'd seen a picture of her when she was twelve—long braids, short bangs, a bell-shaped skirt. A sorry-looking baby brother on her hip. How was that the mother he knew?

Ryder felt strange sleep creeping into his skin, shivering down the backbone. His hanging leg seemed part of the hospital, not his own body. He needed to make his words come clear, to ask questions before waking into forgetfulness.

"Twenty-five days?" he said again.

"If you can stay tough, Ryder, and trust your bones to heal, then twenty-five days will get you mighty close to coming home. It's going to take all the stamina you got."

Ryder tried to spell that one on the mind window. He was so tired. S-T-A . . .

"What do you mean, stanima?"

"Manly courage. Patience in hardship."

"Like, Han Solo in carbonite?"

"Yes. That's a good example."

"Then what?"

"Well, you'll be in a cast a while. Maybe a wheelchair. I told you, on the other side of this, time won't mean what it does now. You just have to believe that."

Ryder pictured the grown boy who drooled and wagged his head at church, in a wheelchair with a little motor. He tried to not think bad of him, but he felt his fists curl into his chest, as if—

Evaleen leaned closer. "And we—you—will most likely have to come back to all this. More surgery on the leg bones as you grow. Because those rods they put in your femur and tibia won't grow along with you. And there's broken pieces down by your ankle, and up by your knee. It will be hard for them to grow in the right shape of a man's big bone. This will be a big job. For all of us. I won't lie to you."

Which brought him to the next thing.

"But you did lie to me."

"Ryder. What are you talking about?"

"Why didn't you tell me? Am I the only one who didn't know?"

"About . . . adopted? Honey, look—"

"Did Ferron and Kenty already know?"

"Well, Ferron, probably. He was old enough to see I wasn't fat with a baby like Maura. You didn't come same way as Kenty. But you came in your own way! You know how smart Ferron is. If you don't tell him he knows anyhow."

"Did you tell him not to tell me? Not Kenty?"

"Ryder, you were our baby. Our son. I couldn't stand to tell you anything that would make you question that. Not until you were old enough to understand. And I didn't want your friends to treat you different from other kids."

Ryder looked at the cardboard calendar—busy Santa, and elves and reindeer and Mrs. Santa, joyfully preparing for Santa's big ride. Around the whole planet. In one night.

Wait a minute.

He couldn't lift his eyes to her. Because he was so tired. But also sad.

"Mom. Everyone's lying about Santa Claus, too."

"Ryder."

"You lied to me about being adopted. You lied about Santa. Maybe you're lying about my leg getting better. And your best sister. I never heard you say anything about her."

"Ryder!"

The bear stood up, far away against the red hills, bellowing with no sound.

Against his will, the oblivion of sleep.

Awake. A new day. Was it? He couldn't tell.

His mom sat in the corner below the TV. She looked like his mother, but also looked peculiar and unfamiliar.

"Once Uncle Doug told me I got delivered in a truck. Is that why you named me Ryder?

Evaleen's lifted her head. "What? Damn that Doug. Of course not. We flew to Washington when they told us you were coming."

"In a truck?" Ryder pictured a full freight of babies, shelved in delivery baskets along the walls, wrapped in flannel. Fat caterpillars.

"No! To the hospital, Ryder! You were coming—getting born—in a hospital in Washington."

"Like, from the government?"

"Not that Washington. Seattle. Lots of trees. Mountains even higher than La Sals. And ocean."

"Did my real mom and dad give me to you? Did you see them?"

"I'm your real mom. Your dad is your real dad. We've been over this—"

"But the first ones –"

"No. We never met them. You were our baby, our son Ryder. It's just how you came. To *us*. You were sealed in the temple to Alma and Evaleen Mikkelson for time and all eternity. You're our son forever and ever, long as we're righteous."

Ryder's brain made a picture of his dad drinking beer. At the campfire. Ryder erased it. Went back to caterpillar babies, lined up for delivery.

"How did you know I was there?"

"At the hospital? They called us. Told us to get on a plane because you were coming."

"Who?"

"The hospital people. The social worker."

"Was my name already Ryder?"

"In a way. We figured it out for you just before you were born. Coming to you. First time either one of us got to fly in a jet."

"I mean, did they have a name, too."

"Who?"

"The other mom and dad."

Ryder's mom looked a little bit angry, but her voice was gentle. "I don't know."

"Did you know I was a boy?"

"No. We had a name for a girl, too, just in case."

"What was it?"

"Laura, after my sister. But we knew you were a boy."

"How?"

"We just *knew*. We named you Ryder for your dad's great, great-grandfather, Jericho Ryder. A sailor, like his father and grandfather, and probably further on back. They rode the water. Jericho was the last Ryder. He had three daughters, no sons, so they kept the name alive by naming at least one boy Ryder, every generation since."

"I never heard of any other Ryders."

"Well, your dad had a cousin with the name. Killed in Vietnam. And there's others."

"Was Jer-Jericho Ryder a hero or something?"

"Probably no more than any other sailor, but you had to be brave to go to sea. Who knows where that man went, what he saw in his life? His daughters must have loved him, seeing how they kept the name running after he was buried in the ocean. People's lives are little and large at the same time. They deserve remembrance."

"How did he die?"

"I don't know. Stories get lost. But it's a good name, and it's a little part of a life that has come down to us."

"But . . ."

"But what?"

Sleep.

THIRTEEN

A big girl named Julie—who wasn't old enough to be a real nurse—came to visit him some days, pushing a cart with puzzles with too many pieces (and how would he put one together, flat on his back?), beat-up games with missing parts (how could he play Mousetrap without twisting to reach?), and, below on a rack, picture books. Until he was stuck in a bed with his leg hung up, Ryder didn't mind books. Now, though, the squeak of Julie's cart, the sight of it turning into the doorway, made him hungry. Like the smells of Sunday dinner.

He liked the stories, but the best part was how the words lit up images in his mind. Made his hand twitch to hold a pencil and draw—which was tricky, lying flat, but one of the nurses had given him a clipboard from the station, a busy hive he'd never seen.

But he could listen. Usually it was boring nurse talk—whose turn it was to take "meds" to the patients along the hallway. Who had to answer the squawking call machine. Which patients had "voided" or not; Ryder figured out that the nurses meant peeing. He was shocked they were so interested in that.

He could hear the crumpling paper sounds of TV applause, the bursts of fake laughter of game shows, soap opera moans in other rooms. He had a TV of his own, mounted up on the wall like a hunting trophy. It made him think about Jimmy Jet and his TV set. Ryder knew he wouldn't turn into a TV. But in this closed-in place, some things worried him. Ryder couldn't even make himself watch cartoons. The sounds screeched in his head, scraped along his skull and made scary shapes in frightening colors. Made his hanging leg quiver like he'd touched an electrified fence.

Julie, the big girl in pink, said she was in eleventh grade. She wanted to go to college to become a real nurse. Her school let her out early on Tuesdays and Thursdays to learn hospital things, to help her decide if she was on the right career path. "But they just ignore me here," she said. "I'm only old enough to give people ice and push this dumb cart around."

Her eyes darted about the room. She leaned in to examine the pulleys and weights that suspended Ryder's leg—a Mousetrap affair of its own. He pushed the sheet down to bunch around the cathe-ter, remembering how much nurses—even wannabe nurses—liked to think about people peeing. And who knew what other stuff? He hated the bedpan, but the thought of soiling the bed was so horrify-ing he always pushed the call button right away.

Julie's eyes were light blue, and close together like the headlights of a jeep. Her lips were dry. She picked at them when she wasn't lick-ing them wet. Her eyelashes were white, and soft-looking white hairs grew down the sides of her pale pink face. Ryder kind of wanted to run his finger down her furry cheeks where they went flat, but his parents had taught him to keep his hands to himself.

Something about the Julie situation made him want something he didn't understand. But those weeks in the hospital, hammocked leg, catheter, no regular clothes and largely unbroken days were nothing *except* wanting. He wanted to go home. He wanted to walk. Run. Hop from rock to rock. He wanted his own bed, the company of his cousins, his mother's cooking. His father's amble at the river-bank (the quick turn of Alma's fingers as he tied a fishing lure).

Ryder wanted the big desert, the shifting sky curdling over gray cliffs, the fresh-cut hay fallen along the roadsides. He wanted his bike. The roll of a saddle under his jeans. He wanted to sit on the bus, leaning in to tell Sami dopey jokes he'd read on Bazooka wrappers. He wanted to ask how she figured out the fifth or seventh or tenth story problem, which maybe meant he wanted to go back to school.

The storybooks, ratty as they were, filled up endless hours even as they set up a new kind of wanting. Julie was a good reader—better than Ryder's mom, who stopped too often to comment and lost her place, or Ryder's dad, who stumbled over the words and got angry and embarrassed. But after Julie had read the same books two or three times, word-after-word-after-word, Ryder became impatient. He grabbed for them, open-fingered, when she read them wrong.

"I'm not reading them wrong!" she said. "The words are right here. I'm saying them exactly how they're put. And I'm showing you every picture."

But not long enough. One quick glance and she'd turn the page.

Little Monster's voice needed to sound more like Kenty's. If he read it in his head, Ryder could make it sound the way it should. He could make Ferron's voice read from the Sidewalk book, that eagle poem, all scary and serious.

Julie got the words right but made them sound like math charts.

"This poem is wrong," she said. "It's not *flied*. It's supposed to be *flew*. He just did that to make it rhyme, and it sounds stupid. And if you died, you couldn't say you had."

"Can't you give me some of the books for a while and let me read them by myself?" Ryder asked.

Julie looked doubtful. "Well, they belong to the hospital library."

"I'm in the hospital. I can't go anywhere."

"Yeah. I guess. Maybe someone needs ice. Other people might appreciate my attention."

"I do like it when you come here. I just want to look at the books. Longer."

Julie said, "Want this one, then?"

"Can I have more than one?"

"You can't *have* any of them. You can borrow some."

"That's what I mean," he said. He wanted to add, ". . . stupid," but she had the books, so he said, "Please."

"Yeah, okay. You can borrow *Where the Sidewalk Ends*. And here's one with no words, so I can't read it to you anyway. You can give them back to the nurse or something later."

"Or tomorrow."

"Just don't steal them. I'll get in trouble."

"I can read. I don't just need picture books. And how the heck would I steal them?"

"I don't want to get in trouble, that's all. I know you can read. You said you wanted to look at the pictures more. And there's lots in those ones. Have fun."

"Yeah, right."

When she was at the door, Ryder remembered his manners. "Thank you, Julie. I hope an interesting nurse thing happens today."

"Me too."

"An explosion or something."

"That would be cool. Then they'd have to let me help."

"Yeah. So cool."

FOURTEEN

Of course he could read, but too many letters made him tired. Pictures opened his eyes wide awake, made the blood jump in his veins. Drawings seemed like writing, a special language he knew how to read in a different way. Like the pictures on the rocks and cliffs, people talking from long ago time into now. The longer he looked, the more the lines told him. And also hid.

The book on top of Julie's stack seemed to want him to pick it up. The cover was a city of skyscrapers drawn in very thin lines. The colors that filled them in—light yellow, purple-gray, pink and small squares of sagebrush green—reminded Ryder of springtime desert. He thought the pointy yellow skyscraper might be the Empire State Building. Another had a flat top, and Ryder could make out the words "Pan Am." A tiny King Kong stretched his arms on top of a low blue building, sneaky, probably making his way to a higher one. Two in the bottom corner were decorated like American flags. A street opened like a canyon floor.

Ryder lost track of where he was, and why. He floated into the pictures on the page. In this city there were no cars. Tiny people walked and played along the glimpse of street. Best of all, an elfish guy on a horse looked to be passing through.

What Ryder thought was sky turned out to be water. A distant ship was made of dots and lines. Ryder turned the book over to see where it was headed. The water went on. A green field wrapped around a huge waterfall. Fluffy autumn trees spread across meadow grass. Tiny sheep ran in front of a tinier dog. Bison walked behind a man with a long stick. Pioneer cabins rose from the grass.

It was like pioneer times and now-times were happening together.

He turned the book over again. Anno's U.S.A.

Ryder shifted on his aching back. His hanging leg swayed. He pushed the buttons on his bed to lift his head a little higher.

He flipped through the pages: so many lines! Did Anno draw them? Small clusters of people. Parades and fairs. A boat pulled by horses. A huge church with a tiny wedding at the doorway. People playing basketball and pioneers playing in bands. Cemeteries. Horses. Dogs. Cats in windows. Sheep and cattle. Deer in the woods.

Each page showed the little horseman traveling onward.

At the end of the book, words about Anno. A photograph: black and white, an old-fashioned kid about Ryder's age in a soldier's cap and a uniform. Anno was a Japanese boy who wondered what was beyond the sea. When he grew up, he went to other countries and drew what he saw as he traveled.

Ryder hoped the traveler had passed through the part of America where Ryder and his cousins lived. He went back to the beginning and turned the pages slowly. There it was. The kinds of red stone shapes just south of his own town, down to where Sami went home in the summers. High buttes rising from the desert floor. A small cavalry. Pioneers burying somebody dead. Indians on horses walking in a neat line, a child riding in front of its mother.

The book excited and unsettled him. That guy Anno. Did he really ride a horse, or did he only draw himself that way? What part of this was true? Was imagining a kind of lying?

Ryder thought about how many ways he imagined going home again.

But he was adopted. Was it really his home? If it wasn't—what was he? Who were Evaleen and Alma Mikkelson, if not his mother and father? Who were Kenty and Ferron, if not his cousins? What would anything be?

Ryder's head went round and round until he settled on one thing that was true. One thing he could recognize: the little boy Anno must have drew and drew. And then grew up and drew more. Ryder had made so many pictures for Kent and Sami that he understood that Anno's only looked easy. To make a pony appear in just a few lines! Its true self, in its true home!

Ryder's pencil hand twitched. He thought of his home in tiny Etna, how nobody knew where it was unless they knew all the other places, too. Pretty near Wellington. South of Huntington. East of Orangeville.

Above the river.

Top edge of the Swell.

On the way to Moab, but you'd have to detour.

Coal town. Farm town. Mormon town. Catholics over there. Greeks up to Price.

Base of the Book Cliffs. Edge of the quarries, where Heavenly Father put dinosaur bones to test the faith of the Mormons—people who had choked corn and alfalfa out of the dry gray earth, learned the twists and turns of the San Rafael, fought Paiutes and shared provisions both ways, chased stolen cattle through stone labyrinths where the Utes could disappear a herd like summer clouds.

He thought about the smokestacks at the power plant, the thick coal seam that ran along the highway beside it, the miners and machines inside the mountains. Dead men sealed inside as coal dust smoldered and popped. Rich ranchers above. Lonesome cowboys and sheepherders in the highlands.

His brain kept running. What else for it to do? He thought of the mothers and teachers, the no-nonsense Ute lady school nurse who knew how to set things right and send kids back to class. The pale red-haired woman who never got married and worked forever at the hardware store. The polygamist families up in the canyons. Rafters on the river. The Japanese grandma and grandpa who ran the Mexican restaurant.

Ryder wanted someone like Anno to see how strange, how regular, how beautiful were the nooks and heights and cliffs and river hideouts of his own home. Ryder had never thought of it this way, but now, taken from it, stuck in a bed, unable to walk, asking to poop, longing for his own people and familiar visions, he almost burst with pride—and about broke down with yearning.

He wished he could write a letter to Anno. That night, when his mother came, Ryder said, "Can you bring me some paper next time? Not school paper. Not the kind with lines already on it."

He couldn't write in Anno's language. But maybe he could draw in it.

FIFTEEN

On Saturday, seven advent doors open and seven chocolates eaten, Ferron came to the hospital with Alma. Right after breakfast.

"Kenty will come one of these days," Ferron said. "He was pissed when we pulled out without him. Threw rocks at the truck."

"Chinked the back window," Alma said. "Little shit. Good thing it was already cracked."

"We'll have to keep him from climbing the walls. Sometime when we won't stay so long. Hospital will freak him out."

Alma stood behind skinny Ferron. "Ferron brought you something," he said. "Get a load of this."

"We gotta clear off that table first," Ferron said. "Wipe it clean and dry."

Ryder said, "What is it?"

Alma said, "Well, be patient a minute. Did you eat your food?"

"Not the gross Malt-O-Meal. Eggs though."

"Stack up the dishes. We can put the tray over on the windowsill till the lady comes."

"Man. Ernesto on weekends," Ryder said.

"Okay. Man." Alma looked surprised. "Is he Mexican or something?"

"He's from here."

"Speaks English?"

"Yeah. He doesn't sound Spanish at all."

"Why's a grown man who speaks good English doing a woman's job? You think he's a perv?"

Ryder said, "He's not—"

Ferron said, "Come on, Uncle Alma. Let's get this going, okay?"

Alma moved the breakfast tray to the sill. The sky was bright blue, but that's all Ryder could see of outside. He wondered if it was cold. His mother had told him that he was eight floors up, too high to see other buildings. No trees, no streets or cars or people. No mountains, even, but his dad said that was because his window faced south. Ryder figured if he could get over there to look, he'd see some of the lake, and big Mount Nebo rising beyond it, and he could make sense of where he was. And where his home was.

But from here, all of it was memory or imagination. Only the boring hospital room, his hanging leg, and the pictures in his mind.

Ferron said, "Ryder, look."

Ferron reached into a sack and pulled out an extra-fat drawing pad. The paper was thick and white. Ryder ran his hand down the front sheet.

"Feel it," he said to Ferron. "Dad, look."

Ferron reached into the sack three more times: a flat metal box filled with nestled pencils and a sharpener; a true watercolor set (not the cheap drug store kind); a handful of fine-tip drawing pens and paint brushes.

"You got all this time on your hands," Ferron said, "And you're a good artist. See if you can fill up the whole pad before you come home."

"If you don't scribble and don't tear out the pages, I'll buy you a new one when this one runs out," Alma said.

Ryder turned page after page, running his palm down the smoothness. He examined each pencil even though they were all exactly alike. He opened the watercolor box to admire the squares of rich color, running a dry brush over each one.

He loved the pens the most. Tiny points, color by color. He could make lines like Anno's if he practiced.

"This must have cost a million dollars," he said. "How did you buy it all?"

Ferron smiled. "The teachers put a box in the office. Just about everybody put some money in it. Look at this." He pulled a scroll of brown paper towels from his backpack, a yellow ribbon tied around its waist.

"Unroll it," he said, handing it to Ryder. "See what it says."

The ribbon pulled free once Ryder figured out it was tied like a shoelace. They must have used half a roll for all the messages. All the kids in the elementary school. Teachers, too. Even some of the big kids in junior high and high school. Moms and dads, the counter lady at the drugstore, the principal. Even Mrs. Willins! No message, but she signed her name. Mr. Aramospe had drawn a picture of a guitar. Mr. Milavich drew a picture of Linda Ronstadt. Some kid drew a horse, but by now Ryder was sure he could do better.

He couldn't wait to begin.

SIXTEEN

Every day he had a new set of drawings (a page of tiny horses; his whole class playing kickball in the schoolyard; elk moving down the mountain . . .) to show his mom, or his dad, even Aunt Maura when she came with Kenty. But that day the visiting ended quick because Kent kept pushing the buttons on Ryder's bed and burping into the intercom. He took off his boots and slid across the polished floor in his socks, slamming himself into the wall. He flipped the channels on the TV, round and round, and then he pulled one of the traction weights up like a pendulum and let fly. Ryder felt the jolt through his whole body and yelped.

Maura grabbed Kenty around the waist and hauled him out like a rolled-up rug, cursing like the drunk parents in the Little League bleachers. Kenty hollered, "I'm sorry! Mom! I'll settle down! I want to see Ryder!" but it was too late. Aunt Maura seemed more fed up every time Ryder saw her.

"Wit's end," Evaleen called it. "Kenty's manifesting the family discord. He's got to express it, some way. We have to be patient with him."

Ryder loved his cousin. More than anyone. Kenty was the smartest kid Ryder knew, some ways even smarter than Ferron. Soon as Kenty was on a horse, soon as he was leaping from stone to stone, soon as he was balancing along a narrow ridge, throwing a baseball, tracking a cat or rabbit or skunk, he had amazing things to say. He knew the names of stars and constellations. All the kinds of tools and tackle—who knew how? He knew the names of cars and airplanes, and most of their parts. Once he told Ryder that the Indian pictures on the sandstone walls were called "rock writing," *not* pictographs or petroglyphs. "They say something," he said. "All of them. All the little differences in shapes and horns and legs and dots. The goats are people, going in certain directions. They all mean stuff."

"What do they mean, though?" Ryder asked.

"I only know a little. My mom's cousin Edwin says the writing used to say where water is. Who died in some places. How far a journey was. Sometimes they tell stories about fights. White people coming. Making moccasins. They were talking to each other all the time, but not only with words. Hand signs too. Rock writing."

Ryder wished he could send a signal to Kenty now. What if it was his cousin stuck in a bed like this, leg hanging? It was a good thing this had happened to Ryder, if it had to happen to someone.

For a moment he felt heroic—like he'd saved his cousins, maybe even his father and Uncle Doug and Aunt Maura, from a dark force in the form of a coyote, sent to remind them that danger lurked at every turn on the trail of life. He imagined he had been chosen to take the fall. To spare them. Maybe that's why he'd come to his family so strangely. Like a guardian angel.

Even so, Ryder was awash in sorrow and homesickness. Maybe he would never be himself again, never see the rippling cliffsides of Emery County. Never ride a horse again. Never pedal his BMX. Never sit with his friend Sami on the bus, looking out at the winter sky.

He reached for the pad of paper. Sharpened a pencil to a perfect point. Set to drawing—to picture-writing—a message to his cousin Kent, now thrashing in his seat belt as Aunt Maura barreled toward the twisty canyon climb, the long plateau, and the drop down the other side that would take them home.

On this page he drew things he'd never thought to put on paper before. He didn't know why he thought of them now. His hands did their own work. Ryder felt like he was watching a show, wondering what would happen next, and next, and then after:

A tall white man with an old-time hat and fancy shoes, walking along the high Steamboat ridge, a bear trap biting his leg. A little dog yapping at his ankles. Lightning striking the chimney of a far-away pioneer cabin. Three spotted fawns trailing a woolly mammoth with long curling tusks. A dinosaur—not just the bones but the whole beast—awakening underground, pushing at the rubble of its hard bed. Old-time Indians swimming in the river, deep under and strong like twirling fish, breathing water. Strange-colored bighorn sheep and antelope coming down the rocks, growing feathers as they drank at the shore. Vultures with human heads in the cottonwoods. Coyotes calling up to them.

Ferron in the sky, all his own—not a cloud, no sun, no moon or stars. Only Ferron, floating high as a red-tailed hawk, waving to his brother and cousin below.

PART TWO

TROPHY BUCK

Opex, Utah

SEVENTEEN

G reat Grandpa Yeadon's place in Opex looked like a junkyard, complete with a growling part-Jindo named Auriferous. High at the end of a dirt road running above Opex Street, the house was an accumulation of half-finished additions clinging to the original company cabin. West, the Tintic Valley—its blue hacksaw ranges, peach-fire sunsets—shimmered like watercolor, dry as it was. East, the black carp mouth of a defunct silver mine breathed across the pooling valley air, sometimes scenting the V-shaped town with something like dank sea water. The hoist house stood beside it, stout. Grandpa said it could still function, anyone had a mind to tune it up.

"Temperature don't change down there in the shaft," Grandpa explained. "Sometimes it burps. When you can hop along better, we'll hike up there."

It was annoying to be fourteen and helpless—*again*—listening to a man past ninety challenge him to a rocky trek. At least Ryder wasn't stuck in a hospital. His leg was pinned and braced after the surgery, protruding in front of the wheelchair like a cattle guard. But he was home—if crowding into a ramshackle house with a chatter-box great-grandpa he hardly knew was "home."

And considering he couldn't get around, living in a junkyard was a kind of adventure. And Auriferous, who thought showing his teeth was smiling back, only growled as conversation. The dog was devoted to Grandpa, but Ryder was a novelty, maybe an object of pity. Auriferous seemed eager to show his new friend all the interesting stuff.

"So, what's that?" Ryder asked Grandpa, as Auriferous peed on it.

"Well, it's the platform of a old bumping table," Grandpa said, as if Ryder was crazy not to recognize such a thing. "Run slurry acrost, bump out a line of gold powder. Got other parts around here, too. Maybe we could rebuild it sometime."

"Okay, how about that thing?"

Grandpa ambled closer to peer into the debris. "Which one?"

"I don't know. The spirally thing."

"Well son, that's a worm coil."

"But what is it?"

"Some folks used to make moonshine whiskey up in the nooks. Back in Prohibition, right? No law's stopping miners from taking refreshment after a shift. It ain't moral.

"See that old green tank? Coil goes in it, filled with cooling water. Brings the vapor back to liquid. The kind with a kick. Look around, you'll see some like it, different sizes. Not all of 'em copper, but the best ones are."

Ryder grinned. "Did you . . ."

"Naw. Course not."

Wink, wink.

Grandpa was in a reminiscing mood.

"Old Opex might look like a ghost town, but it's been busy. Look around. Silver City, just over that hill, first of the boom towns. Opex, up here, brought up silver, gold, lead, copper—you name it. Couple rail lines, transporting ore night and day. Once you get up, I'll take you out to walk the old trestle."

Ryder had something to contribute. "I've been in the Sunshine Mine, past Wellington. My aunt and uncle work there."

"Over there they bring out the black stuff. Whole other animal. Coal sets down flat like cheese in a sandwich, made of dead-dinosaur mud spread over swampy ground a long, long time ago. Coal miners hold up a whole mountain above them as they bite it out. I give 'em credit. Hell."

Grandpa gestured up to the black mouth on the hillside: "Over here, we're hard rock miners. Follow the lodes wherever they go. Up, down, snaking and spiraling every which way. I ain't saying one kind of extraction's more dangerous than another. Each gots its hazards. But not the same. Out here, the earth's been zigzagged by the heat of perdition.

"Your sorry butt is perched on top of a magma cap. Flowed over the older mountain range, covers it like a hard blanket. That's why nothing this side looks like them big ranges acrost the lake. Lava came up from the deep, wrenched the innards, reamed wormholes. Broke the surface some places, flowed over the peaks and valleys. Hardened up. Again and again. Then water shot through the worm-holes—water so hot it carried liquid metals up from the mantle. You pay attention in school? What's the mantle?"

"Under the crust. Melty."

"That's right. Smart boy. Live someplace like this, you ought to know what you're standing on." Grandpa coughed in approval. "Sitting on, I mean. You still listening, buddy?"

"Uh-huh."

"Boiling water lined them magma tunnels with the shining riches of the planet. Cooled after a lot of million years. Left us to go down with our shovels and picks, bring up the gold and silver and copper ore for the overlords."

"Overlords?"

"Fitches. Knights. McIntyres. Chisholms, Derns. More, but not near so many of them as us. We did good, some years. Some of them miners who stuck it out over to Dividend made out like kings. But mostly it was folks never swung a pick that walked away with the money. Maybe them Wobblies was correct. Town wouldn't let 'em in, though."

"Is there any left down there?"

"Not much. Silver and gold take so long to lode, once it's out, it's out. We're left here with the holes. We'll go up there, take a gander when you ain't stuck in that chair no more."

Ryder could barely imagine not being stuck in this chair no more.

"Grandpa."

"Yessir."

"At church they say the earth is six thousand years old. They say science has the math wrong."

"Well, boy, I guess it don't hurt anybody to think so, but hell's sake. Look at them layers upon layers of sand turned to rock, all that coal where you come from, mashed and made from the same chemistry as plants and animals. Picture what it takes for them giant sheets of rock and dirt and stone and water and extinct heat to lay down and shove back up. I don't want to mess with your mama on this. She believes what she needs to. But I've spent my life gandering at the minerals and metals we stand on, look up at, dig into, leave behind after living our tiny lives. We live in one big demonstration of how this world was made, and six thousand years don't cut it."

Grandpa unbuttoned his shirt to cool the skinny flab of his furry chest and stomach. He waved the tails to create a breeze. Ryder considered pulling off his T-shirt, but it seemed too much bother. And not much cooler.

Grandpa whistled for Auriferous, who ambled into sight from behind the house.

"Now you shut your mouth," Grandpa cautioned, "about such things around your good mother. There's no call to give her grief. But a old man knows old when he sees it. And a old man also knows not to put his hand in a hornet's nest. Not calling Evaleen a hornet. But I know better than to take on that swarm over to the Sunday School. You'd benefit from the same wisdom, Ryder McCorry . . . what's that other name? Your daddy's?"

"Mikkelson."

"That's right. A good man. Working hard for your mama and

you. Keep an eye on him."

"How can I keep an eye on him? I hardly see him anymore."

"You know why. He's out there to the Depot night and day. Burning up poison never should of got made. It's them poisons we used in the war—the old war—stopped me believing in any god I'd kneel to. You coulda seen my uncle, come back a nerveless fright, you'd know what I'm talking about."

"Grandpa, what?"

"Poison gas took away all his feeling, which might of been a good thing considering his face and chest was melted and twisted like this mountainside. But then he burned himself to the bone, right here at home, leaning against a hot radiator he couldn't feel. Died of infection, because how in the world—"

Grandpa cut off. Walked behind the cooling shed, where Ryder couldn't follow. Auriferous settled in the shade of Ryder's protruding leg.

EIGHTEEN

Grandpa's stories never dried up.

"My wife, you know, was connected to fame. You got your middle name after McCorrys. Quite a lot around here back in the day, mostly Silver City. Most left when water come up the tunnels, but some clung to claims all about these hills. Her uncle was so touched in the head by the idea of that Dream Mine, he got baptized Mormon. Channels of revelation and such."

Grandpa talked as if Ryder had always lived right alongside him. Ryder shut up while Grandpa was on a jag and took in what he could, hoping to remember names and places when the chance came along. School library. Questions for his parents when he remembered to ask. Ryder liked new words. He murmured them to himself, repeating until they settled.

"Anyhow," Grandpa resumed. "McCorrys. My wife was cousin to Mary. People say Mary had a little brother needed an operation, some kind. I don't know. Maybe she just wanted to be a motion picture star. Don't need a brother to want that."

Ryder looked at his screwy leg. It might be cool to have an older sister.

"So," Grandpa said. "Off she goes to Hollywood. Only job at first was one a them Bathing Beauties—not reputable but that didn't mean nobody watched them little films. It does say how pretty the girl was. Whole family was pretty, even the boys. Where you think you got your good looks from?"

"Grandpa, I'm adopted, remember?"

Grandpa looked confused, then brightened again. "I don't think that makes much difference. Children come to resemble their families. Universe marks them as kin."

Ryder pictured his dad, short to start with and bent by life. Ryder registered Alma's unease over his son's lengthening physique, but Ryder didn't know how to make it better. And even though Evaleen's legs were long and straight, the rest of her sat heavy on them. "Just like my daddy," she'd say. "Built like an ice cream cone. Except worse, once my boobs came in."

Alma: "Evaleen, you are one beautiful woman. Don't talk about yourself that way. You turned me 'round the first time I saw you and ever since."

Right now, the chair kept Ryder at a child's height. But as soon as he could stand again, everyone would have to get used to new configurations. Well, maybe not Grandpa Yeadon, not prone to re-think much at all, although his mind was a long and busy record of the past. Not much room in there to stow more recent information, but eventually he could find a little space on a backroom shelf.

"So, Mary McCorry's prancing with them pretty girls on the California beach, not much clothes on for them days. Even though, golly, if they could see what the camera shows us now, right there on everybody's television—you seen old Joan Collins? What's that show about them rich people? How about that—what's her name? Last name like a spigot. Married the Six Million Dollar Man?"

"Um. Farrah Fawcett?"

"That's the one. You seen that red swimming suit she—"

"Grandpa! She's old, too."

Grandpa paused clanking around to deliver a firm glare.

"No she ain't. You're just a kid. You ain't old enough to be taking part in this conversation. What are you sitting around here for?"

Grandpa's blotchy bald head stuck out of the tennis visor he'd taken to wearing in the searing August sun. Sweat rolled down the pate to soak the filthy terry lining, then dripped in dirty streaks down his cheeks and neck. His work shirt was worn thin enough to see through, buttoned or not. Grandpa's khaki pants hung low, but somehow clung to his concave butt.

"Fourteen," Ryder said.

"What?"

"Grandpa, I'm fourteen. You asked how old I am. I'm sitting around here because my leg got broken. Again. By the doctor. And they put in a lot of screws and, um, cadaver paste, because pieces were coming apart from the first time I broke it. Because I grew a lot."

Grandpa dropped the rusted object he was holding—barehanded in a hundred degrees—and picked his way over to take a look. Ryder's jeans were cut off extra high at the right leg, safety-pinned along the seam-ripped outer line, so he could get out of them at night.

"I'll be damned."

"Grandpa . . ."

"Got yourself all tucked up in t'other leg, I hope."

"Grandpa!"

"Whereat did you break it the first time?"

"Up in the Book Cliffs. Hunting with Dad. I was seven. Remember? That's why we moved here. To be closer to Provo, where the surgeon is."

"I mean whereat on your leg."

"Oh. All over the place. The ones they fixed this time are tibia and fibula, up by my knee. All the pieces were skewampus. The doctor says when I'm done growing she'll put a new nail down through the femur, because the one in there now won't be long enough."

"What did you mean, cadaver paste?"

Ryder was sorry he'd mentioned it. "Like, ground-up bone from dead bodies. They make it into a paste and stick it into gaps and cracks. Like—Play-Doh. Sort of."

It wasn't exactly that he was grossed out. It was about wondering, more and again, whose DNA was in him. Who *else,* now, lived in his body without his knowledge? Grandpa seemed concerned, but not for the same reason. "Well, hellfire and damnation. That's got to be costing your folks a lot of money."

Ryder was relieved to change the subject. "Well, you're letting us live here for free. Remember? So Dad can work out to Dugway and get paid better. And benefits. And Mom can work at the school in Gemini."

Grandpa looked pleased. He swiveled in the direction of the Army Depot, northwest, beyond the Vernon hills. Then he craned as if he could see Gemini over the high ridge. He wrenched off his tennis visor, wrung it out, and said, "Well ain't that good of me."

"Well, yeah. It is. I know my folks appreciate it."

"That reminds me of another boy once who needed surgery. Lived in Silver City. His sister went to Hollywood, back in the early days of motion pictures, and become a movie star so she could pay for it. Did a picture with Buster Keaton, you know of him?"

"I don't think so."

"Family's family, you know that? Family is people who look after one another. And, you know? Your mother's a fine cook. Good for everybody. Simple as that."

NINETEEN

Also in Opex, there was Russell Overland, a mournful kid who looked like a scarecrow Frankenstein. Maybe he was taller than Ryder. Whenever Russell rambled over, Ryder could watch him come down Opex Hill, across Silver Avenue where it forked off Main, then across Ajax and Godiva Streets and then up Gold Way toward Grandpa's place on the south slope of Gemini Mountain. Usually midmornings. Russell didn't talk much (unless he was pointing out old mines and their names or speculating about hunting spots) but he hung around, which meant he viewed Ryder as a friend. He'd stay for dinner when Evaleen invited him, which was most of the time.

"That boy has got a story to tell," Grandpa murmured once as they watched Russell labor up their side of the almost-ghost town. "It ain't pretty."

Russell always wore the same baggy jeans and dirty blue V-neck. Beat up sneakers, poor protection on the sharp mountain rubble, aggravated his odd gait. He combed his coarse hair forward so it hung over his eyes like a sunshade. His ropey neck and forearms burned scarlet in the unimpeded sun.

Ryder felt soft and formless even as his ribs caved over his stomach. His arms and legs were stretched like wire. Everything he ate went first to mending bone, then to growing. He was hungry again as soon as he ate breakfast, lunch, or dinner.

Ryder was afraid the strung-out leg wouldn't grow like the other one. In bed every night and morning, he'd sit up against the headboard and bring the good leg against the other. He couldn't be certain, but so far it seemed disaster was averted. But he was sick of all of this. His butt hurt. His leg ached and itched. He saw the same three people every damn day. He couldn't go anywhere.

"Hell's sake, boys," Grandpa said after Ryder and Russell had polished off an entire box of sugared cereal and most of the milk in the fridge as an afternoon snack. "You need something that's gonna stick. Eggs. Cheese. T-bone. Russell, how about we go get us a deer, come October."

Russell perked up. "My dad and me, we're going for elk up to Wyomy. November. I can bring back some steaks. We'll make jerky."

Ryder said, "Did you say *Wyomy?* Can you even read? It's Wyo—"

Grandpa whacked Ryder upside the head. Shut him up. Turned back to Russell: "That right, buddy? I'm glad to hear it. Where is your dad these days?"

Russell's head dropped, but he lifted his eyes to the old man. "Cody, I think."

Grandpa went to the sink, grabbing a smudgy glass on the way, allowing him to show Ryder a skeptical side-eye. Like they were compadres again. Grandpa filled the glass, took a sip. "Russell, you look grown enough to give Shane's bow a hard pull. Think you'll take it up?"

Russell flinched, as if Grandpa had thrown a dart. There was something going on that Ryder didn't get, and it annoyed him. Grandpa's eyes were fixed on Russell. Kind. Ryder's friend rolled his shoulders back, opening like a butterfly. He stretched his left arm in front of him and pulled an imaginary string back with his right, squinting for aim.

Then Russell deflated. Took a seat at the table and put his head in his hands. "Not this year. But I want to. I think my mom put that stuff in storage somewhere."

"She's saving it for you, ain't she?'

"Don't know what she's doing. Comes home from work, lights a cigarette, plays her accordion. Then she opens one of them romance books and reads the whole thing while she finishes the pack. Then she goes to sleep."

"She could burn that house down one of these nights. You keep alert."

"I will."

"Sleep near a window. Try to make sure she does, too."

Ryder rolled backward to the sink, gave the bowls and spoons a half-assed rinse. Russell pushed a finger along the Formica swirls on the kitchen table.

"Um, what . . ." Ryder asked.

"I don't want to talk about it no more," Russell said. "Actually I gotta go. Ryder, I'll come back tomorrow. I got an idea for something to do."

Russell let himself out the side door.

After dinner, Grandpa told Evaleen: "I don't see that going well over there."

Evaleen stretched over the sofa to look out the front window.

"You mean Doris? Russell?"

"Uh-huh." Grandpa leaned beside Ryder's mother. They stared across Opex at the house that was supposed to shelter Russell.

"You ever see Doris come out of there?" Evaleen asked.

"Nope. Not since . . ." Grandpa looked over his shoulder at Ryder. "Someone's bringing her cigarettes. Or she gets out once the case is smoked up."

"Not since what?" Ryder demanded, hot. Sweating. Suddenly fed up. "Why's everyone so secret about everything around here?"

"I hear the accordion wafting up, when the breeze is right," Grandpa said.

Evaleen answered Ryder. Brusque. "It's not our call to tell you about it. It's Russell's. Don't you like it best when you can explain your own life to people? Don't you keep reminding us how much you hated it when everyone knew you were adopted but you?"

"Mom! That's the whole thing. Everyone knew except me! And now everyone knows something about Russell except me! He knows what everyone's talking about. Nobody's keeping some secret about his own self from him."

Evaleen sighed. "I guess I should of hung bunting on the wall of your baby room. 'Welcome home, Baby Ryder! You're adopted! Run and tell your cousins!'"

"Maybe I would have if you'd given me a chance. And when *were* you gonna tell me so I could tell Kenty? Huh?"

"Kenty wasn't even born yet, remember?"

"Nobody tells me things. I'm not a little kid anymore."

"I think Russell would want to decide how his new friend learns a hard story. You of all people should understand that."

"Mom, you're twisting this all up. Like you always do."

Evaleen zeroed in like a mother eagle. Ryder rolled back. Hit the wall. Evaleen stepped closer.

"You're the one twists things up, Ryder! All you got to do is think a minute about what I'm saying, without kicking it back like a jackass. Some things ain't related to other things."

"You're the one making them all related, Mom! You got whatever happened to Russell all gummed up with whatever happened to me and now you're telling me I can't—"

Grandpa yodeled in: "Hold on, young man! No one in my house talks to his mother that way!"

"I'm just trying to explain! Why don't you guys ever stop yelling at me so I can explain?"

"Don't shout at her, then!" Grandpa shouted.

Ryder choked his voice back down into his throat, but not before reaccusing his mother of shouting, too. "And she's not listening!"

Grandpa struck a rhythm on the paneled wall with his thick fingers as he hollered, "Well! She's your mother! It's within her purview to rebuke her son when maternal duty requires. Especially when you're acting up like a damn coyote!"

Back to the wall, Ryder tried to lift himself up from the wheel-chair. Grandpa put his hands on Ryder's shoulders and pushed down. "Boy! Don't go hurting yourself that way!"

Ryder grabbed the wheels and spun hard to the doorway, tip-ping a kitchen chair with his stuck-out foot. His mother sprang to the frame to stop the leg with her body before Ryder could slam it against the doorjamb.

He backed up, facing his mother and great-grandfather—a pathetic but impenetrable defensive line.

"Take it easy, son. I'm only reminding you to respect your mother. I know this is a hard time for you."

Evaleen glared. Done with talk.

Ryder's gut boiled. Magma.

This ramshackle hut on a miner's dry hill. Dead-eyed souls hiding behind heat-bleached walls. Ryder, sitting on his sorry ass with an old man and a broken friend, waiting every day for his mother to come home with food, week after week afraid his father would die in the poisoned desert for the sake of a doctor bill. His cousins were a universe away. He'd start school among strangers in a couple weeks, plopped in a rolling chair, leg splayed, kids he didn't know, teachers who had no answers to any questions worth asking.

The thought of Russell, the saddest, loneliest guy Ryder ever knew, striding the valley like a butt-hurt Sasquatch, pissed Ryder off most of all, because Russell—whatever his sad story—was exactly why Ryder couldn't feel as sorry for himself as he wanted to.

Ryder took it out on Evaleen: "You're not my mother. I don't have a mother."

To Grandpa Yeadon: "She never had a baby in her life. She's got no more maternal instincts than you do."

And now here he was, out on Grandpa's crumbling porch, hungry as hell, door locked behind him. The hot sun set behind his protruding foot. Diesel rigs, shrunk by distance, blew north toward Tooele, headed for I-80. Or south toward Delta into hard-blown desert, strange rough ranges. Ryder squirmed in his tired seat. Soon as he could stand on crutches, he was out of here. He'd wait until Grandpa was snoring and his mother was dead asleep, tired out from work and worry. It would make things lighter for her. He'd ease down to the streets of Opex, crutch down Main and head for the turnoff.

He knew he could do it. Once he hitched a ride with a sympathetic trucker, he'd rest his leg all the way to California, walk it back to strength on the sandy beach. He'd sit on a pier sipping Seven Up at sunset, taking in the lapping surf. Might try a beer. He'd set up an easel and paint pictures of cowboys and good horses, pretty Indian girls, the hard hills and twisting trails he'd left behind. He'd line them up on a sunny sidewalk and sell them one by one.

Maybe a movie star would walk by, ask about his lonely vigil and fall in love. Maybe he'd find his real mother and father, Hollywood types, descended from the kind of girl who ran off to be a Bathing Beauty.

It was a good plan. Another few weeks and he'd be up and gone.

His mother opened the front door.

"I got dinner set. Want to come in? Wash up?"

"No."

"You plan to sit out here and starve out of spite? Who will that hurt? You got a leg to mend."

Ryder grumbled. His gut did, too.

"Fine."

"Grace us, Your Majesty."

"Mom. Stop it."

"You."

"No, *you.*"

TWENTY

Ryder sat hungry but still angry—more furious than he could think of reasons to be—watching sunset orange give way to twilight blue. Long mountain shadows reached across the silent cooling Tintic Valley.

No lights came on in Russell's house, but Ryder knew he was there, probably settling in to watch *Melrose Place* with his mom. Eating a boxed mac and cheese dinner. Ryder's house—*Grandpa's house*—smelled of hot shepherd's pie. Ryder had peeled the potatoes and grated a pile of cheddar cheese while his mother was at work. He'd been anticipating this all day—hamburger and soft onions under a pile of cherry tomatoes, halved from his mother's tiny hand-watered garden. Mashed potatoes sealing them in, stretchy bubbling cheese to top it all off.

But he couldn't humble down and go in.

Headlights appeared on the highway. The vehicle turned at the Opex road. His father's carpool. No wonder the fancy dinner. Ryder felt a surge of relief. How long would his dad be home? Maybe Ryder could convince him to drive to Nile Valley, out to see Ferron and Kent. Ryder could sit in the back seat of the Monte with a little bit of creative seat-belting. Only a couple hours' ride. Sit at the river—his cousins could do the hoisting. Hamburgers at Roy's.

"Mom, you didn't tell me Dad was coming!"

"Didn't come up, now, did it?"

Evaleen stepped out. Grandpa came around from the back,

where he'd been sneaking a smoke. How old was that guy? He gave Ryder a different number every time he asked. Bad habits seemed to strengthen him.

All three watched the long sedan crawl up the steep drive to Grandpa's house, slipping on gravel. Four men sat inside. Alma opened the left rear door and stepped out. The driver killed the engine and handed Alma a key to open the trunk. Alma retrieved his duffel, closed the trunk, waved goodbye, and approached.

"Dad," Ryder blurted. "Can we go to Nile Valley this weekend? We could stay at Grandpa and Grandma Mikkelson's. Please?"

Alma walked right past.

Evaleen said, "We got dinner all ready and waiting. Welcome home."

Alma kept going. "Too tired. I had a late lunch at the cafeteria. I'll eat leftovers tomorrow."

He didn't even slow down. He stepped to the back room, where the queen-sized bed nearly touched every wall, and shut the door.

Evaleen made a tight line with her lips. Grandpa said, "Well, I sure am hungry."

Ryder muttered, "Well, screw you too, Dad." Evaleen glared.

"Fuck this shit," Ryder said, bucking up. "Soon as I can walk, I'm going to California."

"Get used to eating out of trash cans then," Evaleen said. She walked back into the house, dished Grandpa a plate, and took the rest out to the garbage bin. Scraped the skillet clean.

TWENTY-ONE

S he came out to the porch two hours later.

"Door's unlocked, you know. Nobody's keeping you out here."

"I know."

She pulled up a rickety chair. They sat together. Ryder feared that if he opened his mouth he'd spew venom, and he didn't want to. He could see stars to the south and west. East, the cornering of Gemini and Opex mountains glowed eerie blue under a half-moon. North was behind them, obscured by the walls of Grandpa's house. Ryder hadn't seen the North Star—nor the big and little bears—since he'd come home from surgery, almost five weeks.

Evaleen offered: "Not long and you can get up and walk with crutches. Once the leg is cast. And it will come off soon enough. You'll be yourself again."

Ryder started to say, "*Not* soon enough," but clenched his teeth.

He thought again about starting school in an unfamiliar place. In a wheelchair. Everything about him a spectacle when he liked to lie low and get a school day done. Normally he looked forward to being with his cousins and friends, even if some of his classes sucked. But here, he only knew Russell, and who knew what that might mean in a place like this?

Hell, maybe Russell was class president material.

Maybe he was the loser to avoid if you wanted to talk to girls.

Whatever. Nothing to do but surrender.

"Mom, I'm so hungry."

"I'm sorry I lost my temper. But you can't be saying things like that."

Both worked to stop the next words that sprang to mind. Evaleen managed the right ones. "I can make you a sandwich."

"Okay."

Ryder fought tears. His family was falling apart. Also he was thinking about shepherd's pie in the garbage bin.

She returned with a crispy grilled cheese on a napkin. Stretchy and hot.

He choked out his own apology. "Mom. Sorry."

He wanted to say more but didn't trust himself.

The west mountains looked like an open gap between heavy sky curtain and flat Tintic floor. Looked like a portal a walking boy could duck through to enter a dimensional world beyond.

"Let's drive out to Fish Springs one of these months," Evaleen said. "Grandpa can come if he wants."

"Where's that?"

"Pony Express Road. Way past the Depot, almost to the Nevada line. I like the river desert where we raised you. Especially in fall when the light comes sideways. But west, it's desert and more desert, passes and ranges and valleys. Wild horses out there. And all of a sudden, acres of spring water, cold and blue. More birds than most of us could name. Herons and ducks and loons, cranes, geese, kill-deer. Funny little burrowing owls turning their faces upside down. Birds I never seen anywhere else. Takes a few hours to get there—dirt road, too rough for your leg, but soon. You'll come back to the good world, Ryder."

Ryder was confused. Since moving back to her part of the state, it seemed to him his mother had become sharper, more impatient. But, also, more willing to tell stories, to show herself.

"Why haven't you told me about the springs before?"

"I grew up in all this. Sometimes I forget you don't know it like

I do."

Ryder: "I never knew you missed this place."

She sat that one out a minute.

"It brings hard memories. Probably I didn't tell you about the springs because it's the last time I spent a good day with my dad, out there to see the water and birds. He was in a mood to restore himself, is how he put it."

Ryder had heard plenty about his mother's father. From just about everyone. But this was the first time Evaleen had told a real story. Everything else was stuff about his restless nature. Charming and talky some days, silent and contemptuous others. Fixed on striking the last silver mine. Wandering the Ruby badlands. Wheedling in Caliente. Coming home to re-impregnate his wife and disappear again, months at a time, and, finally, for good.

Woodwards don't marry west of the Tintic line, Ryder had heard at some of the rare but rowdy Woodward "reunions." *They never know how close they're related.*

Guffaws.

As far as Ryder could tell, there wasn't much marrying going on. But there were lots of kids. No wonder his mother couldn't make sense of infertility. Woodwards were witty and brash, tight and contentious, hard-working when they wanted to be. Gun polishers, dead shots. Machine heads. They rode dirt bikes like Mikkelsons rode horses. Film crews paid them cash for illegal movie stunts.

Alma said he didn't know how Evaleen kept track of them all, signaled by the trailers and dirt bikes littering properties in every slip of a town west of Highway 6. "I don't," she said once. "But I babysat so many of them kids, I can put names to more than most."

Ryder's mind returned to his mother. "How come your dad took you out there that day?"

"I wonder if he was telling me goodbye, but I don't know if he was capable of making plans bigger than the day's impulse. I don't know that much about him. He had folks around Delta, on out to

Ely, all along the Lincoln Highway to the California line. But he spent a couple years growing up in Oregon. Out in the woods.

"Something awful went on there. A bad stepfather. My dad had a scar running from his left eyebrow all the way back to his ear. A piece of the ear was missing. Must of taken a hit with a bat or a big stick. A pipe. Whatever it was, it made him run. He was your age when he hitchhiked back here to be near his mother's folks. But it was too late to find home. Fourteen is a hard passage for Woodwards. I loved him, Ryder, but my dad was a mess."

"How old were you when you went out to the springs with him?"

Evaleen laughed, bitter. "Fourteen."

Crickets chirped in the darkness—one directly beneath them, under the porch planks. Bats whirred through black-blue air.

"Mom."

"Hmmm."

"Is Dad okay?"

"I'm not sure."

"Mom."

"What?"

"What happened to Russell?"

She reached to rub her own neck and shoulders. Gave herself a minute.

"Look, you need to hold this in until Russell's ready to talk with you, okay?"

"I will."

"He had an older brother. Shane. Four years older. Rough boy. Took after their father. Not the bonding kind. But Russell worshipped him, same way he adores his no-good runaway daddy. This is the way I heard it, from the women I work with at the school. Shane gets a girl pregnant. Maybe consensual, maybe not. Her dad comes up from Delta or somewhere, threatening, shouting he'd better step out and own up. Shouting every night outside Russell's house. Girl's dad digs up dirt to use against Shane. Turns out Shane's been running drugs across the Nevada line. Maybe DEA had been looking the other way, since it wasn't organized, just saying yes when he got opportunities. But it had become regular and there was folks in a mood to see him locked up.

"I don't know if that's all it was. Russell don't come from a happy family. Something dark in the DNA. Russell's a sweet kid, takes after his mother, misplaced among the men he's made by. I don't know how much of all this he can put together. But one night, about a year ago, Shane's hiding out in the house right down there."

Russell's house sat, dark. Blue TV light flickered behind a broken shutter.

Evaleen picked up. "No urgent sign of trouble, nobody coming after him, everything quiet. Russell was probably thrilled to have his brother under the same roof.

"Shane gets up early. Stands in front of Russell's bedroom door, pushes it open, says, 'Hey, Russell, watch this.' Russell sits up, Shane raises a pistol, shoots himself under the chin, blows out the top of his skull."

The dark deepened. Ryder blinked into warm night but couldn't make out what his eyes were searching for. The moon rose above the summit line, silvering mesquite and sage.

"Ryder, I'm not pretending things ain't hard for us right now. They are. It's not your fault. You didn't make bad things happen. Neither did your dad. Or me. Life is a rough ride. Sometimes we take a tumble. But we're okay. We'll figure it out."

Ryder was trying to see inside the walls of Russell's house.

He wondered if there was a bullet hole in the roof. He couldn't help himself.

"Ryder."

"Yeah. I know."

"Okay. One more thing. Your cousins aren't doing too good. Maura's up and left. Doug lost his job. Can't lay off the painkillers after that back sprain. Gained almost a hundred pounds—drug weight—so now he really can't recover. Sits in his La-Z-Boy. Mean. But he's helpless. I don't know how much Maura's in touch with Ferron and Kent."

Ryder turned the wheels to face his mother. Horrified.

"How come I haven't heard anything about this? Kent and Ferron are stuck with their dad?"

"Well, they're not really telephone callers, are they? Do they write letters? No. You know they've been keeping to themselves. There's details, but I only heard about Maura a couple of days ago. Doug called your dad. Your dad called me at work. He'd talked to Ferron a little, but we don't know enough to put it together. You've got to leave them be while they find a way to present."

Ryder examined his ugly dry toes, sticking up from the rubberized fabric gripping his stupid screwed-up leg. He attempted a small lift. The wasting muscles in his butt and back strained for purchase.

"Mom. That really sucks."

"Ugly language, but I agree."

"Mom."

"What, Ryder?"

"I want to sleep out here on the porch. That room is going to close in on me. The mattress is horrible."

She went in the house and came back with his flimsy twin mattress, a body-high shield. She laid it along the beat-up wooden railing. "It'll do better without the broken springs under it."

Auriferous plopped onto the pleasing new resting spot and looked at Ryder. Evaleen went back in, brought out blankets and a pillow, pushed the dog away, and spread the bedding neat on the mattress. Auriferous reclaimed his place.

"Let those old stars remind you how young you are," she said. "Your life is so new, Ryder, you hardly know what it means yet."

"Thanks, Mom."

"Sleep tight. If you can't sleep, you can look at the sky. Can you ease down? Want help?"

"I can do it."

"Move over, Auriferous."

She closed the front door gently behind her, and then the bedroom door, too.

He wanted to see the Dipper—which was also the Big Bear. Little Bear. Cassiopeia. But Grandpa's house was in the way. But he could see the swan, fleeing the hunter, approaching but not yet arrived.

TWENTY-TWO

Ryder's dad was home for a week, until the next stint at the Depot. He stayed mostly in the bedroom, door closed. Evaleen threatened Ryder and even Grandpa Yeadon with her wrath if they talked too loud, banged dishes in the kitchen, turned up the TV. Grandpa stayed outside, tinkering with old parts, re-sorting. Auriferous divided his time between junkyard rounds and naps on the porch beside Ryder.

Sometimes Alma burst out of the bedroom, then the house, disheveled. He'd walk to his truck, climb in, and disappear for an afternoon, or morning—and return only to shut himself back in the bedroom. Every weeknight, Evaleen came home from work, made dinner for everyone, and took a plate to Alma. Ryder could hear them murmuring.

Russell's instincts for avoiding other people's trouble kept him distant. Ryder watched him sway around his hard dirt yard. Or he'd see Russell heading up the slope—south into the unknown hills. He'd return at sunset. Or not.

"Mom," Ryder asked, blocking her entrance when she returned from the school. "What's the matter? What's wrong with Dad?"

"I don't know, Ryder. If I understood, I would explain it to you."

He looked up at her frightened, tired face.

She said, "Let me by," and he wheeled to open passage. Auriferous eased aside.

.   .   .

There was no blank paper in the house—not even the school kind with lines. Plenty of old newspapers, though, stacked up the walls of what Grandpa called the parlor.

"Will you bring me a marker?" Ryder asked his mother. "Maybe you could swipe one from the school?"

"Ryder!" she said. Next day, she pulled a whole set from her bag. The stinky head-rush kind. All the colors.

Ryder took up the newspapers. Drew Russell's house. He drew the steep Opex Valley, and then the wide, flat Tintic—once a lakebed, Grandpa told him. He drew Grandpa puttering in the yard.

"A whole lot of this," Grandpa reminded him, "is mighty valuable stuff. Scrap metal, at the very least. But if I put parts together, reassemble the way they used to be, they could be museum stuff."

Ryder drew strange parts, remade into weird creatures, Mad Max vehicles, metal people.

He drew Russell lurching about the hills like Bigfoot.

Grandpa lined the inside walls of his workshop with the pictures. He tacked some on to the entry door. He'd stand back to admire each one, as if they imparted magic.

On Monday morning, the carpool sedan pulled up the still-dark road to Grandpa's place. Alma, slicked up and dressed clean, stepped past Ryder's rumpled bed, now a fixture on the wooden porch. Ryder pushed himself up with his arms. Auriferous whined.

"Bye Dad," Ryder murmured.

Alma surprised him, low-voiced: "Goodbye, son."

Alma opened the rear door. The interior light illuminated the faces of the men in the seats.

"Dad!" Ryder called. "How long will you be gone this time?"

"Ten days," Alma said, and got in, and the sedan made a seven- or eight-point reversal to face the valley. Ryder watched the taillights disappear behind the sharp slope of Gemini Mountain.

TWENTY-THREE

"Your dad is doing something heroic," Evaleen said at breakfast. "Not just for us and our family. But the world. Those poisons out there to Dugway were made to kill in horrible ways. For once, the army's doing the right thing."

Ryder was shocked. "But we have to defend ourselves from the Russians, don't we?"

"How's killing our own kind, right here, with bomb tests and poison leaks, defending anybody at all? We ought to be smarter than that, Ryder, and your dad's out there helping get rid of some of the deadliest stuff humans ever cooked up. Decades of it, stored up, waiting to kill. Russians like being alive too, I bet. At least the regular ones."

"My history teacher said they got weapons worse than ours."

"They ought to burn them up, then. What have we told you? Two wrongs don't make a right. Your Dad is out there acting on that. You can respect him for it."

"Mom, I do respect him."

"Don't forget what he's doing out there. Working hard for us, in unfamiliar ways, and he don't like unfamiliar. But he's making sure we can pay for your leg to grow and heal. And he's making the world safer for everyone, whether they appreciate it or not."

Ryder thought about what his teacher had told him. For a long time he'd imagined that teachers and parents just said true things, all the same, served like school lunch. But here was his mother, flat out contradicting Mr. Harris from Ryder's old school. Mr. Harris's face got red and shiny when he talked about America. Evaleen thought what she wanted to think, and when she decided to spell it out, she just said it. Pushed her hand into the air like she was warning a barking dog. It was true even in church, although she always told Ryder he'd better obey the commandments. Follow the prophets.

"We're not about making trouble," she'd say. "Folks get worked up when their beliefs are crossed. Don't stir the pot unless the soup's about to burn."

His mother made him nervous when she got this way. Like he didn't know her at all.

TWENTY-FOUR

R ussell was one sly son of a gun.

Weekend before the school start, as soon as Evaleen's car vanished behind the base of the mountain—Russell returned. And he wasn't swaying up the rocky path on long legs and bad sneakers. He was riding shotgun in a grinding short-bed Jimmy pickup, traversing on the rough doubletrack that cut across the steeper mine roads. The truck turned right and headed up, tilting along an iffy route toward Grandpa Yeadon's place as Ryder rolled to the edge of the porch.

A kid with wire-rimmed glasses and a lank bowl cut sat at the wheel, while a younger, heftier version—same haircut, no glasses—stood in the bed, gripping the rollbar and stepping side to side to mitigate the bumps. The chunky boy looked up and grinned. He gave Ryder a quick half-wave before grabbing the bar again.

"What in the Sam hell . . ." Grandpa said, shading his eyes with his hand under the tennis visor.

Once the truck got close enough for Grandpa to make it out, he said, "Them's Rigby kids. From out to the junction." Then, hollering: "Curtis Rigby! Why you got to drive across my yard like that?"

The driver stuck his head out the window. "Don't look like a yard to me."

"Well does it look like a road?"

"We were checking a route. On up."

Grandpa squinted. "You'll roll that thing, tilting like that."

Russell pulled himself out smooth by way of the uphill window.

The hefty kid stepped up on the panel and leaped, light as a squirrel. Curtis opened the driver's door to plant his harness boots in the rough dirt.

Ryder envied them all. He figured he looked like splayed roadkill.

"Gimme a hat," he muttered to Grandpa.

"See, this is why you comb your hair first thing in the morning," Grandpa said. "So you can look good for company."

"Yeah, I'm gonna start combing mine straight forward, like Russell."

"Better'n it looks now." Grandpa handed him a smashed gob with a blue bill. Ryder yanked the trucker over his tangled curls.

The three ambulatory boys paused at the bottom step. Curtis looked like a city kid, sharp in a red golf shirt. Gold-rim glasses. Wide-leg blue jeans. TV haircut. Only thing gave him away was the harness boots, beat to hell. The younger boy obviously tried to copy his brother, but he was a mess. His gut hung out from under his tee shirt. He filled his jeans tight enough they might as well be Wranglers. His copycat cut was greasy but achieved zero smoothness. He had a gray tooth, right up front, like he'd taken a fall (or a punch) and killed it. He grinned up at Ryder.

Ryder smiled back.

"This is Mike," Russell said, poking in the kid's direction. He pointed at the big brother. "You already heard this is Curtis."

Curtis gazed coolly toward the highway, chewing gum and assessing the basin beyond.

Mike said, "Russell says you can't get off your grandpa's place. Because," he moved his arm up and down, as if he were whitewashing Ryder's sole with a long-handled brush, "you got that leg all up in a mess."

He leaned forward to examine it. "You got metal sticking right into your leg."

"All the way through the bone," Ryder bragged.

"Does it hurt?"

"Not as much as it used to."

Curtis turned to take a closer look. He stepped up the stairs, leaned over, took his time.

"How'd you fuck it up?"

"Hey, what's that talk, Rigby?" Grandpa cut in. "Ryder here don't got virgin ears, but you might not want to bust right in with talk his mama won't like."

"Yeah but she's at work," Russell said. "We was watching until she turned up to Gemini. I told them she's a nice mom. We don't want to hurt her feelings. But Ryder's about to go apeshit sitting here. What goes on in your head is as much trouble as . . ."

Russell's face went blank.

"Men have to get some things done when there's no women around," Curtis declared.

Grandpa snorted. "That's some big talk from a child badger. How old you now, Curtis?"

"Sixteen. Got my license a few months ago. But you know I've been driving for my dad since—"

"That don't make you *men*. Mike, I guess you're what—eleven?"

"Almost fourteen," Mike said. "How do I look eleven?"

Russell said, "Mr. Yeadon, we come to take Ryder up to the steam shaft."

Ryder felt like a calf under barter, but even so. He sat up straight. Leaned forward. "Grandpa—"

Grandpa said, "How the hell you gonna do that, *men*? See that leg? See how it's all wrapped up in straps and metal and form fitting cushions? Them little rods sticking in? See how there ain't no crutches? Ain't no vacation from keeping that leg quiet another month. You know that, Russell."

"Not a month, Grandpa. Maybe I can get a cast in a couple of weeks."

Mike: "We got a plan. Curtis is gonna tell it to you."

Grandpa snorted. "Sure, buddy. Shovel that bullshit. We could use some entertainment."

Mike giggled. "Shoulda brought you some popcorn, then."

Ryder grinned.

Curtis poised his long hands to support a point-by-point proposition.

"Okay, so we brought ATV loading ramps in the back of the truck." Curtis tilted his arm and hand appropriately. "And we got good tie-downs. The ratchet kind."

"What else we got is walkie-talkies," Mike added.

Curtis said, "Don't interrupt, Mike. I got voted to do this part of the job."

Grandpa glanced toward Ryder. The visor rose with Grandpa's eyebrows. Ryder felt like he was about to explode, he was so sick of sitting day after day after day after day. His dad was out to Dugway and lost to himself. His mother would not bend the law. She was right and he knew it. Damaging the surgical work now would mean starting all over again, at best. Worst, the bones might fall apart for good.

Still. How would it help anyone if Ryder went insane? He could turn into an axe murderer! Ryder opened his mouth to offer this insight, but Curtis resumed.

"So between the three of us—" he pointed to himself, then Russell, then Mike (who raised his hand), "we carry Ryder down the stairs, in the wheelchair. Russell and Mike on each side. Me holding the handles in back. We'll tip him back so he don't fall forward. Mr. Yeadon, you can walk right along with us, or in front, make sure we don't miss one single step."

"Hell, what will I do if you take a tumble? Catch the four of you?" Grandpa yanked up on the visor and tossed it onto the porch swing. "Stay here," he ordered. "I'll be right back."

He came back wearing a beat-up straw cowboy hat. "I see what you're leading up to, but I want to hear it piece by piece. All the emergency details."

"Grandpa! You're letting me go with them?" Ryder sounded like a horny goat.

"I only said I'll hear them out. Let 'em make asses of themselves as I entrap them in their scheme."

Russell shot Ryder a wicked grin, and suddenly Ryder understood how much Grandpa wanted to give something good to Russell. Russell was the most bone-deep saddest person here. Ryder was annoyed to be caught, again, feeling so deeply for his friend.

Curtis rose to Grandpa's bait. "Mr. Yeadon. Hear me out. We've thought of everything."

"Well, yak on."

"So we walk super careful to the truck. You can trust us to drive slow because we'll walk slow to prove it. You can check the ramp, make sure it's hooked up level. We push him up and turn him around in the air. We ratchet that chair down tight as a Tote Gote. We'll tie Ryder down too. We won't ratchet the leg, but nothing's gonna shake."

Mike ran for the truck. He reached in to retrieve a full-chin motorcycle helmet, glitter gold. A mirrored face shield. He waved it high as he came back. "Motocross!" he crowed.

"Here you see," Curtis said in his smoothest school presentation voice, "we'll equip him with the very finest headgear. Note the roll-bar on the Jimmy, installed by our dad who is a welder. I will now show you a map of our route to the steam shaft—"

"For hell's sake," Grandpa cut in. "I know every route to the steam shaft. Including straight up the rockslide. I worked them mines long before you was thought to be born. I've drove these hills in anything can get up there. Including mules. What you'll do is drive back down to Opex. Then down to Adkins trough, swing north and follow the ridge road."

"That's exactly our plan, see?" Curtis waved a hand-drawn map.

Mike said, "I drew it."

Grandpa said, "I'm getting in that bed with Ryder. I knock on the window, you stop. That exact second."

Curtis looked pained.

"Well, you can, Mr. Yeadon, but our plan says Russell sits in the back with Ryder, see? We got you down here as Command Central. You can supervise from the comfort of your, um, yard. Remember, we brought the walkie-talkies. Good ones, from my dad's—" he glanced toward Mike. "I mean *our* dad's piping outfit. His men go all over the West Desert. You can talk from here all the way out to Rockwell's. We'll leave the main unit here. You'll have the large view. Only point you won't see us is when we drop over the ridge to the steam shaft. But you can still check on us with the walkie-talkie . . ."

Curtis dried up.

Russell gazed up the hillside.

Mike grinned.

Ryder said, "Grandpa, please. None of us will ever tell. I have to get out of here."

Ryder watched Grandpa figure: how to carry a broken boy down rickety stairs. The terrain to the Jimmy. The strong muscles of each boy's arms—even hungry Russell's. The ramp. The route.

Everyone sweated in the rising heat. The sun bore down and the rocks answered up. The sky was more yellow than blue, atmosphere burned to dull molecules.

Grandpa said, "Anything happens, boys, and I face the wrath of Evaleen Woodward. You got any idea what that means? You will, once you start school again, see her waiting for you. Not to mention I can't stand to think of this boy hurt again. Hurt more."

Ryder: "Grandpa. I have to get out of the house."

Russell: "Mr. Yeadon, we'll be so careful. We don't want to hurt Ryder. We just want to help him not go crazy."

Grandpa looked about to reach out and take Russell in a wiry embrace.

He appeared to feel less tender toward Curtis.

Mike kept grinning.

Grandpa Yeadon: "I don't believe I got much longer to live on this hard ground. I might look unsteady, but you hurt my great-grand-son and I'll haunt every one of you the rest of your shortened lives. Especially you, Hotshot Rigby. I know your daddy."

Everyone took a breath and stared toward the skyline, a hot shimmer.

Russell said, "Let's get going then."

Grandpa told everyone to hold on one damn minute. He paddled back into the house, returned with an egg in his hand.

"I'm putting this in the bed, once you get Ryder strapped down. I expect you to hand me that entire egg, uncracked, when you get back. Can you do it, Rigby?"

Curtis bugged his eyes, intrigued. "I don't want yolk messing up the back of this truck. I'll bring it back all good."

"No cheating."

"Nah. I want to see if I can do it."

"You got till four thirty to get him down safe. His mother comes home at five."

Russell piped up. "We can watch her car from the steam shaft. Just in case she starts back early."

That hazard had not occurred to Grandpa. "You see her leave early, you won't beat her back without shaking this boy to match-sticks."

"Grandpa," Ryder said, trying to keep his voice steady, "you know that won't happen. Never once in her entire life has she left work early. Not church, not PTA—nothing."

Grandpa stood, hand on his chin.

"Grandpa, come on . . ."

Grandpa shook his head clear. Auriferous whined, eager to jump into the truck.

"No, Auriferous. You'll be too rowdy in there."

"Get Ryder in," Russell whispered to Curtis and Mike.

TWENTY-FIVE

Down the stairs, over the rocky yard, up the ramp. Grandpa held the big dog's collar, shouting admonitions.

Straps around the armrests, through the rims, around each bar, looped back up and ratcheted so tight Ryder feared the chair would collapse. "Ease up," he said, and Mike released a couple and carefully cranked to retighten. Chocks under the wheels. Russell pushed up to close the tailgate, then climbed over to sit with Ryder.

"Gimme that egg," he told Grandpa. Russell set it gently in the center floor grooves, back against the gate. Then he slid up to sit against the cab.

"Let's go."

Curtis fired up the truck. Mike floated into the seat beside his brother.

Starting up the high ridge road, strapped down tight and gold-en-helmeted, Ryder felt like a captive Roman warrior being carried into an alien land. Or maybe a wounded god, backing into the heavens that spawned him. The Tintic Valley expanded as the truck gained altitude. He sensed the magnitude of the ancient lake that had once covered most of his home state, blue glittering water filling the flats, lapping against mountain slopes—*right on into Nevada, all them ranges islands or yet unborn,* Grandpa had told him.

"Doing all right back there, Russell?" Curtis called from the wheel. "We got ruts coming up. Steep. Might slip a little 'cause I can't get a run at it. How's the crip?"

"Whyncha ask him?" Russell said.

Mike's voice chirped from the rack window. "How ya doin' Ryder? Push yourself down in the seat. Clench, man."

The walkie-talkie squawked in Ryder's hand. Grandpa hollered from the box. "You all! Stop and test the tie-downs! How you feel, Ryder?"

"Good," Ryder said, not convinced. His leg felt strange, wilted muscles strained.

Russell ran his palms along the taut extensions, anchored to the loops bolted into the floor. He cinched a little tighter.

"Don't want to break the wheelchair," he muttered. "What kind of shocks this thing got?"

"Hold that egg a minute," Curtis barked through the window.

"Nope," Russell said. "Drive easy, like you said."

"Fuck you."

"Come get me."

Curtis held the brakes. The truck clung to rock like a whiptail. The grind of tentative gears ran up through Ryder's wheels and slung seat. Up spine and skull. Russell worked to look casual, but his knuckles were white on the rollbar. Curtis revved. The truck rolled backwards, gearless. Ryder feared it would buck like a rodeo steer, but once he found purchase, Curtis eased the clutch so gentle it took a second to feel the Jimmy moving forward. The egg rolled ridge to ridge as if caught in shallow water.

Up they went. The wheelchair strained against the tie-downs. If they broke, Ryder would fly thirty feet at least before he hit ground. Forehead first. He'd dream this for the rest of his life—the break, the flight, the terrifying jolt of awakening . . . at least if he didn't sail now and die. He saw Grandpa standing small and vigilant below. Auriferous barked like mad, straining on the leash. The dog wrenched out of his collar to run up the hard slope, heading toward the marvelous boys in the escaping truck. He veered as he ran, calculating speed, slope, and meeting point.

Ryder closed his eyes. Curtis called back: "Almost to the top, now."

Mike took over the narration, from the sliding window:

"Look. We can see Gemini. School down there, see? What's your mom drive?"

Ryder choked it out: "Monte Carlo," but he couldn't make himself look. "Purple."

The angle eased. Curtis stopped the truck.

There it was: his mother's car, parked in the front lot.

"Look, there's our house," Mike pointed, but Ryder couldn't turn his head far enough.

Ryder looked down the other side for Grandpa, who waved madly.

"You scared of heights?" Russell teased.

"No. But usually I'm not tied down. I can jump out if the truck wants to roll."

"Didn't you do a bad jump down a mountain already?"

"Shut up, Russell," Ryder laughed.

The ridge road dropped steep off both sides. One wayward turn of the steering wheel would send them rolling *way* down, splattering pieces of boys against the rocks, one still strapped to a bashed and burning truck. Ryder felt a rush of familiar joy. Danger. Friends. Altitude. Big landscape, bluing in the distances.

"Check out Auriferous!" Russell said.

Auriferous was halfway up.

"Come on boy!" they shouted. "Keep climbing! You can do it!"

Curtis took his cue to drive on.

Auriferous tuned his trajectory and kept coming, body half-mooning like a dolphin's. Dodging stony outcrops, tangled debris, quick stops to pant and calculate.

Ryder felt the road tip over and down. The egg wobbled toward him. He stopped it with his good foot. Russell leaned to pick it up.

"We're up here now. We'll set it at the cab end when we go back down. We gotta show your grandpa."

Auriferous caught up. Curtis parked. Russell hopped out, strode to the back, dropped the tailgate and Auriferous leaped in. Russell calmed him, then let him lick Ryder's hand.

"Lemme see the egg," Mike said from the ground.

Russell waved it in the air like a magic stone.

"Whooee!" Mike said. "Curtis, look at this!"

Russell dropped the egg into Curtis's hands. Curtis pretended to fumble but lifted it intact. "Told you I could do it."

Ryder didn't say, "Yeah, but . . ." because he was still the new guy. Russell muttered in Ryder's direction but let Curtis preen.

"Guys, get me down," Ryder said.

"We got you," someone said from the front of the truck.

Footsteps crunched around the Jimmy. Three dark-haired boys, built small and lean, appeared in unison.

"These are Medinas," Russell said. "They live in Gemini. Brothers. That house, down there, see? Behind the rectory."

"We came up our side when we saw Curtis's truck," the oldest-looking one said.

"It's our dad's truck," Mike corrected.

"We told them we were bringing you up here," Curtis said.

"Jeri's coming," somebody said. "Hear it?"

The groan of a dirt bike sounded from the lower knolls, Gemini side.

"Come on," Ryder pleaded. "Get me out of here!"

Mike laughed. "Get him down. See how he likes the steam shaft."

Ryder caught the scent of wet sulfur and a strange, heady green.

Everyone not in a damn wheelchair reached in to release a tie-down. Metal clanked against the truck bed.

"We can just lift him out of the bed," Curtis said. "Everyone grab whatever don't spin. Watch the leg or we're screwed."

"Especially him," the smallest Medina said, meaning Ryder.

"Yeah, but Ryder's mom will throw Curtis down the shaft, anything goes wrong. Old man Yeadon will drop a car down on top of him."

Russell, Curtis, Mike, and oldest Medina assembled at the open tailgate. The tiniest Medina stayed in the bed. It took all Ryder's willpower to keep his hands off the wheels, trusting a foul-mouthed pixie to stop the front spinners at the edge. Everyone took a firm hold to ease Ryder down, then turn him east. The lake, and the high Wasatch peaks, rose beyond. Closer: rounded hills scarred by tailings, hoists, rundown stations.

A motorcycle roared loud as it cleared the edge, other side of the steam. A girl with long braids under a custom helmet landed the jump and killed the motor. She waved.

"What are you guys doing up here?" She swung a high-booted leg over the bike and disappeared behind a puff of steam, reassembling as she emerged. The stink of mildewed dirt and sulfur stifled Ryder's lungs as the breeze shifted.

Mike said, "This is Jeri."

Jeri stared, friendly. She was cute. She said, "Who the hell are you?"

Ryder checked the high-cut leg of his jeans, making sure all was in place. It was, but he still felt exposed.

"Um, Ryder."

"What did you do to your leg?"

Ryder pulled the helmet off and set it in his lap. "I broke it when I was seven. Then I grew. Had to have an operation to help the leg grow too."

"Where do you live?"

Russell spoke up. "His grandpa's Mr. Yeadon. Up on the Opex hill. Other side from me."

"Oh, wait," Jeri said. "My mom works at the elementary school. She's the lunch boss. She said there's a new lady working at the high school. That your mom?"

"Maybe there's more than one new lady at the high school," Curtis said.

"There isn't. It's just the one. And she says she has a kid with a messed-up leg. My mom likes her."

"Your mom a dyke like you?"

"What? Shut up, asshole."

"Yeah, shut the fuck up, Curtis," Russell said.

"What's your mom do in the office?"

"I don't know. Lots of things." Ryder looked the brothers over. "What are your names?"

The smallest one: "Angel."

Angelito, everyone said.

"He ain't no angel," Curtis said.

"He has the biggest cock. Everyone knows it," Russell added.

"And the tallest girlfriend," Jeri said, punching Angel on the shoulder.

"You?" Ryder asked.

"Hell no. Brigitta. You'll see."

Angel grinned. Stood on his toes. Held his arm high, tipping the hand flat to show how tall Brigitta was.

"Don't get him started. I'm Tomás," said the middle one. "Our big brother is Felipe."

"Him?" Ryder asked, pointing. He didn't say *doesn't look very big to me*. Ryder could tell they were tough as cactus.

"Yeah," Felipe said.

"That all of you?"

"What, Medinas? Yeah. Well, we have cousins."

"Me too. Nile Valley."

Jeri: "You starting school here?"

Russell: "He's in my class. Me and Tomás. And Mike."

Jeri: "Mine too then, dumbass."

Russell: "That's what I meant."

Russell and Jeri looked at each other. Lost everyone else. Ryder wondered if they were going steady, but it didn't seem like that. Not exactly.

Curtis broke their trance. He walked to the edge of what looked like a hot spring, throwing sharp rocks down the slope and kicking away beer cans as he went.

"Come on, assholes. We don't got all day."

TWENTY-SIX

A strangeness—seeping, dark, mostly invisible to Ryder from his low sight line—hushed them all.

"What is it?" Ryder murmured.

Russell said, "Deeper they went for the silver, hotter it got down there. Sometimes boiling water sprung up. They dug shafts to release the heat. Certain point, though, no miner could stand it."

"This one's really deep." Mike followed his brother to the apparent edge. Nothing signaled the presence of a vertical shaft but Mike's sudden halt. Ryder registered the remains of a pulley erected to move what came up from a long-ago excavation. Eroded tailings humped over the dry slope.

The Medina boys lifted the chair, levitating Ryder in a semitrance: leg disembodied, hot high air cut with the scent of abyss.

The dark mouth enlarged as he floated toward it.

The hole was twenty-five feet across. Thirty? Perfectly round. Ryder imagined falling, the metal chair tumbling with him.

Auriferous whined and held back.

The brothers set Ryder down at the rim.

Mike sat, feet hanging over the edge, placid as the Buddha. Curtis stood, arms folded, neck and shoulders arced as he leaned sideways toward the blackness. Jeri stood with her hands on her hips. She put on her helmet. Tipped the face-shield down, then lifted it again. Then she took it off. The Medina boys spread around the rim: Felipe and Tomás sat and swung their legs over. Tomás scraped gingerly with his heels, sending pebbled dirt into oblivion. Angel dropped to his hands and knees, palms on what Ryder first thought was grass. Here in the desert heat: wet moss.

"Angelito," Felipe warned.

"I'm just getting a better look," Angel said.

He put his head in the hole. He stood up, casual. "Don't look, Jer," he said. He unzipped and peed: the golden arc glittered like Ryder's borrowed helmet until it was swallowed by dark.

"Jeez, Angel," Jeri said. "Gross."

Mike leaned back to pick up a fist-sized rock. "Watch," he said. The rock dropped into the void.

Ryder, leg planked over the hole like a diving board, leaned forward a half inch at a time. Wet, stinking air filled his sinuses, catching at the back of his throat. He coughed. "Do you know how deep it is?"

"Nobody does. Didn't you hear that rock? Never landed."

"It can't go on forever."

"It feels a little bit cool in summer, like now, once the air gets to the top. But winter, it feels hot. Your grandpa says it's the same temperature. The moss grows all year, even in snow. You can come up here and get warm."

Jeri said, "Listen to this." She leaned in sideways, cupped a hand to her mouth and shouted, "Hello down there!"

Ryder expected an echo, but the hole muffled Jeri's voice like a pillow.

"Fuckin' hell. I hate this place," she said. "Why does everyone always come here?"

Ryder leaned back, dazed. He remembered what his great-grandpa had told him: below them were twisting wormholes, man-made and natural. Broken crust. Boiling salt water, wrenched rock, old machines, chutes and tracks to nowhere.

Rotting tools and mule bones. Forgotten miners.

He took a breath, leaned forward once more. His leg throbbed, a dull silver current. His mind furred. Something in his skull—not a voice, but an ancient rumbling (was it the bear?) told him to let go.

Fall.

In his mind but not, he could see the bear turning mid-shaft in a slow float, swimming toward light. He thought to back away, but he feared the unstable traction beneath his one working foot. The narrow treadless wheels. He kept still.

The screech of Curtis's walkie-talkie nearly pitched every one of them forward and down.

"RYDER!" Grandpa's voice crackled. "You got to talk to me RIGHT NOW."

Curtis stood up and walked around the edge to reach Ryder. Grandpa's voice squawked the entire distance. Ryder pushed the talk button.

"Grandpa, what? I'm fine. We're all just sitting here. Everyone's fine. Over and out."

"DON'T OVER AND OUT ME! YOUR MOTHER IS COMING HOME EARLY. IT'S A EARLY RELEASE DAY. LOOK DOWN TO THE SCHOOL!"

Felipe leaped up.

"Mierda!" he called back. "They're all coming out. Even the principal!"

Grandpa's voice squawked while everyone but Ryder ran to see for themselves. "You gotta come back! Only thing might save us, she called to say she's stopping for milk and eggs. She heading for the Kwik Stop yet?"

"HEY! You guys! You see my mom's car still?"

"Oh shit," Jeri said, returning, eyeing Ryder, then the dirt bike, then Ryder again. "Don't your mom know you're up here?"

"No! Look at my leg! If she finds out I've been four-digging, I'm screwed! Grandpa Yeadon will be screwed! She'll probably hunt down Russell and Curtis and —"

Jeri looked hopeful. "Rip their balls off?"

Mike grinned. He walked back to pull Ryder away from the edge. Ryder strained in the seat. He could see the upper streets of Gemini but not the school. He opened his mouth to yell at Curtis, but the whole pack was already on the move.

"She's coming out of the school," Russell yelped. "We can get you down but we gotta go another way."

Curtis groped his pockets for the start key as he loped toward the truck. Felipe directed his crew in Spanish. Ryder recognized one word: Ándale! The return to the truck bed was anything but dream-like, but the boys carried and hoisted with hardly a jolt.

"Jeri," Felipe commanded. "You guide. We're going around the shaft. Then down the Dane Town road around the tanks. We'll come into Opex the back way. Know what I'm talking about?"

"Sure."

"Watch for shit. Wave back."

"I know, stupid."

Tie-downs secure. Helmets on. Jeri kicked the Honda into a roar.

"Okay Ryder," Felipe said. "The first part's steep as hell. You'll be looking at sky. Hold your neck. Russell will brace the chair at the bad parts. It's further than how you came up, but after Payback it's easy road. Curtis can speed up. We'll beat you to Opex so we can warn you guys if we see your mom's car. Jeri will peel off."

"Go," Ryder answered. "Wait. Where's the egg?"

"Mike's holding it."

Jeri toed into gear. Curtis fired up. Ryder looked down the shaft as the tires lipped the edge. Steam licked his face.

Then the truck dipped sharp and all he could see was sky.

He thought to pray but didn't dare. Summoning Heavenly Father might bring wrath upon him and his new friends, which reminded him that he didn't want to believe in God anymore. He was tired of it, same way he was tired of reporting every damn thing he thought or did to his teachers and parents. Not praying was an intermittent distraction as he rode trussed and helpless, dependent on the capabilities of kids he barely knew, down a dry hot mountain he couldn't see.

TWENTY-SEVEN

The road—if that's what it was—graded into something even a Monte Carlo could navigate. Sky dropped to meet regular gray-green hills. Curtis stopped for anti-gravity Mike to circle the Jimmy and turn back the hubs. The door slammed behind Ryder's left ear, and the truck was moving again.

If Ryder's mother wasn't in Gemini, Russell explained, they could have been to asphalt already, but they had to take the other way—the long part of a circle running along base and canyon back to Opex. "If Johnetta's slow as she usually is, it'll use up time at the register. How's your leg?"

It hurt.

"Fine."

Russell tapped his knuckles against the glass behind Curtis's head. "Little faster."

Mike dispatched through the gun window as Curtis jammed along the smoother stretches, decelerating at tight turns and loose descents. Ryder saw barricaded mine roads, KEEP OUT signs, rotting towers, wrenched iron, cable tangled like yarn, giant buckets. An archaeology of technologies, tools and debris, rust. Then he saw rolling hills and undulating flats, yellow, blooming with purple flowers.

"Okay, we're stopping before the Opex turnoff, where the hill still covers us," Mike shouted. "Jeri's gonna signal and circle back."

The Medinas pulled ahead in Felipe's Jeep, Tomás standing up to crane.

Angelito waved back with a thumbs-up, and the Jeep blew off, curving around the old miner's cemetery.

Curtis wanted a third opinion. "Russell. Get out and run ahead. We'll pick you up if it's safe."

"What if it ain't?"

Ryder knew the answer: "We're all dead. Or *everybody* gets a broken leg. You can go straight to your house and skip it."

Curtis said, "Go Russell go."

Russell put his hands on the panel and flipped his long legs over, landing hard on the gravel. He gasped on impact but then he was loping toward the tapering hill. He stretched to see Opex, leaning one way and then the next.

"Can't see her car! Let's book it."

Curtis eased the Jimmy forward. Russell pulled himself up to stand on the bumper, facing Ryder. Curtis spun dirt and rocks behind them, then remembered his cargo and slowed to a sweating crawl. Couple of mechanics at the diesel garage came out waving.

"'Bout got it," one of them called. "We heard you on the walkie-talkies. Take 'er easy."

The truck tilted up, finally on the road to Grandpa's place.

"You see him?" Ryder asked Russell.

"Yeah. He's trying to come down the hill to meet us."

"Grandpa!" Ryder arched his neck, trying to throw his voice behind him. "Don't walk down! You'll have to hike back up!"

Grandpa was red-faced and pouring sweat as the boys reached the yard. He looked so sorry, Ryder wished he could leap out and wrap around him.

Mike flung his door open and galloped to Grandpa's side.

"Mr. Yeadon, we made it! We'll get Ryder unstrapped and he'll be down quick. Don't worry." He set a cupped hand on Grandpa's shoulder and a dirty (cheating) egg in his hand. Curtis and Russell got busy releasing tie-downs.

Up high and jobless, Ryder was the one who spotted his mother's car. He'd only looked down a minute to urge Mike through a jammed release and there she was, at the bottom end of Opex. He could see her craning, alert to an extra truck. Industrious bodies.

"Oh, no, no, no, NO. GUYS—"

"Oh, shit, she's coming up." Russell said. "Hurry! Get this—"

Everyone got frantic and clumsy.

"No!" Curtis said. "Stop! We might drop him. More guilty we look, the more busted we are."

Grandpa said, "Oh my Lord, we got it coming now."

First, Ryder thought he'd keep the helmet on, but then he took it off to look innocent. Gold glitter sparkled in the sun. He leaned sideways to set it down in the bed. Something pulled at his hip. He sat back up, breathless with pain, air popping around his eyes.

Mike took a seat on a rock, lapsing into his standard grin. "Everyone get ready for broke legs."

Curtis said, "She looks badass."

Ryder, gasping: "She is."

Russell: "She's a nice person. But then I never seen her mad."

Ryder had. And, come to think of it, she'd never done anything awful when she was mad, except throw away a shepherd's pie. She'd never raised a hand to him. Grandpa Yeadon was the only one ever did that, one time, in defense of Russell. What were all these big guys—including Grandpa, including himself—so afraid of?

Everyone stood (or, in his case, sat) paralyzed below the eyeballs as they watched the Monte Carlo advance. Weirdly, in Ryder's vision, it was distant one second, right up to them the next—like a video skip. And then she was out, long legs in green rayon pants, striped knit shirt making her broad shoulders emphatic, tight-permed hair wilting in the heat. White shoes wrong for her stride as she stormed into the arrested fray *What in the hell are you doing with my boy / who even are you people / get him out of that truck now or you won't see the light of morning / Ryder, they better be abducting you because if you or Grandpa got anything to do with this I swear—*

Everyone leaped. Ratchets released, straps slackened, tailgate dropped and ramp hooked into place. Helmet back on.

Three strong boys lifted Ryder to the ground.

He couldn't tell whether they'd parked him and fled or stood yet to face the wrath of Ragnorra. His head felt heavy, vision curtailed. Ryder swung his face hard right, then left, partly to shake it all clear and partly to count the troops, which made him recall he was wearing a glittery helmet with a darkened face shield.

"Take that off your head right now," Evaleen commanded, and right there in front of his new friends, like a three-year-old, Ryder obeyed. He quelled a flush of rage.

How long would his mother see him as a child?

How long would he believe her?

Long as you keep acting like one, she'd snap if he asked out loud, which he didn't.

Grandpa stepped in. "Look here, Evaleen . . ."

She shot him a thunderbolt. Grandpa stumbled back but stayed upright. "Evaleen, this is my fault. I'm the one should have—"

"It's Ryder responsible for his own choices. These boys can go home and answer for themselves. I'm talking to Ryder."

"Mom—"

"And I don't need to hear your yip yap unless I ask you a question."

Mike piped up. "So, can we go? We didn't mean any—"

Evaleen exploded. "Just where did you think you were going to take him? Answer me. You look like a Rigby kid. Am I right? I know your people. Good folks capable of mayhem."

Mike said, "Yeah. Me and my brother—"

Evaleen turned to take in Curtis. He stood, exactly between cowed and defiant.

Evaleen: "Yep. Rigbys. Think I'm afraid to have a talk with your folks? Think again. This boy's got a seriously broken leg. He's been through surgery that's got to work, or he won't walk normal ever again. And it's cost more money than any of your dads make in a year. Even Rick Rigby."

Russell tried appeasement: "Mrs. Mikkelson, we'd never want to hurt Ryder. We just—"

"Don't start with me, Russell. I don't care what you 'just' anything. If I hadn't come along *just* in time, if the principal hadn't called an early day, you fools would have got Ryder up in that truck and tried to take him who knows where. You wouldn't of said a word about it until you rolled that rig or bounced this boy hard enough to pop brains out all your ears. It's dishonest and disrespectful. Which is almost as bad as dangerous, which you already know it is."

Ryder's brain made a little click.

He saw Grandpa shift. Grandpa hopped over to Ryder's side and gave him a little whack. He shoved Ryder's shoulder with a hidden hand. "What did I tell you, Ryder? I tried to explain to you boys, but you had to try to get him to Russell's to play them video games. Evaleen, I used all my powers of persuasion, but I was weak, and I am abjectly sorry. I let these boys plead me into taking Ryder over to play that—what do you call it?"

"NINTENDO!" Mike hollered. "Mrs. Mikkelson, it was a dumb idea, but Russell has a big TV, and we thought it would do Ryder good to go somewhere, he's been here so long and couldn't do anything fun over the summer."

"With school starting," Curtis said, "seemed like a chance for Ryder to get to know some friends, make it easier for him next week when he's in a new, like, environment . . ."

Russell went to Evaleen and put his arm around her shoulder, tentative. Evaleen flinched, suspicious, but it was Russell, so—

"We're sorry, Mrs. Mikkelson. We could of sat here on the porch and took turns with a Game Boy. It's just—Mike's got this new game all of us can play and we got excited. But see? We brought Ryder a helmet. We was going to strap him down, only drive that little ways."

"Yeah," Mike said, so earnest Ryder figured Mike already believed himself. Ryder was nearly convinced, too, but for the thread of silver pain running up and down his leg, looping into his back between the shoulder blades, reminding him he'd just come down from the brink of a bottomless steaming hole on a dry mountain, strapped into the bed of a pickup truck, driven by a sixteen-year-old man-boy fast regaining his overconfidence.

The grind of Jeri's motorcycle above them bore into Ryder's eardrums. Auriferous barked from a high slope. Ryder felt bad they'd left him to meander home. He said, "Mom, I got stir crazy. Russell felt sorry for me. So did Grandpa. They didn't mean anything bad."

"Ryder, I know it's hard," Evaleen said, softening. A little. "But you're almost past the worst part. We have all got to help you get there."

"We'll help, Mrs. Mikkelson," Curtis said. "We'll make sure he's safe at school when we go back. We won't let nothing happen to him."

Evaleen knew a smooth talker when he was talking to her. She sniffed a dismissive sniff. She shot Grandpa a *what's really going on* glare.

But the fort was erected. Grandpa gazed up to the sound of Jeri's bike. He was whistling a breathy Hank Williams tune.

"Let me help you carry your stuff, Mrs. Mikkelson," Mike volunteered.

"I don't need your help. Get on home, Rigbys. Come back when you ain't here to sneak. Russell! Spaghetti and meatballs. Come when you can smell it from your porch. I won't be as mad by then."

Curtis nudged his brother, winsome and hungry-looking, toward the Jimmy.

"Bye, Ryder. Bye, Mr. Yeadon. Nice to meet you, Mrs. Mikkelson," Mike called as he climbed into his seat.

Curtis offered a suave left-hand wave between reverse and forward, then cranked the Jimmy downhill. Ryder pushed himself up, trying to stand on his good leg to see the brothers disappear.

"Sit down," Evaleen said, and Ryder did, contrite.

But something didn't settle the way it usually did after a squall.

"Here comes Jeri," Russell murmured. "I'll go meet her on the trail. She'll give me a ride home."

She'd gone up for Auriferous. The dog bounded over the trail to Grandpa, who made a point to say, "Hoo boy. What were you thinking, chasing that girl?"

Russell held his long legs off the ground, a two-legged spider seated behind compact Jeri, who turned straight down and held the bike steady on the scree.

TWENTY-EIGHT

Ryder awakened near midnight on his porch bed, unable to quit the sensation of falling into a hole. Rocking and descending backwards in an invisible pickup truck. Pain shot up and down the length of his leg, stiffened his back, cut his breath. Auriferous pressed against his strong side.

He felt bad about lying to his mother. But it would be crazy to expose the criminality of his grandpa and new friends, not to mention Evaleen's own son. What good would it do her to realize she'd cleared the ground for her own deception? It was best to bury this, like the memory of his father's hunting beverage. Like Grandpa's intent to make moonshine. Like knowing the difference between a six-thousand-year creation and the millions of years the steam hole exposed.

Keeping some things from his mother was a kindness to her. Then again: five guys conspiring to make a fool of Evaleen. He knew they'd remember her for this. Repeat the story.

He accepted the pain as punishment, hoping that's all it meant. Hoping it was an effect of adrenaline and unaccustomed motion. Near morning, it subsided—all of it—and Ryder slept. When he awoke, the sun was high and hot. His hair dripped with sweat. The blanket smelled like a panting dog.

TWENTY-NINE

Evaleen had her back to Ryder, who sat at the kitchen table, chin in a hand. The new blue fiberglass cast stretched over the wheelchair rack. It didn't fit under the table but Ryder pulled it tight as he could against the periphery. His father had a way of striding past, oblivious, no matter how many times he nearly tripped over Ryder's extended limb. And Grandpa was too farsighted to navigate the unexpected in close quarters.

Evaleen dropped pink chicken legs into a lunch-sized paper sack half full of flour, pepper and salt. She put a flat palm to the bottom, rolled the top, and shook the bag as she launched into a speech she must have been practicing. Because the subject had kept coming up.

"Ryder, it don't matter how you came to be our son. What matters is you are. Heavenly Father's got different ways of bringing children to their parents, and one's not better or more real than any other."

She gave the chicken bag a vehement shake. Her forehead was sweating at the hairline from the kitchen heat.

"Are you listening to me? I don't need you getting all smart about this. I'm telling you the truth. I'm saying something that matters."

Ryder didn't always feel surly. Or sullen. He felt lots of things. He loved his mother. His mother annoyed him. The girls at school were, in general, interesting to look at and talk to. The boys were, most of the time, his friends. Ryder felt tender toward his father, suddenly a small and anxious man, even from Ryder's sitting-down sightline but especially when Ryder stood with crutches. His father was funny, quick with a joke—often a good one—and he had a way of seeing things that made Ryder want to look closer. Great Grandpa was good company, a motherlode of crazy stories.

But lately it didn't matter what Ryder felt on the inside. Everything he said came out like an argument. "Ain't you become a little shit," Aunt Maura, back to try again, had said last trip over to Nile Valley. "Just like Kenty. Crutch on out of my kitchen. I'll throw sandwiches out to you mutts in a minute."

Plus Ryder's leg hurt in an aggravating, itching anthill way, and he wanted to be outside, not stuck here in Grandpa's cramped kitchen, not trying to look all earnest for a heart-to-heart about who he belonged to. He did mean to say something reassuring to his mother. But his mouth kept blurting out stuff he didn't even know he was thinking.

Maybe the insufferable itching made him contentious. Yes, the leg was getting better. Yeah, he could get out of the wheelchair, and he was getting faster on crutches. Back to his full height—five eleven if he balanced on his left leg. Almost six feet! But would it ever end? And would he ever again believe—really believe—he wasn't fundamentally crippled?

"Well, if it doesn't matter how I got here then how come you kept it a secret? Did you think I'd never wonder why I don't look one thing like you or Dad or Kent or Ferron or any of the kajillion cousins I got spread out over this freaking desert?"

Evaleen turned her back to melt shortening in the cast-iron skillet. She reached into the paper bag, extracted a white-powdered leg, shook off the extra and dropped it in the oil. She reached in for another, and another, agitated but careful with the heat, and then the sizzling made it hard for Ryder to concentrate on anything but greedy hunger.

He wanted to say, "That smells good," but instead he said, "Huh? Did God want the whole family to know except me?"

Evaleen turned the gas down, threw the sack and the extra flour into the trash can under the sink, and said as she turned, "In this family, we say 'Heavenly Father.' And we wanted you to know once you were all settled. When it felt natural."

"It didn't feel natural to anyone? I thought everything was pretty natural."

"Well then, why would we mess with that? What would it do to a little boy to wonder why his mother—I mean, the woman who birthed you—gave you away like a bag of rocks? *That* is not your real mother. Your real mother wanted you more than anything, waited and suffered for more than twenty years for you. I was thirty-eight years old! Everyone my age had kids in high school. Some had grandbabies. I'm the one who changed my life and made sure your father changed his too. For you, Ryder! Because we're the ones that wanted you.

"Your real mother is the one who would fight tooth and nail if anyone tried to carry you away. Wouldn't have handed you over no matter what. The one who takes the baby and loves him with all her heart is the mother! That's the truth, even if I didn't know how to tell you about it."

Evaleen wiped her wet forehead with her meaty palm. Then she wiped her dripping nose with the back of the same hand. Then she wiped it all onto the front of her apron. She turned the faucet and filled a glass with water. She drank it without taking a breath and slammed the glass on the counter. It broke from the bottom, shattering up to her fingers.

"Don't move till I clean this up," she said, as if Ryder might hop over to slide his toes through the broken pieces.

"Don't you want to turn the chicken?"

Evaleen turned toward the stove, then back to broken glass. She lifted a bleeding hand.

"Mom."

"It's not bad. Just a little cut. My mind got away from me."

"Fix the cut. Turn the chicken. The glass will wait."

"You think you're so smart, don't you?"

"Mom, I don't."

"You argue no matter what I say. Can't you just let me tell you the truth and leave it be? You *are* smart."

"*Mom.*"

THIRTY

At night the leg had a way of seizing up, rigid like a huge boner. Breathless pain, twisted nerves, waking him just as he sank into chaotic dream.

Then he was stuck awake thinking. Following obscure trails toward places he didn't want to go. Which is why he didn't want more of his mother's explanations during the daytime. He hated his father's forced cheer when he returned from work, averted eyes shielding resentment. His teachers assailed him with questions that didn't matter, or worse, set his mind turning all night.

Variables, for example. The obnoxious thing about algebra was that it never produced real answers. Just what if a. Put this in b but if you put something else in b or c or x it's a whole other answer. Another what if. His brain spun variables all night and then his math teacher wanted him to do it every freaking day in class. And then homework, setting him up for a / b / x maybes all night again. Until he woke up because his leg had a hard on.

Josh, up at the Red Dumps, sitting on the hood of his brother's K10: "What if you go for some hot chick and you, like, do it with her, and then you find out she's, like, your cousin? Or your sister? Wouldn't that be weird? Remember when Mr. Haynie said people who are too closely related make messed-up babies?"

Out to Jericho, scout activity, dirt bikes and three-wheelers parked and grill pit ablaze. Patrick: "What if your real dad is Ted Nugent?"

Everybody: "That would be so cool!"

Mike: "What if he's Axl Rose? You're a good singer. It would make so much sense!"

Josh: "What if he's a rapist? Maybe he'll get out of prison and come looking for you. You'd have to shoot him dead."

Mike: "Yeah, Josh, like you're gonna kill your dad when he gets out?"

Josh: "He ain't a rapist."

Mike: "Far as you know."

Pause.

Josh: "She was a slut. How come she ain't in jail? Ryder, what if your dad's Ted Bundy?"

Brother Nelson: "Any woman Ted Bundy got pregnant would have had an abortion. At least if she surv—"

Curtis: "What if your real mom is Princess Diana? Then they'd call you someday and say, 'Hey buddy, you're the actual King of England.'"

Brother Nelson: "They would not. The king line goes through the dad."

Curtis: "What if your real dad is Prince Charles? Someday he'll call you up and make you move to England and be the king and kick the shit out of those weenies."

Adam: "Ryder's too pretty to be one of them royals. Diana married a dog."

Patrick: "What if your dad is, like, Duran Duran …"

Hot sand hills shifted and rolled in the wind, like a slow ocean.

Dr. Hoffman, the bone doctor in Provo: "If you were Evaleen and Alma's biological son, we wouldn't worry too much about further growth, but there are signs of real height in your genes. How tall are you now?"

"Five eleven."

"See what I mean? If you keep going like that. . ."

Years later:

Ryder asked, "You don't have any white blood in you, do you think?"

Sami said, "In this country? Who doesn't? I think I had a French trapper grandpa. At least."

Ryder: "My great-great-great-grandma is full-blooded Cherokee."

Sami shook her shimmering mane. Set plates on the table. "Very funny. You better not find out your family has Ivies. I know I had a Paiute grandpa from out by Scipio."

Ryder: "What if I do? Would you have still married me if you knew I did?"

Sami: "Sure. But you wouldn't sleep quite so well at night, would you?"

Ryder: "Kit Carson?"

Sami: "Divorce."

Ryder: "Really? What if you found out your very own kids were descendants of Kit Carson? Would you run them off?"

Sami: "What if *you* did? How much do any of us really want to know who's floating around in us? In our children's blood and bones?"

"I thought Diné revered their ancestry."

"I thought Mormons were genealogy freaks."

"I'm not Mormon. No more than you anymore. Quit that."

"We're always what we used to be. A little bit."

Ryder opened the window over the sink, inviting the winter air. "Let's not find out any more than we need to."

Sami: "What does it mean? We're here. Our children are here. Made of what we're made of."

Ryder: "Would you want our grandchildren and great grandchildren to know something about us? Do you think they'll want to?"

"I don't know. Maybe they should just live their lives in their time and not worry about us. Not much they can do about it by then."

He peered out. White sandstone sentinels glowed in chilly moon-light.

"If there's anything left for them."

"We have to hope so, don't we?"

THIRTY-ONE

School was out to open the deer hunt. Alma was still out to the Depot but he said he'd take Ryder to Nile Valley to meet Doug and his boys next weekend. Russell was hopeful, as he had been last year, that his father would come down from Wyoming and they'd head toward Notch Peak. No sign so far.

Curtis and Mike were up in the Stansburys with their family, where their ancestors had staked land and built cabins back in pioneer times.

Brandie's dad and brothers and all their girlfriends set up camp up toward the top of Lady Jane, above the tailings where everyone in Gemini could see them, and proceeded to drink and shoot. There was some talk about sending a warden up, but the appeal of collaborating with Fish and Game versus slowing a random bullet with a car or front room window was sixes, so everyone just held their breath. Not like those people didn't drink and shoot in the hills the rest of the year. Just not all together at the same time.

Grandpa Yeadon kept Ryder and Russell distracted with stories of hunting glory, but Russell was restless, hoping against history to see his father pull off the highway and rumble up to the house he'd left his wife and remaining son to inhabit like ghosts. Holler up the hillside. Wave a couple of rifles. Russell intended to keep the road in his sight, but he consented to hike to the hoist house. Then a little further up to sit lookout.

Russell kept his eye on the valley. Ryder's leg felt all right, a little more than a year out of the wheelchair and cast, crutches, and cane. He wished Russell would go over the peak with him, spot for bucks, but Russell would not be distracted.

Ryder didn't let himself see how barren Russell's nutritional life had become until Evaleen said, "He ain't strong enough for the height he's putting on. The kid is failing, he's so hungry. I don't know what they eat down to the house, besides the sound of that infernal accordion."

Ryder reflected. He'd only been in Russell's house a few times; Russell usually kept him waiting in the yard when Ryder showed up to draw him out. But when she tuned in, Russell's mother said, "Come in here, Yeadon kid. How's your grandpa been?" as if she were a friendly Kool-Aid mom. "You boys want something to eat? Help yourselves."

Moldy stuff in the refrigerator beside greasy cans of Diet Coke. Empty cans of stackable potato chips. A sack of shriveled potatoes in the corner. A box or two of mac and cheese with the kind of powder cheese that disgusted Evaleen. Russell cooked the noodles over a camp stove when he went "trudging," as Grandpa called it. Once, Ryder watched Russell pull one of his mother's Winstons out of his pocket and eat it—paper and all—down to the filter.

Russell fared best when school was in session, when he could wolf down whatever was on the lunch menu, polishing off whatever got left on anyone else's tray. That, and Ryder's mom's cooking, was probably keeping Russell alive.

Ryder's dad made it home by Thursday evening. Ryder had everything loaded into the truck. Grandpa Mikkelson had horses to loan, since Cadillac was too old for anything but kiddie rides in the pasture. Doug said Kit Carson could still carry good weight, so Ryder packed chocolate bars and Jiffy Pop, sodas and Oreos, sliced ham and a block of sharp cheese. Eggs, pre-scrambled and sealed in a plastic jar. Barbecue potato chips. He'd considered ice cream, but his mother said, "Just make snow cones, how about? All that Orange Crush. All that snow. Just make sure it's clean."

"We'll bring the brewskis," Maura, home on marital truce, said on the speaker phone.

"Don't want to hear any of that," Alma said.

Evaleen actually laughed.

Ryder had asked if Russell could come. Alma said yes, but Russell couldn't convince himself his own father wasn't on his way. "I talked to him last week. We're heading out to Notch."

Ryder could see Russell sitting at the edge of his mother's porch. In a hunting hat. Russell waved.

"I want you to take a good one this year," Evaleen said, urging them into the pickup. She nodded down the hill. "We got people to feed. Both of you bag one if you can."

Ryder wasn't sure he could do it. His hunting time beyond the fall had been limited. Ferron had shot good bucks three years in a row now, making up for his father's hotheaded long shots, erratic misses, and one gut-graze from the truck window that Ferron and Kent had spent a full day tracking to finish off.

The storm got serious as soon as Ryder and his dad turned down the Opex road. Already it was twilight. Alma was quiet and distracted, like all the time lately, but more. He muttered from the back of his throat, clicking back his teeth, lips barely moving.

"Dad?"

Alma turned onto the highway. Ryder sat quiet until his father swung right again, headed through Gemini.

"Dad?"

Alma looked startled. "What is it?"

"Are we going by Grandma and Grandpa's? Or are we meeting up at the cliffs?"

"Doug says he'll leave horses at Swasey's. If the weather allows, on up to Nefertiti."

"Can we take the truck that far? In this?"

"Some of us can."

Snow came at the windshield like fireworks. The road was pure white. Neither spoke the whole stretch below the lake. On through Spanish Fork.

"Canyon looks like a nightmare," Ryder said.

"You think I don't know how to drive snow?"

"No, Dad. I know you can. I'm just saying."

"Well, shut the hell up and let me concentrate."

Ryder sat back, stung. He stared out the window, guessing at sources of dim lights in the distance. He pictured Escalante's cross, shoulders weighted by snow, high on a jutting foothill as the pickup traced the wide rising curve toward the canyon's mouth. Usually Alma said something about it—the Catholic priests grasping their way through a bewildering beautiful hell. A confusing journey for the wrong version of Jesus—Aunt Maura's Jesus. In Alma's mind, Maura's god let sinners cheat, let them off too easy with a string of beads.

Alma kept both hands on the wheel. Eyes strained forward. Snowflakes like a meteor shower as the canyon walls closed in. Alma sucked at his top lip but said nothing.

Ryder waited a mile or two, or three, then said, "Dad?"

"What."

"I got Atomic Fireballs. Want one?"

"No."

Then: "Yeah, sure, buddy. Gimme one."

Ryder reached down for the bag at his feet. Rummaged. Head against the dash, Ryder felt the back of the pickup swing hard, pulling them into a skewed, steady slide. He sat up.

The truck kept sliding, off the road into loose rock, wet under a foot of heavy snow. The tilt sharpened. The truck shimmied, looking to roll.

Alma said, "We're going into the river! We gotta get out, now," but the old Ford stopped in an accretion of rocks and snow. They sat, breathing hard, and then Alma pushed the stick into first gear and tried the gas. The tires spun. The truck flailed at the rear. Rocks rumbled and rolled.

Ryder said, "Dad! Stop!" and Alma said, "You get us out of this mess, then!" and both peered into darkness.

There wasn't much to see—fuzzy black and pelting snow—but Ryder knew what was out there, likely steps away: the river, running fast under thin ice. How close was the brink? He turned to beseech his father, but Alma's eyes bugged to the windshield, hands gripped white around the steering wheel.

"Dad?"

Alma opened his mouth, wordless.

"*Dad!*"

Alma's head turned, robotic. "I hear you've been sassing your mother. Too regular these days."

"Dad, what?"

"Talking back to me, too? What an ungrateful little bastard you are. All the things she's been through for you."

"Dad. We've just been talking. Sometimes we get a little excited. I don't think that's . . ."

Ryder petered out. He'd never seen this expression on his father's face. His eyes bore into Ryder but didn't seem to see.

"Dad?"

"Quit saying that word, you little faggot."

Hard gusts shook the pickup. Ryder could not believe his father, who spent his life figuring things out, was not addressing the predicament.

"I've been thinking," Alma continued in a voice that wasn't his, "about breaking my word to my good wife. We made a holy vow in the temple that we'd live by every jot and tittle of the gospel. A sacred contract to protect our baby son. I was hard drinker but I promised to abstain. And I did. Cold turkey. And then I let Maura shame me into drinking that beer, and you broke your leg, and I been paying ever since."

All Ryder could think of: "Dad. People drink beer all the time and their kids don't break their legs. Things just happen to people."

Alma curled his lip like a snarling dog. "You think it's your call to tell your mother and father what's truth and what ain't. You dispense wisdom to all and sundry. You been to college? You been called up as bishop? I broke my promise to the woman I love and kept a secret. I've give her up to you ever since.

"Now we got doctor bills we'll never pay down. We sold our land in Etna. I sleep out to that godforsaken Depot, burn poison all day long, and when I come home it ain't home. I live in a shack in a junkyard in a ghost town with a ingrate and a coot just so I can be with the woman I love. We can't keep food on the table longer than the half minute it takes for you and that half-wit kid can't stop coming around to inhale it."

Alma's hair dripped with sweat.

"Then Evaleen hollers to take two bucks? She might just as well shout down the whole valley what a poor provider I am." His eyes glazed, like they were taken by frost.

Ryder was terrified. Words erased themselves. He began to cry. He thought his father would berate him, but Alma was beyond register. It occurred to Ryder that there might be nothing beyond the darkness.

THIRTY-TWO

"Here they are," Alma said.

"Who?"

"The firemen. They'll put it out."

Ryder peered into the dizzy snow. No firemen. No fire.

He'd heard the muffled passage of big rigs and hunting outfits above them. Faint glow of moving lights. How long ago? He couldn't measure. Ryder guessed his father's truck was a hundred feet below the shoulder. How close was the chasm? How deep the river? Could he step out on his side? Would his boots hit ground? What had stopped the pickup? A rock? Debris?

Unhelpfully, he recalled a phrase from his science class: *angle of repose*. Had they stopped because the weight of the vehicle, with its passengers and rifles, sodas and potato chips, had found its steepest point of hold? Ryder knew his mother would insist that Heavenly Father had stopped them here, protected by the Fathers' cross—right religion or not. Her family protected by a righteous bargain.

Alma sat agape. Ryder might have given his father some lip, mustered courage or indignation to defend himself, if they'd kept on the highway. But the man beside Ryder now was hardly his father.

"Dad? I think we're about to drop into the river."

Alma said, "Don't you imagine it would have untimely flew."

"Dad, what?"

"The sands of the dunes outnumbered by stars. Behold the mighty phragmites."

Dread iced Ryder's spine. "Dad," he whispered, "do you think you can open your door, slow, and get out? I'll slide up and follow you."

"Hearken to the gopher, a most lowly herald."

Ryder considered reaching over his dad, opening the uphill door to climb out, pulling Alma behind him. But Alma might panic and fight.

Ryder calculated the moves it would take to pull the rifles off the rack behind their heads, open the sliding window, and squeeze into the shell and everything he'd piled into it. No trusting Alma to not break his trance and thrash, or pull Ryder back into the cab, or start the ignition and spin the tires.

Ryder sensed a presence at his window. Nothing, and then something—the bear, pressing her paws against the glass, morphing face, black eyes intact and piercing into Ryder's.

A mother's voice in his mind, strange as if through water:

Move slowly. Wrap warm. Tighten boots as you speak to him quieting. My heels brush the brink above the fall. Measure well, and all.

Ryder sucked in one hard, catching breath before he spoke, low and reassuring.

"Dad, I'm going to open my door. I'll come around to you. Unlock your door."

Alma obeyed, docile and contrite.

Ryder enunciated, soft: "If the truck slides, get out, but wait if you can. Until you feel me holding your arm. We'll hike up to the road. I heard driving up there."

Ryder bent over in his seat, cautious not to pitch his father into motion. He tied his boots double, zipped his coat and grasped Alma's, lying on the seat, in his left hand.

"Dad, please stay still until I come around."

Alma murmured, eyes wide and unblinking, fixed on a menacing thing beyond the blowing snow. Ryder tried to assure himself that whatever his father saw was not real.

Ryder eased the latch. The door swung hard and the pickup shuddered. Ryder stuck his head out. He heard rushing water directly below. He put his feet in the snow, still facing his father.

"Dad, hold on, okay?"

Ryder's bare hands gripped the doorframe. He feared they'd freeze to the steel. He considered reaching back in for his gloves, but his father's form was dire. Ryder stepped left, grabbing at the gap between cab and bed. He pressed the door shut.

Ryder guessed it would be safest to inch around the front of the pickup.

No, murmured the bear. *This way.*

He turned his feet, tick by tick, until his back pressed against the panel. He kept his shoulders and butt against the truck as he sidestepped. He grabbed at the wheel well and, holding, ape-reached for the bumper. The pickup felt stable. He moved more quickly up the back, then tapped along the driver's side, afraid of slipping under the chassis.

He crept toward Alma's window. It seemed Alma hadn't moved at all but when Ryder peered inside, he saw that his father had removed his woolen shirt, the thermal shirt underneath, and even the thin layer sewn with temple symbols. His flap hat was, however, pulled down over his heavy-lobed ears. Alma sat childlike, round-shouldered, furry and pink, softened belly spilling over his belt. Ryder hadn't seen his father so nude since old days at the river. Summertime, jumping off rocks into deep green water. The man at the wheel looked nothing like the sinewy swimmer.

Ryder tapped the glass with near-frozen fingers. Alma startled and cranked the window down. He flashed a bright smile.

"Well hello! When did you get here?"

"Dad, why did you take your clothes off? We have to hike up."

"I got hot. What are you talking about?"

The cold air coursing into Alma's window did not persuade him.

"Dad. We have to get you out of there."

Alma rolled his eyes. "Lemme put my shoes on."

Ryder pushed his head in the window. "No. You got boots on. They're good. I have your coat. I'm going to open the door."

"Wait. Does Pop know we're here?"

"Who?"

"He'll take a belt to our butts, we don't get this load to Huntington."

Ryder cracked the door. He snaked a hand in to rest on his father's shoulder. Alma jumped like a rabbit.

Alma said, "Get in!"

"Dad, can you come out a minute? I need to talk to you about something."

Alma cocked his head. "Okay. But we do have to get on the road. Is Dougie in back?"

"Doug's fine. How about let's talk on the way up?"

"Can't we talk in the cab?"

"No."

"Get out of my way, then."

Ryder backed off. Alma pushed the door open and stepped out, hairy-shouldered and blotched red. Ryder reached around his father to set the coat on him.

"Can you put your arms in, Dad? We got a hike."

"I'm fine."

"It's a ways up. Slippery."

"What you telling me how to walk for?"

THIRTY-THREE

His father was, even under hard circumstance and age, a man of the mountains. Sure feet, strong uphill pace, slick snow be damned. Alma's rhythmic steps churned straight up the fall line. Ryder traced a tight zigzag behind, ready to catch, but his father's instincts drew them to the highway.

They stood at the shoulder. No headlights in sight.

"Where's my truck?" Alma said, surprised. But he sounded like himself.

"Umm, in the shop, remember?" Ryder answered, breathing steam.

"No it ain't."

Was this his dad, returned to him?

Ryder paused, uncertain.

Alma spoke again, direct. Imploring. "Buddy. I don't . . . why are we standing here?"

Ryder watched his father assemble clues. Heavy clouds cascaded down black canyon walls. The empty highway was indistinguishable from its whitened shoulders. Alma tilted his head to pick up the sound of water. He looked down at himself, coat clinging like a cape around his shoulders, soft stomach wet and shining in dull light. He put his arms in the sleeves, thoughtful, and zipped.

"Spanish Fork Canyon?"

"Yeah. Dad, we slid off the road. Almost to the river."

"How did we get back up here?"

"We, um. Hiked."

"My goodness. Ryder, are you okay? Son, are you hurt?"

"I'm all right. We took a slide."

Alma reached up to grip Ryder's shoulders.

"Really, son, you're not hurt?"

"Dad, I'm okay. I think you are too. But we can't bring that truck up ourselves. We have to get a ride out of here."

"You seen any rigs?"

"I did for a while. I think. I've kind of lost track."

"Seems I lost track of a lot more than that."

"Dad. I'm just glad you're . . . back."

"Did I go somewhere?"

"Kind of."

"Without you?"

"Kind of."

Alma looked so small and defenseless, Ryder could hardly bear to face him. "Dad. You're okay now. Except we're stranded in a blizzard. Are you up to trekking across the lanes? Get over to northbound?"

Alma was regaining his figure-out instincts.

"Sure, but do you think anyone will be coming over the plateau? It's snowed two more inches while we been standing here. I bet they closed the highway at Helper. Could be closed a mile, two, three down this side too. How long ago did we—how long ago did I take you for a slide?"

Hours ago? Forty-five minutes? It was true; Ryder had seen no sign of passage up here for—what? Whatever a long time was.

"How far past the mouth do you think we're at?" Alma asked.

"A few miles. We weren't driving too fast."

Alma peered into the night. The valley lights were obscured, but the clouds above them glowed. Dull but reflective. Ryder summoned the word: *albedo.*

THIRTY-FOUR

Only one more weekend of deer season. Russell was disconsolate in school on Friday. Ryder sat a few seats behind, diagonal. Russell's bony chest and shoulders covered his desk completely as he slumped in a school-day coma. A guy named Murphy—way shorter than Russell but muscled across the neck and shoulders—sat directly behind. Ryder's classmates knew him; Murphy had returned to Gemini on and off since elementary school, depending on behavior swings in a school in the valley, where his mother tried to keep him. When he was here, Murphy lived with his dad and other in-and-out men in an abandoned mansion up the high end of Gemini.

Murphy kept poking at Russell with a pencil while Miss Peterson went on and on about documentation, which made sense to nobody, probably not even her.

"Look," she said. Miss Peterson was barely older than the seniors. "I don't love this part any more than you do. But the state of Utah requires that you learn how to write a basic research paper your sophomore year. A crucial part of research writing is presenting your sources in standard form. Let's get this over with so we can move on to more interesting developments. The exciting part is that you can choose any subject you want to learn more about."

"Can I write my paper on female anatomy? I'm already doing the research."

"Can I research how to hide a body in a mine shaft?"

"Miss Peterson, can I research how to burn down a—"

"No. We can discuss your proposals when the time comes. But you cannot research any of those subjects."

"You said we could research any subject we wanted."

"Well, I take it back." She lifted the little pamphlet to her face, pretending to refer to the text.

A wad of wet pink bubblegum flew from the back and splattered on Miss Peterson's desk, but hardly anyone noticed; a more compelling spectacle was building toward climax.

Murphy made a big deal of turning his pencil in a little silver sharpener he'd dug—with great messy effort—out of his overstuffed backpack. He poked Russell again, reaching under his desk for the eye-shaped expanse of skin showing between Russell's T-shirt and jeans. Russell stirred like a large sleeping carnivore. The class tittered.

Miss Peterson said, "What's going on over there, Murphy? Russell, wake up, please. I need you to give me your full attention."

"Why do you *need* Russell's attention?" someone behind Ryder asked, and Miss Peterson, who came from the lake valley—obviously the rich Mormon part—blushed and turned back to the board. Then she turned around, pulled a tissue from the box on her desk, picked up the glistening pink blob and dropped it into the trash can. She consulted the little booklet and turned back to speak to the chalkboard.

The class turned their full attention back to Russell and Murphy—except maybe Mike, who could concentrate on everything all at once and recite it back like a tape recorder.

Ryder's mom's official job was keeping books and inventory in the school office, which was also the district office (because there was one more school in the district, twelve kids who met in a house in the far desert). But Evaleen covered many other needs, including talking kids through teacher or student meltdowns, bouts of morning sickness, or effects of huffing tailpipe exhaust during lunch hour. Evaleen had told Ryder to help Miss Peterson find her way. "Sure she's young. You're all too much but give her time to learn. She might figure out how to drag your sorry butts to graduation."

But right now Miss Peterson had about as much influence as a housefly when it came to Murphy on a tear and Russell lost in mournful yearning. Ryder figured 350 pounds of hard muscle between them versus her hundred or so, if you counted the coordinated pink and gray outfit and all the hair spray. Ryder considered running down the hall to alert his mom—far more capable of talking big boys down than the clueless teacher.

But he didn't want to look like a mama's boy.

Ryder glanced toward greasy Mike, who looked pleasantly empty-headed. But his right foot tapped sideways against the leg of his desk, steady as a metronome, and Ryder knew Mike was on alert.

Russell didn't lift his shoulders, but he reached back to swat at Murphy, who leaned back and smirked, untouched.

Miss Peterson had no idea what was brewing.

Did she? She kept her face to the blackboard. Maybe she was frightened.

"Russell," she said, then turned. "Please sit up in your seat. Nobody can pass tenth grade without writing an acceptable research paper. I need your attention."

"What about me?" Tomás inquired in a smoky voice. "Do you need *my* attention?" He unbuttoned the top of his silky shirt, stroked the fine fur beneath a plate gold chain with his index finger.

Miss Peterson pursed her lips.

"Shut up, Tomás," Jeri said. "You don't have to talk dirty every time you open your mouth."

That swiveled Murphy's head away from Russell. "I seen *you* open your mouth, Jeri," he said, vicious enough to raise the hair on the back of Ryder's neck. "I seen you with a cock in it, at the Rendezvous. And your pants were down. I seen."

The only two girls in the class besides Jeri, dough-faced Mormon cousins from Vernon and mostly wordless, gasped together. "Oh my heck, shut up, Murphy," one of them said, and the other might have been about to speak when Russell rose up like a breaching whale. His desk flipped and flew, and then Murphy's did too.

"What the fuck did you just say to Jeri?" Russell roared.

Murphy sat, exposed in his deskless chair, opening and closing his leering lips. Flaring nostrils. "Hey, all I said was what I saw. What's she expect when she's drunk as a skunk and taking a squat—"

Miss Peterson stepped toward Murphy.

"Get out of my classroom," she said. "Get out of this building. Now."

Murphy grinned. He was missing a couple of bottom teeth. "That's against the law. You're trying to make me truant."

Ryder glanced toward Jeri. In school, without her motocross armor, she hardly looked like the Jeri he knew—and right now she was unrecognizable, up against the wall, ghostlike, wide-eyed and seeing something in front of her that Ryder did not want to picture.

But he did picture it. He couldn't help it.

Miss Peterson moved fast. She was a good four inches shorter than Jeri, but at this moment she looked like a real teacher. She passed his desk. "Ryder, go get your mother. And notify the principal."

Ryder leaped and ran. By the time he returned with Evaleen, Russell, Mike, and massive Mr. Harrold from the next classroom over had a spewing, howling, kicking Murphy pinned to the wall, and just about every kid in the school had crowded in to watch. Tomás stood in front of them, cursing Murphy in Spanish. Miss Peterson had Jeri's upper arm, not restraining but holding her. She signaled to Ryder, and he stepped over five rows of desks to reach them.

Murphy screamed, "Hey, bitch, don't you want to show the class what you learned at the Rendezvous?" and Jeri cowered, shut her eyes tight.

"You. Do not leave her," the teacher said. Ryder slipped behind Jeri and draped his arms over her shoulders. She sagged under the weight. He took her under the arms and half-carried her to Miss

Peterson's desk, setting her on the teacher's chair.

"Okay if I keep my hand on your shoulder?" he asked. She stiffened, then softened, then slid to the floor to crouch in the little cave where the chair tucked under the desk. She reached a hand up to pull him down beside her.

"Everybody was drunk," she said. "I had to pee. There was this guy walking around with his pants open . . . I couldn't go anywhere. I puked beer and pizza down his jeans . . ."

Ryder's mind erased itself. Ghoulish images and strange letters flickered in the fog of it. "It's okay," he said. "You don't have to explain."

He could hear his mother, across the room at the wall with Russell and Mike, and Tomás and Mr. Harold, and Murphy—more distinctly than he could hear Jeri. Maybe it was because his ears were attuned to Evaleen at high authority, but also he didn't want to hear what Jeri was telling him. He'd been at the Rendezvous. Everyone had. The celebration in town was wild: wannabe "mountain men" and parents drunk and cursing, T-shirts and candy and snow cones for sale alongside lewd speculations. A gigantic bonfire fueled by pieces of abandoned houses and rotting mine structures, the high school teachers effigied and burned for Homecoming. Nice families sitting on their lawns, bake sales on the sidewalks. Neighbors calling to one another. Fireworks smuggled from Wyoming. Whoops and howls, street brawls, muzzle loaders.

But he'd also seen what went on beyond the city limits, even among the kids his age. He hadn't thought he was a prude, but his brain and gut had reeled at the lurid scenes, the cries and calls and howling curses, the puke, the shit and puddles of piss. The rustlings beyond the firelight. Grown men he'd never seen, come in from who knows where, following girls Ryder knew and didn't, willing and unwilling, experienced and childlike, into the sage and mesquite. A couple of girls and a few grown women had taken Ryder by the hand, pulling him toward the darkness. "What, are you a faggot?

You're pretty enough," one of them said when he resisted. One drunk toothless woman had said, "I got to pee. Come with me. I need protection," and Ryder, not sure that's what she really wanted, had turned and fled.

Had Jeri been speaking to him all this time?

. . . he was back at the fire. Didn't even clean up. Walked around with upchuck pizza on crotch. Laughing. Murphy was following him all night, said it was his uncle . . .

Ryder stood up. The room was cleared of kids but for Russell and Mike, still holding writhing Murphy, and Tomás who stood before them like a livid Latin priest. Tomás looked more fierce and quietly furious than anyone in the room. Mr. Harrold stood to the side, red and quivering, out of breath; Ryder guessed he'd tried to throw a punch before Evaleen stopped him. Miss Peterson, behind Ryder's mother, remembered Ryder and approached the desk. She was coming for Jeri. Mrs. Spendlove, the square-shouldered psychology teacher with a man's haircut, stood next to Ryder's mom, speaking calmly, connective notes between Murphy's outbursts and Tomás's rhythmic sermon.

Mrs. Spendlove said, "As soon as you're ready for Russell and Mike to release you, Murphy, I'll give them the signal. But you need to show us you're calm enough. I need me to tell me you're calm."

"Fuck you, dyke bitch," Murphy spat, and Russell leaned in to pin Murphy's right shoulder against the wall. Murphy strained, enraged as a bull, but didn't stand a chance. Ryder wondered how Russell found the power, starved as he was. Murphy let loose with an animal scream, banging his head against the brick until blood ran and his eyes rolled. Still he howled obscenities, out of his mind, and Evaleen called back to Ryder and Miss Peterson, "Put something behind his head. Get the girl out. Make sure the principal's called for help. Keep Jeri safe in the office. Ryder, leave her with your teacher and go outside to flag the medics. Russell, Mike, are you holding up?"

"Fuck yeah," Mike answered. "Want me to tell you about documentation while we got all this time?"

Russell was a blind, wordless force. Tomás maintained his blasphemous sermon.

Evaleen said, "Try not to say *fuck* in school, okay Mike?"

"Sorry, Mrs. Mikkelson."

"Try not to say *pendejo* in school, okay Tomás?"

Ryder nudged Jeri and Miss Peterson toward the main office. He set them in the lobby where they could be alert to developments, but Jeri followed him back out and then kept walking. Out the front doors. Across the parking lot. Miss Peterson called, "Jeri . . ." and then wandered out too.

The school was nearly empty. Students and teachers milled in the sharp wind of the parking lot. The principal, a razor-thin guy with a combover, strode out to meet Gemini's single cop car. Miss Peterson followed him, walking fast, clearly upset that help had come so late. A camper-style ambulance appeared over the brink of the canyon curve, up from the valley, and Ryder shouted, stupid, "She's okay! She's not hurt! I think she just needed to take off a while!"

And then he understood the medics weren't coming for Jeri.

They were here for Murphy. A beat-up Pontiac station wagon pulled up behind them and a haggard woman came out crying.

Murphy's mother.

THIRTY-FIVE

Evaleen woke Ryder early the next morning, well before light. Told him to put on his warm clothes and gather hunting jackets and hats.

"I already called Russell's mom," she said. "He'll be ready."

"Wait. Really? What about Dad?"

"He says he wants to sleep."

"Can I ask him again?"

"Sure you can."

Ryder went to the bedroom. Sat down lightly on the foot of his parents' bed. Alma said, muffled under blankets, "Take this opportunity, buddy. She ain't picked up a rifle since before you was born. It's something you got to see."

"You'll help us when we bring it back?"

"Your grandpa and me."

"For sure."

"All set up."

"Ok."

"She's been awake, cleaning the thirty-ought. She told me what happened yesterday. Go."

"Wait—what?"

Alma sat up, flimsy still but clear-minded.

"No," he said. "Just deer hunting. That's all."

THIRTY-SIX

Ryder slid to the middle of the bench seat, straddling the stick shift to make space for Russell. Russell threw a duffel into the shell and closed it tight. Russell reached in to mount his gun on the rack and then folded himself into the cab, carp-mouthed and wide-eyed.

"You'll be warm enough?" Evaleen asked.

"Yeah. Got Shane's down coat in the bag. Gloves too."

"Good. You got padding under those jeans? Good socks in the boots?"

"Union suit. Good."

Ryder looked at his own feet, tucked into brand-new size-twelve insulated leather boots that nobody in the whole stretch of his family could fill. Russell's fourteens were beat-up and old-fashioned, but they made him look like a badass pioneer. Ryder wondered how many men in Russell's family had worn them.

Not resembling anyone in his family was yet another way Ryder was expensive. He didn't want to think about it. Another thought flickered in its place, vague: maybe someday he'd have a son who could wear these boots, fill these sleeves and pantlegs. What would that even—

"Ryder, lean that knee over towards me," his mother said. "Make sure I can change gears."

That meant pushing his leg against his mother's, which felt too cozy even though she was packed into a canvas coverall.

"That's good," she said, "but now you got to try not to put friction on the steering wheel."

"Mom, can't we push the seat back a little?"

"I'm already stretching for the wheel, see? My arms ain't long as yours."

Evaleen pushed the stick into reverse, held the clutch while she opened her window, stuck her head out facing backwards, and guided the truck down Russell's long driveway. She J-hooked and braked on the uphill, neat, pushed the stick into neutral, coasted thirty feet and slid into second without engaging the clutch at all. Then after a smooth gain, third and fourth.

Half a mile and she stopped, holding the brake where the Opex floor was built up to the highway, waiting out a groaning Kenworth, and then a couple of oil trucks, and finally a tricked-out Dodge Ram with four dudes packed all intimate in the cab. Ryder pushed himself up, then down the back of the seat. Russell tried to shift his knees.

"Ryder," Evaleen said.

"What."

"Do you want to drive?"

"Really?"

"You're about to get your learner's. You need practice. Russell needs leg room."

"Yeah but I've mostly tried the Monte. Not too good with a stick."

"No time better than now. After we pass through Gemini it'll be dirt roads anyway. Just Russell and me will witness the stupids."

Russell giggled. "I won't tell nobody you dropped the transmission outta your dad's truck."

"Well if you do, we'll have to live off the kill 'til springtime," Evaleen said. "We won't want to come in and admit it. So bring your smartest head to this."

"How many heads you got?" Russell asked.

Evaleen said, "He gots about as many as you, I guess. Boys your age manage to be something different one hour to the next."

She let the truck roll back to a flat spot. She opened her door and stepped out.

Ryder couldn't move. Russell gave him a cheerful shove.

"Mom, can't you just get us up to the highway first?"

Evaleen beckoned. "Nope. You can do it."

Ryder squeezed out. Sharp wind took the breath from his throat. Evaleen climbed back in, and Ryder squeezed himself into the driver's seat.

"Okay," she said. "Now you can push the seat all the way back."

The top of Evaleen's head barely doffed Ryder's shoulders. She sat between Ryder and Russell like a hefty little girl. Her mom voice didn't falter.

Yesterday, the whole school had seen who she was.

"Best thing we can do from here," she said, "is get up the rise and stop on the shoulder. That might be the hardest part, but you can do it. Then we'll stay patient until it's all clear. Give you all the time in the world to shimmy out a few times if you got to. Then you can take us up to speed."

"Mom. I don't think I can do that jump to the shoulder. I'll run up so fast I'll jam on into the road. And I can't see if there's cars there."

"Well, you better think it through and get it right," she answered. "You got three lives depending on it."

"Mom!"

"You can do it. Russell, you want to get out, wait up to the shoulder?"

"Nope. I want a ride."

His mother's voice was calm but unyielding. "Okay then, Ryder. Drive us up this little hill so we can get on with the hunt. Clutch goes in, left foot. Keep your right soft on the gas. Don't push until you're ready to ease up on the clutch. Then go steady on both, meet in the middle. You'll feel a little click under both feet. Then pull off the clutch and press the accelerator. Right foot, just like the

Monte—don't gun it, but stay steady as the truck starts to move. Don't lose your nerve, don't overreact. Now, sit quiet and think it through, step by step, before you leap into it."

"Mom—"

"Do what I'm telling you! Go through the steps in your mind. And that's good advice for more than stick shifting, ain't that true? Ryder, you got your dad back up from the river's edge, brought him down to safety. Directed the winch crew back to the pickup. How did you do that?"

"I—I thought it through. I planned the parts and then . . ."

"You did them. Only way it could have happened, and you came through. Now do it here in a situation that ain't so dire. It's just driving. Something grown people do every day."

Ryder hunkered over the wheel to think about the steep rise to the highway. He pictured a smooth transition into motion: the truck going up easy, coming to a gentle stop where the asphalt began. Then he envisioned himself a few weeks into the future, suavely rolling down the window of his father's truck, arm resting on the wheel, chatting up eager girls in the school parking lot. Two or three clambering in for a ride to the Pick and Shovel. A whole flock chattering at his table—

"You going or what?" Russell asked, and Evaleen said, "Ryder!" and Ryder put the clutch down and the stick into first gear, pushed the gas nice and assertive but not overexcited, and the truck leaped forward exactly as he had feared, stammering to a mortifying stop.

"See, Mom, I told you!"

"Try it again. Calm down and do it right."

Russell snorted.

Ryder said, "I bet *you* can't—"

Evaleen: "Stop fooling around."

He took a breath, and then another. Closed his eyes and put his mind through each move. Especially the little click between clutch and accelerator.

"Are you ready this time?"

"I think so."

"Russell," Evaleen said. "We'll do the same thing once we're out by the Slants. Start thinking now about what it will require to take a buck. We'll talk it through once Ryder gets his mind on the road."

Russell murmured.

Ryder pushed the clutch. Slid the stick into place. Eased the left foot as he applied the right, feeling every line of old break and surgical pinning—but that just kept him alert. The truck engaged, climbed the rise, came to a stop at the shoulder exactly where it was supposed to. Ryder hit the brake and the engine killed. But no jolt. Didn't roll back.

Evaleen said, "Good job on the first part. Start her up again. You got some big rigs coming from Tooele way, see? Wait 'em out. Don't cling the clutch."

Three diesel tankers approached like bombers, nearly blowing the pickup back down the rise at each pass. Ryder held the brake and tried to focus. All was quiet, but then another rig appeared in the distance, coming up from Delta.

"It's a good ways off," Evaleen said. "Think you can come out clean?"

"Not sure."

"I don't mind waiting," Russell said sensibly.

The toy monster grew big, blew past, and diminished north.

All quiet.

"Ready?" Ryder asked.

"Good to go."

In, out, engage: first, second, third, fourth: full speed. Smooth as butter.

"Whoa," Russell said.

"See?" said Evaleen. "Here on out, second nature."

"I can't hardly believe it," Russell grinned.

Ryder laughed. He couldn't hardly believe it, too.

THIRTY-SEVEN

"What's your opinion, Russell?" Evaleen asked as they rode through cold, quiet Gemini. The Tintic hills were gray-brown and not too wet—same tones as the herds this time of year. The high Wasatch peaks across the invisible expanse of lake rose pure white beyond. Snowy continents, sun still rolling along their shoulders.

"Well," Russell answered, obviously wishing to impress Ryder's mother, "the Slants drop a ways after the first mile. Deep brush. I seen bucks down there year-round. Big ones, but it's hard to open a shot."

"Okay, we'll think about how to do that," Evaleen said. "Let's remember, boys, we're hunting this year for meat. No heroics. No trophies. Steady thinking and straight shooting."

"My mom won the state big buck record out past Topaz before I was born," Ryder bragged.

Russell leaned forward to look back at Evaleen. "Really, Mrs. Mikkelson? How many points?"

"Seven. It was a big guy. But I was just out looking to pack a freezer. Got lucky."

"That's not what Dad said," Ryder said. "He told me you were the best shot in the whole West Desert, and everybody knew it. Dad says the head's mounted in the Elks Lodge."

"Uh-huh. Maybe you two upstanding young men can check it out next time the Elks host a strip show."

"Shane went to that. It was only a fundraiser."

"That ain't all it raised."

"*Mom.*"

"What. Women's the show but women can't talk about it?"

Russell squirmed. "So, how'd you get it?"

"The buck? I was the most careful shot," she said. "And since you're going out with me, you'll shoot to my standards. Russell, how about up there around Pinpoint, if we go the other way?"

"You mean up past the—uh—steam shaft?"

Ryder clamped his jaw.

Evaleen said, "Steam hole still wide open, waiting to swallow another dog? Or kid?"

"Well—"

"When I was young, we lived further out, down toward Delta. But we all knew about the steam shaft—there was a story about a guy that got mad at his girlfriend. Everyone knew somebody who knew the fiancée who got pushed over the edge."

"I heard it was out to Nutty Putty," Russell said. "Squoze her down a wormhole and took up the ropes."

"Lots of holes around here. Sometimes I get thinking the entire meaning of these towns is underground."

What was Ryder's mom getting at, chatting with Russell like this? Ryder had never seen Russell so talkative. Ryder got that weird feeling again: he didn't really know his own mother. Russell's mom was at home in that barren house, probably playing an accordion waltz. Evaleen had been through plenty herself, but so far she hadn't lost—well, a living son. She'd lost plenty of partly-made babies. A sister she loved, a mother gone to mindlessness, a father run off. What held her up? Ryder remembered the pale, desperate woman—Murphy's mom—who stepped out of her car yesterday in time to see the ambulance take her raving head-bleeding son away to—where?

Ryder straightened in the driver's seat. He took a big look at the scene before him: the school coming up on the left, jutting hills contoured by tailings, wooden derricks, zigzagging doubletrack, gaping holes, sliding rock. The sudden down-pitch of the twisting canyon that led to the wide lake valley, the mountains that had nearly engulfed him and his father.

Was that only two weeks ago?

Up the slopes to the right, whole towns had been built and obliterated, some within his grandfather's lifetime—huge ironworks and concrete walls rising, then collapsing to the riddled ground. Ryder was overtaken by a vision of vanishment: his parents gone to where parents finally go, a world so wrecked, so hostile, so finished with its inhabitants it only offered heat, or biting wind, or barren rock.

"Ryder," his mother said. "Where's your mind at? You got this turn coming up. Have you been listening?"

Ryder wiped his eyes. Gripped the wheel.

"Gear down easy to second, and then you can release to neutral as you come off the blacktop. Pull off where Russell says. But I got something to say to you both. Stop at the turnout."

The stop was not excellent. Ryder hit the brake too soon. The truck killed hard.

"You can't do that too many more times," his mother said. "We need this truck to last."

Russell said, "I knew we'd be coming out to pick up the transmission, some point."

"Shut up, Russell," Ryder said.

"You know I hate that word," Evaleen said, and Ryder almost retorted *Which one? Shut? Or up?* He didn't, but he did mutter "You try this, jerk," which almost made Russell tell him to shut up, it looked like. Then they both shut up and got out.

The air was cold but smelled of clean sky and distant snow. Faint but immediate sage. Instinct sent them up the draw toward a crumbling cement foundation. Evaleen said it was the one-time Dane Hollow school, dismantled—along with houses, mercantile, a bank ("see the old vault there, back in the scrub?"), and a saloon—by the mine owners once the lode was depleted.

"Boys," Evaleen said, "We'll bring home a couple of good bucks, so don't get impatient. We have all day. Sun looks to be warming. Have a sit on these old stairs and let me give you one good talking to. Deal?"

Ryder glanced toward Russell, who looked more interested in enduring an Evaleen talking-to than her actual son was. Maybe his mother saw Russell as her son, too. She'd picked Ryder out of the universe. Why not Russell too? He quelled a small resentment. Was this how Ferron and Kent felt about each other? Ryder had never considered it. He'd always been the one glorious gift.

"You two," Evaleen's voice cut in. "We need to talk about what happened yesterday in school. It's hard conversation."

Ryder glanced toward Russell, who looked about to melt like a summer snake down the cold ghost-school stairway.

"Mom—"

"I talked to Russell's mother late last night. She gave me permission to talk this over. Russell, your mom is a good woman, and smart, and she believes in you. She's just had too much happen. You too, but you're going to be okay. You are."

Ryder was shocked to see Russell sit up, dip his head toward his knees, and cry. Silent, but tears rolled off his bony chin.

Evaleen didn't wait. She'd probably been thinking about this all night and morning. Even while she was teaching Ryder how to drive stick. "I grew up all around this place. I went to high school a year in Gemini—same old building, same classrooms, same good and bad feelings about it. Any of us live here, we're proud of it. Right, Russell?"

Russell said, head down but vehement: "Right."

"Ryder, you come from here as much as you come from the cliffs and the river. You got deep roots here. I see you wanting to say you don't really come from either place, but if you're adopted into a family, your home is where you've spent your time, where your life takes form among your people. And here you are in Gemini, already a year and a half. More."

"Mom, I know."

His mother took off her hat, blinked in the rising sunlight, ran fingers through her perm-frizzed hair, and forged on: "But any place has got its share of darkness. Bad history. Maybe Gemini's got its own brand.

"Young men can get set on the wrong path. Maybe they see too much too soon. They're strong, full of juice, too much power but not much at all. Some learn to wield what force they can. Do you understand what I'm talking about?"

Russell looked up at the sky, face wet.

"Jeri," he said.

"Russell, I can see that you love her in such good ways."

"Since we was in kindergarten," Russell said. "Even before, because we went to the Methodist church. Our moms brung us."

"Did you know what happened to Jeri that night? Rendezvous?"

Russell looked sick. "Murphy's dad lives up with the ex-cons that rent cheap up to the old Bailey house. Ain't all of them bad but some are. Shane had a room up there a while, hardly costed him anything. But he came back home, said it was too rough even for him."

Ryder stood up. Climbed the full staircase, surveyed the foundation, came back down. Sat, twitching. His leg hurt like cold mercury.

His mother said, "You don't got to account for it, Russell. I just wonder if Jeri was packing that all by herself."

"She never told me." Russell said. "But that guy was walking around all night, hanging his—you know—"

"Was it Murphy's dad?" Ryder asked.

"No. Some guy that lived up there. Murphy was following him around, laughing and chugging one of them milk jugs you could fill from the keg for a dollar. We all did, but you know how Murphy is. Fucked up. Sorry, Mrs. Mikkelson, but that's the word for it. Him and that guy was watching for girls—any of 'em, don't matter how old they were—going out past the lights to pee. Everyone had to pee.

THINGS I DIDN'T DO

Lots of beer. But the girls had it rough. Maybe some of them wanted to be followed, but—"

"Russell!" said Evaleen. An edge in her voice pulled Ryder's nerves tight. "Any girl goes out to the bushes to pee deserves to go out there to pee. Not one male person ought to decide she wants anything else, let alone follow her, pants open or zipped, parts—penis—in or out, hands in his pockets or out to grab."

Small wind, cold. The early sun warmed one minute, failed the next. Ryder watched gray clouds roll across the eastern valley. Bringing snow.

Russell sat stricken.

Ryder said, "Mom, we know. I can't believe you're even saying those words to us."

"Ryder, you're not a little boy anymore. Saying you know something better mean you do. Not just in your brain but your whole body. Your soul. Not just here, but out in the sage, up in the pitches, in the locker room or parking lot when everybody's talking big or quits talking—turning into something inhuman. You've seen it. I know you have. I have too. I never lived in a rosy bubble."

Russell heaved up, straightening his back, rolling his head like a cautious dog. "Mrs. Mikkelson, I get what you're saying but my brother Shane said plenty of females do want it. Deserve it, way they behave. Then men get the blame. He said look at the way a buck goes after a doe. Shane said when you get out there in nature you can't deny that's the way of things."

Ryder's vision rolled into a dark place in his mind. Mean wanting. Cold black water below him. Ice and raging heat. Lust. Familiar, terrible, strange.

He brought himself back, accusing: "Mom. You've said the same things yourself. You told me that my real mom—I mean my biological mom—was probably some cheap girl who couldn't say no. Who—"

Evaleen stood up on the corroding school stairs.

"I was raised same ways you boys were. Same attitudes, same ugly excuses. Same nastiness, and I can fall into its trap. I lose my mind when I think there's another woman on this planet who loves you as much as I do, even if she don't know you. Ryder, I'm sorry for that. But right now we've got to think about Jeri. What you know of her, how you call her your friend, how some man in drunken lust told himself she wanted it, that she deserved it because she was out there, or she was drinking, or because she acts tough, or because she has a body that wants food and drink, and pleasure, and plain relief."

She walked to the top of the stairs, stared into the foundation.

She put on her fluorescent hat, flaps down, pulled it snug. Her hair stuck out the bottom, every which way. Her face was blotchy in the cold, lined deep at the corners of her mouth.

"This is a world of blood and cum," she said, "and a little bit of water and salt. If we go up that canyon to shoot, we ought to remember we're killing our kind. But also they ain't our kind. Don't matter how a buck mounts a doe. Sex is something different to us, and it matters. We can't be animals, no matter how blind, drunk, stupid, or damaged we are. Drunk and stupid—and vicious—belongs to humans.

"Jeri will be okay. I'm not saying she's not hurt, bad, in ways that will stay in her. And I'm not giving more sympathy to Murphy than to her. But Jeri has a good mind and a strong heart, and she has a loving mom and dad to go home to even if they don't look like a picture book. They'll stick with her and she'll find her path, even if it seems a strange destination to you."

Evaleen came back down the stairs. Seated herself a step below them.

"That's probably not true for Murphy. You two saw. We had to scrub the blood from the back of his head off the classroom wall. That boy is a broken thing either one of you could of become, had your lives tilted a little more far one way or another. That's a hard kind of broken to fix. Plenty of boys like Murphy grow up and get set loose in the world—poor, rich, strong, weak, don't matter. It's a bad recipe, passed down generations. I don't understand it, but I've seen it.

"Both of you got strength could overcome about any woman—a woman who fears you, a woman who loves you, a woman who's got no real choice but to trust you. Every time she's near a body like the ones you walk in. I'm not talking negative about your brother, Russell. But you can be a better man than he got a chance to be. What makes us human is we learn to take care of one another. Today we're taking care of your mom. We're making sure you ain't hungry this winter. We'll take from nature what nature will give, and we'll do it with respect. You boys ready to do that?"

Ryder didn't feel ready to do anything. Ryder wondered who, exactly, his father was—and he didn't mean the one quailing under the covers back at Grandpa Yeadon's house. Is that what his mother was getting at? Did she think Ryder came from –

Evaleen said, "Russell, how long since you cleaned that rifle? Is it good to go?"

"This morning. I been up since four-thirty."

"You took it apart? Oiled the barrel? Tested the safety?"

"I did. Shane taught me way back."

"Clean ammo?"

"Yes. New box."

"Ryder."

"What."

"Lead up."

"From here?"

"See that double track? See how it narrows into trail past that little knoll? We're heading up to traverse the one above it. Then we'll summit and sit quiet. It's a good-sized basin. Deer will walk right out of the scrub.

"I'm telling you now: we'll sit it out to get familiar. Then we take our pick, and we aim careful. No gut shots. No legs. No butts. No shooting at all until they're close enough, out in the open, to kill clean. Chest. Neck. One shot.

"We see two good ones—which is what we're waiting for—you'll need to shoot at the same time. Know who's shooting at what, stay out of each other's line. Then you two can hike down, field dress while I come back down for the pickup. I'll drive around that side, you can carry them down to the road.

"That's the plan. It's the *only* plan. If it don't look to turn out that way, we don't shoot. You got me?"

"Yes."

"Yes."

"Get your rifles. Load. Lock in the safety. Come back and let me inspect. Then Ryder leads up. He sets our positions, but Russell calls the shot. Can you do that, Russell?"

"I think so."

"Can you?"

"Yes."

"Ryder."

"How's the leg?"

"Weird in the cold."

"But you can hike strong?"

"Yes."

"You're good men. This world needs you in it. I'm sick of talking. Let's go."

THIRTY-EIGHT

It happened so much like his mother said, Ryder wondered later which rendition was real and which was its mirror. The whole sequence left him off-kilter and dazzled, then re-grounded by hard dirt and blood, viscera steaming in a sharp, spinning wind, the brute dead-weight carry, twice, down scrub oak and piercing tuff to the pickup.

They lifted the five-point into the bed under the shell, tailgate dropped for the rack to protrude. The huskier four-point went up on the hood, tied secure, head on Russell's side so Ryder could see to drive. They took the back road home, same one Curtis had driven with Ryder poached and secured.

Ryder thought again what a cheap trick it was to maintain that lie at his mother's expense. He nudged it out of his mind as he eased his dad's truck over the twined streets of Opex, pulled the stick into a lower gear, and tilted the pickup and its gorgeous, awful cargo up to Grandpa's place.

The truck killed with only a minor shake. Alma was already at his window, beaming.

"Didn't I tell you, son?" Alma crowed as Ryder rolled down the glass. "You got to see that woman in action, don'tcha think? Whoo-ee, look at that beauty!"

"We got a five-point in the back, too," Russell said to Grandpa, who was knocking at the other side. "I shot that one. Not as big, but it's big."

Grandpa said, "Come out of there and let's get them cleaned up right," and Evaleen said, "Back off so we can open the doors."

Ryder stepped out. His dad clapped him hard on the back. Alma reached in for Evaleen's hand. She shimmied toward him, her chest in her heavy coat grazing the steering wheel. They stood above Ryder on the slope. Ryder felt like a little boy as he tipped his face up to meet their smiles.

"Can I call my mom?" Russell huffed, and Grandpa nodded him toward the house. Russell's voice rose and dropped inside as he recounted the thrilling tale. By the time he'd stretched the cord to gesture with his bloody hands, Ryder and his parents had hoisted the bucks away from the pickup. Grandpa took the hearts and livers Evaleen had enclosed in the carcasses. He set the hearts in buckets of salted water.

"Get off the phone, Russell," Evaleen said. "We need your strong arms."

"Russell, is it okay if we do the processing here?" Alma said. "We can hang them both in the shed. We ought to skin them now, cut the tenderloins. You can take those home with you. Liver too. Your mama will cook them up right. We'll send you with onions. Cold looks to stay, so you can come back in a couple days to help cut the rest. Rigbys say we can grind for burgers and sausage over to their place. Lay out jerky."

Russell looked like he'd eat the liver raw.

"Okay," Alma said. "Let's get this done."

Ryder and Russell did the heavy lifting. Alma and Grandpa hooked and hung.

It was exciting, but Ryder strained to keep his mind on the work. He did wish to inherit ancestral skills. He hungered for the winter meat. But he had to quell a certain horror. The image of these beautiful creatures stepping out, trusting the forage and cold light. The terror of the fleeing herd. The spilling, steaming guts. The stinks of bladder, glands, bowels. The blank, dead, clouded eyes.

How strangely, cut by cut, a quick animal was turned into meat.

How easily a hunter could slip into the wrong dark place in his mind.

Russell and Ryder stood back as Evaleen and Alma rose to their skillful tasks. Ryder's parents murmured and joked, called memories to one another's minds. Laughed quiet and content. They cut, circled, pointed out, grunted and tugged, moving in tandem.

Once, Evaleen stopped to stare blank and uncomprehending at the blood on her arms and apron. She plunged her hands into the water bucket, scrubbed them clean. She dried them carefully on a clean towel.

She turned back to the rendering.

"This is the last time," she murmured to Alma.

He nodded. Whispered.

Ryder felt like he was sinking down in time, their voices garbling into underwater sound.

He saw his parents clearly: young, in love in their funny ways. Blissful.

Innocent of the blood and sorrow coming.

Then, *him*.

PART THREE

EGYPTIAN QUEEN

Nile Valley, Utah

THIRTY-NINE

Ryder's father never returned to work out to the Depot. Something had broken in the blizzard. But behind the broken was a person Ryder hadn't known, at least since he was small. Evaleen said the "nervous breakdown" had retrieved something of the open-hearted kid she'd fallen in love with. Took her back in time.

Things were going in another direction for Uncle Doug.

"They had a hard upbringing," Evaleen told Ryder, out on the porch, warm sun, as they watched Alma and Grandpa take a wrench to yet another rusty object. "Your dad had an easier life than me, material-wise. Land, livestock, enough to eat. But I never heard one kind expression from his folks. Your dad caught hard discipline. Doug got neglect. Don't know which was worse. Your dad was made with deep emotion. Maybe Doug too—look at his boys. But Doug ain't got it in him to rise. Maura's given him every chance and more. You need to understand."

Ryder wasn't certain what he understood. But he was happy to be moving back. Only a couple hours but a whole world away. It meant Kent and Ferron. Horses. A two-year-old gelding, already fifteen hands, that Grandpa Mikkelson said Ryder could train, buy with a little cash at a time. Discount if he'd feed and water the family herd, clean the stables.

FORTY

Grandpa and Grandma Mikkelson were too old to maintain the family place. They were satisfied to move into the old bunkhouse, especially since Alma was coming home to help fix it up. That left the main house, a squat brickish-rockish affair, for Alma and Evaleen and Ryder. Eighty acres that Alma knew as home, much of it studded with sandstone but decent pasture. River front. Water shares for Evaleen's garden. Ferron intended to come in after work to grow watermelons on fifteen acres. Not enough to make a living like the big producers, but Ferron said he liked to watch the vines grow. Loved playing at old-time irrigation. A little extra money. He'd bought an old box truck, cleaned it up, and he was learning how to restore the engine. He wanted Ryder to paint a logo on it.

Alma would keep up twenty acres of alfalfa, which went to the horses. Doug was supposed to get better so he could help. And Alma could return to masonry when jobs came up. He'd missed it, hard as it was in rough weather.

Grandma Mikkelson's force of will was gone a long time ago. Kent said she sat on her old recliner and gazed out the front window. Ate bologna sandwiches Maura used to make in weekly batches and stack in the freezer, thawed one at a time for her breakfast, lunch, and dinner. Now Grandpa made them—white grocery store bread, yellow mustard and precut cheese. Considering what a coot he was, Grandpa deserved a brass band and a medal for cleaning her up every night and putting her to bed, almost tender.

"Folks are full of surprises—haven't I always told you?" Evaleen said.

Alma said, "She waited on him, hand and foot, more than sixty years. Least he can do."

Ryder wondered how his father was made by those people. Only time Ryder ever saw the likeness was the night Alma slid off the highway in the canyon. Accusing. Suspicious and single-minded. Scriptural. It was like watching a forgotten home movie reeling behind his father's eyes, shredding in its own heat. Ryder didn't want to recall it, which meant he would. Forever. Alma had no memory of that night until reaching the brink of the highway. Ryder hoped it would stay that way.

Only thing that set Ryder off about homecoming: Kent had a girlfriend. He wouldn't tell Ryder who she was.

"You wouldn't understand," Kent said on the phone. "You've been gone too long. We'll talk about it when you get here."

"It's not Sami though. Right?"

"Sami didn't come back after ninth grade. Went home to Redhorse. Probably hooked up with some hot sheepherder in a pretty canyon."

"Shut up, Kent."

"She deserved to get out of that goddamn spook alley. Harmony, Charity, already married to polygamists. Maybe the same one. I heard Ephraim got thrown out. Works on the river. I think he sees Sami sometimes."

"Really? Like—"

"I don't know. Sucks for you though, right?"

"Who's your girlfriend, asshole?"

"Worry about your own lonely pecker."

"I'll ask Ferron. You sleeping with her?"

"Maybe."

"Talk to me, Kenty!"

"Later, dude."

"What the hell is wrong with you?"

"Lots. Come home. You been gone too long."

Mittened and ear-flapped, Grandpa Yeadon said, "Look here. Your dad filled the coal bin for me, up to the brim. I got venison in the freezer, thanks to you and your mama. A topped-off water tank. I been getting along right here, more'n five times your lifetime. I ain't leaving this place till the Lord your mama believes in pulls me off this dry earth. And if it takes too long, I got a plan.

"I hope you come see me though. And Russell's by. Go on now with your folks, let them pick up the lives they left when you came here. How's the leg?"

"Good enough."

"How'd you break it so bad, anyhow?"

"Fell off a pack mule, Grandpa. I've told you that a thousand times."

"I remember. Just teasing. Who ain't walking around a little screwy, anyhow? This is just your way of it. Helps you walk sideways on the mountain. I mean traverse."

Ryder laughed. "Long as I'm going clockwise."

"I'm happy I got to know my great-grandson. Your mama, she's best of this lot by far. Always was. You take after her."

Ryder didn't know whether that was a statement or admonition.

"I'll come out, Grandpa. I've got friends here, besides you. Auriferous needs a hike every so often. I'll help you put that still together."

"We'll get up to the piles, pick about. And we'll strike one last pocket of silver. I know where to look."

Auriferous showed his big teeth.

"Or, gold," Ryder offered.

"We'll be rich. Even richer than we are now! How about that? I'll take it to California, live on the beach. Now, get on. Don't look back."

FORTY-ONE

It was Jerusha Beeson. The worst girl in elementary school.

No wonder Kent wouldn't say. Ryder couldn't spend more than a minute with his cousin without Jerusha butting in.

"She's different now," Kent insisted, but it appeared to Ryder she was the same self-righteous know-it-all since the day she showed up at San Rafael Elementary. First-grade tattletale. Fourth-grade snot. Now, tenth-grade cousin-stealer.

The spring Ryder's family moved to Opex, Jerusha was launching her campaign to be ninth-grade class president. Now, sophomore year, she was a varsity cheerleader. Co-captain of the girls' volleyball team. *And* vice president of the National Honor Society, whatever the hell that was. Worse: Kent, the rat-tailed kid who couldn't resist pencil-darting the ceiling, who leaped from desktop to desktop in elementary school, who twisted like a chipmunk on a Sunday School chair, was now on Adderall and a student officer for the Future Farmers of America. Plus, National Honor Society treasurer.

Alma had a wood fire roaring in the inset. The rooms were stifling. Ryder put the phone to his other ear. Stretched the cord out to the front porch. Snowflakes spun between him and the riverbanks, but the ground was hard and clear.

"What, like, you sit on the hoard?" Ryder said. "Like Smaug?"

"I collect the dues. Keep track of expenses."

"Like what?"

"Publicity stuff. Trips. Stuff."

THINGS I DIDN'T DO

"Trips?"

"Sometimes we meet with clubs in other schools. Academic decathlon. Speakers. Socials and stuff."

"You keep saying *stuff*. Sounds super important, Kent. Come on."

"Ryder, you're good at math. You're a real good artist. And even when we all had to help the teachers get what you were saying, you knew the answers to the social studies questions. You could remember the science words. Ferron read whole books while I was bouncing off the walls. My mom was valedictorian at her high school out in Colorado. I want to be smart too."

"You are smart! Smarter than all of us. You have *ideas*. You never lose a trail. That's got nothing to do with this preppy shit you got going. You're trying to impress the most conceited girl in the whole valley. Don't you remember how she tattled on Sami that time? She called her 'that Indian girl.'"

A sharp gust sent Ryder back in, but he kept the door cracked to mitigate Alma's fire.

Kent was talking from Ferron's place, somewhere at the bottom of town. "Her dad's a big shot in the mine office. Her mom's some poet type. They think they're better than everyone, but Jerusha hates that bullcrap."

Kent paused to muster his argument. He had a cough, so it took a minute. "But that doesn't mean she don't—doesn't expect a lot from herself. She's going to college. She's trying to decide between Northwestern or Princeton."

"What? Jeez, Kenty! Listen to yourself. You know what's going to happen? She'll get set up for college to please her mommy and daddy. Then she'll drop you on your hands and butt."

"I didn't say I'm trying to go to Princeton. I want to go to Colorado, or Arizona State, or University of Wyoming. I'd go up to Salt Lake if they gave me a scholarship. You know I want to understand the cliffs. The Swell. The Reef. Jerusha and me can get together in the summers, and when we graduate we can—you know—"

184

"You? And Jerusha Beeson? Get *married?*"

"That's a long way off. Right now I'm just trying to become a better person for her."

"Gaaa! Kent!"

"We have a good science teacher. A lady. She came from Pittsburgh to teach here in Utah because she loves this *geoscape*. She's a women's libber but she says she'll help me apply for college, and for money to pay. She's wack but you'll like her."

Evaleen called, "Ryder, you in or you out? Shut the door!"

Saturday, Kent came over with Jerusha to help Ryder arrange his new bedroom. Ryder had not requested help, but Jerusha didn't mind.

"Still smells like Grandma," Kent said, cranking the window open. "Ben-Gay and shit."

"I'll stink it up," Ryder said.

"Just takes a few farts. Wet dreams. Dirty socks."

Jerusha: "Kent. Don't be gross."

"He's trying to pass himself off as not gross?" Ryder said. "You been in his room? Snot wipes and shit stained jocks. Right Kenty?"

"As long as his family calls him Kenty," Jerusha said, "He'll respond like a child. He's older now. He deserves to be addressed respectfully."

Kenty turned the butt of his high tight Wranglers toward Ryder and gazed out the window. This time of year, under these clouds, everything was gray and still. A no-color photograph.

Another problem: if Ryder had worn his Nile Valley jeans—even once—to school in Gemini he would have been creamed. Good thing his leg was messed up long enough for him to figure that out. They didn't exactly dress like city kids up there. But even though the high school was even smaller than here, Gemini was no country-western town. They listened to metal and rode their motorcycles and went four-digging up the dumps and tailings. They wore baggy jeans and tanks, big T-shirts cut to sleeveless sails. Nikes. Pullover shirts and basketball shorts. Back now among his cousins and elementary school friends (and enemies), Ryder had a wardrobe problem.

He couldn't borrow from his cousins; Kenty was a wiry five-seven, Ferron an inch taller but nowhere near Ryder's almost six-one. Ryder's shoulders strained the seams of his shirts and jackets. He pulled at the hems of his T-shirts to stretch them longer.

Ryder's mother said no more new clothes until his wrists and ankles stretched out from the ones he had. "Not like you're getting fatter. You'll have to stick with these till you've topped out."

Ryder wondered how much higher. Kent and Ferron could look at their dad, or Ryder's dad, or scattered uncles and know what to expect. Or try to avoid. Neither had grown since eighth grade. They just had to hope they'd follow Maura's brothers into lean, lifelong cowboy physiques, or work around their father's burger, beer, and butter diet to keep their stomachs behind their belts.

Jerusha was picking stuff up, looking everything over, arranging piles, folding Ryder's jeans and stacking them on the unmade bed. Yakking about creative window coverings.

Ryder said, "I don't want to cover my window."

Kenty said, "Aren't you afraid Bigfoot will look in, see you sleeping buck naked?"

Jerusha said, "Kent, stop it. I'm trying to help Ryder feel at home again."

"Creative window coverings won't make me feel at home. I want to see the cliffs. The moon."

"My mom had an interior decorator do our house. It looks nice. I learned a lot. I'm just trying to do something good for you, Ryder. People are happier in aesthetically pleasing spaces."

"Kenty, shut the window. It's cold."

"Wuss."

"Don't call him Kenty."

"What the hell, Jerusha? He's my cousin. I can call him what I want. Right, Kenty?

Kent didn't answer.

"You guys get out of here," Ryder said. "I'm doing this myself. It's my room."

"Don't smell like your room," Kent said. "Smells like Grandma's room. Have fun folding your nightgowns."

"Shut up, Kenty."

"Don't call him Kenty!"

"What the fuck, Kenty! Can't you talk for yourself? Is Jerusha your mommy now?"

Kent stiffened, unrecognizable. Then he was just Kenty, livid. He strode back to the window. He lifted a pointed boot flat toward the screen and kicked it out. He planted his butt on the sill, swiveled like a barstool, and dropped to the ground.

"You forgot your jacket, sweetheart," Ryder called after him, and Jerusha, still standing at Ryder's bed, said, "You're such a jerk." She picked up Kenty's coat, wrapped it around herself, and stormed out the proper exits.

FORTY-TWO

Ryder called Kent later, after dark.

"I'm not sorry about the other stuff," he said, "but I'm sorry about—you know. Your mom."

Kent said, "Go back where you came from." The line clicked.

Ryder asked his father if he could borrow the truck. Go to Kenty's.

"Can't drive after dark with your learner's license, can you?"

"I'll be careful. They only got the dummy in the cop car this time of night."

"It's rough over there," Alma said, at the sink, rinsing dinner dishes. "Doug's turned into a fat pile of garbage, sitting in garbage."

Evaleen said, "Alma."

"I'm not saying I wouldn't of gone the same way, Evaleen, if I hadn't had you to pull me through. Not saying I never been garbage. It runs in the family. Lucky you, huh Ryder."

"Dad, what?"

"Look at us all. Heads popping like corks. I got brothers and sisters all over the place, not a one hasn't dropped the ball on good sense. You know Earl and Elroy each got their boys patrolling the fence line between their properties, neither won't let the other's family lay a toe across. All of them busy shutting in for the Last Days, stocking their bunkers. One of these days somebody will shoot. Then what will we have."

Ryder pictured his father's brothers—stout, ruddy, nasal scrabblers with plenty of land and no water to ease it. Evaleen explained way back that the kids near his age on the properties were like as not the children of his first cousins. Ryder had played on the "ranches" with some of them, following tiny creeks for tadpoles, jumping on trampolines until they were delirious, riding bashed-up three-wheelers so prone to tipping his mother had mortified Ryder by putting a stop to it. BB guns, then .22s: no tin can was safe, no rabbit untraumatized. He'd recognized some of the kids in other classes in elementary school. Ferron knew each of them by name. At this point, Alma said, most of his brothers' grandchildren were grown or "homeschooled," which in their case meant "no-schooled."

"Kent wants to go to college?" Alma said now. "He'd be the first ever."

"Yeah but Dad—"

"Go on now and see your cousin," Evaleen said. "He needs you."

"He needs Jerusha."

Alma: "Maybe so."

"I can't stand her."

Evaleen: "Well, that's why she's not *your* girlfriend, right? Best thing you can grant a person you love is their own trail through life. You owe it to make it easy on each other."

She handed Ryder his coat.

"Kent and Ferron's dealing with plenty of heartbreak," Alma said. "And right now, you're the best family they've got."

Ryder stepped out into bitter cold. Sky: winter black and clear. Blinking stars. Thin snow squeaked under his boots; he wished he'd brought mittens but didn't want to turn around.

He retracted his hand into the too-short sleeve of his denim coat to open the pickup door. He shivered as the engine turned. Cold coursed from the vents as the wipers arced over unyielding ice. He got out again to scrape the windows—not well but now the temperature was kicking up inside. He opened his palms to the blowing heat.

Grandpa Mikkelson held the bunkhouse curtain open to watch

the truck slip by. Ryder waved and Grandpa dropped the fabric.

Ryder turned left out of the long driveway, onto the river road toward town. He peered for the narrow track that led into the cottonwoods where Uncle Doug had turned his old fifth-wheeler into a "residence."

Besides the most recent pickup, this was all that was left of Doug's long train of customized rigs. Ryder recalled it new. The trailer had even made a trip to Opex, Doug smirking from the double cab pickup. Maura sat in the shotgun seat, too pissed to speak, Kent surly in the back. Ferron had already moved out to live in a wall tent above the creek.

After a night camped right there on Opex street, Doug hollered Kent down from the porch where he slept beside Ryder. Doug pulled out, and in, and out, nearly hitting the Ockleys' fixed-up boxcar before losing patience and bumping forward in a wide U-turn over rocks and a side ditch: on to Jericho. Alma and Ryder drove down to meet them, watched buggies and three-wheelers fling over the dunes, ate hotdogs boiled up in the deluxe RV kitchen. Listened to Rush Limbaugh blaring over the sandstorm from ten rigs at least; came home to Evaleen.

Soon after, Doug strained his back building props for Sunshine. A doctor in Price prescribed OxyContin, and Doug's career was done. Once she got Doug on disability, Maura left. Kent said she'd found a job in Salt Lake, come back a few times, left for good, lived with a boyfriend in West Valley until he beat her up and took her credit cards. She got a ride with a distant cousin to Powder River where the mines wanted office skills. She'd wanted out of coal, but here she was again.

No word since, far as Evaleen or Alma knew.

The grounded trailer sat on cinder blocks, rising like a short-necked monster from stripped sage and rabbitbrush, head fringed in willow whips. Grime dripped from the casings. A cord stretched from the trailer to a tilting power post; the lights were on.

Ryder tapped the horn, hoping Kent would come out. They could take a ride somewhere. Go into town for hamburgers. But Kent opened the door and gestured. Ryder cranked the window.

"Dad wants you to come in and say hi," Kent called, then mouthed "sorry" with a grimace.

Ryder opened his door. Kent came out to meet him.

"Just stay a minute," he said, "and we'll cut out."

Uncle Doug lay half reclined in a red leather chair that filled up most of the RV's common space, even with the extensions pulled out. Ryder was shocked by the size of him. Maybe once he would have smirked at Doug's girth, but this was massive and shapeless. Doug's face looked like a dirty marshmallow moon. His eyes darted and peered behind puffed lids. His lips were dry and peeling. Horribly, Ryder saw his father's likeness in the clarity of the brothers' noses, the only intact feature.

Kent looked miserable. The confident boyfriend and scholar beyond these walls slumped like a stringless puppet in the unwashed smell of his father's disintegration.

Doug barked, "You come to take this sorry little bugger out to play?"

Ryder said, "What?"

"That all you can say to your Uncle Doug? Thought you'd honk and I'd let him run off? Neither of you got no respect. Lemme talk to you a minute. Kent won't tell me nothing."

Kent sat down on the little stairway that led up to his "room."

"He got the best spot in the house," Doug pointed out. "Up in the master suite. I can't climb stairs. He thinks that makes him the master."

Ryder expected a retort from his cousin, but Kent gazed toward the doorway. Ryder churned with anger. Nausea.

"Okay. Sorry. Hi Uncle Doug." He strained for a respectful tone.

"That's better, smart-ass," Doug said. "Kent. Bring me a drink of milk. Make me a sandwich before you go." He rolled his head back toward Ryder. "How's the little shit doing in school? Now his mother's gone off, it's me has to keep track."

Kent stood up.

Doug reached toward the folding table beside the chair. He kept an eye on Ryder as he felt for a plastic pharmacy bottle, shook it, and set it down. "You seen that faggot Ferron? Kent won't tell me where he is."

"No."

"No you ain't seen him, or you telling me no, same way Kent does?"

"I have not seen Ferron, Uncle Doug."

Doug reached again for the pills. "Kent! You bringing me milk?"

Kent poured and served. Handed his father white bread with a slice of bologna between. "Dad, leave Ryder alone. We need to go."

"Find me the remote. And bring me something decent when you come back. Cheeseburger."

"Yeah."

"Don't be out late. Stay out of trouble."

"You got it, Doug," Kent muttered. He grabbed Ryder's arm and jerked him toward the door.

"It's cold," Ryder said, almost whispering. "Get your coat."

"Fuck it. Move along." Kent jiggled the bent doorknob and shoved. Air like ice water.

"Shut the goddamn door," Doug hollered. Kent hopped out behind Ryder and obliged.

Ryder jammed up the heat in the truck, but Kent shivered like a bunny.

Ryder said, "Where's Ferron live? Should we pick him up? Get something to eat?"

Kent stared forward.

"Kent. I didn't know it had got so bad. I didn't."

Kent slid his butt toward the front of the seat, sinking his head below the back window line. He took off his boots and put his stockinged feet on the dash, above the vents. Ryder sent all the air to them. The heater was loud. Ryder dried up and drove toward town. He knew Ferron had a room down by the tracks. He guessed the old Riverbend Motel, where migrant hands and summer workers could rent cheap all summer. Winter, cheaper.

"Here," Kent murmured, too late for Ryder to swing a pickup left on the icy road. Ryder dropped the gear and tapped the brakes. The truck slid on, fishtailing, but came to a stop. Ryder backed up, made the turn, and aimed for the dilapidated motel. The old neon sign was long dead—an awkward rendering of Nefertiti's head, uninterpretable to anyone who didn't know the landmark.

Ferron stood in silhouette at the open door of the farthest unit, expecting them. Somebody must have called. Kent exhaled and relaxed a little, although his hands trembled. He opened himself out before Ryder could ease to a full stop. Both brothers stood to draw him in by the time Ryder managed to park and pick his way.

Ferron's little room was clean, and compared to outside, warm. Ryder recognized stuff Aunt Maura had in the old place—a striped chief's blanket, passed among family until Maura had gotten hold and held on, lay neatly folded at the foot of the bed. A lamp with a pieced-glass shade, set on a crocheted grandma-style doily. Ferron's well-used saddle sat graceful as sculpture on a sawhorse taken from Grandpa's shed.

Kent sat, transfigured by relief, on a cane-seat rocker Ryder recalled from the back porch of Doug and Maura's old Etna house. Doug had demanded his share of inheritance in cash a long time ago; his brothers hocked their own properties to buy him out. Doug bought trucks and trailers, pedigreed horses, a "ranch" out by Thompson that the credit union repossessed. Technically the home place would all go to Ryder's dad, and then supposedly to Ryder, but Grandpa Mikkelson had reservations about deeding the remainder of the "estate" to a grandson who didn't carry true family blood. Alma told Ryder, "The old fart can't last forever, can he? He's too old and confused for anything but flapping that mouth. Long as none of you think you have to go big, I'll make damn sure the three of you got claim. All of you, a place no one can take away."

Ryder wondered whether Ferron and Kent knew about Alma's promise. Right now, too much to know and not know. Family, Ryder was beginning to think, was a re-tangling clusterfuck. He said: "Have you heard anything from her?"

Ferron pulled a beat-up manila envelope from under the mattress. Reached in to extract a clean fifty-dollar bill. Handed it to Kent.

Kent recoiled. "What's this?"

"She's doing better. Decent job. She didn't want to send this any way Doug could catch wind. She says she'll send money to you, steady as she can, at least until you graduate. You can get out from under him the minute you're eighteen."

Kent stared at the money, took it, dropped it on Ferron's scraped-up spotless floor. "What the hell? That's more than two years. Bitch runs off, leaves me alone with that moron, thinks she can buy me off?"

Ryder eased toward the bed. Sat down. Pushed back to lean against the rough-paneled wall.

Ferron said, "Kent, take the money. She's working hard for it. She's doing what she can for you."

Kent's anger reheated the room. Ryder felt sick. He wanted to go home, or go get something to eat, like he'd intended. He hated thinking about awful things. He hated the rock-in-the-gut sensation of feeling sorry for someone else. Even Kenty. Especially Kenty. Kent's misery was harder to push out, ignore, or cover up than anything Ryder felt himself.

"Look," Ferron was saying. "I'm arranging for home care for Dad with social services. Things take time with them, but they want to help. They've been guiding me through the paperwork and they'll get it set up. Nobody thinks you should be Doug's caretaker, but right now it's on record that he's the parent, that he's supposed to be taking care of you. Kent, if we aren't careful, they'll come in and commit you to foster care."

Kent went pale.

Ryder was shocked.

"Can't he just come live with us?" Ryder asked.

"Not if Doug won't give permission," Ferron answered. "That's what I'm working on. We need to document he's incompetent. That he's dangerous or negligent, or too sick to take care of himself, let alone his kid. Then Kent can come live with me. Or with you and your mom and dad."

"Why'd you leave him there alone? Can't you be with him?"

"Dad took a shot at him," Kent murmured. "Thinks he's—"

Ferron shut him down. "Kent's still a minor and Doug's the custodial parent since Mom left, so we have to go through all the shit to show he's not fit. We do something rash and it goes haywire. Listen to me, Kent. Give me a little more time. Make sure you don't look like a truant or delinquent. You're doing so good in school. Buck up and stay on it. Uncle Alma goes over to look in on Doug, which means he's looking in on you. I'll be over there any way I can, Aunt Evaleen says she'll bring him dinners, and you can be over to their place, or mine, or at school, most of the time. It's good Ryder's family's back. It's going to help. A lot."

Kent stood up, fists clenched. Ferron stanced like a boxer.

Kent shriveled. Ryder stood up. He towered over his cousins, but he felt like the smallest person in the room.

"Kent," he said.

"Shut it, Ryder. Your mother lit out on you, too."

It took a second for Ryder to catch Kent's meaning. Then it threw him backwards.

Ferron said, "Kent. What the fuck. Maura took it and took it.

How long can you expect a grown woman to—"

"Long enough to not leave me in that hellhole alone with the guy she promised to—to stick around for what she signed up for. Stupid bitch."

Kent took a swing. Ferron dodged. Ferron's arms were longer—just enough to put flat hands against Kent's chest and step him back against the wall—not rough, but iron-man strong. Kent writhed like a pinned bug. Got one good kick at Ferron's shin. In a way, Ryder welcomed this: old Kenty. Ryder's cousin, not Jerusha's preppy boyfriend. Ryder figured if Jerusha saw this, she'd light out like a cat.

Ryder knew he was being a selfish jerk.

And he thought he was laughing.

"Ryder!" Ferron said. "Stop whimpering, fool. Help me out!"

"I'm not whimpering!" Ryder said, but he was, and he quit it, and picked up the chief blanket, shaking it out as he walked. Ferron stepped sideways to help Ryder wrap howling, kicking, flailing Kent tight as a burrito. Ryder picked him up and laid him on the bed. Ferron threw himself over his brother, full body pin.

"Get off me!" Kent yelled.

"Soon as you calm down!" Ferron said. "Get a grip, you little jackass."

"Fuck you, faggot! Get off!"

Ferron leaped up like he'd rolled on a snake. First time, ever, Ryder had seen him out of his mind. Ferron gave burrito Kent a hard boot-heel kick to the ribs. Smashed a palm against Kent's sweating forehead and balled his other hand into a fist. It took all his strength, but Ryder pulled him off. Ferron took the fist to the wall: bam, bam, bam, bam. Slivered, bleeding knuckles. Iron jaw. Shaking, pale.

Kent struggled up to an awkward sit. Stood up, undulating to shake off the blanket.

Brothers quivered like wolves. And then Kent was crying.

Ferron whispered, "Kenty. I'm doing my best. We'll get you out of there. We'll get help for Dad. He's really sick."

"Hope he dies in that goddamn chair."

"Kent—"

"I need to tell you something." Kent wiped his cheeks dry with his thin cowboy sleeve. Leveled up.

Ryder stepped closer. Ferron's eyes narrowed, body attuned to his brother's.

"Kent—" Ferron said again.

Kent opened his mouth. Two words dropped like gumballs from a penny machine.

"She's pregnant."

Ferron stepped back.

Ryder spun.

Ferron said, "*Who.*"

Kent dropped his head.

Ryder said it for him.

"Fucking hell. Jerusha."

Ferron's face at Ryder's open window. "Go home. Both of you. Keep your mouths shut, hear me? We'll talk about it later. Jesus Christ, Kent. What were you thinking? You're not even old enough to drive."

Kent kept his face away from them, but said, "What were *you* thinking, huh? Out in the hills with that—keeping that shit under your—"

"Did it make anyone pregnant, fuckhead? Fuck you."

"What?" Ryder said.

"Fuck you," Kent and Ferron said together.

"What the hell did I do?"

"Go home. Shut your mouths, like I told you."

Ryder backed up and hit a trash can.

"Leave it," Ferron said. "Take him home. I mean it, you two. Don't say *nothing* until we have a plan."

FORTY-THREE

Ryder's mom drove with him to register for school.

The counselor was a jerk. Kept trying to make Ryder sign up for basketball.

"You got height like that," Mr. Bridges said, "you owe it to your school. To the team."

"I don't like basketball," Ryder said. "I didn't get tall on purpose."

"Don't you even want to try?" Evaleen asked, like the kind of mom a school counselor might approve of.

"No."

"Come on, my friend. What's your problem? Do we have an attitude issue?"

Ryder was not his friend. And he didn't want to go on, but school counselors weren't made to lay off until they got explanations.

"I don't want to stay for practice every day. I got a horse to train."

"You don't look like the cowboy type to me."

This offended Evaleen.

"What do you mean, cowboy type?" Ryder's mom asked. "This boy has a fine hand with horses. Besides, he hurt his leg. It don't work for gym sports."

"When's it getting better?"

Ryder and his mother stared the man down. Evaleen said, "How about we sign him up for classes? We intend for him to graduate."

Mr. Bridges said, "So, he's not up for a good manly sport? We need a forward."

Ryder said, "I don't pivot. I get on a horse the wrong side because the right leg won't swing up."

"What did you do to it?"

Ryder almost said, *fell off a mule.* But he didn't want to defend his horsemanship.

"Broke it."

Mr. Bridges blinked several times. He didn't stretch himself over the desk to take a look, but Ryder could tell he wanted to.

"So, what *are* you good at? Looking here at your transcript, you need another couple math classes. Doesn't look like Gemini over there had much to offer, but your grades are good. Think you can keep up in our new trigonometry class?"

"I don't know what that is."

Mr. Bridges blinked more. "Something about triangulation. You got geometry under your belt. Why don't we give it a whirl?"

Ryder liked geometry. Geometry made him think about the Book Cliffs in interesting ways. The canyons, and the shapes of the Swell. Houses and barns.

"Yeah. Okay."

"You need English. Let's put you down for third period. Just before lunch."

"Fine."

"That gimp leg of yours disqualify you from taking Phys Ed?

"What?"

"Are you handicapped?"

"No."

"But you can't try out for basketball."

"I can. I don't want to."

"I think a guy blessed with your height owes his community."

Evaleen put her hand on the counselor's desk. "Enough about basketball. He don't want to play."

"I'm just saying. How'd you get so tall anyway?" Mr. Bridges asked Ryder. "Aren't you Mikkelsons from around here? I've never seen so many inches on a Mikkelson."

Ryder glared out the tiny window.

Evaleen said, "Let's stop with the basketball."

Mr. Bridges rolled his eyes. "Okay, you got history in the morning. Science right after lunch. It's that new teacher, out here from somewhere back east. Libber. Just pay attention to the science and you'll be fine. Then you got a couple of choices. Do you play an instrument?"

"No."

"Woodshop?"

"Maybe."

"Drafting?"

"Like, blueprints?"

"Uh-huh."

"Yeah."

"Okay, that leaves one more. You already got a sort of drawing class, so not art."

"Yeah, I want that."

"Drafting *and* art?"

"Yes."

"Think you're an artist? Where's the money in that?"

Evaleen was fed up. "Just get this done. He's not signing up for a lifelong career, is he."

"I'm just saying."

Evaleen stood. "Are we through here?"

"Unless he's thought better about basketball."

"We need to sign him up for seminary."

"That's a separate thing. We can't put him in it from here because some people make a big deal out of church and state. Here's the number though. 6:30 sharp, every morning, over to the 2nd ward."

"Mom, I don't want to do that."

Mr. Bridges: "Whole lot of things you don't want to do, is what I'm seeing."

His mother's grip on his upper arm made him wonder if he was the one in trouble. Ryder stood up, or maybe got pulled up.

"Let's go," she said.

Mr. Bridges said, "Pick up the class schedule from the secretary. I just sent it out to the printer."

The office lady said, "Evaleen Mikkelson! So good to see you back! And my heavens, is this great big guy your little Ryder? I can't hardly believe it!"

Evaleen cheered up. "Neither can I. How in the world can they grow so fast?"

Ryder felt like a 4-H calf.

"How does it feel to look down on everybody?" the office lady asked Ryder.

"Weird. Good, I guess."

"Honey, I remember holding you first week you came home to your mom and dad. They brought you to church for your name and blessing. Your dad looked about to faint, he was so overcome. You were so tiny! So perfect! Shock of blond hair, bright eyes taking it all in like you'd been waiting to get right where you belonged. You had such long fingers, I told your mama, this will be a tall one! Didn't I say so, Evaleen?"

"Well, I'm sure you did, you remember it so clear."

Other kids in the office seemed more interested in the office lady's gush than whatever business had brought them there.

"Ryder Mikkelson," the lady went on. "I never in my life seen folks so happy to bring a baby home. It makes no difference how you come to them. Heavenly Father sent you straight into their loving arms."

"Awwwww," some kid in the truant chair crooned. "Ain't that special."

"I didn't know you were adopted," a girl at the counter said. Ryder recognized her from church at Grandma and Grandpa's old ward.

A voice from the beat-up chairs behind him: "Hey, do you play basketball?"

Ryder ducked out.

Kent was in the cold space between the outside and inside doorways, mushing it up with Jerusha. Her hair was silky and yellow, cascading down her back. Her bangs stood straight up like she'd witnessed a crime.

"Get a room, losers," Ryder said.

Kent said, "Go jack off somewhere."

"Mack away," Ryder muttered as he pushed the door open to concrete. He stuck his head back in. "Watch out. My mom's coming."

Jerusha pulled off, patting the back of her head. She rummaged in her purse for lip gloss.

Ryder stepped in. "Okay. I'm sorry."

Jerusha's evil eye.

Kent's tight jeans made his butt about as wide as a salad plate. His bowed legs looked too thin to hold him up, but his chest and shoulders rippled lean under his pearl-button cowboy shirt. Kent was already shaving. Ryder's face was smooth as a ten-year-old's.

Kent turned to face Ryder, took an ominous step toward him.

Ryder said, "Really, Kent. I'm sorry."

Ryder's mom arrived. "Look at you three. What are you doing here in the cold?"

"Hi Aunt Evaleen," Kent said, a little hard. "We're waiting for lunch break to end."

"We're just talking," Jerusha said. "Are you glad to be back, Mrs. Mikkelson? We all missed Ryder a lot."

"It's good, I think. And it's just in time for Ryder's birthday. Sixteen on the Sixteenth! That's Tuesday. Come by for cake and ice cream. Kenty, bring Ferron."

Kent melted a little. A pup wanting a mother. "He likes mint chocolate chip, remember?"

"Now I do. Tell him I'll buy it special."

"Thanks, Aunt Evaleen."

"Ryder, can you find your classes?"

"Yes I can, Mom."

"Okay. I'll leave you kids to it. Stay out of trouble, you little demons."

Out she went, into the wind.

She stuck her head back in.

"Kenty."

"What, Aunt Evaleen?"

"Come see me. I don't mean Ryder. Me. I want to hear how you are. From you. You up to that?"

"Yeah."

"Soon."

Kent's voice was thin. "Okay."

Evaleen reached for Kent, stopping short of touching him. "Love you, buddy."

"I love him too," Jerusha piped up.

Evaleen stood back for a shrewd appraisal.

"Okay," she said, neutral. "He needs all he can get. His mother loves him, too, you know. She loves him."

Kent muttered as he pushed back into the foyer. The door came hard to its frame.

"I mean it, both of you," Evaleen said to Ryder and Jerusha. "He needs caring for. Don't ask too much of him."

Ryder said, "I need to go to class."

Jerusha stood rigid.

He left Kent's girlfriend standing there, in the space that was not inside, not out.

FORTY-FOUR

Ryder was grateful for the three classes he and Kent had without Jerusha. But he was anxious. They carried on as if nothing had changed; Ryder began to wonder if Jerusha was blowing smoke. She showed up on Fridays wearing her skimpy cheerleading outfit. Kent stayed after school to watch girls' volleyball practice, where Jerusha continued to dominate.

She was perky as ever in English, which they all had together. Some days, Kent was his funny and exuberant self. Ryder was surprised by his cousin's interest in class discussions—Kent had a quick memory and asked real questions. This was not cool at Nile Valley High School, but Kent didn't care. *Dulce et Decorum est.*

But other days, Kent was fogged. Jerusha held her pert posture, spoke in the chipper tones she'd practiced since elementary school, no matter how Kent behaved.

There might be no depth to her at all. Or maybe (he did not want to grant this) she was shoving it all too far down to reach. Not just this. He thought of his friend Jeri—not at all like Jerusha, but girls lived strange lives. Ryder didn't like thinking about girls and their problems. It messed him up. Ryder disliked Jerusha too much to grant her so much energy. Or concern. She took his cousin away. She might take him away forever.

At home, Ryder was engrossed in training the gelding. Grandpa had named the colt Mailman but hadn't spent enough time, Ryder figured, for it to take. Ryder changed it to Traveler, and the horse answered like he'd been waiting to be recognized.

Ryder loved caring for the horses. Didn't mind the weather. Unlike Gemini, set high in glass-brittle hills, Nile Valley didn't pick up much snow—at least not on the floor. Still, the sharp winds shot through the warmest sheepskin. Ryder's baggy jeans froze stiff and his boots cracked. But the animals were big and affectionate. Nuzzling and eager. Ryder felt like he was swimming in a warm pool as they milled around him.

Alma returned from a job in Price one night and strode to the corral. Ryder was moving the horses toward the lean-to stalls for bed.

"You're doing so good, son," Alma said. "You got a way with them."

Ryder's heart pumped in gratitude. "Grandpa comes out to tell me how I ought to do it different. No matter how I do it, it's supposed be some other way."

"Well your grandpa used to come out to criticize me and my brothers, too. Only he'd do it with a shove into the muck or up against the posts. Don't mind him. He don't know how to turn his hard world over, but he's harmless now. Mostly."

Grandpa Mikkelson used to own land speckled over three counties. Four if you counted the piece that straddled into Duchesne, but most of it was hard valley floor. Ryder's uncles had taken over the distant plots, settling however Mikkelsons knew how to settle. They'd cut out soon as they could, far from the old man's watch. Alma was third oldest but he'd stayed closer; Grandpa yielded property only when he was satisfied there were grandsons, with his name, to prop his legacy.

Ryder came so late he aligned with Doug's boys. As far as the old man was concerned, an adopted grandson was an imposter come to take land from blood family.

Alma said now, "It's a good sign the old bastard comes out to give you a hard time. Means he's claimed you, in his way."

Ryder considered. "Yay? I guess."

Alma folded himself between the crossbars into the corral. He stood close to Ryder as if he was about to tell him a secret. Instead, he reached a chapped hand into the pocket of his hod-hardened canvas coat. He pulled out five twenty-dollar bills, smoothed out, faces up. He reached for Ryder's coat pocket and stuffed them in.

"You been working hard," Alma said. "And I'm glad you got a good horse in the making, but you got all wrong clothes. Take the truck on Saturday and get yourself some nice pointy shit-kickers. And jeans that don't flap in the wind."

Traveler raised his head and dropped it over Ryder's shoulder, pushing his chest and neck into his boy. Ryder reached to give the flat jaw a scratch.

"Dad, a hundred dollars? Mom said I can't get new clothes until—"

"Big shot boss in Price been tipping me twenties every couple days for the fancy work. I been dog-toothing the top of a six-foot wall. Goes all the way around his front acre. I can unload the paper any way I want, can't I?"

"Well, yeah, but Dad—"

"You're doing good in school. You're working hard out here with the stock. I don't want you taking a cash job until summer. You'll be wanting it, but this'll help you stall until school's out. I talked to Roy. He'll be hiring for the tourist season. Just bussing but won't pay bad. Might mean you start while classes are still on, but they'll end quick. I can help with the livestock."

Alma chucked his tongue and held a hand toward the horses. They were shaggy and rough, fortified against the February cold.

"Give them oats yet?"

"I was about to."

"I'll help you walk 'em in."

Traveler stuck close to Ryder, following easy. Ryder loved his long swagger. The others arced around father and son, ready for night shelter.

A handful of oats for each. Old Cadillac nickered for more and Alma obliged.

Evaleen was in the kitchen, lights on. A tower of glowing sandstone rose behind the house—six hundred feet, breaking into a ledge of eroded skyline chimneys. The shapes of Ryder's first memories, so familiar he'd believed these were the forms that defined the world. Now, coming back, he saw how strange they were and he loved them more.

Alma said, "I shared that downstairs bedroom with three brothers. Window so small we couldn't hardly tell if it was day or night. Didn't spend much time sleeping, though. Every damn day, up before light."

"What about Aunt Nora and Aunt Kathy?"

"They had the small room upstairs, but it was luxury because there was only two of them. Dougie slept upstairs in the closet until he was two. By then Lamar was out, married young. First wife. They already had a baby, but she left him and took the kid. I'll point her out sometime. She's your cousin but so much older you wouldn't know her even if Lamar had raised her."

Alma blew into his hands. Tugged his boots off on the porch, laid them neatly, heels against the wall, for tomorrow. He liked to put them under the dash to warm up while he drove to Price.

Ryder leaned against the wall to pull his corral boots free. Set them beside his father's.

"I could about put my boots right into yours," Alma said. "My land you've got big."

Ryder stood up straight. He had to stretch the right leg to level out. Push down at the toe.

"Dad," he said.

"Yeah, buddy?"

"Thanks."

"You're welcome, son. You know I'm so proud to be your dad."

"Me too," Ryder said, which was a dumb way to put it, but they both knew what he meant.

FORTY-FIVE

Grown Kent is a shapeshifter in Ryder's eyes: small rat-tail Kenty bangs inside the walls of smirking libtard Professor Mikkelson. Cowboy Indiana Jones. Small Ryder inside the tall husband and father doesn't know what to make of a self-respecting straight guy from Emery County with a rainbow sticker on the back window of his pickup. Just below the gun rack.

Plus, just beneath, three black letters: "BLM." Either meaning in this county might incite a mob.

"This is how you let on you're queer?"

"Probably Ferron was."

"Aren't you afraid you'll get your window shot out? Get yourself killed on the back roads?"

"Ferron did, in his way. Just because he beat them to it doesn't mean it wasn't them. Whole country's guilty and they ought to know I know it. Besides, plenty of assholes out in the hills happy to pull a trigger just because you married their high school girlfriend. Because your binoculars gazed upon their sickly two-point. Because their uncle hates your uncle, way back."

"What the fuck, Kent."

"What the fuck, Ryder."

"It's not like I have anything against them," Ryder says now, on grand beautiful Ursula, up Westwater, riding alongside Kent. "I don't make it hard for anybody."

"Hard for who?"

"Quit doing that Socrates thing."

"Well, not having anything against 'them' takes about no effort at all. Besides, Ferron wasn't *them*. Whatever he was. All the things. He was us. So's the seriously brilliant environmental geology student I lost over holiday break."

"What happened to him?"

"Her."

"She do it to herself, like Ferron?"

"Ferron didn't do it to himself. No more than she did."

Ryder pulls the reins. Lifts his straw knockoff and runs his hand through sweaty hair. Wipes it dry on his pants. "Look, I hate the snake flags and guns and big talk. I know your dad worships hyenas. I can't live with an Indigenous wife and kids and buy that shit about getting great again. But it pisses me off I'm supposed to make a stand every damn day just to prove what I'm not. What I don't do. How come we have to make everything into politics? I hate it. Like you college lefties got something figured out?"

"Sami's got her masters."

"She's not a snob like the rest of them."

"You've met them all?"

"She looks after kids at the schools. Gives them help we never got."

"Yeah, well, college helped her learn how to help. Helped her get better at what she was good at. What's the matter with that?" Kent takes off his Stetson, shakes his glossy hair, puts the hat back on. Like a dude. "The difference between people isn't college and not college. The difference is people who stop thinking and start shouting, versus people trying to hear better stories. Better than the crap we got from the bishops and priests and mayors. And most of our teachers, sure. And our parents. Nobody's a prophet, nobody's a pope, even if they got the title.

"Ferron wanted to think about stuff. He had the best mind of any of us and he asked questions. He had to do that all alone. And it had nothing to do with going to college or not, but I wish he could have. And nothing to do with who he wanted to get it on with."

"Maybe it did. He told me the Greeks got educated by hooking up with philosophers. Like, for real hooking up."

"Well, maybe sex and brains went better together back then."

Ryder laughs. Sami likes to think about things while they're having sex. Ryder does not. She thinks conversation and sex are more or less the same thing. (*It's called intercourse for a reason, Ryder*). The difference messed them up a while, but now they have a system. He comes first, working his way from some place deep behind the word window. Then they start talking (how blue the sky against the clouds, something amusing from Ryder's day, or Sami's, or a memory drifting up), then Sami comes. Almost foolproof. Ryder knows what he'll talk about tomorrow night after the first mute pleasure: this May in heightening sun. The chasm's contours as the light begins to drop. Smoky lavender, deepening under back-beam gold.

She'll make him describe the southward colors: tanned hides. Coral pinks. Deep ferrous rust. That exact shadow blue before the red seeps in. It makes him want to turn back now, but Sami sent him up here. She said don't come home until he's hashed through a hard question with Kent.

Ryder is still not ready.

"I took a ride with Ferron along the west line," he says. "Less than a month before he . . . took his own route. We stayed west and rode the edge. Stuck the big views. He was happy, going on about cosmic repetitions. But now I see he was getting at—"

Ryder dries up.

Kent clicks up the gray. Late geld, prone to tantrums, but nimble under Kent's confident rein. Ursula knows to keep back, or pass wide, because Schist is like to kick.

Ryder picks up. "He said something weird. He told me he can't make pictures in his mind."

Kent says, "Whoa." He twists in the saddle. "Ryder, what?"

"I mean—couldn't. Didn't dream in movie ways, how I think most people do. Couldn't recall things by seeing them in his mind."

Kent turns the horse fully round.

"He never told me that."

"He said you probably didn't either. See in your mind, I mean. That I do because I'm not the same genetics."

Kent's eyes are wide, like he's seen Godzilla.

"I do, though. I can see him here, with us, plain as truth. I can see my mother, sitting on the cooler in that scruffy meadow, bawling out Doug. I can see every horse we've ever run through this family, just by naming it. Probably not as vivid as your superman talent, but I can see them fine. I dream stuff so real I wonder if it's not the regular world, if this one here is the illusion. I dream about that bear. I can see her, three-dimensional."

Ryder says, "He only told me that once. Like maybe it was so normal to him he hadn't realized it was odd."

Kent says, "It's called aphantasia. Sometimes it's inborn. But sometimes it happens after a traumatic event. With Ferron? That's my guess."

Ryder is washed in grief. Ferron made the worst parts of childhood bearable. He was the umbrella. For all of them.

"What happened to him?"

"What didn't? I don't really know his life. Especially the earliest parts. I knew him better than anyone, but he shielded me from who knows what. All of it. Gropey cousins. Stupid, self-indulgent father. Helpless, angry mother. Grandpa Mikkelson had this habit of taking out his anger at Doug by humiliating Ferron. Like, what? He was teaching our dad a lesson by beating up on a little kid? Shutting him in the old outhouse? I should have taken a chainsaw to that thing years ago.

"And I remember watching Dad hold Ferron under the water. Dragged him into the river because—I don't know. I couldn't have been more than two. No sense of cause and effect at that age. Just wide-eyed watching. Sometimes I wonder what I might have been if I'd tried to raise a kid in—holy shit, Ryder—tenth, eleventh grade. I look at you and hope I could have been like you. But what are the odds? Most kids live in spook alleys."

Ryder's mind runs to hot little writhing bundles, the terror of bringing them home. The long-wailing little-animal nights. A memory: Ferron at the door. A sobbing baby Stella, calming in his arms. The image of him, out there in the moonlight, whispering to the tiny girl . . .

Kent, here and now: "Doug held him under so long I thought my brother would come up dead like a catfish. And if he was dead, I knew Dad would turn on me, because Ferron wouldn't be there to run interference. I knew I lived in a volatile world, and I'm sure it messed me up. But I never got hit. I never got grabbed or groped, not by anyone. I never got strapped into a chair with Grandpa's belt, never got dunked in the river even though I was a little beast and Ferron was something wiser and better than all of us, right from the get-go."

Kent wheels the horse, abrupt, and heels him up the scrabble.

"How about," Kent says, somber, "another hour in and we make camp."

"Sure."

Kent slows where the trail crests. Stops to survey as Ryder catches up. The terrain up here is meadowy, fluorescent in spring light, rolling. Summits pitch northeast. Small canyons break shallow and deep. The sun casts long shadows off sandstone towers, striping the trail.

Kent scopes pines for night enclosure. Still thinking about his brother.

"Maybe he just wanted a dumb, ripped, rugged cowboy. Or some hella tough woman who could keep stride on the mountain, like your mom. We never got time to know. He never had a chance to love like a grown man, at least not that I know about. Deal with that any way you want, Ryder, but I'm not hiding what I am and who I've loved. Not here, not in Collins. Sure not in fucking Laramie, not goddamned Provo, not Texas or Florida. Not anywhere. I loved my brother and he should be here. With us. On this huge beautiful *escarpment*, if you want the technical term. Here. Now."

"He wasn't—" Ryder starts and stops. Tries again. "He wasn't just some damaged homo, don't you think? He was moody, and he lived inside himself, and he would have been complicated on the inside whether or not he wanted to—fuck guys."

Kent rides on.

Ryder calls, "Don't you think?"

Kent pulls Schist to hard stop. Turns him to face Ryder. Kent's eyes are obsidian black.

"How's that an insight, you moron?"

Ryder has no answer.

Kent spins his horse back up the trail. He calls back. "What do you think we've lost here, you jackass? A homo?"

"That's not what I meant, Kent! That's exactly what I didn't mean!"

"No shit."

Schist's gray butt moons placid Ursula as Kent flickers under the light of quaking aspen.

Deep night, moonless, embers. Horses asleep on their supple hooves.

Bedrolls on soft sand, saddle blankets for pillows.

Ryder asks, "You got a girlfriend up there? Fort Collins?"

"Sometimes."

"One? Or you still playing the field?"

"Too tired to play."

"Why sometimes?"

"She's an anthropologist. Ancient American migrations."

"Like, Clovis point ancient? Or gold plates ancient?"

"No plates. That's how she got interested in anthropology though. Her mom was converted in Alaska by some missionary from Idaho. He took her away for a globe-trotting life in the Civil Service. Erased the Tsimshian, made them Mormon. Deep state flunkies." Kent laughs. "That used to be patriotic. Now it's treading on the snake. Anyway, she went home to grandparents. College in Fairbanks. First course that gave her authentic Indigenous history, she was in."

"Is she a professor?"

"Yeah. She's out in the field a lot. So am I."

"Which is why you say sometimes."

"Yeah. But it's good. You know I'm not the domestic kind. Neither is she. But we're good cooks when we have time together."

"What's her name?"

"Margaret. Meg."

"Are Tsimshian people Athabascan? Like Diné?"

"No. They're just Tsimshian. No language tree. They just came out of the ground already Tsimshian." Kent smiles. "Or dropped from the sky. Like you."

"They had to come from somewhere."

"Isn't that what we're supposed to be talking about? How much of your own anthropology you want to excavate? Sami gave us an assignment."

"I think I'll be ready tomorrow."

"To . . .?"

"Talk about it. Let me sleep on it, one more night."

"Got it," grown up Kenty murmurs, and then he's snoring.

FORTY-SIX

"Sex outside of the bonds of holy matrimony is a sin," Brother Larsen proclaimed, again, in seminary. He exhorted in Sunday School, too—so rote that Ryder and his classmates, ten or fifteen of them (depending on how many were kicking against the pricks), had to sit through it six days a week. Same tone, same arm-flapping, same follow-through: "Don't get me wrong. Nothing is more glorious than the physical union of a righteous man and his wife, coming together to bring valiant spirits to inhabit bodies fit to usher in the Millennium. But toying with this sacred power courts destruction and damnation."

Ryder wondered unhappily if he and Brother Larsen had the same annoying problem with language: once certain words blazed up in their brains, that's all they could deliver. That's why Ryder worked to cover mind words with pictures, with memories of trails, or canyons, or faces. Sometimes he still needed window writing to loosen his tongue, but once he got going he had to turn away or the engraving would harden, and then he could only say what the writing said, and mostly it was stupid crap dredged up from Primary lessons, or pieces of Sacrament Meeting talks woodburned into ten-year-old brains. Ryder hated it.

Same words over and over, same simplified answers to complicated questions.

Right now he hated church most because he knew Kent and Jerusha had sex. There was no pretending it didn't happen. Jerusha came to school in peculiar dresses and oversized shirts. Kent was struggling to keep up his college-bound image against the misery of living in a filthy fifth-wheeler. It was all bad enough without the Mormons and Catholics, the born-agains and town scolds going on about sin. And as awful as it was all going to be for Kent, Ryder had to acknowledge that Jerusha would carry the brunt.

She was pitching toward crisis, and it would be easy for Jerusha to pin it on Kent, to cry and point and run to her rich daddy. But she hadn't. She insisted she loved her boyfriend. Ryder feared she might mean it.

And plenty of busted lovers before Kent had showed this town how ruthlessly boys could blow off their pregnant girlfriends—call them sluts and turn friends against them. Bring in the church or the law. Kent could destroy her, even though he was poor and his family was pretty famously screwed up, and Jerusha came from money and prominent folks.

Ryder knew he wouldn't.

It was all nasty, and not in the ways Brother Larsen went on about. If sex was nasty, it was because a town could make it so. Or it was the kind that had gotten into Murphy's head, back in Gemini. Stuff Jeri knew. Ryder suspected Aunt Maura had been through some bad shit, too. Before Doug. Maybe that's why she married him. Doug was a jerk, wanted a wife to argue with, and Kent said he hit her. But that seemed to be all he wanted. Shouting and hitting weren't sex. Were they?

Ryder's mom and dad acted like sex was just goofy fun. They teased each other, grabbing about. Now that they were in the new house, further from Ryder's hearing—did they do it?

Would all the adults declare Kent a sinner, declare "premarital sex" a crime almost as bad as murder? Would Ryder's mom call Jerusha a slut? A mother who didn't deserve the child her own body produced? Ryder did not like Jerusha, but the thought of it clutched at something.

And there was—in all of this—a baby. A little mashup of Kent and—Ryder shut it down.

Ryder got up for seminary every morning, left on time, but began to skip the exhortations once or twice a week. Then he cut it out entirely. He was envious that Ferron and Kent never had to sit through seminary. Or church, anymore, of any kind. They were about as good or bad as anyone else Ryder knew, with or without the pious harangues. Better.

Ryder started hanging around the school building, distant enough to look innocuous, until the office ladies showed up to open the doors. Then he went to the art room to draw until the school busied up. Did extra homework.

English Paper
By Ryder Mikkelson
Mrs. Iordanu 10th Grade
March 3, 1995

For my English Class I was assigned to write about an interesting question I don't know the answer to. So, a question I've been thinking about for a really long time is, what do I think about being adopted.

I think this is a good question for this assignment because I'm supposed to explore some ideas about why the question matters to me and talk (I mean write) about some ways I will maybe follow some of the paths it leads to in the future. Maybe my teacher means in college but I don't know if I'm going to college, because I like horses and animals and my dad is teaching me construction and masonry, plus I think I can take care of my grandpa's farm if I learn some skills to make extra money. My mom and dad have already paid a lot of money to fix my leg, which I broke when I was seven. So I picked a question that I will probably think about for a long time even if I don't go to college.

I didn't know I was adopted at first but when I was 7 I fell off a pack mule when me and my dad and my cousins were hunting in the Book cliffs. When I was at the emergency room out to Grand Junction my dad freaked out when he had to answer questions about me, like my family health history and how I would probably grow, and he blurted out that I was adopted. He thought I was unconscious or I was in too much pain to pay attention but I wasn't so that's how I found out. I was super upset about it because it meant that I wasn't really my cousins cousin and I felt like I didn't have any true family anymore, and also I was upset because I felt like my mom and dad and everyone who knew me who was older than me had been lying to me all that time. And I hate when people lie to me. My Mom said they were'nt lying that they just hadn't told me yet but looking back, I was upset for a long time that she hadn't told me. Now I think I understand better why she didn't tell me I think she was just scared I wouldn't believe she was my Mom anymore and she had a hard time having babies and her heart was broken.

So this leads me to the questions I'm asking now that I'm older the main one which is do I want to know anything else about being adopted or should I just let it be and forget about it. Because I do feel like this is my family and we've been through a lot together and my cousin Ferron says we're made by the lives we live and the Universe isn't really so easy to change anyhow. Ferron reads a lot of Philosophy and he says when you really think hard about things like the Philosophers do, most of our first Ideas fall to the wind while Great Ideas stand like stone. I don't know what I think about all that but that's a question for another paper. That I hope I don't have to write.

Some questions about being adopted do stay in my Mind though, I don't know if they'll ever go away even when I try to leave them alone. Like, I know how my mom and dad (Evaleen and Alma Mikkelson I mean) got me but when my Mom tells me the story of getting on an airplane and going to pick me up in Seattle, Washington,

I can't help thinking about the other Mom who had me on that very same day and in some ways it almost seems like I remember her. I don't mean to be gross but I had just come out of her and I had been in her for nine months probably and so it seems like I would at least remember the feeling of that. A little bit anyway. And it bugs me that she probably remembers all of it and I wonder if she wants to know where I ended up even though for some reason she didn't want to keep me.

I also wonder about my Dad (I mean the biological dad) and if he loved my biological mom or if it was just a mess like I've seen around here sometimes. And I wonder if he was tall because no one in my adopted family is tall and now that I'm really reaching full height it makes me feel like I stick out like a sore thumb. My cousin says more like a middle finger but I probably shouldn't mention that in an English paper. I wish I knew how tall I'm going to get and also I wonder about some talents I have that no one else does like I'm good at drawing. Like where did that come from. And I like math, especially geometry and I'm liking trigonometry at school. My dad is teaching me masonry and he's real good at it instinctually, but I've been able to tell him stuff that really helps him because I get the math. He's not bad at it he's a really smart guy but he says I have told him some things that he never would have realized, and I explain it clear, and he says maybe one of my biological parents was super good at math.

This brings me to my last thought which is that my dad (Alma Mikkelson) is pretty easy going about talking to me about where I might have come from before I came to them, but my mom (Evaleen Mikkelson) is definately not. Which is why I would appreciate it if you didn't talk about this essay with her. My dad and me had a hard time for a few years while he was going through some things, but we can talk about most things better now. I think he knows I love him and I will always call him my Dad. But it's harder for my Mom maybe because she's had a pretty hard life and she always wanted to be a Mom and to love her own child or children so when I came to be her Son she must have thought she had to hold on tight. It's weird because she's taught me lots of important things. She's the one who talks to me about the hard things in life and she's not scared of anything but then again she can't talk about this subject without kind of falling apart so I just avoid it with her. Mostly because I don't want to hurt her feelings but also because it's not worth the hassle. So right now I don't think I'll look for any answers because why should I ever hurt my mom, Evaleen Mikkelson.

To summarize I have a lot of questions about being adopted, mostly right now whether I should even keep thinking about it at all or if I should let things lie. But I do think I might understand my self better if I knew some things about being adopted. But then again what if I found out that my biological parents were horrible people or something, or if their dead, and how would that affect the way I see my self. My mom and dad that adopted me taught me to be a good person and I don't want to make that harder than it already is. So I know I'm not supposed to answer my main question in this essay, just explore it, but I do think I have one answer, that I won't look for any information for now, and I'll try to stop thinking too much about it. I know this paper is supposed to be 1,500 words but this is all I can come up with, so I understand if I don't get an A. The End.

FORTY-SEVEN

In March, Social Services made Ferron Kent's legal guardian and Kent moved into the Riverbend. Medicaid sent a kind but overworked home care nurse to see to Doug three times a week, which made Doug think he had a girlfriend, and he bucked up a little. Evaleen sent Alma over to the fifth-wheel to deliver a healthy one-man dinner every night, plus every Monday on the way to work she dropped off a weekly stack of beef or turkey brown-bread sandwiches, wrapped to keep in the freezer for lunches. No cheese. This caused Doug to heave out of his chair and shuffle across the room to the fridge at least once a day. And back. Exercise.

"You eat them all in one sitting, Doug, and you'll have no lunch until the next Monday," Evaleen said on the phone to him, not mean but matter of fact. "Do it any way you want, but that's how it goes. One a day, and then wait for dinner. Eat your cereal in the morning. I'm back to work at the city office now, so this is the schedule."

Evaleen insisted on pulpy orange juice and skim milk. He was still too weak to lift himself into his truck even if it could start, which it couldn't because his breathing was so bad he hadn't turned the key in months. No beer runs. So Doug started to get healthy despite himself.

Evaleen, in league with the social worker, told all three boys to keep away from him for the time being, and Ryder saw the weight lift from his cousins' backs.

Sometimes Ryder went to the Riverbend to make dinner with

Ferron and Kent. They cooked over the firepit in what Joe Gonçalves, who passed as the manager, liked to call the courtyard. Foil dinners with hamburger, and potatoes and onions. Black pepper and garlic salt. Evaleen advised carrots. Or they grilled brats and sauerkraut. Alma came over one night with venison steaks from Grandpa's freezer and Ferron got fancy with side salads. They ate popsicles for dessert, no matter the weather.

Other times Ferron and Kent drove up in the fenderless Altima Ferron bought on auction in Salt Lake County. "Ugly, but it runs," Ferron said. "Gets me to work. And I'm getting the produce truck in really good shape. When you coming to paint the logo, Ryder?"

"Spring break?"

Alma said, "When you're ready, pull it out of the warehouse and I'll go over each part of the engine with you. We'll take a look underneath while we're at it. We'll give it a power wash."

Ferron looked relieved.

When he was in Evaleen's kitchen, Kent carried on like there wasn't a thing wrong. Devoured whatever Ryder's mom put on the table. Brought his homework. Kept his nose in the ACT study guide. Answered questions politely.

Except one: *Where's Jerusha?*

In which case, Kent's eyes veiled over. Lips pressed bloodless.

No one at school had seen her for weeks. The cheer squad had no leader, the National Honor Society no president. The Beesons, up in their big house on the slope, seemed to have no daughter.

Kent, no girlfriend.

FORTY-EIGHT

In April, Ferron backed his fixed-up box truck out of Grandpa's warehouse for a sunlit once-over with Ryder's dad. Ryder had drafted ten thumbnail logos for Ferron's inspection. After dinner, everyone pored over them at the kitchen table. Vote by vote, double elimination, they narrowed them down to three:

"FERTILE CRESCENT Produce and Delivery" with the first C green like the river, wrapping around the rest of the word like a horseshoe bend. "Produce and Delivery" in smaller letters cutting across. Egyptian reeds festooning each side.

"PHARAOH'S BOUNTY We bring it to you" with the first O adorned with a Rameses headdress. "We bring it to you" in smaller letters above.

"EGYPTIAN QUEEN Nile Valley Produce" with EGYPTIAN QUEEN arced above Nefertiti's head, "Nile Valley Produce" draped like a necklace below.

Everyone liked the third one best, but it was for sure the trickiest. Ryder was afraid he'd mess it up. And he'd have to do it on each side of the truck. He'd talked to his art teacher, Mrs. Roundy, about what kind of paint would be best. She suggested stencils and a spray gun for the main parts. Because she was also the drafting teacher, Mrs. Roundy emphasized the importance of precise measurements. Ryder knew his dad and cousins could take care of that. Mrs. Roundy said she'd give Ryder full credit for his final project in both classes if he pulled it off. She said she was proud of him for taking on a real-world challenge, and made a point of saying it to the other students, which made him nervous all over again.

Ryder and Kent drove to Price for stencil and paint supplies: X-acto blades and coated paper, a small spray gun with change-out cans to attach to Alma's compressor, and auto paint. Slender brushes for detailing. On the way home, Kent gazed out the window, but it didn't seem to Ryder he was taking in the views. Granted, it wasn't exactly scenic out there: RVs and SUVs clogged the southbound lanes; idiots kept trying to pass a line of cars racked with mountain bikes, trailers loaded with boats, motorcycles or four-wheelers, Jeeps with Kokopelli stickers, German tourists on rented Harleys, pretending to be Hell's Angels. Everyone was headed to Moab or bound for Lake Powell. Everyone aimed to fill their tanks in Nile Valley.

Plus, the usual shipping rigs blew black smoke in both directions.

Ryder cursed as a kid-sized mountain bike flew off a rented trailer two cars ahead, followed on a second trajectory by a bench-sized cooler. A northbound Peterbilt blasted the cooler and its contents off the shoulder, but the bike lay like a booby trap for the next vehicle blazing north.

"Should we pick it up?" Ryder asked, mostly to make Kent respond.

"Pick what up?" Kent answered, and Ryder quit trying until they were off the highway, nearly to Grandpa's lane.

Ryder rolled to a stop along the ditch.

Kent sat fused. His face was pale, bluish under the fine fur.

Ryder said, "Kent. Where is she?"

Kent pressed his face against the window.

Ryder: "Is she okay? I know I was a jerk. But I never wanted—"

Kent held his face away from Ryder. Spoke to the willow thickets at the waterline. His voice grated like a handsaw.

"Her dad came to the motel a couple nights ago. Knocked real hard. Called me *Kent Fucking Mikkelson*. Kicked the door and said I'd better come out."

Ryder pictured Jerusha's father, usually dressed in a suit and tie or department store chinos, polo shirts. The guy had thick, stand-up hair, gelled into a motionless wave. Five o'clock shadow no matter what time it was. Overtly sociable but dangerously pissed off—a dam nigh to break. Picturing that man banging on the cheap motel door, defacing Kent's name, made Ryder sick.

Kent resumed the sawing sound: "I didn't want him to think I was hiding so I stepped out. He said I owed him for half an abortion. Said he'd taken care of the part that was her mistake, since he was one of the men responsible for this 'oil slick.' But I was the other one and I better pony up."

Ryder dropped his grip on the steering wheel.

"How—how's he figure he's . . .'"

Ryder tried again. "How's that . . . how's he being . . . responsible? He can't make that choice for . . .?"

Ryder cracked his window. Kent rolled his down all the way. Stuck his head out, gulping like he'd been pulled from the river.

"Does Ferron know?"

"He came out. Gave the guy money."

"Kent. Holy shit. How much?"

"He showed Ferron the receipt. I don't know. Dude got back in his BMW and squealed out. Ferron said shut up about this. We don't need trouble."

"Do you think *she* wanted to get rid of—"

"We talked about how we'd take care of each other. I was thinking I'd work up to Price, or maybe Castle Dale in the mines. Pay's good right now. Or the power plant, until she graduates from here. Then we could move up by the state college, or maybe down to Ephraim or Cedar. We were talking to Miss Neerings about how to get Jerusha in and find a way to pay for it. I would have done it, Ryder. Jerusha said she wanted the baby. But then she was just gone. And her dad came to find me. He said she was at boarding school and if I tried to contact her he'd kill me."

Ryder felt like his guts were wrapped around his ribs. "Well, *I'm* gonna kill *him*," he said. "He can't—"

"Ryder, we have to drop it. We do. What the hell I was thinking? Anything I do will make it worse. You can't tell anyone. It's you, me, Ferron. And Jerusha, and that mean fuck. That's it. I guess Miss Neerings too. She told me I need to get on with my future, same way Jerusha does. I want out of this town. There's a science scholarship at University of Arizona. She thinks I can get it. I want to be a geologist. Not the kind that finds coal and oil, like here. I don't know what other kind there is but I'll find out."

Kent wrapped his arms over his head, pulling it into his lap. He took hard heaving breaths. He sat up. Rolled his window partway up. "Right now, that's all I want. Only thing I can think about."

Ryder put in the clutch, turned the key. Brought his hands to the steering wheel.

"I didn't know some feminazi would help out a guy, you know?"

"Ryder, go hang out with Doug if that's what you think."

"Have you heard from your mom?"

"She's still sending money. I'm saving it up. Ferron won't let me pay him back for the—he says load up for college any way I can. He's about to make manager at Lin's. Mom doesn't know about any of this."

"For sure."

"Let's go fancy up Ferron's truck."

"I want us to help him."

"Grandpa can come out and cuss at us because we're doing it wrong."

Ryder pushed the pedal.

"Ryder."

"What."

"I know they'd try to help, but don't tell your mom and dad. It's got to go down the river and drown. That man could make hell for the whole family. He's itching to."

Alma's pickup was getting old, but Ryder knew his dad would drive it until it turned to desert dust. He felt a rush of love and admiration for the squirrelly guy who claimed Ryder as his own.

And guilt. Another secret, now, to keep from his kind and forthright mother.

FORTY-NINE

While Ryder penciled measured letters on the coated paper, Evaleen took Kent around back to the pile-it shed. They dug out an old kitchen table with a still-smooth top. Kent looked shook up as he helped his aunt haul the heavy piece into the garage; Ryder knew Evaleen had coaxed some of the story.

"Here you go, Ryder," she said, wiping the tabletop clean. "Cut to your heart's content. No damage done. Call when it's time to paint because I want to watch."

"Don't think we'll get to painting until tomorrow."

Kent went in with Evaleen to gather extreme-cleaning supplies.

Next day, Kent and Ferron showed up early to measure and mark the scorched-clean, sanded circles awaiting the grand queen. Ryder intended to practice his brushwork, but he was distracted by his cousins. He liked to watch them move and murmur together. No person who saw one within a hundred feet of the other would fail to see their likeness. Dark hair and eyes set on sculpted faces. Hard, flat chests, lean muscled backs, delicate waistlines over matchstick legs. Tenor voices popping with little profanities. They worked the ladder, levels and markers, tape measure like they drew each intention from the same well.

Ryder felt an old pang of yearning. He wanted to be their blood, complicated as it was by generations of strain, disorder, alienation. He wanted to be Alma's son so he could be their cousin. He wanted

Evaleen to be his mother so Great-Grandpa Yeadon could show him where he was headed. If that meant ancient Opex junk collector, fine. He wanted to live among his family and assume—never dream otherwise—that he was among his own, decreed by DNA, reiterations of likeness.

"Who would have designed and painted my truck, then?" Ferron would say if Ryder had tried to explain. "Think what a mess we'd have."

Ryder turned back to the practice queen on the concrete floor. The stenciling looked good. Ryder would have to repeat the success now on sheet metal, horizontal. No goofs. He drew in his breath, knelt with his good leg on the hard cement, splaying the right one so the bone screws wouldn't punch through the skin at his knee. He took a fine brush to Nefertiti's deluxe mascara. Then the graded sheen of her high cheekbones, then the cherry red of her lips. A pretty line to define the chin, the descent of her long neck.

He stood up, annoyed.

Hard-on.

"I'm gonna take a walk. Clear my mind," Ryder said to his cousins.

"Okay, this is it," Kent said. "It's all you, Ryder. I'll go get Aunt Evaleen so she can watch."

Evaleen came in with brownies, which Alma, Kent, and Ferron ate, delicate. Ryder shoved one into his mouth and washed his hands. Then he loaded up the green, attached the slender hose, flipped the switch on the compressor. The noise startled everyone. He took a deep breath. He climbed the ladder.

"Wait a minute, son. Come down."

"I got it," Kent said. He took a hod mask from Alma's hand, then stepped up to give it to Ryder.

"Want to spend your life coughing like I done?" Alma said.

Ryder put it on. Then he sprayed, evenly as he could, along the lettered arc of EGYPTIAN QUEEN. Paint dribbled down his wrist, into his sleeve, but he tried not to let it distract him.

He climbed down. Switched the paint to black for *Nile Valley Produce*. He worried about spraying outside the edges of the stencil paper, which would put the lettering in a sloppy border. He adjusted the pressure. Perfect. He was eager to pull the stencils away—but this was not a thing to rush.

"It's gonna look so good!" Alma said. "Now that I'm watching, I can start to picture it in my mind."

"It will be beautiful," Evaleen said. "I can't believe we got ourselves such a good artist. Who would have ever thought something like that?"

"Now comes the queen," Kent said. "The old girl herself."

Ferron kept the thumbnail design in his hands, referring to it then looking up with happy wonder, which almost made Ryder cry. Doing something that mattered to Ferron was like witching water.

Ryder stepped down the ladder to mix again: night sky hue. Nefertiti's high hat was the biggest block of color. He needed to keep it from dripping down her face. He took it slow, putting it down in thin layers, blackening his fingers.

Finally, the face and neck. He decided to spray the whole cut a dark tan. Then he'd keep the stencil in place to hand-paint the emerald eyes and the lips (that dangerous cherry red). Clean black lines to finish.

He thought everyone would drift out after a while—the work was slow and meticulous, but nobody budged. Even Grandpa wandered in. He took a gander, said nothing, went back out. And then he came back in to say, "Well I'll be damned," and went to get Grandma. Alma seated them on lawn chairs, handing each a brownie and a glass of milk while Ryder detailed the stenciled jewels.

His head spun with fumes and concentration. His shoulders were bunched into tight knots. Alma said, so close he made Ryder jump, "Here, son, hand me them colors. Brushes. I'll clean 'em up for tomorrow. Come down and rest. Eat this last brownie. I fought Kenty off it."

"Think we can do all this again tomorrow?" Evaleen asked.

"Sure we can," Alma answered. "Kent, Ferron—be here first thing and we'll measure out the second side."

"Never can do the same thing twice," Grandpa muttered.

"Should we go get pizza?"

"No! Tourists out there."

Evaleen said, "Okay, then. It's a weenie roast. Boys, make us a fire."

The week after it was done, Mrs. Roundy said, in sixth period art, "Okay, everyone. Put your work away early. We're taking a little field trip, out to the parking lot."

She walked over to a window. Tilted it open. She put out a hand and waved it like a flag.

An air horn blared.

"Clean up right," she said. "You won't want to come back once the last bell rings."

Fifteen art students buzzed through clean-up and zipped their backpacks, awaiting the signal to go.

"Find your way to the student lot. I asked the principal if the drafting students could come. They'll be waiting in front of the office. Go out the main door. Don't get rowdy."

No one got rowdy. They were too curious. Ryder took up the rear—his height made him conspicuous in a group and he didn't like it.

"Pick up the pace, Ryder," Mrs. Roundy said. "You're the man of the hour. I want you up front to answer questions."

"What?"

The horn blared again. Ryder pushed out the front doors and rounded the corner.

Ferron stood on the running board of his excellent box truck. Grinning.

Mrs. Roundy said, "Students, Ferron Mikkelson accepted my invitation to bring his delivery truck for you to admire. That beautiful logo is the work of your classmate Ryder. Now this is what I've been trying to convey! What you learn in your classes has real world applications when you rise to your abilities. Look at the execution! Walk around the truck to appreciate the personal touches."

Ryder stood like Lurch as his classmates plodded around the truck. The girls said, "Oooh!" The guys maintained stony faces. Ferron walked over to stand with Ryder as Mrs. Roundy gestured the students into listening formation. "Ask Ryder some questions! Take this opportunity to learn from one of your peers!"

General silence. Then somebody asked, "How long did it take you to do it?"

Ryder said, "Well, uh . . ." and lost his words completely.

Ferron said, "Kent and I helped him get the surface clean, and we measured it all out while he cut the stencils. We taped them up on one side and he mixed the colors and sprayed. Took him about two hours. Then he did that cool brushwork to make her pop. And he'd already spent a lot of time on the sketches. Right, Ryder?"

Ryder said, "Uh-huh."

"Next day we did the same on the other side. How many hours total, Ryder?"

"Um, about, forty?"

Ryder wondered whether he should have counted the drive to Price and back. The spring break traffic jam.

"Any other questions?" Mrs. Roundy asked.

Everyone was as tongue-tied as Ryder until the bell rang. Then the whole class crowded around him. "That's so cool, man!"

"You're so talented!"

"Will you paint my car, man? How much would I have to pay you?"

Ferron gave him a ride home, blaring the horn at waving kids along the way.

FIFTY

End of junior year, Ryder returned to his job at Roy's, so he was always busy. School for a couple more weeks. Livestock, early mornings, since his mother had surrendered over seminary. Bussing and dishwashing in the hot kitchen of the town's busiest tourist café. Roy usually let Ryder and the other underage employees go home by ten, but sometimes, when the roster was short or river trippers came in, Ryder worked past midnight.

One night, early moonrise, the wide Green River lit and lapping high behind the fast-filling dumpsters, Ryder walked past a young couple leaning against an old wood-panel Wagoneer, deep in conversation. Sometimes lovers came out here to argue, or make out, so he tried to show that he was minding his business. He carried heavy trash bags in both hands, veering to keep the scent from wafting over.

"Hey Ryder," the guy called as Ryder passed. Friendly. Familiar.

Ryder kept moving toward the dumpsters. "Um. Lemme drop these bags, 'kay?"

It was a high toss; trucks came tomorrow and the dumpsters were billowing.

"They gotta send the tall guy out?" Wagoneer said. "Man, you got vertical."

Ryder turned and stepped closer, wiping his hands on his apron, squinting in the dim greenish light. The guy looked like a tourist: river sandals, cargo shorts. T-shirt with an outfitters' logo, matched on his canvas baseball cap.

Ryder couldn't believe it.

"Ephraim? Holy crap. I haven't seen you in . . ."

"Long time, right?"

The woman—girl—woman! beside Ephraim turned her face into the moonlight. Toward Ryder. Dark eyes vivid. Long hair shining.

She smiled. Ryder's legs turned to static.

Sami.

"I—gotta go. Another hour on shift," Ryder managed, backing away.

"Well, hey. School still in session here?" Ephraim asked.

"Another week."

"You work tomorrow?"

"No."

"Well, come out to the campground then. We're setting up, but we aren't pushing off for a couple days. You're one of the only people in this town I wouldn't mind talking to. You and your cousins. And Sami's been keeping an eye out for you."

"Are you two—like—" Ryder couldn't make himself say it.

Sami laughed. Ryder thought he'd pass out cold.

Ephraim said, "Together? We're kind of brother and sister, remember? That would be a little weird."

Then: "She wants to catch up."

Ryder took in garbage air. Coughed it back up. Turned to face her.

Ephraim: "With you."

"Really?" he asked. Her.

She said, "I do."

FIFTY-ONE

Sami wasn't old enough this year to run the river with Ephraim and the raft crew, but Ephraim, a capable and convincing guy, had persuaded management to hire her on for reservations, prep, customer welcome and return. She'd made herself valuable quick enough to score a shared wall tent for the summer at the reserve side of the state campground, a nice place where the river lapped shallow. Willows hung shady and low.

"You hardly ever talked when we were in school," Ryder said. "Now you're talking to tourists just about every day."

"I was a little kid, far away from home," Sami said. "Placement people told me to hunker down and not call attention to myself. So I didn't."

"Plus, what. You lived with—well, you know."

Sami held up a hand, a stop signal. "They were probably the best family I could have lived with. They didn't make a fuss over me, and I didn't want them to. They did old-time things I recognized. Cooked on a wood stove. Kept a garden, bottled and canned all fall. Planted in spring. They grew and butchered their own meat—not sheep, like I knew, but one year they did it for me. I felt so important, showing them how we did it at home."

Ryder was ashamed. All he'd ever thought about the Johnstons was *loony*. Fanatics.

"Well, yeah," Sami said now. "But who isn't? Didn't seem any loonier to me than any other people up here. And they weren't mean.

Those kids took a lot of meanness from other people—even grown-ups—at school and church."

Sami's voice was bright and rhythmic, dipping on certain syllables that dropped lower than most men's, even while the top notes stayed true. It only lasted a second, happened every few. Ryder made himself concentrate on what Sami was saying, because the sound was wildly distracting. He felt the chords in his chest. And legs. And...yeah.

"They were super religious. Ephraim's dad was always going on about the Lamanites. Said I'd be white someday if I proved I deserved to shake off the curse of my ancestry. But everybody told me something like that. That was just stuff to—Ryder, are you even listening?"

"Yes!"

"How about you?"

"What do you mean?"

She laughed. "What do you think I mean? You were lost in your own world, too. Especially after that leg broke. How is it now?"

"Fine. I had to keep going back to the doctor. Did some more surgeries. My dad and mom sold the place in Etna and we lived with my mom's grandpa up to Gemini. Closer to the hospital. I pretty much busted my mom and dad paying for it all."

"It was easy to see they loved you. I bet they didn't care you were expensive."

"Well—"

"Does it still give you trouble?"

"What, the leg? I get up on a horse the wrong way. It's a little short, but not too bad."

"But finding out you were adopted changed you, too. I remember that."

Ryder sat up. Small sticks and sand stuck to the skin on his bare back.

"It's weird to feel like I have two possible lives. You know?"

Sami said, "Yeah, stupid."

Sami lay with her arm shielding her eyes. From sun. Or his blinding white chest.

"Hell, Sami. Of course you do."

She rolled her lower lip under her top teeth.

He said, "I hate the way I get all caught up in my own sob story. Forget who I'm talking to. You, I mean."

"We're not telling sob stories. We're just telling stories. I had two pretty okay lives, considering. All the trading out messed with my brain, but at least I could picture them both. I decided to stay in Redhorse after ninth grade. My family was doing better. It took a long time to feel like I belonged with my Diné family, in Diné places, even though I knew most of them and they *all* knew me.

"Navajos don't express it same ways as white people. At least the ones I know. I had to learn that they loved me and wanted me back."

The moon, a mottled arc in diminishing daylight sky, rose over the water.

Ryder thought she was finished, but she sat up and said one more thing: "You kind of got left wondering. That's a different thing to have to figure out."

He couldn't help ladling himself a little bonus sympathy. "It's weird to not look like anyone in my family."

"What are you talking about? All you white people look the same."

Ryder laughed, nervous.

She said, "What? Does that hurt your little feelers? Anyway, you sure got tall."

"Thought I'd never stop growing. But it's not as bad as I was afraid of. Six-two. I think I'm done."

"Taller when you put your boots on." She poured a handful of sand into one of them.

"Hey!"

The current was high. A rolling sound, like faraway thunder.

He could hear rocks grating against each other in the depth. Ryder thought about snow, sculpting and dripping on the high slopes, running in a million small streams, headed for this primordial bed.

He wished to reach for Sami's hand but lost his nerve.

"Gotta start my shift," he said. "You want a ride up to the bridge?"

"Sure."

They stood to wipe sand off their jeans. Nearly collided as they turned toward Alma's pickup.

He shook out his T-shirt and pulled it over his head, suspecting he looked like a toddler as he punched around for the sleeves. He smoothed it down over his stomach, suddenly mortified by his skinny frame.

She brushed the back of his hand with hers.

He yelped like the dog he was.

She took his hand. Hers was so small. And desert-rough. The top of her head just reached his collarbone. It made him want to cry, even though he was so happy his brain fizzed like shook soda.

FIFTY-TWO

Senior year was good enough. Ryder just wanted to get it done, get on to summer. Sami was coming back, now old enough to ride the rafts, help cook breakfasts for the clients.

"They love the idea of having a real-live Indian girl on the trips," Ephraim said. "Photo gold. The Germans go crazy for that shit. French too."

Ryder didn't know what to think of that. But then again, he did. "Is she on your crew? You'll be there with her, right?"

Ephraim had the pinyon-trunk core of a desert farmer, bulked up at the shoulders and arms after four seasons of river work. Hard, boxy hips. "I think she can take care of herself," he said. "She's small but she's tough as rocks. Most of them tourists are gym rats, only interested in their own physiques. Or pudgy corporate dudes. But— yeah. Some think they've paid good money for a week of Wild West grab-n-go. The shifty ones ain't hard to spot, most of the time, but I have been surprised."

Ryder couldn't believe this guy was the same Ephraim he knew from school. Sure, a local sound to his talk, but the difference between the greasy, formless kid at the bus stop—the blank mush of his face, pale expressionless eyes—and the muscular sociability of the river guide was surreal. Ryder thought how stupid it was to imagine he knew anything about anyone. People were like the river: never the same water as a minute ago.

Ephraim said, "Bring this up with Sami. See what she does. Have fun with that."

By now Ryder knows very well what she does: transforms into stone. Nefertiti. Turns her back.

Mind your own damn business, is what she says. *Like I want white men stepping in to save me from white men. For that matter, Indians either.*

"I don't need you, Ryder," she reminds him when he needs to be reminded. "I love you."

Not the same, according to Sami. One rules out the other.

Do not confuse opposing things.

FIFTY-THREE

Ryder still had a few weeks of school, but the novelty of being eighteen was beginning to dawn. The world saw him as an adult. Kent's birthday was in June, so technically he was still Ferron's ward. But Kent was accustomed to living apart from his parents. Taking care of himself. In plenty of ways, Ryder felt like a kindergartener among his cousins.

Kent was the darling of the Nile Valley High School faculty. He'd done what he said he would: aced the ACT (glitchy in the grammar section, but the science department in Tucson didn't give a damn), applied and interviewed for the scholarship. He had other offers, too, but he was going to Arizona. The whole family "couldn't hardly believe it," in Alma's words, that a Mikkelson from Nile Valley was going to college, and that the college was *paying* him to go there. Ryder wondered if Jerusha had heard about it, wherever she was. Her parents must have: Kent's picture was on the front page of the *Nile Valley Papyrus*, with an article that took up most of the rest.

But Kent had shut his mouth about Jerusha for good. It's like he'd put it all in an ammo box, latched the lid, and buried it in quicksand.

Ryder was trying to blunt the resentment he'd felt when his cousin had staked everything on a girl. Woman. Whatever. Because now it was Ryder pounding the stakes. Ryder wanted to be excited about Kent's adventure. But all he could think about—mind and body—was Sami.

This month, before the tourist season ramped up: one perfect hour after Sami got off work and before Ryder clocked in. He'd meet her at the bridge, or the campground, and they'd walk the shoreline, turning where the willows leaned low and the grass stood high. One time, he saddled Traveler, rode back trails and doubletracks at full gallop to the highway. He sat suave in the saddle, waiting on the tall horse when she emerged from the warehouse.

"If it isn't the Marlboro Man," she said. "I'm reining, then."

He swung down, wrong side, the way he did.

"He'll let you come up either way," Ryder said. "But he's used to the right."

She reached high for horn and latigo, left side, and swung up in a smooth arc. She leaned forward as Ryder mounted behind the saddle.

"Where'd you get the Navajo blanket?" she asked.

"Been in the barn forever. I cleaned it up. My grandpa rode on it—I saw it in a picture on the wall. It's pretty, huh."

"It's older than your grandpa."

"Could have been stole. Want it back?"

"Maybe. Let's see how it rides."

The blanket rode fine. The saddle was squeaky and soft, an old roper, no wings. She sat supple, legs slack.

"Want me to raise the stirrups?"

"No. You want 'em?"

"No."

"Good horse you got."

"Traveler."

She leaned forward over the horse's neck. "Heya, Traveler."

She clicked her tongue. Gave his neck a gentle flat-hand push to the right, and Traveler swerved, joyful, as enamored of Sami as Ryder was. She nudged him left, speaking words Ryder couldn't catch. Traveler went west, sudden but smooth, then straightened his path and picked up for the cottonwoods at a bumpy gallop. Ryder leaned forward, adjusting to the momentum, and Sami leaned back. Ryder said, "Let me have the reins a minute." He reached his right arm around her, took the leather in his hand. Traveler loped through the airy trees; the ground opened to rolling gray tuff. The horse veered instinctively toward a wide ATV trail.

"Here we go," Ryder murmured in Sami's ear. Ryder pressed heels to flanks and the horse leaped to speed, kicking dirt and burnt gravel behind them, blazing toward sinking light and long horizon.

"Want to take him while I'm at work?" he asked, back at Roy's.

"Sure," she answered. "I'll bring him back to you. About eleven?"

"Sure."

"You smell like a damn mustang," Roy said when Ryder clocked in. "Run over to the truck stop. Tell 'em I said take a shower."

When she came for him, moonlight. She rolled off Traveler's right side, stood silhouette as Ryder approached.

"Did you take him out?" Ryder asked.

"Along the river. A good ways. I took the saddle off to ride. Put it back on for you."

"Blanket?"

"Felt like spirits."

The river rolled behind her, on beyond this dry diesel-scented pit stop, toward the plunging gorges and twisting oxbows, toward the approaching Colorado, into Sami's beautiful conflicted homeland. Struggling along its thwarted bed to Mexico. To ocean. Standing here with Sami felt like time and no time. He wondered if he was dreaming—the kind of dream that stretches a long distance even as he tries to cover it. But when he stepped toward her, she was warm in the rising heat of spring and the light sweat of a big horse hovering.

"One more ride," he pleaded. "Just a little ways and I'll take you back."

He reached to unbuckle the leather strap around Traveler's girth.

He uncinched and pulled the saddle away. "I'll come back for it tomorrow," he said. "Roy won't mind."

He made a hammock with his hands, and Sami put her foot in. Spotting her up to the horse's back made it clear she was corporeal.

"I need a rail," he said. "Don't want to pull you off. This leg pivots funny."

She held out her right hand. "Good enough?"

Ryder hesitated. "Maybe."

She patted Traveler's neck with her left hand. "Hold steady, pal."

He took a little run at it. Caught her hand. Swung up clean.

He said, "Holy shit."

She laughed. "I found a pretty spot. Grass. Sand. River makes a nice sound. Quarter mile. Want to see it?"

"I do."

FIFTY-FOUR

It seemed to Ryder that his religious life had been one endless sex talk, colliding two four-letter "L" words—love and lust—into a mess. The ugliness of Jerusha's father's terminology, his spiteful bill collection, made Ryder queasy. Watching Uncle Doug and Aunt Maura sink into a pit mine of hate was disillusioning. Ferron gave no sign, ever, that he might pursue love. If he lusted after other bodies he hid it within the cinder block shelter of the Riverbend. Brightly as Ryder's parents expressed their affections, sex had wracked them.

Nothing in Ryder's world showed him what love ought to look like where he stood now. Or what mad lust had to do with it. Ryder kept trying to level his mind, and heartbeat, and boners. To think beyond his sweaty, dirty dreams.

Was this how the world he knew was made?

How *he* was made? All the stories of his special, starry route. Heavenly Father's great design, bouncing baby Ryder like a pinball from—what? He'd sprung from bodies unknown, traced in his stature, the shape of his hands and feet, his two-toned hair, green-gray eyes, his lust and longing. He wasn't just paperwork.

His brain went into overdrive. At Roy's he kept an eye on the couples who came in—young and old. They arrived from everywhere: Germany and France. Korea, Japan. New York. Salt Lake City. Los Angeles. Brazil. It wasn't hard to spot the angry ones, or distracted, or sick of each other, everything lined emphatic in what was for them an exotic (and expensive) landscape. Strain shone bright on the faces of people here to relax. To "find themselves" in nature. Sometimes men came in together—bonding, chugging brews, happy to escape their wives and jobs. Sometimes groups of women; Ryder thought they were, equivalently, taking time away from husbands and children, but Roy said plenty of them were lesbians—many of them rich, some of them lovers, here, semi-invisible together. Ryder tried to pick out which ones—lovers, that was. Rich was easy. Smart and angry, not too hard. He wondered how lesbians knew they wanted each other's bodies.

Sami said, "Well, how do you know I want you?"

How *did* he know? His lust was unfakeable, painful, impossible to hide. Her lust was an aura he had to trust himself to believe in. Was it the same as her love? She was not the kind to demonstrate in public. She didn't squeal or flutter or touch for show.

But she waited for him at the river. Did it mean everything he hoped?

All summer, they took their good hours. They did not speak of past or future. They murmured at the colors of sky, reflections in the water. Pointed out snakes and rabbits, the brazen white butts of does at the shore, pronghorn in the sage. They rode on the Navajo blanket on Traveler's back.

All summer Ryder burned with lust. She drew him into her as they lay in grass and sand at water's edge. As Traveler stood by.

FIFTY-FIVE

Kent showed up at Roy's the night before he left for Tucson. Roy clapped him on the back, said how proud he was of a local kid like Kent, off to show the world what Nile Valley was made of. He told Ryder to have a sit with his cousin, order up some burgers.

"I told your girl to come in too," he said. "Why are you skulking around with her like that? I had a girl so pretty, I'd be showing her to everyone."

One last night: the three of them, ratty kids from the Etna school bus. Ryder would have been happy to bring Ephraim in on it, but he'd taken his days off to guide a pack trip up the Henries. Corporate guys from New York. Ephraim was collecting cash like a son of a gun.

Sami had one more river trip and she was done for the season. She was also headed for college, all set for Grand Junction. She already had a year of credits she'd earned in Redhorse.

Roy said Ryder could double down on shifts until the tourists thinned out. Also, he wanted Ryder to paint a mural on the long brick wall of the tavern, facing the tourist byway. Not in Ephraim's league, but good money.

The dining room was a clatter of human sounds: talk of the river. Forks tapping on plates, clinking bottles, kids hollering. Bursts of laughter. Old-time cash register ringing beside the beeping card reader. Cars and trucks blazing along the highway.

Kent said, "How are your folks, Sami? They'll be okay with . . .?"

Sami's eyes widened. She gave Kent a half smile, then stretched her lips in a comic grimace. "Guess they'll have to be, right?"

She shot Ryder a funny glance.

Kent said, "What about—"

She said, "I'm thinking. Figuring it out."

Kent looked at Ryder as if Ryder's pants were down.

Ryder said, "What?"

Sami said, "Won't you miss your cousin when he's so far off?"

Ryder rolled his eyes. "Yeah. But I got stuff to do. Got bricking jobs with my dad this fall. Horses. Ephraim says he might need someone to help guide a couple private trips in the La Sals. And I'll be driving out to Junction to see you, if you let me."

Sami narrowed her eyes. Ryder didn't want to push it. Didn't want to hear that this had all just been a "summer fling," as his mother would put it.

Didn't want to sit here and feel like the stupid one who wasn't going to college.

Kent said, "Open your eyes, dumbass."

Ryder said, "What?"

Early morning, still dark: Kent hardly looked like he was driving off to college in a city ten hours away. He had a few clothes and boots in the trunk of Ferron's decrepit sedan, plus books, a sleeping bag, and a shaving kit on the backseat floor. Next to him—the reason he was taking the whole drive in one shot, in a car that didn't lock—a brand-new desktop computer, still in the box, covered under a quilt. Kent had bought most of it with the stash of his mother's monthly fifties—more than a thousand dollars—augmented by the whole family's cash contributions. He had another grand, surplus.

"You buy groceries with that, Kenty," Evaleen said. "Good food. I mean it. Your brain needs vitamins and protein. Don't skimp."

"I won't, Aunt Evaleen. I'll stay healthy, I promise."

Alma said, "Don't be scarce, now. With that internet, you can send us a letter in a flash. Ferron's set up in the warehouse to open it anytime."

Doug, back on his feet and a cane, home nurse at his elbow, thought it was witty to say, "Get on now, you ungrateful shit."

Ferron said, "We'll come down, Ryder and me. We'll come in the truck so we can bring back what they grow in Arizona. Oranges maybe."

Kent put on his cowboy hat. Pressed it down. He said, "Appears to me Ryder's gonna have his hands full."

Ryder said, "What?"

Evaleen reared her head like a startled mare.

Alma said, "Well, that's true. Just because he ain't going off to college don't mean he'll sit idle. Plenty of ways to be smart. Plenty ways to make a living."

"Don't we know it, Uncle Alma." Kent climbed into the driver's seat. Beckoned Ryder close. Ryder leaned down to the open window. Kent whispered: "You know what you've done. Think like a big boy for a goddamn minute. Rise to it, man."

"Think that car will hold up acrost that whole desert?" Alma bellowed.

"I bet it's broke down before he gets to Salina," Doug quipped. "Twenty bucks. Any takers?"

Kent started the car. Everyone watched and waved as he drove out to the river road, then turned south and disappeared beyond the cottonwoods.

Ryder said, "Dad, can I take the pickup? I need to check on something."

He ran for it.

FIFTY-SIX

The morning sun lit the river like foil. Some staff dude was at the bank, testing patches. Ryder broke into a gallop.

"Jeff, you aren't leaving today, right? Trip rolls tomorrow?"

"Yep."

"You seen Sami?"

"Yeah. Looks good in shorts. Long black hair. I think she might be an Indian."

"What the fuck, Jeff. Is she here?"

"Inside. Packing the coolers."

"Will they let me in?"

"Go around the side. It's open."

Ryder turned toward the building. Took a couple of steps. Turned back.

"She seem—ok?"

"What do you mean?"

"Nothing. Thanks."

Ryder tried to walk casual. Breathe level. Then he tried not to look hysterical as he quickened into a sprint. He rounded two corners of the warehouse. Poked his head in the open door, blinking in the dimness. Gaped like a sucker. The room smelled like a cave. He heard Sami laughing with a couple of the other girls. At him.

"Sami?"

He rubbed his eyes. Squinted to make her out.

He could see her smile, the shape of her shoulders as she

approached.

"Need a seeing eye dog?" she said. "A cane?"

"I guess I need more than that."

Her hand on his forearm brought tears. How could he be so blind?

"Can we go outside a minute?" he whispered.

"Sure," she answered. She called back to her river friends. "Hey, I'm taking a little break, all right? Back in ten."

"Take your time."

Was he the last to know what was somehow obvious to the world?

Seemed like the temperature jacked up a degree with every step. Ryder thought about Kent in that awful car, rattling toward Tucson. He saw Kent's exasperated face. Heard his voice. *Rise to this, dumbass...*

Ryder turned, careful. Stood in her path, full face.

"Sami."

Now she was crying.

He said, "How long have . . ."

She wiped her face with the back of her hand.

"I'm keeping it. You can do what you want."

"I want—it. I want you. We can do this, can't we?"

She sat down, right there in the dirt.

He said, from way too high above her: "Have you been sick? Do you know for sure? How did Kent know? I'm so sorry. So stupid! It should have been me that saw it."

He angled his right leg and lowered himself like a carjack with the left. Put his hands down, then his butt.

"Is this okay? Can I sit by you? Are you mad at me?"

She lay back, shielding her eyes with cupped hands. She said, "Which of all those questions do you want me to answer? Ten-minute break, remember?"

He said, "Sorry. This one: have you been sick?"

"Not too bad. Right now it just feels kind of heavy and tight."

"How long have you known?"

"Two periods, now. But I knew, one night out there by the river. Knew it as soon as it happened, I think."

What night? Plenty of nights out there. He hadn't sensed a damned thing. Except . . . release. A surge of anger at himself, but it turned on her: "So, most of the summer? And you didn't tell me anything? What the hell, Sami?"

She sat up. "What do you mean, *what the hell?* You're pissed off that you didn't have a clue? You needed Kent to figure out I'm pregnant, but you cuss me out for needing time to figure things out? Screw you, Ryder. I don't have to tell you shit."

"Sami! I'm sorry! It's just kind of a shock."

"Tell me about it! And why's it a shock? What do you think happens when boys and girls roll around in the grass?"

"But I wore a—didn't I?"

"Didn't you?"

"Yes! You know I did! I paid a little attention in health class."

"I'll bet you did."

"Hey! That's not fair! I never acted dirty with you. I *never* did."

She stood up. Brushed dirt off her butt. She looked so good in shorts. Ryder was ashamed: Now. In the middle of—

"Sami—"

He corkscrewed up. "Sami, please. I'm sorry. I'm sorry I made you deal with this all alone. I wish I'd been smarter. I'll catch up, I promise."

She stalked toward the warehouse. "I have to get back to work."

"Wait, what do you mean? You're going back out on the river? Like this? Can't you tell them you're—"

She whirled.

"Don't *even.*"

"But what if you hurt yourself? What if it's too much of a strain? What if . . ."

He'd heard the facts of his mother's grief a hundred times. Now, impact. Fear of nature. Blood menace. His father's helpless, implicated sorrow.

She said, "Ryder. You want to stay in this, understand the rules. I get on with what I do. This planet makes babies. You get one part. I get another. Don't tell me how to do mine."

Ryder sucked in his breath. Wiped his slobbering lip.

"Okay?" she said.

"I'm sorry. Yeah."

She looked like she might cry again, then toughed up. "I'll be back in a week. My mom wants me to come home but I'm going to college. We can make decisions. *Only if you want to be part of this.* Decide while I'm gone because you only get one chance."

"I do, Sami."

"Take the week. Think hard."

She left him standing. She moved like mirage. Her hair flashed silver in the sun as it swung across her back.

Ryder was twice alien on this hot upended tilting plummeting landscape.

Sami walked the contours of ancient home.

God.

FIFTY-SEVEN

He talked to Ferron, manager of the Riverbend since Joe Gonçalves followed a woman to Phoenix.

"I've been thinking," Ryder hedged. "Because Kenty went off to college. I want to feel like I graduated, too. I'll go back to the farm every day to look after the horses. I'm bricking with my dad sometimes. I got painting jobs lined up. So I want to try living on my own. Learn some cooking. You got one of those kitchenette rooms I could rent?"

Ferron lifted his eyebrows. "River rats are starting to go home. Probably a couple weeks. I can hook you up with that one on the south side."

"How much?"

"Hundred a month. If you clean it up, give it some paint, I can let you off the deposit. Make a mess of it though, I'll call Aunt Evaleen to come and kick your ass."

"I won't! I mean, I won't make a mess of it."

"I've been thinking about grubbing up some cash from Melendez. I think he'd buy the paint for you to spiff up the whole place. Doors and windowsills and stuff. And the old sign nobody can read. He's not looking for overnighters, but I think those four rooms off the west end would open up nice for it. Right now they're full of old beds and stuff, but you and your dad could fix them up. Only problem is the plumbing. Uncle Alma does that, right?"

"Not the deep stuff. But anything above the floor, yeah."

"That's all it needs. I've been working up the math to show Ron. He'd make it up over a good summer. We'd have it up and running by April or May, and we can raise the rates for a nicer place. I've been meaning to talk to Uncle Alma, see if he wants the job. If it works out we could get you in that little kitchenette free a year or so."

"Really? Holy crap, Ferron! That would be great!"

Ferron shook his hair out of his eyes. Sudden, precise, he gave Ryder a two-handed shove. Ryder backpedaled, hard, before he could stand up straight again.

"What the hell was that for?"

Sami.

Ryder asked his dad to drive down to Roy's after work. Ryder said he'd take his dinner break soon as he saw the pickup pull in.

Ryder bought Alma a cheeseburger and led him out to a broken picnic table out back.

"You have to sit on the good legs," he explained, which set the two of them awkwardly side by side. It helped, though. It let them talk without figuring out the right faces to make.

"Dad," he said, soon as he saw Alma take a big bite.

"Dang, old Roy still makes a good burger," Alma sluffed.

"Dad, you think I could buy your truck? Don't you think it's getting to be a hassle for you, every time I take it out? We both got jobs to make, and Mom shouldn't have to share the Monte. You deserve something new after all these years."

Alma kept at the cheeseburger. He stopped halfway through to chug some Coke. Ryder thought his dad was getting ready to speak, but instead he picked up a sprig of fries, dunked them in pink sauce, and filled his mouth again.

"Dad, I'm eighteen. I need to start up my own life. Kent's off to college, Ferron's been on his own a long time. I like living on the farm with you and Mom, but—"

Alma swallowed the fries. Took another swig. Big rigs and SUVs jammed along the parkway, nearly bumper to bumper. Gasoline and diesel fumes blew from the truck stop. For a minute, Ryder saw Nile Valley through the eyes of the many strangers passing through. Hot and shocking. Barren. Colorless and desolate even while traffic roared like a raceway.

"Ryder," Alma said. For a second, Ryder didn't recognize the sound of his name. Didn't even recognize it as a word.

"Ryder!"

He turned to face his father, expecting to look upward, as if he were still a little kid. But the top of Alma's head barely surpassed Ryder's shoulder; it was the father who had to lift his gaze. Ryder felt a rush of shame, or guilt, a feeling without a word. How could he betray his dad, making him small this way?

Alma pushed the paper plate away and backed out of the table's entrapment. He walked around to the other side, placing his palms flat on the planks to face his son.

"Have you gotten that girl pregnant?"

Ryder thought he should stand up. Be a man. But he put his fists on the table and dropped his head to them. "Dad, I'm taking responsibility. I love her! This is what I'm telling you. I'm trying to grow up for this!"

"Do you, Ryder? Do you love her? Because you got a lot of things working against you here. You think you know things, but you ain't been on this planet much longer than a dog's life. Just about everything in that head of yours comes from somebody else's experience. That ain't the same as living it."

Ryder couldn't lift his head. "I know, Dad."

"You say you do, but you don't. Not until it's on you, and now it ain't just you. A wife and baby to—"

Ryder sat up straight. "Dad, you were about the same age as me when you married Mom. And she was sixteen. You did okay, didn't you?"

Alma reared back like a crow, trying to take flight. He spoke in rhythm with his flapping arms. "*Okay*? What do you think *okay* is, son? I'll bring all this around to tell you, Ryder, that once you're in a predicament, you don't call it a mistake. You call it your life and you rise to it. But if any of us knew what's coming at us once we step into the big stuff, we'd sure think again. How can you expect me to tell you this is the best way to go about it?"

"Mom was pregnant, right?"

Alma slapped the table so hard he pulled his rough hand back up to his chest, tucking it in, palm flat against the soothing fur. He pulled it out again, shook it like a dishrag. Poked his chunky fingers in Ryder's direction.

"Pregnant she was. And I loved her. And I didn't have folks one bit willing to talk to me about what to do. My dad mean as a wolverine. My mama dead tired. I had no idea how to be a husband. Me and Evaleen went up to live on the farm, making do in the old chicken coop, I kid you not. I fixed it up, closed it in best I could. You know your mother—she had it clean as a whistle. Guess the old pioneers would of seen it as luxury, but even so. And then, right after her seventeenth birthday, I don't want to tell you what we woke up to. We didn't have no bathroom. We'd been running to the outhouse …"

"Dad—"

"Ryder, it might not even be a baby that changes your lives. We didn't get you in ours until after I turned forty. You can't guess what you'll go through together, babies or not, and you're a good boy, capable, but you ain't had the time to get ready. For none of it."

Alma stalked to the dumpster. Strode back, speaking as he came.

"And who knows if she's ready? Do you truly know anything about her? Do you know her people? Do you know where they live, and how, and what they expect of a man—a white man—who brings the kind of change you're bringing their daughter? Their sister? You two don't come from the same worlds, even if they cross into each other. And there's other things. You think you got the wherewithal

KARIN ANDERSON

to deal with the white people that took her in out to Etna? We might say we're same religion, but—"

Ryder pulled one leg, and then the other, out from under the picnic table.

"Dad! I have to go back in to work. I get what you're telling me, but I need to punch in. I'll talk to you more in the morning, all right? But don't tell Mom yet. I want to talk to her myself."

"You think she don't suspect?"

"I'm the one has to tell her. Think about the truck, okay? And talk to Ferron. He's got a job we might want to take."

Ryder ran toward the kitchen. Stepped in to steam and colliding dishes. He put on his apron. His rubber gloves. Plunged his hands into hot soapy water.

He knew his mother would want her son married by a Mormon bishop.

"Ryder Mikkelson! Haven't seen much of you at church these days," Bishop Pace said, all back-slappy when Ryder slunk into the church foyer. "You finally come in to fill in your mission papers?"

Ryder said, "No. I need to talk about something else."

The bishop retracted his handshake hand. Put it in his gabardine pocket.

"Well, come into my office, then."

Ryder sat like a pathetic mutt. He didn't want to sit on the other side of a big shot's desk ever again. Bishop Pace set himself behind the polished expanse and leaned back in his leather office chair.

"Can we close the door?" Ryder asked.

"Whatever you want. Nobody here but you and me, though."

Ryder stood up to shut it tight. The bishop was taller than Ryder. Thick meat on heavy bones, softened up twenty years beyond second-string football up to BYU. Bishop Pace dispensed wisdom in sports analogies.

Ryder wasn't in the mood. "I just need to ask you a question."

Was the bishop hiding a smirk? Ryder plunged in.

"I'm wondering if you'll . . ."

He lost the words. Erased.

"If I'll what, now?"

Ryder painted them, letter by letter, on the wall behind the bishop. Up and around the picture of Jesus.

"Do a . . . marriage. Me and my girlfriend. I mean, f-fiancée."

The bishop flexed his jowls. Leaned forward on his elbows.

"Who's the lucky lady?"

Ryder's neck burned. He wanted to get up, never come back, but respect for his mother held him. "Maybe you remember her. Sami Begay. She lived with the Johnstons out to Etna, but she went back to Arizona, ninth grade."

Bishop Pace sat back. Templed his fingers.

"Lamanite, huh?"

The word took Ryder aback. He hadn't heard it since he'd quit seminary.

"Diné," Ryder said.

"Those people can call themselves what they want, I suppose. But we who have received higher knowledge understand who they are. I'm not racist, but the plain fact of latter-day revelation is that the Indians bear a curse for their ancient rebellion. The Lamanites were a violent people, marked with darkness to warn the fairer children of God against intermarriage. If you breed with an Indian, Ryder, your children will bear that curse. Now, I know you're adopted, but it's clear as day that you come from European lineage. That's not a blessing to be trifled with. Best to leave one kind of people to their business, and us to ours."

Ryder had heard this kind of talk his whole life. Maybe he'd even believed it, some ways. Now it was—no word came. Just a perfect image of Sami, on the saddle blanket. On Traveler. At the shining river.

He said, "Well, it's too late. I got her pregnant."

The bishop stood. Ryder did too.

Bishop Pace said, "So, you've come here, *Brother Mikkelson*, to confess the grievous sin of premarital sex. That's the issue we'll address before we consider the sacred ordinance of marriage. Your parents must be devastated."

"Address—how? I came here to take responsibility. I want to marry her, and I know my mom will want it to happen in a church."

"Your mother is a good woman, and she has mourned over the negligent quality of your faith. But your mother has nothing what-soever to do with your decision to fornicate with a girl—regardless of her race—before you've troubled yourself to make it sacred in the eyes of God. What we must do first is weigh your worthiness to remain within the fellowship of the church. You must cease your carnal relations and go through the proper process of repentance. I will refer this to the Stake Presidency, and you'll need to appear before the High Council.

"How the Indian girl chooses to confront her sin is her affair, but if she expects me to solemnize her relations with you, she'd better come in for a serious talk."

Ryder tried to imagine it.

No way in hell.

"Carry on how you want about sin," Ryder said. "But we're going to the courthouse. Down to Redhorse, in fact."

"Do you really want to break your mother's heart?" Bishop Pace called after him. "After all she went through on your behalf?"

FIFTY-EIGHT

Ryder showed up early morning at Roy's to talk about painting the wall. Roy gave him cash for color and tools, and Ryder drove to Price. Roy said he'd cover the café shift, so Ryder was waiting on the burning asphalt of the runners' lot when the trucks came in, stacked high with rafts and oars over lockboxes, dry bags, empty coolers. Ryder could see Sami riding with a couple more girls, back of the caravan. Rafters tumbled out, dirty and tired. Staff people came out of the offices to greet them.

"Sami!" Ryder called. "Sami, I need to talk to you!"

Sami waved as if she was greeting a local buddy, noncommittal, and turned to the tasks of unloading.

"Can I help?" Ryder asked, approaching Jeff, who was already cussing over a tie-down strap twisted in the ratchet teeth.

"Technically, not without employee insurance. But go around the other side. Catch the strap when I throw it over. You know what to do."

Now Ryder couldn't see Sami.

The rafts sprung up like buoyant whales once Jeff and some other guy managed release. The light ends flew high; Ryder felt for slack and yanked up, freeing his side to send it back over.

"Sami!" he shouted as he worked. "Sami, let me come talk to you! You can hear me, right?"

No answer. Another strap flew over. Ryder pulled hard where it was squeezed tight around a low crossbar. The rafts jumped again.

Jeff came around to assess.

"Okay. Let's leave this one until we got more hands."

"Jeff, I really need to talk to Sami."

"Chill, man. You know she won't come running. You look like you escaped from a doghouse. Go wait for her at Roy's or some-place."

"Will you tell her I'm under the bridge?"

"Like she won't notice?"

"Can't I help with the other trucks? Everything go okay on the water?"

Jeff looked at him funny. "Dude, I know she's pretty. But let her do her job. Get outta here."

The heat was too much. Like the end of the world, and here Ryder was, trying to begin in it. He lurched toward the water, kicking up dust, stumbling on rocks. The sudden tilt toward late-summer shore-line nearly pitched him into a face-plant. He straightened to catch his ragged, half-bawling breath. Didn't calm down. He traversed the slope toward the highway bridge, dodging sage, scratching his arms on tamarisk.

It was hardly cooler under the structure. It rattled like an earth-quake every time another Kenworth or Mack groaned over. Diesel fumes lapped against the pylons like foul water.

Ryder took off his shirt and boots. Then his socks, trucker hat, and insufferably tight jeans. He considered the boxers, but he stood in clear view of the tourist cabins on the east bank.

He stepped into the water, sinking ankle deep into saturated sand. The channel opened a few feet beyond, deep olive in the bridge's shade. Near turquoise, edged with yellow, where the sun lit it up beyond. He aimed for depth and dove in.

He came up, shaking water from his hair. Backstroked down-stream into sunlight. An empty cattle rig blared its horn. Ryder raised a finger. Kicked back up to the bridge, slow. He pulled on his jeans and cap. He found soft sand and grass and lay back. He tipped the bill over his eyes, slept, and dreamed: deep tucks, tight rolls in strange water.

"Ryder," she said.

He opened his eyes. She stood above him, blocking the sun, a foot planted on either side of his hips. From Ryder's angle, prone in the prickling sand, she looked a mile tall, lined with fire like an eclipse.

"Sami," he said.

He started to cry. He let the tears roll down his temples, pool in his ears.

She said, "You're gonna cry harder when you start to feel that sunburn."

She reached down to cover him with his sand-scented shirt. She pulled her right leg over him, turning as she sat down on his broke-leg side.

Ryder lifted his head to look at himself. Jeans had dried in the falling light. His crotch was burning, and not from mad desire. Slack as a melted candle. The seams of his back pockets pressed into his butt, damp as he pulled himself up to sit. The motion stung like bees on his stomach, chest, neck, and (most strangely) his chin and jawline, like a flaming Amish beard where the bill of his cap had run. He reached up to touch, heating his fingertips.

She said, "Let's get you into the shade."

"How long's it been?"

"Don't know how long you swam, but you tripped off more than two hours ago."

"Aw, hell."

"Get up. Want to cross to the park? Or sit under the bridge?"

"Can we drive up the canyon a ways? Nefertiti, maybe?"

She stood up. Offered her hand. "Sure. How about I drive?"

In the canyon it was already twilight. The bumping agitated his flaming skin.

"Let's get out here," Sami said, past Swasey's. "We can walk the last part. I like coming up on her."

The cooling air stung. No relief. He couldn't bear to snap the shirt against skin. Her touch on his stomach was painful, but withdrawing it would be worse.

She took his hand and led him to the water. Helped him drop the shirt from his shoulders. She bent to the water, brought her hands up dripping, and covered him—the burning red of him—palm by palm, fingertip by fingertip, with fine silt. Gave him a wet beard, coated his neck and shoulders, sculpted him into a two-toned statue. His unburned back took the cool breeze. He shivered and burned.

She said, "Can you make it up to bow to the queen?"

"Yes."

They rounded the final bend as the moon rose over the eastern lip. Nefertiti lit up, towering over the waterline, Queen of the Green. The current shimmered like ancient writing. Pygmy owls piped from the thickets.

Ryder said, "Sami, I want to do this with you. I've loved you ever since we got in trouble in first grade. You're the only one. Ever. Please, let me—"

"I know. Me too."

"Really?"

The moonlight made her look like *forever*.

She said, "But I'm going to college. I can go up to Price, but Grand Junction is better. I could schedule most of my classes just two days a week."

"Ferron says I—we—can have a room with a kitchenette at the Riverbend, hundred a month. He'll let us skip rent for a year if I help my dad fix the place up. Ferron wants me to repaint it all. Make a new sign. We'd just need groceries, you know? And college things. And—doctor stuff—when do you think—"

"February. I don't plan to stop school. Can you handle a baby along with the jobs? I mean can we figure out a schedule? Will your mom want to help? We can take the baby down to my mom's when we're busiest. And she'll come up, too."

"My mom will want to help. Will your family be okay with . . .?"

"A pink and white guy like you?"

"Yeah."

"We'll go down there and see, I guess."

"Do they know you're—we're—having a—"

"My mother does. I'll tell the others when I feel like it. Can you help slaughter a couple sheep? That'll impress them. And they'll appreciate your drawing hand. Don't expect anyone to fall all over you, though."

"Okay."

"It's just that Navajos don't get gooey about stuff the way white people do."

"Okay."

"But you have to run twenty miles barefoot through the desert to prove you're worthy of a Diné bride."

"Really?"

"Naked."

"What?"

She laughed. "Let's get you home, Sandman."

FIFTY-NINE

Evaleen stood in the open doorway, backlit by the living room lamps. She'd clearly been waiting: fully dressed, nearly midnight. Tufts of permed hair waved like small plumage.

Sami said, "Looks like we got a conference coming."

Ryder said, "We're in trouble now."

"How much does she know?"

"From me? Not much. Doesn't mean she doesn't magically understand stuff, though."

"You scared of her?"

"What? No. It's just—complicated. I should have talked to her. She'll be mad at me, but she'll love you. She will."

He thought a minute. Remembered his mother bringing cupcakes to his elementary school class every January 16, or close enough. His mother teaching Primary, speaking plainly to the kids, answering their questions as if they mattered. Shutting down antics with a wave of her hand. Little Sami, smiling. Trusting someone, for once. Sidling up to answer Evaleen's special questions, just for her.

Ryder amended. "She already loves you."

Sami dropped into second gear to follow the lawn line, then turned left into the gravel driveway. She stopped neat, barely displacing a pebble, which would have impressed Alma if he hadn't been cowering in the back rooms.

Ryder sat on his shirt, shivering and burning under a crumbling armor of drying silt.

Sami said, "Well, you look great for this. Bet you won't be shaving for a couple weeks."

Ryder moaned.

The kitchen light went on, and then the side porch bulb, illuminating the truck.

Evaleen pushed at the screen door. Stepped out.

"Sami Begay," she said. "I ain't seen you in a few years. You're all grown up. Wish you would of come seen us sooner."

"You don't need to be scared of her," Ryder murmured.

"I'm not."

Sami stepped out.

"I brought Ryder home, Sister Mikkelson. He got a bad sunburn."

"We ain't at church. And you're not a little girl. You know you can call me Evaleen."

Ryder pitched out the other side. He staggered to the edge of the grass and heaved. His head spun. His chin, neck, chest, clavicles, and the fronts of his arms burned like he was standing against a bonfire.

His mother said, "Are you drunk?"

He stood up straight. "Not drunk."

He tried to brush silt off his stomach but quit it because it hurt.

"Hose," he said, and plodded over brown lawn for the pump.

"Oh, for hell's sake," Evaleen said. "Get cleaned up and I'll find aloe. Sami, come on in with me. Are you hungry? He knows the way in."

Ryder found the end of the hose. He carried it to the pump, pulled the handle up and pushed it down, a few too many times it seemed, but the water rushed up sudden. He tried not to scream as it hit his bare stomach, and after a few seconds, the water gave him relief, sort of, which brought him back to the situation at hand: his mother in the late-night kitchen with Sami. With—something beyond them. Among them, already, binding them all.

Inside her, as water flowed over him.

River silt pooled at his feet. Crickets sang quick in the night's residual heat. He could see only his mother through the blue light of the window. Sami sat across from her, obscured.

Evaleen leaned forward over the table, reaching.

Ryder dropped the hose. Cut the flow. He walked toward the house but did not enter. This was, for all his instigation, a thing between them.

Women.

He sat on the concrete stair, shivering like a wet cat. He dropped his forehead into his cupping hands. The crescent of burned jaw-line—a stupid, mortifying clown smile—pulsed with pain. His neck was on fire. He lifted his face to the sky, as if the late-summer stars could soothe him.

PART FOUR

RIVERBEND

Nile Valley, Utah

SIXTY

In his memory, the double arrival was hardly more strenuous than a sequence of graces. Revelations of a planet too sweet and surprising to contain.

Conception a romp in the willows. Sami's disconcerting resilience, poising the disproportions of pregnancy right up to delivery. Her classes, his feverish work.

Late night awakenings, big trout in a small pond. Settling.

Ecstatic jolt of an new, already timeless presence. A wet, inchoate (but fully-formed) *person*—and then, before he could absorb the impact: another! Too much, too fast to stop and marvel, too much to take in but by getting on with daily infinities.

All of it her doing, Sami's aptitudes. Multiplications. Geometries.

The grandmothers leaning in. Naming as affirmation.

Diné cosmogeny.

"No, don't burden a child with 'Evaleen.'"

"How about Eva?"

"Oh. Well. That's pretty. All right then."

"Which of your names, Mama?"

"Stella."

"Yes. Thank you."

Which is Eva?

This one.

Which is Stella?

This one.

Four years later, the boy: unfathomable strain. Something angry in Ryder, preoccupied and diffused, the featureless night of conception. Ryder got up to shower, hoping to cleanse an unhappy sensation that he'd merely *fucked* his wife. Something irretrievable—that flickering stupid moment after dropping a bowl of soup, after backing a truck into a plate glass window. Hitting a deer on the highway: *Wait. No. Didn't mean—go back . . .*

Ryder knew before Sami believed him that there was something in her. Her instincts off, a flailing compass.

Guilt vague and debilitating as he watched her expand. He saw how she quivered under the weight of water and blood and child. Her hand pressed to her back. Calculated intakes of troubled, uranium-addled air. Had he just been oblivious before? Or was this a premonition, a new strain of . . . what? And why?

He knew she was carrying a boy. No need for ultrasound, which, yes, confirmed it and yes, deepened his troubled sense that this was a thing he had done. To her.

"What in the world are you talking about?" Sami said when he choked out a garbled, inane apology. "Sorry for what?"

All of it. Everything. Backward and forward.

"Ryder, I want a boy. We have two beautiful girls. This time, a boy. Like you. What's not to celebrate?"

He couldn't explain.

The boy came, straining, awkward, ghost white.

"That's a big head," said the attending nurse. "Didn't know if we'd get that one through the passage. And the cord kept him back a while."

The twins had met the world with lusty wails. This boy, a thin, one-note cry, no oxygen in it.

Eva and Stella, glossy black hair from the start. Dark eyes, almost as dark as their mother's but flecked with green glass.

This one: sandy hair. Face swollen, eyes barely visible. A hard coming. The air creased and blackened around Ryder, enclosing him like a blanket. Even so he rose like a balloon to the top of the room. The woman on the bed seemed far away, as if he were seeing her from the wrong end of a telescope. Reaching for her only raised the ceiling, only wrapped him tighter. He opened his throat to scream.

He came to on the fathers' sofa. Far side of the birthing room.

He heard the baby wail, strengthening as the fox kit lungs accustomed to air.

The doctor approached. "Whew, Daddy-O," she said. "A little much for you? Sometimes this is harder on the father than the new mom."

"Sami . . ." he whispered, but he wasn't certain he'd made sound.

He swore he'd heard her crying. Then, worse, he feared she'd gone silent.

"Ryder, it's okay," Sami called from the delivery bed, calm, not weeping at all.

Grandfathers, of course, would appear in the sequence, but no clear front-name for this child appeared.

"Not Ryder," Ryder said.

"You don't want your son named after you?" Sami asked.

"Lately it doesn't seem like my name."

"Well? What is it then?"

"I don't know."

"Guess that's why we don't know his name, either."

His. Even that small word wrote itself strange. No match for the order of things.

SIXTY-ONE

"You had a big head too, you know," Evaleen observed, gazing into the crib. Here to help, every day, first weeks of school. Sami back in the classroom.

Ryder said he knew how to take care of his kids, for hell's sake. Traded hours with Sami while she was in college, while he was bricking and painting like a motherfucker, barely seeing each other, happy when they did.

"Don't you say them words around your babies. What's happened to that framing job out to Wellington?"

"Not working for a little while. I talked to them a few months ago, let them know I'd need to be home first weeks Sami starts school. And then you'll be seeing more of this crowd than you want to. You know that."

Evaleen returned to the subject at hand. "Don't know how your—how you managed to push your way out into the world. Took you a while to get proportional. You still got a big hat size, even for a man tall as you."

"Not me," Alma said. "My folks got small pointy heads that fit nice into hats. You could wear my cowboy hat by the time you was six. Also, men in my family don't got parts so big they hurt the ladies. All about nice fits, all around."

"Dad!"

"I ain't saying you got a bad thing going. Just different. Take a look at this fella here. When I changed your diaper, I couldn't shake the sense I was cleaning up another man's son. You don't got that problem, Ryder. What's keeping you from taking to this beautiful boy? It's clear as day he's your issue."

Evaleen said, "What in the world are you talking like that for, here in front of your own grandson?"

"I'm just saying. It appears Ryder's got something in the way of bonding with his boy here. He's got to address it, just like you made me do with him."

Evaleen pursed her lips.

Alma added, "And I'm glad of it. Ryder's my good son. I'm proud to be his dad. But we got to give this boy a name. How long's it been? Two months already?"

"Daddy," Stella petitioned, petting at Ryder's hip.

"Dad," Eva echoed from the front doorway. "Is it time to get Mama from work?"

Ryder looked toward his parents.

"They like when we can walk to the high school and all of us come home together. Doesn't take forty-five minutes. Okay to leave him with you?"

Alma grimaced. "What if he starts that crying jag he does?"

"Just hold him. Let Mom hold him. She's tough enough to stand it. He calms down. Eventually."

"Why don't you go with them?" Evaleen suggested. "You can keep up with a couple of itty-bitty four-year-olds, can't you?"

"We can push the air thing in the stroller, Grandpa."

"The oxygen thing."

"Sami won't mind being seen with a old decrepit?"

"She'll be happy to see you. I'll call Doug to come pick you up if you get tired."

"The hell you will. We don't need to involve Doug in this."

"Okay, then. Ferron."

"Just go, Alma."

Eva and Stella were already out the door.

. . .

September heat was high, but the school year starting made Ryder believe it was autumn. The sun had slipped, changing the shadows. Stella and Eva walked in front, like he always told them to, so he could see them every second. Evaleen had hiked their long hair into high ponytails, unlike the double braids Sami had taught Ryder to bring about. The twins walked welded at the shoulders, fingers intertwined. Who knew what they talked about as they gestured and twittered.

"Girls! Don't get so caught up you don't pay attention to the road! Cars can surprise you!"

"We know, Daddy!" they called back together, without turning their heads.

"I mean it! Pay attention to your surroundings!"

"We *know*, Daddy!"

"You're one to talk," Alma said, huffing along with the stroller in front of him, mini tank tucked in like a steampunk baby.

"I know, Dad."

"Right, fella."

"Eva! Stella! We're almost there! Don't run across the street! Stop and wait until I tell you it's safe!"

Big kids streamed out of the building. Girls cooed over the twins as they walked by. Sami had the principal's blessing to leave with the students, seeing as how she'd come back despite the baby. A good math teacher was hard to find. And she was certifying to become a counselor. The district would do about anything to keep her.

Ryder caught sight of his wife (how was that word still so surprising!) flowing out the side door. He stepped up to take the little girls' hands, afraid they'd run to her. "Let's cross the street. Then you can race."

Alma was sweating. Wheezing a little. Ryder reached to cup a hand on his father's shoulder.

Alma said, "I'll stand right here. Get 'em to their mama."

God, she was beautiful. Black eyes glittering in the near-autumn sunlight. White teeth revealed in a maternal smile. Strong legs striding across the mostly-baked lawn, gray cliffs rising around her—a hue so stark it was barely color. High sage and juniper invisible above the undulating drop line.

Could it be? Did he somehow resent the thought of sharing her love with another male? Even his own baby son?

Was that it? He could share her with their daughters.

What, then?

Evaleen sat on the front steps, waiting to greet them. The baby, so often strained, stiff at the sensation of enveloping touch, sat supple and bright on her bony lap. She pumped his small arm up and down in a puppet wave. His sisters laughed and waved back.

"Wow. Something's changed," Sami said. "Just since I left this morning. Funny how babies just take the next step into themselves, isn't it?"

"Sure is," Alma answered. "We seen it again and again with Ryder. One day he's falling off a mule, another day he's grown six inches. Then he gots to shave . . ."

The baby's hair had darkened since he was born. Now black like his sisters' but somehow, also, palomino gold under the broad sun.

Auriferous.

"He has your eyes, all of a sudden," Sami said. "Your eyes, Ryder."

"River color," Alma said.

"I know his name!" Stella said.

Eva: "Me too!"

Greene.

SIXTY-TWO

Ferron was *finito* with hunting. From now on he was riding for scenery. Today was good because Ryder was scouting. September.

Ferron was going the whole distance. Vegetarian. "How hard will it be? I drive a produce truck. I manage a grocery store. Your mom's garden—"

"You told your dad about this?" Ryder asked. "I'd love to see Doug's face when—"

"No, you wouldn't."

Ryder reined up. "He's still that gonzo?"

"You know him, Ryder. Son of a gun can't piss in the morning if the mirror's askew. Whole world's gotta tick on his sense of meaning, narrated by Rush. That damned Mormon dude—what's his name? Beck. Speaking of meat, Doug's looking for a new girlfriend. Where's he get the confidence?"

Traveler reached for grass. Ryder said, "Why does he care what you eat?"

Ferron looked ready to charge. Ryder backed Traveler off the narrow trail, bunching into serviceberry.

"He wants me to deliver elk steaks. You and Kenty can do that."

"Not siding with Doug, but people have been eating meat since they could throw rocks, don't you think?"

"People have also been trying to make meaningful choices since they could throw rocks."

"Don't plants have feelings? Don't you think all this nice green grass here cringes when the horses bite?

"Don't fuck with me, Ryder. You got shit all figured out?"

"What. I don't get it."

"Neither do I. We live in this bizarre corner of the world. We ride our horses into some of the weirdest terrain on the continent, canyons and bluffs we stole from the Indians, that they stole from each other. We stare at signs on rocks that can't be read but we think we're all spiritual because it stirs something in us. Round and round, thinking it adds up, that the world means something, or it's going to transform us into something new and different."

"Does it have to? Can't it mean whatever it is?"

"Sure. What is it, then?

"I don't know." Ryder took a gander. "It's pretty though."

Ryder held Traveler back a yard so he wouldn't nip at Come Again's spotted butt.

Ferron swung his right leg over Come Again's mane, then his left over the saddle, turning around to ride backwards.

"Yeah. It is. Lots of little beautiful things I hope to see and do again. Some, not so much."

"You think that's a thing? Reincarnation?"

"Not exactly. Seems too easy. I don't have stuff all figured out, but I don't think it puts together into one big system. Kent says the same about geology—any one specialist can make sense of some of the parts, but the big picture never comes together. Drives everyone crazy, but they can't quit."

Ferron kicked his legs like he was swimming. Come Again kept climbing.

"I just read whatever's in the half-ass library. The County library does not contain...multitudes. But there's this one thing I've been thinking about. Nietzsche says what if it's all just a closed system that only has so many ways of putting itself together. Like, at some point, it will all come back around and repeat exactly, because there's only so many possible variations. Forever."

Ferron's skin glowed bronze in streaks of early sun. His lank hair brushed his shoulders. A short curling beard made him look like a Byzantine Jesus.

His eyes flashed opaque when they caught light.

Ferron lived in his lithe form so heedlessly he seemed to splash over his own contours. Water sloshing in a headgate, seeking flow. Ryder could almost predict each shift in conversation because Ferron took on the appearance of it. At this moment he resembled his recently dead mother so vividly it was hard to picture Doug—even something like high school Doug—in Ferron's composition.

Ferron's voice sounded like clean wind in high evergreens. "What was my mom repeating, Ryder? What re-familiar hell is she traveling now? What choices did she ever have except to put up a fight? Or decide when to make it stop?"

Ryder slowed his mount.

"Ferron."

Ferron kept moving, forward but also backwards.

"Ferron, stop a minute. Come Again, hold up! Whoa!"

Ferron's gelding slowed but clopped onward. Ryder nudged Traveler up to pace.

"Ferron! None of us will ever get over Maura. I get that."

Ferron said, "Yeah? What do you get?"

Ryder said, "Boulders. Heads up."

"What?"

Come Again lifted his shoulders and humped up sudden, twisting for footing over the laddering shale. Ferron rose and arced with the horse. Sparks flew under the scrape of metal shoes.

Ryder gyrated on his own tailbone as Traveler scrabbled over the outcrop. Spark-smell of friction against the scent of sage. Back on simpler footing, Ryder said, "So what about *my* mom?"

"What about her? She seems all right. Isn't she? You've had some rough patches. But Evaleen didn't answer with a handful of Valium."

"Evaleen delivered nine unfinished babies before the miracle that was me arrived. I'm Heavenly Father's reward for grief he could have just fixed the easy way."

"I was there before you were. My mother was out of her mind sorry for Aunt Evaleen."

"But I mean the one who bore me. I'm just the body that repeats and repeats for her, some way or another? It's my job, over and over, to roll like a newt, come out and disappear? I'm supposed to wonder, one run after another after another, why she did it?"

"Did what?"

"Do him."

"Ryder, you know why. At least how. If there's proof of eternal recurrence, teen sex is it. You did it yourself, which is why you just spent five years living the good life in a Riverside kitchenette."

"You want me to be grateful? Because I am."

"Hell, you helped me pay the mortgage. Maybe I'll leave the place to you when I die. Kent's got his own life. Give him a room when he comes home to ride. I liked living next to you and her. I'll even miss hearing the kids howl all night."

"We're only moving up to the farm. It's your farm too. And Kent's."

"I know it. And I'm grateful to your dad for making sure it is."

"So what are you telling me? This is how the universe is meant to be, again and again? *This?* Sex, Indian camps, massacres, kitchenette, farm carved off thousand-year-old Indian camps, watermelon trucks, drought, sex, babies, start over?"

"Not meant to be. *Is.* Maybe. Nietzsche didn't lay this down as the truth. It was just some crazy idea floating around. Why do you need your personal arrival on the planet to be so special? We went to high school, for fuck's sake. Didn't you pay attention to the *actual* education? Overexcited teenage boy. Willing or unwilling girl, doesn't know how to say no, can't exactly say yes. You can work yourself up trying to come up with a more touching tale of your conception, but isn't that the exact way I got made too? Is it my eternally recurring purpose to kickstart my mom and dad's dismal destiny? My fate to force them together, watch them tear each other apart, wonder what I could have done to save her, shove him toward something like grown-up capability?"

Ryder coughed. "Damn, Ferron. You didn't do that to them. They did it to themselves."

"Did they? Given the momentum of human nature bearing down? Screw Doug Mikkelson, but even so did he pick to get born after Grandma and Grandpa were plumb wore out? Did he whisper to Grandpa what he had to prove by getting it up at forty-eight? Do you really think my infant dad came to Grandma in a dream, insisting she had to bring one more precious soul to the earth to help prepare for the return of Jesus? What's a woman like Grandma supposed to dream, once she feels another guppy roll? What was *her* mother supposed to dream, and her grandmothers back forever?"

Ferron's horse found a yellow stand of aspens. The sound of open sky dampened under a million quivering leaves. The horses crested again to emerge from the quick forest. The enormous valley spread below them. The gray worm of highway skirted the San Rafael maze. Ryder turned Traveler slow to take it all in: red contours churning toward the Henries. La Sals rising above Moab, lined by river bottoms. Hidden depths of the Canyonlands. Goblin Valley, big Factory Butte, Hanksville hunkering up to the domes of Capitol Reef. The flat heights of the Aquarius Plateau, dappled mass of Boulder Mountain.

Roans at Ryder's back. Rugged Wasatch and Uinta summits beyond. Not the precise scenes Ute and Paiute travelers, or the ancients before them, would have taken in. But, close. How did they make sense of things? How would all this return, and return again, to people he could and could not envision?

He said, "So, I'm the eternal answer to my biological father's urge to poke?"

"Aren't *your* kids?"

"At least I know them. Gave a damn once they showed up."

"Maybe you're like a boulder set where the trail divides. What does the boulder do? Nothing. It's a big rock, sitting in a pretty place. Time passes by. Maybe the rock wants a say. Having a say means we think we got a little power. That's probably why people do stupid shit for the sake of doing it. Feels like power."

Ferron pulled his hat brim low against the climbing sun.

Ryder said, "Think you might be reading too much philosophy?"

"You think I'd be better listening to talk radio?"

"No."

"What do you read?"

"Louis L'Amour."

"Come on."

"Give me a break. I read other stuff too. But sometimes words scribble scary thoughts in my mind."

"Still?"

"I like that the cowboy always gets the girl. Eternal recurrence. Besides, I can always talk to you if I want to lie awake all night, trying to kill the brain movies."

Ferron turned back around in the saddle. Face to the approach. "You know," he called back. "It's the weirdest thing. You can't shut the pictures down. My brain doesn't make any."

"What?"

"I can't make images in my mind. All I see is what's in front of my actual eyes."

"What? How do you remember stuff? How do you never get lost?"

"I remember how it feels. I see it when I get here."

Ryder was stunned. "How can you have memories without making pictures? Can't you see your mother? Like, in your mind?"

"No. I told you. I remember stuff we talked about. I just—think about her."

"In words? How do you dream?"

"I dream how I dream."

"You can't close your eyes and see Eva and Stella in your mind? You can't picture the baby?"

"I know they're cute as all get out. I just can't pull up a mental picture of them."

Ryder said, "Can you see that little meadow up ahead of us?"

"Of course I can. It's right there in front of my eyes. They work just fine."

"But if you close your eyes?"

"The horse can see it."

"I don't get that, Ferron. Of all the things you go on about."

"I wouldn't even know it about myself, if it wasn't for you forever yakking about your magical inner eye."

"I think I'm the regular one. Fuck you."

"Fuck you."

"Let's stop for lunch. Sami sent cheese. Corn cakes. I sneaked candy. Can you taste things in your mind?"

"Yes. I remember taste and smell when I'm hungry. And smell reminds me of things. I always remember how a saddle feels. And grass and rope and sandstone. Tree bark. I don't think I'm unique in this family. Ask Kenty sometime. You sure you're our real cousin?"

SIXTY-THREE

He should have known that ride was Ferron's goodbye.

Six weeks later, Ryder knew Ferron had headed into the cliffs; Come Again and Ferron's tack were gone. No word about where Ferron was going, or whether he was spending the night, but that was Ferron's way.

But after a week, family fears converged. He'd missed two days at Lin's, no word, although he'd scheduled employee shifts two weeks beyond.

Then the sheriff called Alma. Shepherds had staked the spot where they found Ferron's untethered horse, eating frosty grass way up near Pioche Run. Saddle and bridle set neat over a fallen fir. They said Come Again looked startled but stayed put as they approached. The horse seemed grateful for the saddle; he followed meekly down the old wagon road to the sheep camps.

Ferron could have gone anywhere from there. He'd leave no sign unless he wished to.

"Call Kenty," Alma said when he pulled into the Riverside parking lot. "We should of talked to him already. I don't want to bring this up with Doug until Kent's calling the shots."

Evaleen took the little girls' hands in hers to walk toward the swing set.

"Is Uncle Ferron lost?" Eva asked.

"Uncle Ferron can't get lost," Sami answered. "But maybe he's hurt. Or keeping to himself somewhere."

Stella said, "We got to go find him."

"Sami," Ryder said. "You talk to Kent. Please? He'll take it best from you."

She said, "Help Greene eat his applesauce." She took her phone around the building. Ryder sat in front of the highchair, spooning goop into his son's baby-bird mouth as he watched Sami through the window. She paced as she talked, tucking her hair behind her ear with her free hand. She shook her head. Nodded. Looked toward Ferron's unit, curtained and locked.

Ryder had an awful thought: had Ferron returned on foot and shut himself in his room? Would he do that?

No. He was out there.

Sami gestured Ryder out. He pulled Greene out of his seat, dropped him in his little down sack and stepped out to meet her. Holding Greene was like wrangling a small python.

Kent was still on the line.

"He says check Ferron's room," Sami said. "He'll listen while we take a look."

She walked with Ryder to the office. The key ring was where it should be, on the hook behind the desk. Ryder had hung it there this morning. But Ferron's key was missing.

Kent said to Sami, loud enough to be speaking to Ryder too, "Extra one under Maura's urn."

"Why does he keep *that* in the office?"

"He doesn't want to sleep in the same room as his mother."

Sami bared her teeth.

Ferron's room was immaculate, enriched by the objects of his meanings. Vintage tack. Greene reached toward Maura's turquoise crucifix. A striped wool blanket covered the bed, but the chief blanket was missing. A washstand and ceramic pitcher, salvaged from Grandma Mikkelson's kitchen. A braided rag rug Ryder remembered from Grandma and Grandpa's tiled basement. Framed on the wall: Ryder's first rendering of the Egyptian Queen. Beside it, thumb-tacked: seven-year-old Ryder's drawing of Ferron in flight. Evaleen must have given it to him. When?

A red file folder lay on the desk.

"Come, Kent. Now," Sami said on the phone. "Whatever's happened, it won't change before you get here. How long from Los Angeles?"

Ryder heard Kent's voice: *Eight hours.*

"That's too fast. It's at least ten. It's important for you to stay safe. We'll lock his room until you get here."

Kent compromised: made it in nine.

Sami's uncles and brothers drove up from the reservation with their horses and trailers to help search. Her mother rode with Stephen, Sami's closest brother, to help with the kids. Stephen brought Sami's horse from home, and she rode with him every day of the search. Sometimes they each put a twin in front of them, depending on the trail and weather. Maura's cousins came from White Mesa with mustangs only they could control. The Mormon Elder's Quorum called up their ranks—some on horses, some on ATVs, some in muscled pickups. The Relief Society set up a food station and kept it coming. Maura's Catholics came with the Nile Valley Search and Rescue to set up a communications center, and the Forest Service commissioned a helicopter.

Doug sat with the officers, pale and bewildered with no radio voices shouting politics. Ryder could hear his uncle's voice in the background, a high nasal soundtrack, explaining the devil's signs on the U.S. dollar bill, the gold fringe of clandestine martial law. The treachery of university queers and feminazis.

"Keeps him occupied, anyhow," Evaleen muttered. "Anyone wants to believe the least rational man on the premises, go ahead."

Stella Begay kept Greene on her hip, murmuring to him in the rhythmic halts and dips of the old language as she packed ham sandwiches in plastic bags, one-handed. Greene wound his fingers into her hair and clung. Alma tried to lose the oxygen and head up the river trail, but Kent put a hand on his back.

"Anyone finds Ferron," Kent told him, "It's gonna be the sheepherders. Nobody knows that terrain like they do. Stay here, Uncle Alma, and help us keep track of the big picture. Nobody's more capable of that than you."

Thus, the 2003 deer season was upstaged by the search for Ferron Mikkelson, from the Book Cliffs to the Roans, to Strawberry and Tabby Mountains, hard high desert up to Myton and Duchesne. Through the San Rafael Swell and up the Wasatch Plateau, back down to Joe's Valley and over to Fairview, east to Westwater, where Ryder had fallen down and down in what now seemed another lifetime, where a mother bear yet rose and collapsed in Ryder's deepest dreams. Along the railroad tracks in the Colorado River bottoms, where rafters waved in high summer. South toward the Canyonlands. Factory Butte and Goblin Valley, Hanksville bentonite. Up and down the Green, both sides, Dinosaur to the Confluence.

Kent said, "If we find that son of a bitch alive, I'll kill him myself."

If Ferron had wished to be found, he would have been. If love could draw him back, he'd be standing on the next ridge over, or the next, waving as if he'd been there all along. Kent rode Come Again four weeks straight in snow, hail, wind, and sun. Mud and ice.

Kent brought the gray dapple down when it was incontestable: his brother had outfoxed them all.

SIXTY-FOUR

The papers on his desk specified transfer-on-death of the Riverside Motel and relevant objects, including the box truck, to Sami and Ryder. The mortgage had another ten years, but the rentals paid for it and more; profits should go to improvements and the children's welfare. College if they wanted it.

Ferron's share of the family farm was designated to Kent, with sincere thanks to Uncle Alma for making it possible.

"Help Doug keep the trailer in shape. My thanks to Aunt Evaleen for all the dinners and sandwiches she made for him. Give my stuff to people who want it. Saddle to Greene when he's big enough. Come Again goes to Kenty. He's a big ride but trained right, so I hope Eva and Stella and Greene will learn to ride him while the fancy college boy gets his fill of education."

SIXTY-FIVE

Eventually, most things returned to how they'd been, but for the black hole in the shape of Ferron. Or, Ryder reconsidered, back to where they'd been going before. Busy. Kent went back to UCLA to keep at the doctorate. Eva and Stella liked kindergarten. They liked just about anything, long as it didn't impinge on their chattering stories. Something about river mermaids and, for some reason, badgers. Guiding pretend visitors from Japan around the property, stopping at interesting points to teach them English words. Sometimes one or the other took the role of Sami's ancient Grandma Curley, who lived in a hogan in Redhorse. Whichever wasn't Grandma led the old woman by the hand, gentle but overly patronizing, Ryder thought, introducing her to the many conveniences of modern life: a toaster. Cell phone. Power tools, if Ryder happened to be holding one. Best of all, a freezer with ice cream, which Grandma Curley would be invited to sample.

"The real Grandma Curley likes dilly cones," Sami said. "She likes them better than anything we've got in our freezer."

"What's that?"

"We'll take her to the powwow in Bluff this summer. She'll show you two some things. Including dilly cones."

"Will Greene like a dilly cone?"

"He sure will."

Evaleen and Alma took Greene in the mornings while Ryder's "women" were at school. They fed him oatmeal or bananas, scrambled egg and toast. Orange juice. They told Ryder what he liked at Greene's age. Greene was a better eater. Greene was a mush mouth with words, just like his father had been. Greene didn't like pants, same way Ryder hadn't.

Then Ryder drove to the Riverbend to check on things, which were usually fine. Gladys Merton, widowed by a mine accident, had taken over Ferron's old room—and the one adjoining for her single-mom daughter—as part of her night-manager pay. She hired good housekeepers and kept them sharp. Ryder was a little afraid of her. She was made like his mother—hard experience and no excuses.

Business used to wane at the motel after tourist season—really it was only twelve little rooms in two straight lines (Ryder couldn't help it: *the smallest one was Madeline's*) and a drive-up office—but Gladys knew folks who needed winter lodgings, a safe place for a while. She knew people who knew people, an endless stream coming through town, going on to who knew where.

"Decent folks," she assured Ryder. "Ask your mama if you worry I don't got the judgment. I want no truck with troublemakers. But we might's well fill these rooms with paying customers, even if it ain't summer rates, if that's okay with you."

"For sure," Ryder said, trying to sound older than a quarter century to a woman who knew exactly what he was. "That sounds good to me."

"There's a bathroom needs some re-plumbing," she said. "Number eight."

"I'll get on it. Is it empty now?"

"Ain't let it because of the plumbing. Sink drips. Toilet shouts some."

"Okay, I'm on it."

After the Riverbend, Ryder arrived home for lunch and afternoon tasks. He parked at the bunkhouse and walked to collect Greene from his folks. Ryder's parents were trying to convince Ryder and

Sami to trade houses, now Grandma and Grandpa Mikkelson were gone. "There's five of you. Two of us. We like the bunkhouse. Just our size."

Sami said she liked the bunkhouse, too. It reminded her of a rez house. She wondered if white families even liked each other, seeing how they built so many rooms to keep themselves apart.

"Mom. Dad," Ryder tried to tell them. "You deserve a little luxury. You took care of Grandma night and day. Seems like you could sit back and enjoy the space."

"The bunkhouse is good space for two old farts like us," Alma said. "Right now we just got them two extra bedrooms closed off. Basement's clean and empty. What in the world we need all that for?"

Evaleen said, private, "I think it would be good for your dad to move out of the house he grew up in. It's nice to be on the farm and all, but he don't need reminders of bygones every time he turns a corner."

That was persuasive.

"Let's wait until summer," Ryder said. "We'll move when it's warm and easy."

Alma liked to set his tank in the stroller and walk down with Ryder to look after the horses. Greene rode on Ryder's shoulders. Once he got to the corral, Alma pulled the tubing out to enjoy handing out oats. Push a little manure from one place to another with his square-mouth shovel. Gather bale twine. Finger stuff in the tack shed.

Ryder knew Alma had smoked heavy as a teenager. One concrete way to defy his hard religious parents. "Started when I was thirteen," he said. "Felt good to have something in my fingers." He smoked behind the school. Out to the corral. Smoked when he rode the sheep camps. Quitting for Evaleen's sake was a tough go; Ryder knew his father sneaked a few cigs when he was out on a job. "What mason you know don't smoke when he ain't got a trowel in his hand?"

"None, I guess. Can I try one?"

"Hell no. And don't tell your mom."

"How can she not know?"

"Well, it ain't your job to help her know. She thinks it's a sin, and it is. I'm a hypocrite smoking and thinking I deserve to go to church. I gotta give one of 'em up, and it don't seem like smoking is finally the one."

Alma had put in some years in the mines before Ryder was born. Men in his family aged fast. Hard working lives. Alma had already outlived cousins and brothers, and by now he'd quit smoking for real. Had to. Ryder kept expecting his mother to let loose with tough talk on sin. *See? Consequences*, but it seemed she'd surrendered something, too. Given up the sharper edges of faith.

"Come what comes," she said. "Plenty of bad but we can't stop what's coming. Plenty of good in the meantime. Who are we to not hold fast while we can?"

Ferron's truck sat in the warehouse on the farm for two years. Ryder couldn't make himself step into the building. He knew Alma lifted the door and started the engine once a week, kept the battery charged. Ryder stored his own tools in a shed behind the bunkhouse, or in the lockbox in the bed of his pickup. Some local producers—small timers like the Mikkelsons—asked in passing whether he might take over the once-a-week summer deliveries, excess from hobby crops. Dick Chlebek shouldered up to Ryder in the elementary school parking lot, last day of the twins' second-grade year. Chlebek was on the lookout for his sixth-grade grandson, probably eager to take him home for a summer of tractor work.

"I got guys up north wanting melons," he told Ryder. "We all feel bad about your cousin. But you could pick up the run. They sell Saturdays. We can fill the body come July. Ferron used to come back with raspberries. Peaches and pears. Sold 'em fast, remember? Right out of the truck. You won't get rich but you could take your wife to dinner. Something fancy, up to the city."

Ryder rolled his eyes.

"Think about it," Chlebek said. "Anyway, that truck oughtta roll again. It's kind of a mascot, know what I mean?"

"Here come my girls," Ryder said. "Good talking to ya, Dick."

"Think about it, pal. There's three or four of us wanting it. I'll give you a call."

"Yeah. All right. Take it easy now."

"I don't got your number. I'll call your dad."

Thanks to his seasons at Roy's, Ryder was *el primo* dishwasher. Greene, muddled with the tongue and lips but graceful in every other way, liked to sit on the counter and "help" with his feet in the soapy water.

"Da," Greene said, which might have flattered Ryder, but "D" was the only consonant the kid could produce. Eva and Stella were "Da." Mommy was "Da." More complex expressions tumbled out in long chains of rhythmic vowels, musical but unintelligible.

Maybe dishes were "da," but then Eva said, "Dad, he wants you to open the window." It was true: Greene was pleased enough to slap his (pretty damned big) feet in the water, soaking Ryder's shirt.

"Who wants to help put the horses to bed?" Ryder asked, putting the last plate up to dry. Greene threw himself into his father's arms, kicking and wet.

"We do, too!" Stella said. "Mommy, come too!"

"Okay then. Boots on."

Early summer light was still surprising. Greene rode on Ryder's shoulders. Eva and Stella pulled Sami one direction and another, zigzagging to admire blooming mallow or smell the unfolding sage.

"Hi, Grandma and Grandpa!" Eva called toward the bunkhouse. Evaleen and Alma waved from the porch.

"You girls done with school?"

"All summer! And then we're in third grade!"

"Noooo!" Alma hollered. "Stop growing up so fast!"

"We can't help it, Grandpa!"

The horses stood waiting at the gate. The girls picked tufts of tender grass: soft lips reached in response. Greene writhed for Ryder to let him down.

"Stay on this side of the fence, Greene," Sami said, but Greene ducked under the rail and lined himself against Come Again's long forelegs.

"Greene, take it easy." Ryder rolled over the high rail. "Stay right there."

"HORSE," Greene said.

"Daddy, Greene said a whole word!"

Sami bent and slipped between the rails, reaching. The horses towered around Greene, protective.

"Ummaden," Greene said.

Ryder swooped him up.

Sami: "Did he say what I think he said?"

Stella: "Mama, Greene said Come Again!"

Eva: "Did you, Greene?"

Greene twisted toward Ferron's perfect spotted horse. Ryder lifted him to straddle the high back. Come Again craned his neck around to absorb the radiant presence.

Greene leaned forward to run his fingers through the black mane.

A low nicker. The animal tossed his head. Lifted his front foot, fancy, and set it down. Greene sat easy.

"Ummaden."

"I'll come in. Give me a minute," Ryder said, nudging his family back toward the house.

"We're drawing pictures," Eva said. "We need you to help us."

"I will. I just need to check on something."

The overhead bulbs on the warehouse beams all lit up but one. Ryder knew his dad couldn't climb a ladder. He made a mental note to fix it.

"Warehouse" was a generous word for a cinder block building the size of a big RV garage, but before Ferron's truck found home in it, it had been used for the fruit and melons Grandpa Mikkelson grew. When Ferron was harvesting, he'd keep the truck under the covered port, making room inside for the bounty.

The reel of sudden memories convinced Ryder his cousin had been on to something. For a few minutes, a perfect dimension of return:

Ferron in the high school parking lot, laying on the horn.

Ferron on the high rail at Westwater, waving to Ryder and Alma as they approached.

Ferron leaning out the pitching pickup window, spotting his father's foolhardy climb.

Ferron standing over Ryder in the pickup bed, pointing the way to St. Mary's.

Ferron holding his livid, heartbroken brother at arm's length. Ferron pulling a beat-up leather wallet out of his Wranglers pocket; handing hard-earned cash to an angry corporate patriarch.

Reading a library edition of Plato, or Nietzsche, or who-but-Ferron-knew-who, under the porch bulb at the Riverside. Bug zapper going pop, pop, pop . . . Ferron above Ryder on the high flats, riding backwards on Come Again. Waving his arms, pontificating like the great philosopher he should have become, had ever been.

Next morning, Ryder drank hot coffee while small early risers worked cereal and milk.

"Let's see those pictures you drew last night," he said.

They narrated him through the stack:

"This is Mommy being a teacher at school. Look, she's making numbers on the board."

"This is Uncle Stephen on his horse. See the sheep? Here's the one that fell in the crack."

"This is Grandma Curley weaving a rug. It has stars."

"Here's ducks on the river."

"And deer."

"Grandpa Alma fishing."

"Gramma Evaleen, see? In the garden. All the tomatoes."

"Look, that's you and Greene doing the dishes."

"All these men are going up the mountain to look for Uncle Ferron. Here's Mama, too—see? On her rez pony. Here's you with Uncle Kent."

Ryder laid the last drawing of last night's batch on the stack. He said, "I got a big job to do, out by the warehouse. Wait until you see I've pulled Uncle Ferron's truck out to the sunlight. Then you can come help me if you want."

"What's the job?"

"You'll see. Put your dishes in the sink. Wipe up the drippy milk. Gather up all your drawings and bring more paper and your colored pencils."

"Is that Mommy?" Eva asked, gazing up at the Egyptian Queen.

"Nope. It's Nefertiti. Queen of Egypt, long long time ago. Looks a little like Mommy, though, doesn't she?"

Stella: "Did you make her?"

"I painted her for Ferron. Now we're going to paint the rest of the truck. The box, anyhow. It's gonna take a few days. Your mission, should you choose to accept it," (the girls giggled) "is to keep drawing ideas. The truck paint is pretty nasty, so here's how it works: you make pictures on the paper of all the things in Nile Valley. Everything you can think of. And all the things down to Redhorse too. I'll paint them up here on the big panels, okay? I'll show you."

Ryder thought about Anno—the enchantment of that first encounter. He thought about the hundreds (thousands?) of little figures he'd drawn in the big art pad in the hospital. He thought about

Egyptian hieroglyphs, about the generations of human expression on the rocks and cliff faces of the world he inhabited. The real people who experienced this same world and left a record of it. He considered the uninhibited relations between his daughters' inquisitive eyes and flowing hands, their pleasure and confidence as they remembered, reinvented, *created* (and here they were, astounding creations of the world they reflected in each word, stroke of their pencils, press of colored clay).

He began in the center, up high on Ferron's driving side, outlining Ferron in a cowboy hat, sitting backwards on a twenty-inch Come Again. Green grass and dark shale at the horse's feet. Below him, down slope, Ryder himself, seated on his tall gelding.

"Why is Uncle Ferron riding backwards?"

"Because he wants to talk to me."

"Why are you wearing a cape?"

"Because it's a traveler cape. And I'm the Traveler."

"But your *horse* is named Traveler," Stella said.

"In this world, yes. But in the one we're painting, the Traveler is me. You see what I'm doing here? The Traveler has a lot of things he needs to see. We got a lot of pictures to make, and they've got to all add up to a very big one. Both sides of the truck. Back of it, too."

Sami said, "I want some poop clouds in that scenery."

"Dang, your mama's stealthy," Ryder said. "How'd she sneak up on us like that?"

"Greene came too."

"Mom, why do you want poop clouds?"

Ryder came down from the ladder. Moved closer to the taillights, began partway up. "Okay, when you figure it out, tell me what I'm making."

"Mommy on her rez pony!" the twins said together.

"Uncle Stephen!"

"Grandma Curley's hogan! Paint her weaving a rug! Here she is," Eva said, and Stella leaped up to hand her father the right piece of paper. "See? She's in Redhorse. Remember those big pokey things sticking up from the rocks. And the little arch."

"That's what I'm talking about. The Traveler has a big journey. We have to show him where he has to go."

Grandpa Alma building a long snaking brick wall. Grandma Evaleen lifting a bushel of red, yellow, and purple tomatoes. Tiny Greene on great big Come Again.

"Sure, the same horse can show up again. Stuff in this world happens in lots of places at once. And times. Keep talking to me."

Two little boys and one little girl inside the Etna school bus, pressing their faces against the windows. Uncle Kent examining rocks amidst Tucson saguaros. Now tapping his hammer on the Los Angeles fault line.

Tourists bouncing on the river rapids. A small boy lying flat on his back in a hospital bed, leg hung high. Bigger boys bouncing in the back of a pickup truck (Ryder didn't include the wheelchair, or the leg brace). A girl on a motorcycle, braids flying. An old guy with a bald head and a tennis visor, a rundown house and a shiny copper still. Deep tunnels beneath him, glittering gold and shining silver. A smiling dog.

"We still have a lot of space to fill," Ryder said at the end of the day. "Think we can keep it up?"

In the morning, Alma and Evaleen were already seated in lawn chairs, early sun at their backs. They had suggestions. "You tell us them," Eva said, "and we'll draw pictures and hand them to Daddy."

"Good plan," Evaleen said. "You ready?"

A mom and dad with a bundled baby under Northwest pines. An airplane flying above the rainclouds, bringing them home. Small Kenty and Ryder in swim trunks, wading in green water with herons and ducks. Skinny Ferron holding tight to a bucking horse. Maura and Doug cutting into a wedding cake.

Evaleen's prize buck, springing up glorious in the Vernon hills. Scarecrow Russell standing next to his brother Shane. Mrs. Overland on the porch, playing her accordion.

Miners among the deep coal pillars, headlights beaming. A train full of lilacs chugging toward Scofield. Mother Carrie waving from her jail window. Old-time cars and camping trailers jamming for Moab, stopping for burgers at Roy's. Watermelon stands. Pronghorns at the river's edge. The solo line of the Henries, white La Sal peaks rising over red arches. Black Hawk's riders coming out from the Swell, driving fat Mormon cattle to the crossing. Robidoux in a beaver hat. The old Catholic church. Stone pinnacles at the canyon's mouth, Steamboat Mountain, the scalloped overhang of the Book Cliffs.

Eva and Stella drawing on pieces of paper flying away. School kids streaming from the open doorway. Sami and Ephraim, and Charity and Harmony, peeking from the loft of the Johnstons' red barn.

Tall stone Nefertiti rising from the river. Mermaids emerging at her call. A nice Japanese lady visitor. Pioneers in a covered wagon. A woolly mammoth up Skyline Road.

Alma's truck clinging to the edge of the Spanish Fork River chasm. Escalante's cross on the hill above. Flooded houses where the mountain collapsed.

Uncles in regalia at the Blanding powwow. Kids on the fences, eating dilly cones.

Ute Bear Dancers at White Mesa.

Badgers. Jackrabbits. More ponies, black cows with white faces, sage grouse, field mice, stray cats. Ravens, coyotes. Flycatchers, a red-tailed hawk, a horned lark, sparrows in the trees.

"We're coming close," Ryder said to his congregation: Evaleen and Alma. Doug and home nurse. Dick Chlebek and some of his kids, a few more neighbors with casseroles. His official assistants, Eva and Stella. Sami. Greene in the dirt, pushing his plastic horses.

"You got to finish the colors," Stella said.

"We'll give it a good stare in the morning. You can help me make decisions."

"This means you'll be driving the route again, ain't that right?" Chlebek said on behalf of the farmers.

"Guess so," Ryder said. "You got takers up north?"

"More'n we can supply. We'll give priority to the original ones. Springville. Clearlake. Up to Big Horn. They'll send you back with peaches and pears. Raspberries if you can keep 'em cool."

Ryder went back out after dinner. The new summer sun shone from the west, lighting up the busy landscape and its little figures. Ryder took his just-cleaned brush and dipped it one more time into the blue-black paint.

Two little boys, jeans and orange vests, bright caps.

A mother bear, reaching her friendly tongue toward their outstretched hands.

Three cubs behind her, poking their heads up from sage and winter grass, calling her back.

"Would you look at that," Kent said when he came home for a summer spell. "I'll be damned if that's not the best thing anyone's made in this place since—rock writing."

"Will you take us for a ride in it, Uncle Kent?"

"I sure will. We'll be a one-truck parade. How about we stop by Lin's and pick up soda pops? We can drink them down at the river park so the googly-eyed tourists can take a gander."

"Hooray!" they answered together.

"And potato chips?"

"And apples and cheese?"

"Oh heck yeah," Uncle Kent said. "Climb in, ladies. Need me to lift?"

"We're big now. We can do it."

"You sure are. Look at you little spiders go!"

SIXTY-SIX

Mid-July, Ryder resumed Ferron's produce runs over the broad elephant back of the Wasatch Plateau, into the northern valley. He and Sami and the girls had agreed upon a system: each week one twin had a special day riding with dad, and the other had a special day with Mom, making something good in the kitchen, carrying it to Grandma and Grandpa, and helping keep track of Greene, who liked to wander.

Then, trade.

Dad Day meant getting up early to pack a lunch, and safety-check the truck. Seat belt and carefully practiced sentences: "I'm getting out of the truck now, Dad." "I'm walking around the back of the truck now, Dad," and listening for an answer. Stops to load melons as first sunbeams poked through the cottonwoods.

Then, a whole day of looking and talking.

"Daddy, tell me that story about when you and Mama and Uncle Kent got in trouble in first grade 'kay?"

"Dad, how did the triceratopses even get out there?"

"Dad, what's your favorite color of pony?"

"Dad, want me to tell you about Sacajawea?"

Also, music: Johnny Cash and Hank Williams. Ray Charles and Linda Ronstadt. *Mommy says Black-Eyed Peas is ok.* Selena! Wu Tang Clan! Led Zeppelin!

"Dad, how come he's named Led Zeppelin?"

After the long flat road to Price, the highway met the mountain and turned up the canyon like a snake's tongue. Train tracks. River. People in cars craned to admire the pictures on Ferron's truck. They honked, or rolled down their windows and waved.

Twisting climb flattened to plateau, forty miles of giant sky, big Nebo looming. Sudden drop into the north canyon, big-shouldered peaks crowding the curving highway. Cliffs dripping with runoff water, old battle sites, deer walls.

"Dad, tell me about when the mountain came down and the water filled up Thistle town."

"Dad, remember that story about you and Grandpa sliding down to the river?"

The big valley spread from the tight V of the canyon's mouth. Windmills, now, overshadowing the Spanish cross.

"Up that road, see, going west below the lake? I used to live up in those hills. My great-grandpa told crazy stories. That old sucker burned his house down a couple summers after we left. Drove to California. Made somebody take a picture of him at the beach so he could send it to me."

"What happened after that?"

"I don't know. Never wrote again. Maybe he paddled to Tahiti."

"Can we go see where you lived?"

"Someday. I have a friend out there. Russell. Works for Fish and Game."

Two drop-offs in Springville, one at the mouth of Provo Canyon. Then up to Big Horn, where a family of grown brothers—fathers— stood to help them unload. This was the last stop, where most of the watermelons went. It took time, especially because they also packed raspberries and peaches for the trip back.

This is where it was okay to say, "Dad, I'm getting out of the truck now," and open the big door and hop down. The kids there— quite a few—waved their fingers in greeting and offered berries or popsicles. There was a big swing set and a seesaw. Once, when all the men were standing together, maybe figuring out money, Eva ran up behind her father, reaching up the back of his shirt, tickling.

"Daddy," she said, "can I—"

He turned around, smiling, and leaned down to answer her, but something was wrong. It really seemed like him, but for sure he was not. It frightened her deeply, especially when he said, in a voice like her dad's, "What can I do for you, honey? Your dad's up inside the box there, see?"

Eva ran for the cab. Climbed in and hunkered down until her true dad, Ryder Mikkelson, opened the door and said, "Well, babe, it's okay. People make mistakes, you know."

But she was troubled by it, in a way that made her shake inside. She'd never, ever doubted that she knew her own dad. It made her afraid of those people in Big Horn, like they had some kind of power to confuse what seemed familiar and safe. Like they could turn her dad into something he wasn't.

Eva told Stella about it that night in their bedroom. Stella said, "Well, we have the power to confuse them, too," and they made a rule: they would never tell anyone on the route that they were twins. Only their dad would know, so only their own dad, no tricks or transformations, could take them home. Eva and Stella would be the same person, no matter who was having a Dad day, and they would never say their names, because it would show they were two. Grandma Stella had told them: your name is your own power. You don't have to give it to anyone."

Being twins made people look at them and smile, especially on the reservation where people they didn't even know gave them little gifts and murmured, reverent. But, also, being twins made them invisible, strong and safe, because they were like a magic trick. Everyone—except their mom, dad, and Greene—mixed them up.

"I just watch what hand you use when you pick up a spoon, or a pencil, or a rock," their father said. Eva left, Stella right."

"What if we trick you?"

"You can't, once you try to move it."

It was true.

"What if we don't pick something up?"

"Then I have to deploy my secret powers of discernment," he said.

"What powers?"

"The secret ones. Even I don't know how they work."

He never called Stella or Eva the wrong name. But he promised he'd keep their secret and wouldn't say either one when they were driving Ferron's route.

"Mama has Diné names," Stella said. "Do you have a secret name?"

"If I do, it's so secret I don't even know it."

"I think," Stella said, "It's probably Bob."

"*Bob?*" Ryder said.

Eva said, "Or maybe Brad."

"*Brad?*"

Sami laughed so hard she had to step outside. And then take a little walk around the yard.

Even when she came back in, composed, she had to keep her laugh-shaking back to him as she made dinner.

PART FIVE

DOUBLE HELIX

Nile Valley, Utah

SIXTY-SEVEN

Eva and Stella were sitting casually on the patio chairs on the front porch when Ryder pulled up in the pickup. The old engine sputtered a good minute after he turned it off, but that let him roll up the glitchy power windows under the look of distant rain. The temperature was dropping, but the channeled sun made a bright swath over the cliffs.

Eva and Stella never sat on the patio chairs on the front porch. Casually or not. It wasn't a relaxing setup for big kids who preferred to sprawl. Yeah, it was a weekend, but they'd just driven back up to the university after the holiday break. Seemed soon to be back.

Ryder's boots crunched on the hard driveway gravel. His daughters waved, languid, as if they'd hardly noticed he'd pulled in. They were up to something.

"What you two doing back already?" he called.

"Aren't you glad to see us?" Stella answered, eyes wide. The tease.

"Sure. Always. How's gas prices up there?"

Eva: "Better than here. A little." The pragmatist.

"How was the canyon?"

Stella: "Fine. Too many trucks. Windy up top."

"Regular, then. I know it makes you mad but I'll keep saying it. You can't forget for a minute how many ways you can get yourselves killed on that drive. One second of inattention and we lose you both. Can't have it, you hear me?"

He expected eye rolls, but his daughters were favoring him with a peculiar tenderness. He stepped up as they stood.

"What's going on?" he asked. "What's happened?"

"Dad," Stella said, reaching up to put her arms around his neck. "Everything's fine."

They were taller than their mother.

Eva wrapped an arm around his waist. "Don't worry. You always worry."

"That's my job. Let's go in the house. Where's your mom?"

"She's inside. She's making dinner. We helped, don't worry. Greene's back at the barn. Everyone's *fine*."

"Why do you keep reassuring me? I hate surprises."

Eva: "Chill out, Dad. There's nothing bad."

Stella: "Just—a little weird."

"*What*, dammit."

"Come in the house. Everything is one hundred percent entirely *fine*."

The girls shuttled a nervous laugh between them as they pushed him through the entry. Sami was in the kitchen, setting the table for five, avoiding his gaze. Had he forgotten an important date? He was good about remembering birthdays. He never forgot their wedding anniversary. Not even the date they believed was the conception anniversary, the "done deed" night at the riverside.

"What's going on?" Ryder demanded. "You're all smirking like—"

A terrible thought: "Hey! Nobody's pregnant, right? Nobody's engaged, or thinking they're getting—you know—because I'll just tell you right now . . ."

Sami put a hand up. "For heaven's sake, Ryder. Calm down. Your daughters are home. Greene's out with the horses. Go get him and we'll eat."

She held his gaze. No yield.

He heard Stella and Eva burst into laughter as he stalked out the back door.

Greene was draped like a limp octopus over his long-legged black gelding. Link nipped at bits of cold brown pasture grass. The six others—Kent's pinto Tough Beans, Ferron's aging Come Again, Eva's quarter mare Trickster and Stella's Queenie, Ryder's and Sami's matched roans Ursula and Polaris—shuffled around him. Greene lifted his head when his horse sensed Ryder's approach.

"Greene!" Ryder called. "Nudge them this way and we'll break a bale."

The horses ambled over as if they understood, which they probably did. Greene slid off Link's back, stood upright in his beat-up boots and slack jeans.

"Hi, Dad."

"What the hell are your sisters up to?"

"I don't know. Something. I guess."

"You guess?"

"I don't want in the middle of it. They're busting to tell you, so we won't have to wait longer than getting in the house I bet."

Greene ambled over to the barn, picked up a bale easy as a sofa cushion. Ryder watched his son—uncomplicated yet mysterious as the cloud of horses that moved with him. They followed Greene back and stood patient as he opened his pocketknife. The red twine sprang and the bale opened. The horses stepped in.

"I gave them a little oats already."

"Looks like the water's full. Thanks, son. You take good care of these beasts."

"Okay."

"Your shirt's wet. You're gonna smell like horse sweat. Wash up as soon as we get in."

"Okay."

"Let's get this over with."

"Okay."

SIXTY-EIGHT

"Wash up Greene. You smell like a horse," Sami reminded the boy. She put her face to Ryder's neck. "Mmm. Sexy. Sweat and hod."

Ryder sniffed Sami's hair. "Mmm. Enchilada sauce. Let's wait and take a long shower together when the kids go to bed. At eight."

"Dad. Gross."

Sami took Ryder's hand and pulled him toward the hallway. "Just wipe down a bit. I'll come with you. Then we'll eat."

In the far bathroom, Sami said, "Take off that shirt. I don't mind watching."

"Yeah, well that's all good but—"

"Here, let me help—" she lifted his undershirt to his shoulders, and he bent to let her finish, "—white man." She pressed warm hands flat against his chest.

"A curse," he murmured. "The gods decree I must be blinding pale until my people bow to the gospel of sandstone."

"Ha. Nothing's gonna make you brown but a good bake in the summer sun."

"We've tried that. More like pink."

"Speaking of your people—"

Ryder straightened up, shirtless and stinking.

What.

Sami gave him a little shove. "Don't panic. The girls have news. Heads up because I know you hate being taken off guard. Especially about—"

She shut her mouth. Ryder opened his. "Especially about *what*? Is this the first you've heard about—whatever this is? Or is this something all you girls—I mean *women*—been stewing up? You're freaking me out. Greene's agitated too. Back to—"

"I know. Back to 'Okay.' Pony instincts."

"Should I brace for something bad? What the hell?"

"Ryder, please take it easy. Are you up to listening to your daughters? They drove all the way down here to talk to you."

"Well, now I don't know."

Sami reached for his arm. He flinched away. Got a hold of himself. Put a hand on her shoulder.

"Sorry."

"Look, why don't you breathe this out. Go ahead and take a shower. I'll let Greene eat. You can decide when you're ready."

"This all feels onimous."

"Ominous."

"Yeah."

"You'll be fine. Take a shower. Get dressed."

It struck him with the steaming water.

The eerie, sprawling image in his mind he could never write on the window: night blue. Sunken snow in a transparent lake. Ice-chip stars above high shouldering stone.

Desire. Fear.

He knew what this was.

Why did it have to matter now? He knew his life. He'd worked so hard to belong in it.

Oh, Alma.

Oh, Evaleen.

Ryder stepped out of the shower, surprising Sami standing uncertain in the doorway.

"You okay?" she asked.

"Okay," he answered, in Greene's voice.

She laughed. "You figured out what you're in for?"

"I guess. Help me. I need it broken up. A little at a time."

"Sure. We'll just make it dinner conversation."

"Here we go then."

SIXTY-NINE

"Did you all eat?"

"Only Greene. We're waiting for you."

"How you doing, Greene?"

"Fine. Can I go to the corral?"

"It's dark. And cold. The horses are fed and warm. Don't you want to stay in for a super freaky family talk?"

"I don't know."

"Sure, buddy. If I'm up to it, you're up to it, don't ya think?"

Greene stood up from the kitchen chair. Wobbled against his own assembling height. Sat down. "Fine."

Sami laid what was left of the enchiladas, still bubbling, on the table. Extra corn tortillas. Salad and dressing, a bowl of green beans bottled from last summer's garden.

"You," she said to Ryder, "eat." She handed him a serving spoon.

"You two," Sami said to Stella and Eva. "Talk. But take it easy. Stop when he looks ready to bolt. I want to finish this dinner together."

Greene said, "Really, I gotta stay?"

"*Yes.*"

"Dad," Eva said. "Here's the thing. We took a genetics class last semester."

"Together," Stella added.

Ryder said, "Well, that's a hell of a way to come out of the gate."

Sami: "What did you learn about being twins?"

Stella: "A lot. The professor was super into that. We were practically the class mascots."

Eva: "Kind of annoying."

Stella: "But not that bad. He just couldn't get over such a great example of mirroring. We made his whole semester."

"His whole career."

"Did you get good grades for that?" Ryder asked.

"We both got an A, but that's because we aced the final exam."

"I got a 98. Eva got a hundred."

"So much for mirroring."

"I just forgot what alleles were, for a minute."

Ryder set down his fork, hit hard by melted cheese and soft chicken. "You both did great. I'm proud of you. Glad you drove all the way down here to tell me that. You could of told me at Christmas though. Let's do the dishes and watch a movie."

He pushed his chair back. Made a show of standing up.

"Dad!"

"We're just getting started."

Sami said, "Eat some salad."

Greene said, "Can I eat that last enchilada?"

"Eat some beans with it, okay?"

"Sure."

Everyone watched Greene scoop the final cheesy mess. He laid it carefully in the center of his plate, tucked in the dripping edges and laid a circle of beans around it, like sunbeams, making sure no item touched another. He poked his fork into each bean in succession, ate it, and then dug into the enchilada.

"Speaking of genetics," Sami said. "Where'd that come from?"

"What?" Greene asked, mouth full of chicken and cheese.

"I'd say some twist on my cousin Ferron," Ryder said. "But there's no—"

"Dad," Stella said. "That's what we came down here to talk to you about."

Ryder jumped up. Paced an erratic lap around the table. Lifted an already transparent lace curtain to check the weather he'd stood in all day. But now it was dark.

He turned. Took in his confounding, miraculous family. All he could see in them was Sami—but for Greene's eyes and the way they all towered over their mother. They were more familiar to him than he was to himself. It always took a minute for Ryder to make himself out in a photograph. He avoided mirrors. Since he could remember, he'd pictured himself as a variation of Kenty and Ferron, even after *everyone* started saying "How are you even cousins? You must have been adopted."

"Want to sit down in the living room?" Sami asked, gentle.

Ryder strode to his seat. Head of the table. Sat down.

"What is it."

"We didn't have to take a genetic test for the class. We just talked about how they work, the things you can know if you take one, and what the ethical implications might be."

"You said you got a hundred," Greene said.

Eva said, "Not that test, Greene. That was a school test. Now we're talking about a sort of medical test. You can spit in a tube and send it to a lab, and they send back information about where your DNA comes from. And . . . stuff."

Ryder watched Greene's remarkable face click through units of information. Greene's eyes widened. He poked at Eva.

"Did you do that?"

"Uh-huh. We both did. Before the long break. We just didn't get the results until . . ."

Everyone looked toward Ryder.

Stella said, "Yesterday."

It didn't matter what Ryder half-comprehended in the shower. This was a baseball bat to the forehead. He said, "Give me the dishes. I don't want to talk over them."

Everyone stood. Took their own to the sink, rinsing and stacking.

Sami pulled the tablecloth off the clean wood, set it in the laundry room and returned.

Ryder sat uneasy.

Greene launched the new volley. "Why'd you both do the DNA thing? Seems like a waste of spit."

"And money, come to think of it," Ryder said. "I guess those things are expensive. Did you need proof you're twins?"

Eva said, "We each wanted to have our own record. And it helped us trust the results."

"We wanted proof we have the same father," Stella grinned.

Ryder sputtered.

Sami laughed. "So, do you? Maybe your dad and I remember it wrong."

Eva leaned over the table toward her father. "Well, whoever he is, he dragged some family line from way back in Scandinavia. Some white guy with yellowish-brownish hair. Probably tall."

Stella said, "Which means beanpole Greene here most likely came from the same dude."

Greene blinked. His eyes turned toward Ryder.

"You mean Dad, right? Our dad. Here."

Sami said, "Greene. Yes. For sure."

Greene looked relieved.

"Okay, but that wasn't really a surprise," Stella said. "You just have to look at Dad to know most of that. And Grandma and Grandpa Mikkelson are Swedish anyway, aren't they?"

"Grandma's Welsh. At least her mother was."

"What's that?" Greene said.

"A little like being an Indian in America. Except in England."

"Grandma don't look Indian."

The kids quieted. Sami fixed her eyes on Ryder, but he could not return her gaze. His brain flashed pictures. He thought of the little Batman Pez machine, a long time ago in speech therapy, head sprung back to deliver a wan tablet.

He snapped his own head forward.

"You okay, Ryder?" Sami asked. "Need to take a breather?"

"No."

"Which?"

"I don't want to take some time. We're in this now. Keep going."

Eva reached for the light switch. Ryder said, "No. Let's pretend we're camping. Okay Greene?"

Greene leaped up. He lifted Grandpa Yeadon's old kerosene lamp from the high shelf. Reached for matches. Turned the wick and lit it, careful, and set the glass. Everyone sat quiet, admiring the oily flame. The flickering shadows.

"Turns out," Eva began again, murmuring, "that Stella and Greene and I are pretty much what we expected, in a way: half Indigenous. Half European. But it's mixed a little different than we thought. Mama's got some English in her, and French. A way back though. And there's some Iroquois. Don't know how that got here."

"Well, all that trade out of Santa Fe. Busy folks."

"Yeah. And there's Ute, but we knew that. Mom's great-great-grandpa. Mostly though, good old Four Corners Athabascan."

"Yá`át`ééh, Mom," Greene said.

Ryder stood. It was too much. Fun and games for everyone but him. Nothing but affirmation that his wife and children belonged, however fevered the begettings, whatever violence they carried in the colliding histories they embodied, whatever detours and displacements. He'd spent his life, since that night in the E.R. in Grand Mesa broken and bewildered, convincing himself that he belonged to the only people he knew to reach for. To the landscapes his eyes best understood. Wrenching sense from nonsense, ratchet-strapped to a fairy tale—

Ryder slapped his palm on the table. The kerosene lamp shook yellow light across his family's features. They might as well be swimming in an unreachable dimension, all of them together—him at the glass, in the cold white atmosphere, looking in.

"Dad, what," Eva said.

He had to paint the words on the window, so he could speak them clearly. And then he said them too loud, like some bellowing frightened animal.

"I don't want this!"

Sami pursed her lips. Dangerous. But Ryder barely took it in.

He said, "This is my own business, not any of yours. Why do you two think you can go poking around in my history? It's mine. At least you could have asked me."

"Dad—"

"Ryder—"

Greene put his hands over his ears. Laid his forehead on the table and made a humming sound.

Ryder opened his mouth to say more, but nothing came. His brain felt like clouds.

"Give me a minute."

He strode to the door and threw himself out. The frigid jolt of winter night stopped him short. He stood on the porch in stockings and jeans, inadequate T-shirt. He wavered, but didn't want to turn around too soon like a fool, so he descended the stairs to take a mincing lap around the house. He blew steam into his cupped hands. He looked up, following sandstone chimneys and sculpted walls. The whole dome of black sky glittered with stars, so far away they seemed to recede. So close they might reach and cut.

Polaris. Ursa. Orion. Pleiades. Ancient as eternity. Telling him everything. Nothing.

One pure image of Ferron, gesturing, sitting backwards in the saddle, rising up the trail on his gray spotted horse.

Then: the bear, turning.

Did he *choose* to go back in?

Sami at the doorway.

Her voice, smooth and controlled, how it got when she was seriously angry. "You can ride two rivers. More. People figure it out."

Ryder shut his eyes. Nodded.

She said. "You're not an island. This is their story, too."

He said, "I—"

She said, "All of it. Their continent, their history. You can bury your little treasure. Put the ashes in a pot and seal it up. Ride out to the cliffs and disappear while the people who love you reach forever. Or you can answer the circle."

Ryder wanted to bang his head against the doorjamb. "I—I wasn't looking for this! Not anymore. I've been feeling like my life made sense. Like I knew the map."

"You just turned forty-one, and you've seen all you want to see? You've given your family all you have to give? You're done taking what they can give to you?"

He slumped like a bad dog.

Sami wasn't finished. "You want a little ancient Navajo wisdom? *There are more things on heaven and earth, Horatio, than are dreamt of in your philosophy.*"

Ryder pulled his chin off his chest. Met her fierce gaze.

"That's not Navajo."

"Isn't it?"

"Okay," he said. "But . . ."

"But, what?"

"What about Evaleen?"

"What about her? She's your mother. Big stream. Who are you to build a dam?"

Frigid air ghoulish at his back. He wanted to come in.

"Fine, Sami. You win. I give up. It's cold."

No yield. "Stop with the bullshit, Ryder. Don't put this on me. Don't put it on her. This is your passage. She makes her own way. Most of our lives are made up of things we didn't choose—even you, a grown-ass white man in America. All you can choose is how you stay in it, until you don't get to anymore. Why do I have to explain this to you?"

Ryder took a step backwards. Out.

She said, "Shut this door, then. Enough cold's come in."

He said, "Can't we just have sex and forget about all this?"

"Nope."

Greene snorted from somewhere behind her. Stella and Eva broke into laughter, still at the kitchen table.

"Dad," Stella called. "Come back. We have more to tell you. It's crazy."

SEVENTY

Ryder awakens to the smell of coffee. Kent's tight, nearly smoke-less fire.

"I read this book about Crazy Horse," Ryder says from the warm sleeping bag.

"Yeah?" Kent replies. "What about it?"

"It said that white people and Indians could smell each other a good way off. Both thought the other was super stinky. Want to know why?"

Kent puts down a layer of fat bacon.

"Sure."

Ryder sits up. Gestures toward the pan. "This. White people smelled like coffee and bacon. Walked along in a cloud of grease and caffeine."

"What did the Indians smell like?"

"They put animal fat in their hair. Like, skunk oil. Rendered bear blubber or whatever. Made it all glossy. Made them feel connected to the ecosystem."

Kent stands up to admire his culinary wonders.

"Maybe I'll try it," he says. "I could smell like coffee *and* skunk grease. Want to hear about something I read?"

"Yeah."

"Back in the eighteenth and nineteenth centuries, especially here out west, women's shinbones were angled and flat—lengthwise, that is—pretty much like everyone's now. But most men's were cylindrical, more like oboes. Wanna know why?"

"Uh-huh."

"Because," Kent says, squatting to turn the bacon, "men rode horses. Like, from the time they were little kids. Women walked. Men were terrible at walking, A: because they hardly ever did it, and B: therefore their tibias were underdeveloped."

"Really?"

"Margaret says it's one of the quickest ways to tell who you're excavating, at least within a certain time range."

Ryder runs his fingers down his left shin.

Kent goes on: "Almost nobody rides to that degree anymore. Maybe the herders up there. 'Course, if you fall off a pack mule when you're seven, who knows what kind of tibia will come up from the dirt?"

"One with plenty of metal. Strange bumps."

"Anthropologists are interested in that. They find skeletons with mended fractures all the time. Some recovered better or worse than others. They tell a story, transform a generic set of bones into a distinctive individual with a personal history. You got a whole league of kin under your feet."

Kent nudges bacon to the edges with his jackknife, arranging a little nest to scramble the eggs in. He cracks six, one after the other, letting them plop from a gleeful height. "This way they scramble themselves. Hope you like shells."

Ryder stands up to pull on his pants. He fishes his flannel shirt from the sleeping bag. He gazes up as he zips and buttons. Sunlight beams sideways through fragrant juniper.

"I'm gonna go pee," he says. "Don't overcook those eggs. I'll be right back."

"Piss fast. Almost ready."

Women go for cover. Men spray for glory. Ryder makes a happy 360, sprinkling clockwise as he gazes up: clear sky, cloudless, whitening in the morning sun. An array of trick summits, north—always another, higher, beyond. Shingling flats to the south, obscuring the sheer drop to desert floor. Aspens greening into solidarity. Mahogany blooming yellow, tall pines blowing pollen like volcanoes, sentinel stone backboning spruce and fir.

Birdsong.

Schist and Ursula eat thick new grass at the periphery.

"Had your fun?" Kent calls. "Come eat. We have talking to do."

Ryder zips and returns. Kent hands him a plate, steaming with bacon and soft eggs. A big broken shell for garnish.

"No more deferring," Kent says. "Debrief."

Ryder eases down to the sitting log. "Okay. Fine."

He drops the shell in the fire. Fills his mouth with hot scrambled egg.

"You already know the girls did a genetic thing."

"Yeah. And you're all blond Scandinavian and shit. And other white guy stuff. What a surprise."

"Have they told you anything since then?"

"No. Everyone says you have to explain it to me, since you got all butthurt about your family nosing around in their own genealogy."

Ryder eats bacon. Takes his time chewing to annoy his cousin. "Hell. I can't be the only person with ancestor issues."

"Ryder, I don't know anyone had it better than you, parent-wise. And somehow you grew from little dipshit into a damn decent dad. So, whatever random universe cooked that up, you don't have a lot of crying to do."

Kent's breakfast is still in the pan. He'll eat it after three or four more cups of coffee.

Ryder says, "I'm not crying. That's not why we're up here."

"Okay then. Maybe it's me, feeling sorry for myself. Right now you stand to retrieve something you've lost. Sure, might complicate some things, but Ferron? He's not coming back. Mom . . .?"

Kent gulps coffee poured straight from the boiling kettle.

For a moment, Ryder can see nothing but little Kenty. The grown man is built exactly the way he was when he was five, and eight, and twelve and sixteen—small-hipped and lean at the trunk. Wide gray eyes—none of Ferron's feline opacity—under long, feminine lashes. Now, green hipster beanie over dark hair—black from a distance, deep brown up close. Wildness blurs and spins around Kent's deceptively frail figure.

Ryder says, "Even when we were small, I thought that Ferron had already lived a lot of lives. I mean right here. In the cliffs. Vernal and Duchesne. Four Corners. Like he's been some kind of magical wanderer, century after century. Like he's his own ancestors, you know? So maybe his own descendants, too."

Kent pours one more cup. His hand shakes. He doesn't drink it. "We're camping on the world's longest continuous escarpment," he says. "One big failure of a mountain range."

"What do you mean, failure?"

"Just couldn't get the power under it, like the La Sals over there. Uintas, up there. Just one massive shove, broke the surface and lifted it like pie crust. Then, ran out of heat I guess."

Ryder takes a long look around. "Well, I like it. I don't see the failure. It's cool."

Kent stands to brush dirt and bark off the butt of his jeans.

He says, "I know where he is."

Ryder cannot answer.

Kent says, "I don't want you to get distracted. We're here for another reason. But I wanted to come up here because he should be with us. For this."

Ryder stands too.

Kent says, "You were on that mile-high pack when we all rode up here. Dad kept sending me and Ferron around little twists and trails to scout signs of deer. We camped a mile or so past this spot, remember? I know your recall is all trauma-screwy, but I'll show you sometime."

Ryder says, "Where's Ferron?"

"So, we rode on through that opening in the intrusion over there—see where the horses are? There's just a small climb and then it opens big on the other side. Hidden valley, hard to get to the floor because it descends quick. Down there, one of the most gorgeous herds—the record bucks Doug was pining for. Ferron and I had no intention of reporting that. But you can ride on around the sandstone apron there, plenty of flat trail as long as you stay up against the rock. Ferron spotted a little sign where the wall corners in—a spiral, saying to go up. We didn't, because we knew Doug would be hollering, but Ferron pointed out a panel of figures up there. A whole saga, probably happened right here, or close. Off to the side, an upside-down guy. Ferron was really affected by that. He looked at it a long time.

"And a little higher, a small cave. You can see it—a hundred feet up, about? Little pinyon clawing in. Doesn't look like a cave from this side. I imagined that was where that mother bear had her cubs. No basis to that. Just a little kid making connections. Ferron must have made another connection."

Kent downs the coffee.

Ryder feels like he's levitating.

Kent says, "After all that searching, after the parties went home, after the snow started to melt again, the memory told me what I hadn't wanted to understand. I rode up here. Sure enough."

How did he get here, all the way from Pioche Run, without his horse?

Hiked, I guess. Flattened his tibias, I'll bet.

Why didn't you tell me, you son of a bitch? All these years.

I wasn't ready. I'm sorry.

Is he up there now?

Unless something's dragged him off. But I pushed a good-size boulder into the opening. Left room for air to come in and out. He wouldn't want to be sealed up.

Should we go up and see?

Hell no. Let him be.

Should we—tell anyone?

Not their business. Sami, maybe. Ferron loved her. If you bring Greene within a five-mile radius, Ferron will call to him. Keep him away until you can trust them both.

Jesus, Kent. You rode up here all alone and found . . .

He set his boots at the entrance. And his hunting knife across the portal, unsheathed.

For sure it was him inside?

Wrapped in the chief blanket.

How did he . . .?

I don't know. Don't think it was a gun. Just under the little upside-down man, though, italicized toward the cave, he arranged a couple handfuls of stones on the ground. "E R".

Eternal Return.

That must be right.

SEVENTY-ONE

"So, tell him your tale of woe," Kent says. "We got the three of us here."

"Are you serious?"

"Look, I've been flippant. This is a big deal. Life-altering for you. I've told you something heavy. Give back."

"I need a little time to take this in."

"No. Sit down on that goddamn log and start talking."

"I hate dirty dishes."

"Fine. Through the portal we go."

Kent had described it perfectly: the shelf on the other side of the spine dropped into a deep wooded valley. Twenty feet of flat base supported the high intrusion. Kent pointed wordlessly toward the spiral carved into the wall. Ryder looked up, as it directed. Pecked sheep on a flat panel a hundred feet above. Arrows. Human figures with head gear. Bear paws. Deer prints, running. Behind the prominent images, painted butterfly beings. Snakes. Water.

Images behind images. Layers behind layers. An art word: *palimpsest*. How many returns to this place? How many thousands of years?

"Far as we go," Kent said, seating himself. "If he wants, he can hear you. No more hedging. Talk now."

It came in a rush, like spring runoff.

SEVENTY-TWO

O *kay, so last winter I come home minding my own business just after the girls went back up to school, and there they are, sitting on the porch like everything's regular. You've heard this part, but they said they took this genetic test, and they went on about Sami's DNA and then mine, and none of it was too surprising until the end when they said that a whole lot of my genetics had run pretty recent through Clearlake Valley, Big Horn especially.*

It seemed anti-climatic, I mean anticlimactic. All these years wondering and it's just this town a few hours north. The one that's got all rich and full of—

"Republican Mormons. Yeah."

But Eva remembered once when she was little, she'd mistaken this guy we delivered melons to up there, sneaked up on him because she thought he was me, and it freaked her out because she couldn't unconfuse herself. She wasn't used to being around people who look like me or like she says "emanate" like me. She said it was like knowing you and Ferron weren't the same person even though you kind of are. Or like her and Stella.

I don't see myself clear. Sami says it's because I don't see myself physical in family, at least until Greene came along, so what I had to do in my mind is see Greene in those people and then it was pretty convincing. We couldn't imagine how the only people we knew up to Big Horn might be the exact ones I was related to, but Sami said no matter how it happened, we'd see coincidence. Like it could have been one of my schoolteachers or somebody who stayed at the motel or someone we'd read about in the newspaper. Or hired Dad to brick their house.

But I was upset. Felt like everyone was in my business and Sami had to remind me it wasn't only my concern because it also affected our kids, how we're put together as a family. It's their ancestors too. She's right, but it was stuff I put out of my mind a long time ago, so it was hard to plow it up again.

So for a few weeks, I'm convincing myself that I come from these farmers up to Big Horn, which isn't the worst news because they're good people, kind of old-timey like the farmers around here. But also I'm freaking out about how religious they are—they seem like fundamentalists, some of 'em more than others, and I can't figure out why people like that would have sent just one kid away. There's four or five brothers, if looking alike means what I think. But it was better than coming from some of those snooty rich people up there, like—I don't mean this bad about Jerusha, but people like her folks and that's all I'm going to say about that.

Kent raises his eyebrows.

Then I get another call from Eva and Stella, and they tell me to put Sami on too. Greene makes a run for it, but the girls are going on about how there's this internet group of adopted or kicked-out or lost descendants of Big Horn, because weirdly there's lots of us.

"Not that weird. Think how many descendants of Nile Valley are flying out there in the wind."

Well, I hope you find out someday how many are your half siblings, or cousins or nieces and nephews, so you can lie awake and wonder what the hell that's all about. And here's where it gets really loony. They've been talking to this guy from back east.

"The online group?"

Yeah. He came out to Big Horn a couple times because his DNA says something like mine, lots of relatives there. And he was adopted. And he's marked, whatever that means, as closely related to Eva and Stella. He's writing some newspaper thing about discovering his roots in Wild West Utah, so he's been talking to a lady in Big Horn. She doesn't live in Big

*Horn, because she got pregnant in high school and they sent her away
to have the baby and she didn't want to stick around after that. But she
was back in Utah to take care of her mom who's about to bite the dust.*

"The pregnant high schooler?"

*And for a minute the dude thinks she might be his mother. But his
birthday didn't match. But they figure he's the son of the same father, and
straight up it's obvious the guy's an asshole. The father, I mean. Reporter
guy makes him out to be of those rich white-shirt Mormons getting a
jump on eternal increase. The genetics show he's been a busy guy.*

"Wow. Surprising. Not surprising."

*So, I'm not loving it, and I want no more except I'm feeling good that
I was raised by a perfectly good dad right here in Nile Valley, but the girls
don't stop there. The reporter guy says there's a funeral coming up, and
he's coming out from wherever, because it's for the mom of the lady who
came back to take care of her. They're friends now. He mentions online
that she has a son born on January 16, 1979 and if anyone who's on the
internet group knows of him, maybe he'd want to know it's his grandma's
funeral—*

Kent stands up. "Don't these people have names?"

"I told you one of them, back a ways. The old man with the sons
is named Soelberg, on the farm in Big Horn."

"And . . .?"

"He's my—my biological mother's—brother."

"So you've been delivering melons to your uncle's farm all these
years. And all those religious brothers are your cousins."

"Yeah. But you and Ferron are my real cousins."

"What about the reporter? Half-brother? One of the blessed
many?"

"Uh-huh. Probably the oldest. And I'm just three months
younger."

"What's his name?"

"Something that sounds Italian. Eva and Stella like him a lot."

"So, they went up there? To the funeral? You hung back here like a mutt?"

"Yeah."

"This was—when?"

"March."

"Did they meet her?"

"Yeah."

"How'd it go?"

"They liked her. They said she was about to make a run for it, but she stayed after the funeral. There's more but I'm wore out."

"What's her name?"

"Cassandra."

"That's pretty. You know what that name means?"

"She's the Greek myth that told the truth, but no one ever believed her."

Kent laughs. "Sounds about right. Let's go home."

The sky is creamy, creamy blue.

Ryder's worked up now. "She's an artist. Minnesota."

"She out there now?"

"I think so."

"Is she coming back?"

"I think so. Not to live. But she's reconnected some."

"Does she want to meet you?"

"I think. Either way I'll have to see the farmers soon as the melons get ripe."

Kent scrunches his face like the bratty kid he was. Is. And then he's all teacher-ish like the professor he's become.

"You all done living? Made it to forty-one and seen all you need to see? Know all you want to know? Got your little world sewn up watertight?"

"You sound like Sami. I—guess not."

"Buckle up, then."

"I still haven't brought it up with Mom. But she's gonna lose it. She's never been able to talk about—the other one."

Kent's clambering over the rocks. Whistling for the horses.

"That's pathetic," he hollers back. "Quit feeling sorry for yourself. This is her saga, coming for her too. You'd best let her live it."

Saddled up, camp clean, Kent mounts his horse and salutes the high cave.

"Hasta la vista, Ferron. We'll be back."

Kent reins up for Ryder to take the lead.

PART SIX

MISSIVE

Nile Valley, Utah

SEVENTY-THREE

Evaleen is wading in her green irrigation boots, flooding young tomato plants in a quarter-pull of the garden headgate. She's wearing a cheap straw hat that once had green see-through plastic sewn into the visor. Her coveralls are loose in the legs, tight at the torso. Ryder eyes her from a safe distance; she stops to unbutton, releasing herself into the gentler gingham work shirt under the canvas.

Sami is in the house, sitting in front of the computer with miserable Greene, coaxing him through one more week of whatever education has become since the state closed the schools. Her laptop was also open when Ryder left; she has her own work to finish. She threw him out after breakfast, fed up with procrastinations.

"Do it this morning, while I'm working on administrative stuff," she said. "I have face-to-face meetings this afternoon. You can take Greene out to ride. Look at the plants and we'll call it botany."

"What's he gotta do?" Ryder heard Greene ask, but Sami gestured Ryder out and he didn't hear the answer.

Ryder fusses for an hour or more around the property. He shovels shit out of the horse stalls, piling it up neat so he can come back with the tractor, haul it to the compost. He strides past his mother as he heads to the warehouse. He checks on Ferron's truck, which is fine, just as he and Kent confirmed last week before Kent left for Fort Collins.

She doesn't look up, but she's paying attention.

He passes her again, going the other way.

"I'm just gonna walk up the ditch to make sure it's un . . . unob . . ."

"Unobstructed?"

"Yeah. Clean."

"You burned it out a month ago. What are you so jumpy about, *son?*"

Ryder stops to kick a fist-sized rock off the path.

"Nothing. What are you so ornery about? How's Dad?"

"What do you mean ornery? Expecting a squishy hug?"

"No."

"Your dad's okay. He'll be out in a bit, least to the porch. He don't like being quarantined. Doug ain't helping things, yakking on the phone about fake epidemics."

"Kent set him straight, though, didn't he?"

"Doug, or your dad?"

"Dad, of course."

"Yeah, Kent gave him the what-for. Doug's not worth the air it takes to explain good sense. Don't know if Alma will say yes to a shot, but he's respecting the idea of distance. He ain't happy about it though."

She gestures toward the bunkhouse. "Don't have much choice, now does he? Can't come tripping down the stoop without help anyhow."

Evaleen surveys the furrows for blockage. She steps over a row to release a little whirlpool. The water runs, pleasing, but she's got other things on her mind.

"Can I help?" Ryder asks.

"With your dad? Best thing you can do is sit a ways from him on the porch sometimes and let him chew the fat. Stop by once in a while."

"Right. I do, but I'll do it more. But I mean the water. Are you still planting stuff? What can I do for you, Mom?"

She squints. Takes off her hat. Examines the gibbous void where the green plastic used to be. Re-sets the hat backwards for better shade. Bites down on nothing. Temperature's maybe eighty-five, but direct sun feels hotter.

She's holding it, but Ryder can see she's pissed off.

Evaleen furrows her whole forehead.

Now she sets her feet like she's ready to fight.

"You want to help *me?* How about you buck up and talk to me about what you been talking about with everyone else? How about you stop keeping me the last to know something important!"

Ryder shrivels like a busted fourteen-year-old.

"Mom, what?" he squeaks. Like he's six.

"You know what. Why you got to treat me like a wilting violet? Ain't I done all the things to get you to good, grown-up manhood? Ain't I shown you what it takes to get on through life, take care of your people, carry 'em through hard times, put food on the table? Why do I got to plead with you to treat me like an equally smart human being? Quit it, Ryder."

She stomps the water. "I'm your *mother.*"

Evaleen grips the shovel. Ryder thinks she might take a swing. Her upper lip shines with sweat. Her hair drips at the temples. Her pale eyes shoot lasers.

She turns away to huck the shovel like a javelin. It goes way up. Together they watch it arc, and clank and bounce against the rocks beyond the garden.

"Mom. Okay. I'm sorry."

His mother's voice is hoarse. "Is that right? What is it you're sorry about, Ryder?"

What the hell. She's really torqued. Came on fast.

He thinks again. No. Slow. Smoldering. Ignition. This has been coming for years.

He says, "Mom. I'm sorry you had to go through so much to get . . . me."

Evaleen scoffs. "Grow the hell up. You didn't have one thing to do with any of that. You weren't born yet. Don't apologize for things you didn't do. That's just a slippery way to get around the things you did."

"Well, everybody told me my whole life how I owe you for all the suffering you've been through."

"You know that's none of their business, Ryder."

He stalls. "Do you want to walk to the bank? We could sit down a minute, closer to the river."

She sets off. He jogs to keep up.

She chooses a huddle of doghouse-sized boulders. Selects a good seat. He finds his own, none too smooth.

She waits, made of the same stone she sits on, gazing over the water—early summer high and fast.

He fills his lungs. "Okay. Here's something I've been sorry about a long time. I'm sorry I didn't tell you I rode in the back of Curtis's truck when I was still in the wheelchair that one time. They took me all the way up to the steam shaft, and then we saw you come out of the school early. We barely made it back when you pulled up to Grandpa's. We let you think you'd caught us before we went over to Russell's."

Evaleen twists for that one. She's surprised, for real.

"You little shits. You all stood there like goons and lied to me? Grandpa too?"

"Mom, I'm sorry. I really am. I hated lying to you, but—"

"But you did it anyway?"

"Um. Yeah."

"See, it's one thing that you risked your recovery, maybe your life. That's what I should be upset about. But you let me look the fool. Your *mother*. In front of all them little toads. And my own grandpa."

"I know. And, see? I'm telling you I'm sorry for a thing I didn't do. I didn't tell you."

"Or you could just say sorry for going up to the steam shaft and lying about it. Which is what you did."

"Okay," he intones. Like Greene.

She turns back to face the water.

"Also," he says. "I'm sorry I didn't tell you Dad drank a beer before I fell on the mountain. Not like I think he did something bad, or that it made me fall and break my leg. I didn't want to be a nark, but I still feel bad that I was helping keep a secret from you. Because I know it mattered. About who we were. As a family."

"He told me about that years ago. And of course I knew he smoked sometimes. It wasn't your fault. You got set between your mom and dad on that one, and you chose to be loyal, best you could. I didn't raise a tattletale."

She takes a long lungful of river scent. "I'm not looking for this to become a confessional. I bet you could tell me things all day. I know you weren't always an angel. And families got all kinds of things to make up for. But we got something more important at hand."

"Still," he says, working his way to the big stuff. "Mom, I'm sorry I didn't tell you I was skipping seminary. I'm sorry I didn't talk to you about Kent and Jerusha right away, because I know you would have made it better for all of us. I'm sorry I cost you and Dad so much money. I'm sorry you and Dad had to sell the place out to Etna and I'm sorry you had to live in that shack with Grandpa and I'm sorry I didn't show you near enough gratitude for all those trips to the hospital, the surgeries, and I'm sorry I wasn't a better son to you when I'm all you ever got, and I'm especially sorry that I snuck around all that time without telling you about me and Sami, because in every way you were right there ready to help us out. To love her. To love the kids. And I'm sorry you lost Ferron, because I know he was like a son to you, and you loved him so much."

Evaleen whistles a song—a little one, but the whole thing. Ryder doesn't know what song it is.

"It's my mother's tune," she says. "But she hummed it, not whistled, when she was cooking or out in the garden. My dad was the whistler. I don't know what it's called. Don't know any words to it."

She reaches back to take Ryder's hand, but it's a stretch, so she drops it.

"Ryder, I'm sorry I ever said bad things about the mother that brought you here. I know it set a kind of fear in you. I could say it's because I was afraid, too. I could say it was because you were more precious to me than life, and I was desperate to hold on to you. I could say it's because I wanted to believe that Heavenly Father had finally seen me as worthy and given me something only mine, but that's all part of what I'm sorry for. In some ways, I kept Alma from drawing close to you, for too long, because of it. Me and him was having sex earlier even than the kids who made you. We were at it all the time. I was in tenth grade. I got no call to be critical. It's jealousy, pure and simple. I couldn't understand how some could sin and be rewarded with something so sweet and good, when it felt like I was being punished again and again and again for the early lust and carnality. The longing. Those nights in the desert, out under the stars, Ryder. We were so young, but already I felt like I'd lived as many years as my mother. I'd been expected to stand in for her my whole life—"

"Mom. Please. You're the best person I know. I wouldn't wish for anyone else in the whole world to be my mother. I should have told you that a million times by now, but I'm just – a butthead. I'm sorry I'm a butthead. I really am."

Evaleen breathes in, and out, raggedy. Her hand flutters at something invisible. And then she laughs.

"Well, you've always been one hell of a beautiful butthead. I never understood how I got someone so good for the eyes as you. I've never got used to it. And then your babies, too. Maybe that's another reason I couldn't soften my heart to your first people. They must be fine looking folks, and me and your dad, we're only beautiful to one another. I've always been afraid if you found them that you'd run to them, just to stand among all that pretty."

Ryder coughs. Shifts on his hard rock seat. "*Pretty?* Mom, mostly

I've just felt like a gorilla around you all. If I was going off to look like my kind, I would have checked the zoo."

"You got no gorilla in you at all. Didn't your girls find a way to confirm that? Sounds like they figured out what you really do got, though."

"Did they tell you that?"

"No. Greene."

"*Greene*? Really? I didn't think he was even paying attention. You know he lives in his own pecticular—peculiar—head."

"Like his daddy."

"Kind of."

"Well, you're right about that. He's himself, too. And he come to talk to us when you didn't."

"Mom, I just needed time to figure things out. Get used to some new ideas."

"You think he didn't? He was terrified me and Alma wasn't going to be his grandma and grandpa anymore. He thought he was going to have to leave the farm."

"What? When was this?"

"Way back. After the girls came down."

"After they went to Big Horn?"

"No. Before."

"Does he know they've—met her?"

"Have they?"

"Yeah."

She says, "I know."

"Well then, what's all this about not telling people stuff?"

"I've been waiting on you, ya damn gorilla."

. . .

The Green River comes to them from the north, emerging from deep canyon not far from where Ryder and his mother sit. Where it's been, where it comes from? Behind them, the water rolls and turns through the escarpment, ancient bed dropping as the sheer cliffs rise:

Gray Canyon, Desolation—nearly and sheltering as wild as they were in ancient times. Up into the Uinta Basin with its boom-and-bust oil pumps, the fracked-through pockets of gas, stillborn babies. Curves into Colorado, carving through dinosaur sediments, spilling from the Flaming Gorge dam, huge, deep, unnatural but—as Ryder once believed was its meaning—haunted and *gorgeous*. Reservoir recedes back to river near the Wyoming line, cut by freeway. North along deltas and irrigations, high greened-up desert to the mighty Wind River range, alpine lakes almost too pure and blue to bear.

Where was it going? Labyrinth Canyon with its ancient sandstone walls and ancestral structures, Canyonlands, Stillwater.

The Confluence, a gargantuan *intercourse* of ancient gods, the Colorado meeting the Green, Sami's home Nation and the long, tortured, dammed, altered, and often desiccated journey to the Gulf of Mexico, the contentions of the southwest—yet onward. To the sea.

What did this explain?

What, except its journey, is the river?

. . .

"Anyhow," Evaleen says, "I sent her a letter."

Ryder doesn't compute.

"Did you hear what I said?"

"Mom, what?"

"After Greene came crying, I talked to the girls, got her name. Looked her up. You think I don't know how to type a couple of words into the worldwide webbing?"

"Mom! What the hell?"

"I waited a while. But after Eva and Stella told you they'd met her up to Big Horn, I figured I had as much reason as anybody to take hold of new ideas of family."

Ryder is horrified. He hops off the rock, rubbing his butt for circulation.

"Mom! What did you say to her?"

Evaleen grins, wicked.

"I told her she'd best settle herself back down in Michigan, or Minnesota, or Mississippi, wherever M place she's been, and leave my family alone. Told her skedaddle. You're my boy. Them kids is my grandchildren."

She lifts her chin high and square in the summer air.

A family of mallards paddle by, ducklings S-curving behind proud parents.

"Mom . . ."

Evaleen starts to laugh. Hard. It nearly bends her over. She staggers a little, moves down toward the shoreline. Can't stop laughing. Won't.

"Mom, the girls said she was nice! And scared of all this, too. She almost ran away from them."

Evaleen wheezes at the bank.

"Mom it's not funny! I can't believe you did that! You should have talked to me, at least!"

"Well, you didn't come talk to me, did you now?"

"I'm talking to you!"

Evaleen stands up straight. Takes another minute, but she finds her straight face. "How much time do you need?"

She reaches into a deep front coverall pocket. Brings out an envelope and waves it.

Ryder feels faint.

"So you didn't send it?"

"I did. I sent it after her mother's funeral, after she went back to St. Paul. I know where she went. Minnesota."

Ryder strides toward the garden. Evaleen, past eighty, catches up.

She says, "You know, that girl was young enough to be my daughter when she had you. Broke my heart to comprehend it."

"But—you still—"

He turns.

She nearly walks into him. Backs up. She speaks hard. And soft. "For hell's sake, Ryder. Who do you think I am? Of course I didn't say them things. I told her how much you've been loved. I thanked her with all my heart for giving us you, even though she might of had no wish to hand you over and had no idea where you'd be taken."

She's blinking tears.

"I told her you're a great artist, like her. You need to soldier up and see what that woman can make. It's no question you come from her. Don't need a genetic test to prove it.

"I told her you're a good son and a good father. I told her you walk a little funny because we let you fall. I told her you never done nothing—not ever—to shame her.

"And I told her you got a beautiful wife and children, and they love you and you love them back. That you work hard for them. I told her you all understand this river, these gray cliffs, to be your home."

She steps toward him. He draws her in. She's wrecking his clean shirt with snot and tears. When has he ever—*ever*—seen his mother cry?

She says, muffled, "I told her we'd all like to meet her when she feels ready."

She extricates an arm, waving the sealed letter in her hand.

He releases her.

An ink drawing of a baby boy on the envelope, buck naked, little weenie flying as he tumbles though stars and clouds. Addressed to *The Mikkelson / Woodward / Begay Family, Nile Valley* . . .

"That supposed to be me? Is that even legal?"

She laughs. "I decided not to open it until you wanted to. It came last week."

"Mom …"

Greene is crashing through tamarisk, coming their way.

"Dad," he hollers. "I did school. Can we ride now?"

"I'll meet you at the corral, buddy."

Greene runs up the bank. Slides to a halt. Blinks. "Hi, Grandma."

Reverses.

"Okay, Dad, come now!" he calls back. "Mom says, don't forget *botany*."

Ryder turns once more to his mother. "Don't drop that letter in the river. I'll come tonight with Sami. We'll read it together. With Dad."

"I'll hold it safe."

She flies the baby boy – over her head, loop-de-loops—through sunlit air.

Greene shouts, "Dad, come on! Race!"

Evaleen says, "Run after your Greene."

Ryder turns to pursue.

ABOUT THE AUTHOR

Karin Anderson draws from Utah and Idaho generational roots to portray characters, landscapes, and perplexities of the arid American West. A past (but recent) life of on-hand parenting and university teaching gave her enough, and more, to write about forever. She is the author of the novels *Before Us Like a Land of Dreams* and *What Falls Away*, co-editor of the anthologies *Utah Lake Stories* and *Blossom as the Cliffrose*. Currently she wrangles apparitions and leftover pets, plants tomatoes, and re-composes at home in Salt Lake City, Utah.

TORREY HOUSE PRESS

Torrey House Press exists at the intersection of the literary arts and environmental advocacy. THP publishes books that elevate diverse perspectives, explore relationships with place, and deepen our connections to the natural world and to each other. THP inspires ideas, conversation, and action on issues that link the American West to the past, present, and future of the ever-changing Earth.

Visit www.torreyhouse.org for reading group discussion guides, author interviews, and more.

As a 501(c)(3) nonprofit publisher, our work is made possible by generous donations from readers like you.

Join the Torrey House Press community and donate today at www.torreyhouse.org/give.

SPECIAL THANKS

Torrey House Press is supported by Back of Beyond Books, Bright Side Bookshop, The King's English Bookshop, Maria's Bookshop, the Ballantine Family Fund, the Barker Foundation, the Jeffrey S. & Helen H. Cardon Foundation, the Lawrence T. Dee & Janet T. Dee Foundation, the McMullan/O'Connor Family Fund, the Stewart Family Foundation, Kif Augustine & Stirling Adams, Diana Allison, Richard Baker, Karey Barker, Patti Baynham & Owen Baynham, Matt Bean, Klaus Bielefeldt, Joe Breddan, Karen Buchi & Kenneth Buchi, Betty Clark & Gary Clark, Rose Chilcoat & Mark Franklin, Linc Cornell & Lois Cornell, Susan Cushman & Charlie Quimby, Lynn de Freitas & Patrick de Freitas, Pert Eilers, Ed Erwin, Laurie Hilyer, Phyllis Hockett, Kirtly Parker Jones, Emily Klass, Rick Klass, Jen Lawton & John Thomas, Susan Markley, Leigh Meigs & Stephen Meigs, Mark Meloy, Kathleen Metcalf, Donaree Neville & Douglas Neville, Laura Paskus, Katie Pearce, Marion S. Robinson, Molly Swonger, Shelby Tisdale, Rachel White, the National Endowment for the Humanities, the National Endowment for the Arts, the Utah Division of Arts & Museums, Utah Humanities, the Salt Lake City Arts Council, and Salt Lake County Zoo, Arts & Parks. Our thanks to individual donors, members, and the Torrey House Press board of directors for their valued support.